I AM A CAT

Natsume Soseki

I AM A CAT

A NOVEL

Translated from the Japanese by
Katsue Shibata
and Motonari Kai

A Perigee Book

Perigee Books
are published by
G. P. Putnam's Sons
200 Madison Avenue
New York, New York 10016

UNESCO COLLECTION OF REPRESENTATIVE WORKS
JAPANESE SERIES

This book has been accepted in the
Japanese Literature Translation Series
of the United Nations Educational, Scientific
and Cultural Organization (UNESCO).

Translated from the Japanese *Wagahai wa Neko de aru*

Library of Congress Cataloging in Publication Data

Natsume, Sōseki, 1867-1916.
I am a cat.

Fiction.
Translation of: Wagahai wa neko de aru.
Reprint. Originally published: London : Owen, 1971.
(UNESCO collection of representative works.
Japanese series)
"A Perigee Book."
I. Title.   II. Series: UNESCO collection of representa-
tive works. Japanese series.
PL812.A8W313   1982   895.6'34   81-15391
ISBN 0-399-50609-8   AACR2

First Perigee printing, 1982

PRINTED IN THE UNITED STATES OF AMERICA

TRANSLATOR'S PREFACE

The novel-essay *I Am a Cat* by Soseki Natsume is considered a milestone in contemporary Japanese literature. In it, we have a glimpse of Japanese life at the early part of the twentieth century as seen by a cat. This cat, the narrator, one day meets a tragic death by drowning in a rainbarrel. Before his untimely end, however, the cat describes his daily life in the home of a weak-stomached and stupid English teacher and his discontented wife. He tells us about Mrs. Nose, the possessor of a big nose and the wife of the businessman Kaneda, as well as about several of the schoolteacher's friends: a carefree aesthetic, a scientist who does nothing but polish glass balls, an eccentric follower of the Zen doctrine, and a young office clerk. Kushami, the English teacher, has many other such interesting visitors to his home, and Soseki's cat observes these characters with shrewdness and unique insight.

The enthusiasm with which *I Am a Cat* was received greatly influenced *Botchan*, another of Soseki's masterpieces. The author's sophisticated style in these novels is instrumental in making him one of the most popular Japanese writers today.

In this translation, I have been very conscientious in keeping the text as close to the original as possible. Although a few changes were necessary to insure understandability by the English-reading public, the essence remains intact. And because of the naturalness of expression in the translation, I would like to express my deepest gratitude to Mr. Harold W. Price of Doshisha University who rendered great help in revising this work, and to my son-in-law, Mr. Motonari Kai, for his wholehearted cooperation.

Katsue Shibata
January 1961

I

I AM a cat but as yet I have no name.

I haven't the faintest idea of where I was born. The first thing I do remember is that I was crying " meow, meow," somewhere in a gloomy damp place. It was there that I met a human being for the first time in my life. Though I found this all out at a later date, I learned that this human being was called a Student, one of the most ferocious of the human race. I also understand that these Students sometimes catch us, cook us and then take to eating us. But at that time, I did not have the slightest idea of all this so I wasn't frightened a bit. When this Student placed me on the palm of his hand and lifted me up lightly, I only had the feeling of floating around. After a while, I got used to this position and looked around. This was probably the first time I had a good look at a so-called " human being ". What impressed me as being most strange still remains deeply imbedded in my mind : the face which should have been covered with hair was a slippery thing similar to what I now know to be a teakettle. I have since come across many other cats but none of them are such freaks. Moreover, the center of the Student's face protruded to a great extent, and from the two holes located there, he would often emit smoke. I was extremely annoyed by being choked by this. That this was what they term as tobacco, I came to know only recently.

I was snuggled up comfortably in the palm of this Student's hand when, after a while, I started to travel around at a terrific speed. I was unable to find out if the Student was moving or if it was just myself that was in motion, but in any case I became terribly dizzy and a little sick. Just as I was thinking that I couldn't last much longer at this rate, I heard a thud and saw sparks. I remember everything up till that moment but think as hard as I can, I can't recall what took place immediately after this.

When I came to, I could not find the Student anywhere. Nor could I find the many cats that had been with me either. Moreover, my dear mother had also disappeared. And the extraordinary thing was that this place, when compared to where I had been before, was extremely bright—ever so bright. I could hardly keep my eyes open. This was because I had been removed from my straw bed and thrown into a bamboo bush.

Finally, mustering up my strength, I crawled out from this bamboo grove and found myself before a large pond. I sat on my haunches and tried to take in the situation. I didn't know what to do but suddenly I had an idea. If I could attract some attention by meowing, the Student might come back for me. I commenced but this was to no avail; nobody came.

By this time, the wind had picked up and came blowing across the pond. Night was falling. I sensed terrible pangs of hunger. Try as I would, my voice failed me and I felt as if all hope were lost. In any case, I resolved to get myself to a place where there was food and so, with this decision in mind, I commenced to circle the water by going around to the left.

This was very difficult but at any rate, I forced myself along and eventually came to a locality where I sensed Man. Finding a hole in a broken bamboo fence, I crawled through, having confidence that it was worth the try, and lo! I found myself within somebody's estate. Fate is strange; if that hole had not been there, I might have starved to death by the roadside. It is well said that every tree may offer shelter. For a long time afterwards, I often used this hole for my trips to call on Mi-ke, the tomcat living next door.

Having sneaked into the estate, I was at a loss as to what the next step should be. Darkness had come and my belly cried for food. The cold was bitter and it started to rain. I had no time to fool around any longer so I went in to a room that looked bright and cozy. Coming to think of it now, I had entered somebody's home for the first time. It was there that I was to confront other humans.

The first person I met was the maid Osan. This was a human much worse than the Student. As soon as she saw me, she grabbed me by the neck and threw me outdoors. I sensed I had no chance against her sudden action so I shut my eyes and let things take their course. But I couldn't endure the hunger and the cold any longer. I don't know how many times I was thrown out but because of this, I came to dislike Osan all through. That's one reason why I stole the fish the other day and why I felt so proud of myself.

When the maid was about to throw me out for the last time, the master of the house made his appearance and asked what all the row was about. The maid turned to him with me hanging limp from her hand, and told him that she had repeatedly tried throwing this stray cat out but that it always kept sneaking into the kitchen again—and that she didn't like it at all. The master, twisting his moustache, looked at me for a while and then told the maid to let me in. He then left the room. I took it that the master was a man of few words. The maid, still mad at me, threw me down on the kitchen floor. In such a way, I was able to establish this place as my home.

At first it was very seldom that I got to see my master. He seemed to be a schoolteacher. Coming home from school he'd shut himself up in his study and would hardly come out for the rest of the day. His family thought him to be very studious and my master also made out as if he were. But actually, he wasn't as hard working as they all believed him to be. I'd often sneak up and look into his study only to find him taking a nap. Sometimes I would find him drivelling on the book he had been reading before dozing off.

He was a man with a weak stomach so his skin was somewhat yellowish. He looked parched and inactive, yet he was a great consumer of food. After eating as much as he possibly could, he'd take a dose of Taka-diastase and then open a book. After reading a couple of pages, however, he'd become drowsy and again commence drooling. This was his daily routine. Though I am a cat myself, at times I think that schoolteachers are very fortunate. If I were to be reborn a man, I would, without doubt, become a teacher. If you can keep a job and still sleep as much as my master did, even cats could manage such a profession. But according to my master—and he makes it plain—there's nothing so hard as teaching. Especially when his friends come to visit him, he does a lot of complaining.

When I first came to this home, nobody but the master was nice to me. Wherever I went, they would kick me around and I was given no other consideration. The fact that they haven't given me a name even as of today goes to show how much they care for me. That's why I try to stay close to my master.

In the morning, when my master reads the papers, I always sit on his lap; and when he takes his nap, I perch on his back. This doesn't mean that he likes it, but then, on the other hand, it doesn't mean that he dislikes it—it has simply become a custom.

Experience taught me that it is best for me to sleep on the container for boiled rice in the mornings as it is warm, and on a charcoal-burning foot warmer in the evenings. I generally sleep on the veranda on fine days. But most of all, I like to crawl into the same bed with the children of the house at night. By children, I mean the girls who are five and three years old respectively. They sleep together in the same bed in their own room. In some way or other, I try to slip into their bed and crawl in between them. But if one of them wakes up, then it is terrible. The girls—especially the smaller one—raise an awful cry in the middle of the night and holler, " There's that cat in here again! " At this, my weak-stomached master wakes up and comes in to help them. It was only the other day that he gave me a terrible whipping with a ruler for indulging in this otherwise pleasant custom.

In coming to live with human beings, I have had the chance to observe them and the more I do the more I come to the conclusion that they are terribly spoiled, especially the children. When they feel like it, they hold you upside down or cover your head with a bag; and at times, they throw you around or try squeezing you into the cooking range. And on top of that, should you so much as bare a claw to try to stop them, the whole family is after you. The other day, for instance, I tried sharpening my claws just for a second on the straw mat of the living room when the Mrs. noticed me. She got furious and from then on, she won't let me in the sitting room. I can be cold and shivering in the kitchen but they never take the trouble to bother about me. When I met Shiro across the street whom I respected, she kept telling me there was nothing as inconsiderate as humans.

Only the other day, four cute little kittens were born to Shiro. But the Student who lives with the family threw all four of them into a pond behind the house on the third day. Shiro told me all this in tears and said that in order for us cats to fulfil parental affection and to have a happy family life, we will have to overthrow the human race. Yes, what she said was all very logical. Mi-ke, next door, was extremely furious when I told him about Shiro. He said that humans did not understand the right of possession of others. With us cats, however, the first one that finds the head of a dried sardine or the navel of a gray mullet gets the right to eat it. Should anyone try to violate this rule, we are allowed to use force in order to keep our find. But humans depend on their great strength to take what is legally ours away from us and think it right.

Shiro lives in the home of a soldier and Mi-ke in the home of a lawyer. I live in the home of a schoolteacher and, in comparison, I am far more optimistic about such affairs than either of them. I am satisfied only in trying to live peacefully day after day. I don't believe that the human race will prosper forever so all I have to do is to relax and wait for the time when cats will reign.

Coming to think of the way they act according to their whims—another word for selfishness—I'm going to tell you more about my master. To tell the truth, my master can't do anything well but he likes to stick his nose into everything. Going in for composing *haiku*, he contributes his poems to the *Hototogisu* magazine, or writes some modern poetry for the *Myojo* magazine; or at times, he composes a piece in English, but all grammatically wrong. Then again, he finds himself engrossed in archery or tries singing lyrical plays; or maybe he tries a hand at playing discordant tunes on the violin. What is most disheartening is the fact that he cannot manage ary of them well. Though he has a weak stomach, he does his best.

When he enters the toilet, he commences chanting so he is nicknamed "Mr. Mensroom" by his neighbors. Yet, he doesn't mind such things and continues his chanting: "This is Taira-no-Munemori. . . ." Everybody says, "There goes Munemori again," and then bursts out laughing. I don't know exactly what had come over him about a month after I first established myself at his place, but one pay day he came home all excited carrying with him a great big bundle. I couldn't help feeling curious about the contents.

The package happened to contain a set of water colors, brushes and drawing paper. It seems that he had given up lyrical plays and writing verses and was going in for painting. The following day, he shut himself up in his study and without even taking his daily nap, he drew pictures. This continued day after day. But what he drew remained a mystery because others could not even guess what they were. My master finally came to the conclusion that he wasn't as good a painter as he had thought himself to be. One day he came home with a man who considers himself an aesthetic and I heard them talking to each other.

"It's funny but it's difficult to draw as well as you want. When a painting is done by others, it looks so simple. But when you do a work with a brush yourself, it's quite a different thing," said my master. Coming to think of it, he did have plenty of proof to back up his statement.

His friend, looking over his gold-rimmed glasses, said, "You can't expect to draw well right from the beginning. In the first place, you can't expect to draw anything just from imagination, and by shutting yourself up in a room at that. Once the famous Italian painter Andrea del Sarto said that to draw, you have to interpret nature in its original form. The stars in the sky, the earth with flowers shining with dew, the flight of birds and the running animals, the ponds with their goldfish, and the black crow in a withered tree—nature is the one great panorama of the living world. How about it? If you want to draw something recognizable, why not do some sketching?"

"Did del Sarto really say all those thing? I didn't know that. All right, just as you say," said my master with admiration. The eyes behind the gold-rimmed glasses shone, but with scorn.

The following day, as I was peacefully enjoying my daily nap on the veranda, my master came out from his study, something quite out of the ordinary, and sat down beside me. Wondering what he was up to, I slit my eyes open just a wee bit and took a look. I found him trying out Andrea del Sarto's theory on me. I could not suppress a smile. Having been encouraged by his friend, my master was using me as a model.

I tried to be patient and pretended to continue my nap. I wanted to yawn like anything but when I thought of my master trying his best to sketch me, I felt sorry for him, and so I killed it. He first drew my face in outline and then began to add colors. I'd like to make a confession here: as far as cats are concerned, I have to admit that I'm not one of those you'd call perfect or beautiful; my back, my fur or even my face cannot be considered superior in any way to those of other cats. Yet, even though I may be uncomely, I am hardly as ugly as what my master was painting. In the first place, he shaded my color all wrong. I am really somewhat like a Persian cat, a light gray with a shade of yellow with lacquer-like spots—as can be vouched by anyone. But according to my master's painting, my color was not yellow nor was it black. It wasn't gray or brown. It wasn't even a combination of these colors but something more like a smearing together of many tones. What was most strange about the drawing was that I had no eyes. Of course, I was being sketched while taking a nap so I won't complain too much, but you couldn't even find the location of where they should have been. You couldn't tell if I was a sleeping cat or a blind cat. I thought, way down inside me, that if this is what they called the Andrea del Sarto way of drawing pictures, it wasn't worth a sen.

But as to the enthusiasm of my master, I had to bow my head humbly. I couldn't disappoint him by moving but, if you'll excuse my saying so, I had wanted to go outside to relieve myself from a long while back. The muscles of my body commenced fidgeting and I felt that I couldn't hold out much longer. So, trying to excuse myself, I stretched out my forelegs, gave my neck a little twist and indulged in a long slow yawn. Going this far, there was no need for me to stay still any longer because I had changed my pose. I then stepped outside to accomplish my object.

But my master, in disappointment and rage, shouted from within the room, "You fool!" My master, in abusing others, has the habit of using this expression. "You fool!" This is the best he can manage as he doesn't know any other way to swear. Even though he had not known how long I had endured the urgent call of nature, I still consider him uncivilized for this. If he had ever given me a smile or some other encouragement when I climbed onto his back, I could have forgiven him this time, but the fact is that he never considers my convenience. That he should holler, "You fool!" only because I was about to go and relieve myself was more than I could stand. In the first place, humans take too much for granted. If some power doesn't appear to control them better, there's no telling how far they will go in their excesses.

I could endure their being so self-willed but I've heard many other complaints regarding mankind's lack of virtue, and they are much worse.

Right in back of the house, there is a patch of tea plants. It isn't large but it is nice and sunny. When the children of the house are so noisy that I can't enjoy my naps peacefully or when, because of idleness, my digestion is bad, I usually go out to the tea patch to enjoy the magnanimous surroundings. One lovely autumn day about two o'clock in the afternoon, after taking my after-lunch nap, I took a stroll through this patch. I walked along, smelling each tea plant as I went, until I reached a cryptomeria hedge at the west end.

There I found a large cat sleeping soundly, using a withered chrysanthemum in lieu of a mat. It seemed as if he didn't notice me coming, for he kept snoring loudly. I was overwhelmed at his boldness—after sneaking into somebody else's yard. He was a big black cat.

The sun, now past midday, cast its brilliant rays upon his body and reflected themselves to give the impression of flames bursting from his soft fur. He had such a big frame that he seemed fit to be called a king of the feline family. He was more than twice my size. Admiration and a feeling of curiosity made me forget the past and the future, and I could only stare at him.

The soft autumn breeze made the branches of the paulawnia above quiver lightly and a couple of leaves came fluttering down upon the thicket of dead chrysanthemums. Then the great "king" opened his eyes. I can still feel the thrill of that moment. The amber light in his eyes shone much brighter than the jewels man holds as precious. He did not move at all. The glance he shot at me concentrated on my small forehead, and he abruptly asked me who I was. The great king's directness betrayed his rudeness. Yet, there was a power in his voice that would have terrified dogs, and I found myself shaking with fear. But thinking it inadvisable not to pay my respects, I said, " I am a cat though, as yet, I don't have any name." I said this while pretending to be at ease but actually my heart was beating away at a terrific speed. Despite my courteous reply, he said, "A cat? You don't say so! Where do you live?" He was extremely audacious.

" I live here in the schoolteacher's house."

" I thought so. You sure are skinny." Gathering from his rudeness I couldn't imagine him coming from a very good family. But, judging from his plump body, he seemed to be well fed and able to enjoy an easy life. As for myself, I couldn't refrain from asking, "And who are you?"

" Me? Huh—I'm Kuro, living at the rickshawman's place."

So this was the cat living at the rickshawman's house! He was known in the vicinity as being awfully unruly. Actually he was admired within the home of the rickshawman but, having no education, nobody else befriended him. He was a hoodlum from whom others shied. When I heard him tell me who he was, I felt somewhat uneasy and, at the same time, I felt slightly superior. With the intention of finding out how much learning he had, I asked him some more questions.

" I was just wondering which of the two is the greater—the rickshawman or the schoolteacher."

" What a question! The rickshawman, naturally. Just take a look at your teacher—he's all skin and bones," he snorted.

" You look extremely strong. Most probably, living at the

rickshawman's house, you get plenty to eat."

"What? I don't go unfed anywhere! Stick with me for a while instead of going around in circles in the tea patch and you'll look better yourself in less than a month."

"Sure, some day, maybe. But to me, it seems as though the schoolteacher lives in a bigger house than the rickshawman," I purred.

"Huh! What if the house is big? That doesn't mean you get your belly full there, does it?"

He seemed extremely irritated and, twitching his pointed ears, he walked away without saying another word. This was my first encounter with Kuro of the house of the rickshawman, but not the last.

Since then, we've often talked together. Whenever we do, Kuro always commences bragging, as one living with a rickshawman would.

One day, we were lying in the tea patch and indulging in some small talk. As usual, he kept bragging about the adventures he had had, and then he got around to asking me, "By the way, how many rats have you killed?"

Intellectually I am much more developed than Kuro but when it comes to using strength and showing bravado, there is no comparison. I was prepared for something like this but when he actually asked me the question, I felt extremely embarrassed. But facts are facts; I could not lie to him: "To tell the truth, I have been wanting to catch one for a long time but the opportunity has never come."

Kuro twitched the whiskers which stood out straight from his muzzle and laughed hard. Kuro is conceited, as those who brag usually are, so when I find him being sarcastic I try to say something to appease him. In this way, I am able to manage him pretty well. Having learned this during our first meeting, I stayed calm when he laughed. I realized that it would be foolish to commit myself now by giving unasked-for reasons. I figured it best, at this stage, to let him brag about his own adventures and so I purred quietly, "Being as old as you are, you've probably caught a lot of rats yourself." I was trying to get him to talk about himself. And, as I had expected, he took the bait.

"Well, can't say a lot—maybe about thirty or forty." He was very proud of this and continued, "I could handle one or two hundred rats alone but when it comes to weasels, they're not to my liking. A weasel once gave me a terrible time."

"So? And what happened?" I chimed in. Kuro blinked several times before he continued. "It was at the time of our annual housecleaning last summer. The master crawled under the veranda to put away a sack of lime, and—what do you think? He surprised a big weasel which came bouncing out."

"Oh?" I pretended to admire him.

"As you know, a weasel is only a little bigger than a rat. Thinking him to be just another big mouse, I cornered him in a ditch."

"You did?"

"Yeah. Just as I was going in for the *coup-de-grace*—can you imagine what it did? Well, it raised its tail and—ooph! You ought to have taken a whiff. Even now when I see a weasel I get giddy." So saying, he rubbed his nose with one of his paws as if he were still trying to stop the smell. I felt somewhat sorry for him so, with the thought of trying to liven him up a little, I said, "But when it comes to rats, I hardly believe they would have a chance against you. Being such a famous rat catcher, you probably eat nothing else and that's why you're so plump and glossy, I'm sure."

I had said this to get him into a better mood but actually it had the contrary effect. He let a big sigh escape and replied, "When you come to think of it, it's not all fun. Rats are interesting but, you know, there's nobody as crafty as humans in this world. They take all the rats I catch over to the police box. The policeman there doesn't know who actually catches them so he hands my master five sen per head. Because of me, my master has made a neat profit of one yen and fifty sen, but yet he doesn't give me any decent food. Do you know what humans are? Well, I'll tell you. They're men, yes, but thieves at heart."

Even Kuro, who was not any too bright, understood such logic and he bristled his back in anger. I felt somewhat uneasy so I murmured some excuse and went home. It was because of this conversation that I made up my mind never to catch rats. But, on the other hand, neither do I go around hunting for other food. Instead of eating an extravagant dinner, I simply go to sleep. A cat living with a schoolteacher gets to become, in nature, just like a teacher himself. If I'm not careful I might still become just as weak in the stomach as my master.

Speaking of my master the schoolteacher, it finally dawned upon him that he could not ever hope to get anywhere with water-color painting. He wrote the following entry in his diary, dated December 1:

Met a man today at a party. It's said that he's a debauchee and he looked like one. Such individuals are liked by women, so it may be quite proper to say that such people cannot help becoming dissipated. His wife was formerly a geisha girl and I envy him. Most of the people who criticize debauchees generally have no chance to become one themselves. Still, others who claim to be debauchees have no qualifications to become so worldly. They simply force themselves into that position. Just as in the case of my water-color painting, there was absolutely no fear of my making good. But indifferent to others, I might think that I was good at it. If some men are considered worldly only because they drink *sake* at restaurants, frequent geisha houses and stop over for the night, and go through all the necessary motions, then it stands to reason that I should be able to call myself a remarkable painter. But my water-color paintings will never be a success.

In regard to this theory, I cannot agree. That a schoolteacher should envy a man who has a wife who was once a geisha shows how foolish and inferior my master is. But his criticism of himself as a water-color painter is unquestionably true. Though my master understands many of his own shortcomings, he cannot get over being terribly conceited. On December 4, he wrote:

Last night, I attempted another painting but I have finally come to understand that I have no talent. I dreamed that somebody had framed the pictures I have laying around, and had hung them on the wall. Upon seeing them framed, I suddenly thought that I was an excellent painter. I felt happy and kept looking but, when the day dawned, I awoke and again clearly realized that I am still a painter of no talent.

Even in his dreams, my master seemed to regret his having given up painting. This is characteristic of a learned man, a frustrated water-color painter and one who can never become a man of the world.

The day after my master had had his dream, his friend, the man of arts, came to see him again. The first question he asked my master was " How are the pictures getting along? "

My master calmly answered, "According to your advice I'm working hard at sketching. Just as you said, I am finding interesting shapes and detailed changes of colors which I had never noticed before. Due to the fact that artists in Western countries have persisted in sketching, they have reached the development we see today. Yes, all this must be due to Andrea del Sarto." He did not mention what he had written in his diary, but only continued to show his admiration for del Sarto.

The artist scratched his head and commenced to laugh, " That was all a joke, my friend."

" What's that? " My master didn't seem to understand.

"Andrea del Sarto is only a person of my own highly imaginative creation. I didn't think you'd take it so seriously. Ha, ha, ha." The artist was greatly enjoying himself.

Listening to all this from the veranda, I couldn't help wondering what my master would write in his diary about that conversation. This artist was a person who took great pleasure in fooling others. As if he did not realize how his joke about Andrea del Sarto hurt my master, he boasted more : " When playing jokes, some people take them so seriously that they reveal great comic beauty, and it's a lot of fun. The other day I told a student that Nicholas Nickleby had advised Gibbon to translate his great story of the French Revolution from a French textbook and to have it published under his own name. This student has an extremely good memory and made a speech at the Japanese Literature Circle quoting everything I had told him. There were about a hundred people in the audience and they all listened very attentively. Then there's another time. One evening, at a gathering of writers, the conversation turned to Harrison's historical novel *Theophano*. I said that it was one of the best historical novels ever written, especially the part where the heroine dies. ' That really gives you the creeps ' —that's what I said. An author who was sitting opposite me was one of those types who cannot and will not say no to anything. He immediately voiced the opinion that that was a most famous passage. I knew right away that he had never read any more of the story than I had."

With wide eyes, my nervous and weak-stomached master asked, " What would you have done if the other man had really read the story ? "

The artist did not show any excitement. He thought nothing of fooling other people. The only thing that counted was not to be caught in the act.

"All I would have had to do is to say that I had made a mistake in the title or something to that effect." He kept on laughing. Though this artist wore a pair of gold-rimmed glasses, he looked somewhat like Kuro of the rickshawman's.

My master blew a few smoke rings but he had an expression on his face that showed he wouldn't have the nerve to do such a thing. The artist, with a look in his eyes as if saying, " That's why you can't paint pictures," only continued. " Jokes are jokes but, getting down to facts, it's not easy to draw. They say that Leonardo da Vinci once told his pupils to copy a smear on a wall. That's good advice. Sometimes when you're gazing at water leaking along the wall in a privy, you see some good patterns. Copy them carefully and you're bound to get some good designs."

" You're only trying to fool me again."

" No, not this time. Don't you think it's a wonderful idea ? Just wnat da Vinci himself would have suggested."

" Just as you say," replied my master, half surrendering. But he still hasn't made any sketches in the privy—at least not yet.

Kuro of the rickshawman's wasn't looking well. His glossy

fur began to fade and fall out. His eyes, which I formerly compared to amber, began to collect mucus. What was especially noticeable was his lack of energy. When I met him in the tea patch, I asked him how he felt.

" I'm still disgusted with the weasel's stink and with the fisherman. The fish seller hit me with a pole again the other day."

The red leaves of the maple trees were beginning to show contrast to the green of the pines here and there. The maples shed their foliage like dreams of the past. The fluttering petals of red and white fell from the tea plants one after another until there were none remaining. The sun slanted its rays deeper and deeper into the southern veranda and seldom did a day pass that the late autumn wind didn't blow. I felt as though my napping hours were being shortened.

My master still went to school every day and, coming home, he'd still bottle himself up in his study. When he had visitors he'd continue to complain about his job. He hardly ever touched his water colors again. He had discontinued taking Taka-diastase for his indigestion, saying that it didn't do him any good. It was wonderful now that the little girls were attending kindergarten every day but returning home, they'd sing loudly and bounce balls and, at times, they'd still pick me up by the tail.

I still had nothing much to eat so I did not become very fat but I was healthy enough. I didn't become sick like Kuro and, as always, I took things as they came. I still didn't try to catch rats, and I still hated Osan, the maid. I still didn't have a name but you can't always have what you want. I resigned myself to continue living here at the home of this schoolteacher as a cat without a name.

II

DURING the New Year's holidays, I became somewhat famous and I liked being able to feel a little proud of myself.

On New Year's Day, my master received a greeting card from an artist friend. The top was red, the bottom deep green and there was an animal in the middle drawn out in pastel colors*. My master took the greeting into his study and kept admiring its shading. Having looked at it once, I thought he would quit, but no! he still kept examining it, turning the card this way and that. He'd twist his body to look at it more carefully or hold it out at arm's length as if he were an old woman trying to read her own fortune. At times he put the card right in front of his nose.

"If he doesn't stop all this, his knees will shake so much that I'll be falling off."

I then heard him say to himself in a low voice, "What in the world is this picture of, I wonder!" Although my master had admired the colors he could not make out what it represented and was having a hard time trying to find out. I didn't pay much attention at first but later, looking at it through half-opened eyes, I found that that picture was, without a mistake, one of myself. The painter could not have been one who had studied in the Andrea del Sarto school because he had given me the proper shape and had used the right colors, just as a painter should.

Anyone except my master would have known outright that it was a cat and anyone who knows anything about pictures would have been able to see that it was none other than me. But my master was so bewildered that I felt somewhat sorry for him. If I could have done so, I would have explained it to him. Even

---

* Post cards for New Year's Greetings in Japan very often have a picture depicting one of the twelve zodiac signs of the Chinese calendar.

if he couldn't understand that the picture was of me, I wished, at least, that I could have told him it was a picture of a cat. But, unfortunately, the human race is not endowed with the ability to understand the language of cats so I had to let the matter stand as it was.

I would like to remind my readers that you humans all too often carelessly criticize cats with scorn, but that is not right. The idea that cows and horses are the very dregs of the animal kingdom and that cats are less than the excrement of those same cows and horses is a common failing that often exists among ignorant teachers with proud faces. As seen from the viewpoint of a cat, this becomes particularly obnoxious. Actually, we cats might all look identical to you, with no individual peculiarity of character whatsoever; but within the society of cats, we can also apply the human saying " So many men, so many minds."

The eyes, the shape of the nose, the fur, and the personality of each cat are not at all the same. The length of our whiskers, the way we hold our ears, and even the manner in which we droop our tails—all differ in each individual animal. Our beauty or ugliness, our likes and dislikes, our gracefulness or lack of grace differ in a thousand ways.

Though such clear distinctions exist between one cat and another, humans do not seem capable in the least of discriminating between our features to say nothing of our character. This is probably because humans insist too much on their own importance and keep their noses in the air. Man, therefore, is only to be pitied. According to an old saying, birds of a feather flock together; perhaps only a baker can understand other bakers, so it takes a cat to understand another cat.

Even though humans mistakenly consider themselves highly developed, a true understanding of the feline family seems quite impossible for them to manage. Besides, people such as my master who are lacking in sympathy are not able to grasp even the first rule of love—the simple understanding of others. Perhaps nothing can be done about it.

My master is like an oyster. He isolates himself in his study without seeing anything of the outer world. That he believes himself to be extremely learned makes me laugh. Proof that he knows nothing about others can be easily given: when looking at my picture, he could not even make out that it was a cat. He only kept mumbling something about its probably being a bear as we were in the second year of the Russo-Japanese War. He simply let it go at that.

Considering this while dozing on my master's lap, the maid came in with another post card. It was a printed picture with several Western cats "studying" in a row; the first cat had a pen in its "hand", another sat in front of an open book, and so on. There was one cat which had separated itself from the others and was doing a dance on the edge of the desk. Above it, written in black Indian ink, was the inscription: "I am a cat." On the right side, was a poem: "A peaceful day in spring when cats read and dance."

This post card had been sent by one of my master's former pupils and anyone else looking at it could have grasped the meaning immediately. But not so this stupid schoolteacher. He slanted his head to one side and muttered something to himself about the Year of the Cat*. It seemed as if he didn't even know that we cats would be greatly talked about until the following New Year.

The maid then came in with the third post card. This one did not have a picture, but only a greeting. Besides the usual New Year's salutation, though, there was a P.S. asking that the writer's best regards be extended to me, the Cat. My master wasn't any too clever but he was able to understand that. He glanced at me with a "Hmmm." Quite different from the glares he usually gives me, this glance seemed to contain a speck of affection. That my master who had never before received much attention should be suddenly honored, due entirely to my existence, made it seem quite natural that he should show me some respect.

Suddenly the front doorbell began to ring. It meant, most probably, that someone was at the door. If it was some visitor, the maid would announce him. I had decided not to go to the

---

* Actually the Year of the Tiger [1902], one of the twelve animals assigned to years according to the Chinese calendar.

door unless it was Ume-ko, the young fish dealer, making a delivery so I only continued to lie on my master's lap. My master sent a glance towards the door as if a money lender had suddenly called on him.

The reason for this was that my master hated to entertain New Year's guests with *sake*. It would have been more logical, in this case, for my master to take a walk, but he was too lazy even to try to escape such visitors. He was, as usual, revealing his true oyster-like disposition.

Presently the maid entered, saying that a Mr. Kangetsu Mizushima was here. Kangetsu had formerly been one of my master's pupils but now had finished school and I understand in a better position than my master. He invariably talks about girls, though you can't tell if he is very successful with them or not. You can never tell if he is really enjoying life. He often drops remarks that cannot be discriminated as being horrible or just terribly sexy. To think that he drops in to see a wizened man like my master and purposely tell him stories about women is queer in the first place, but what is even more strange is that my oyster-like master agrees with his worldly views at all times.

" Haven't seen you for a long time. I've been quite busy because of the year end so I couldn't come this way until now," the visitor began. He talked while fingering the string of his *haori* coat.

" Well, what's kept you so busy? " asked my master with a serious face. He himself began pulling at the sleeves of his own black cotton *haori* coat because it was a little too small and his undergarments showed about half an inch.

" Oh, I'm afraid that happens to be a little personal," replied Kangetsu, laughing.

Taking a good look at him, I found that he was missing a front tooth.

" What happened to your tooth? " asked my master, changing the subject.

" To tell you the truth, I ate some mushrooms the other day."

" You ate some what? "

"As I was saying, I was eating some mushrooms and when I

tried to bite the top off of one, my tooth broke—just like that."

"You take a bite at a mushroom and break a tooth? That's funny. You might be able to make a poem about such an experience, but being toothless won't get you anywhere with the girls." So saying, my master lightly brushed my head with the palm of his hand.

"Oh, is that the cat you were telling me about? It's quite plump, isn't it? If it keeps growing, it'll be able to stand its ground against Kuro of the rickshawman's. It's a nice cat," said Kangetsu, gazing at me.

"Yes, it's been getting big lately," proudly replied my master who kept petting me. I was happy to be praised but his hand hurt my head a little.

"We had a little concert last night," said Kangetsu, bringing the conversation back to the subject.

"Where?"

"You don't have to be so inquisitive. We had three violins and a pianist. When you have three violinists it doesn't make much difference whether they're very good or not. I played mine between two girls and I thought I did rather well."

"And who were the girls?" asked my master with envy.

My master usually wears the same expression on his face but that doesn't mean he is not interested when it came to women. Once he happened to read a foreign novel and the hero was a bachelor who seduced almost every woman in the book. It was written in a satirical vein but my master praised it and announced that this was real life. But why a man who takes such an interest in sex should remain oyster-like was something which I, a cat, cannot fathom. Some people might claim that it is because of some frustrated love, while others would suggest that it is because of his weak stomach. Still others might believe that it is because he does not have much money and, on top of that, is so cowardly. Whatever the reason, he is not a person likely to become famous in the history of the Meiji era*, so perhaps it doesn't make any difference.

But the fact remains that my master seemed envious of Kangetsu

---

* The reign of Emperor Meiji, 1868 to 1912.

because of the girls he had been with. Kangetsu seized a serving of hashed fish from the plate with his chopsticks. I was afraid that he might chip another tooth but nothing happened.

"No need to get excited about the girl violinists because you don't know either of them," replied Kangetsu with some formality.

"But . . ." exclaimed my master. However, he left out adding "Perhaps I do." Kangetsu's answer only made him more curious.

Kangetsu must have thought it about time to leave because he remarked, "It's a lovely day, isn't it? If you're not doing anything, how about taking a walk? With the good news concerning the capture of Port Arthur, it's quite lively in town."

My master's face seemed to say that he wanted to know more about the girls rather than the fall of Port Arthur but finally he stood up and said, "Let's get going."

Under his crested *haori* coat he wore a padded kimono. He had been wearing the kimono, a parting momento from his elder brother for twenty years. Such quilted kimonos are usually quite strong but even the strongest cannot last forever, much less twenty years. In places, it was so thin that holding it up against the light, you could see the needle holes where it had been patched. My master doesn't have anything special to wear on New Year's. Nor are his visiting clothes different from his everyday wear. When he goes out, he saunters about with his arms folded against his chest under the kimono. It has never been clear to me whether he has any other clothes or whether he is just too lazy to change, but I can positively say that his sloppiness is not due to any frustration in love.

After the two of them had left, I helped myself to the hashed fish Kangetsu had left uneaten. I didn't feel like just an ordinary cat now that I had received so much attention. I now felt equal to the Black Western Cat the storyteller Joen Momokawa describes in his recitations, or to the cat Thomas Gray wrote about in his *"Ode on the Death of a Favourite Cat, Drowned in a Tub of Gold Fishes."* I no longer considered Kuro my equal.

When stealing the fish, I was sure no one would ever find out about it. By the way, this habit of eating by stealth is not limited only to the feline family. Osan, the maid, often eats something especially good when the Mrs. is out. The girls too have this tendency even though the Mrs. is very strict about teaching them manners. Only about four of five days ago, the children got up earlier than usual and sat down at the table while my master and the Mrs. were still asleep.

Every morning they are generally given some bread and, after putting sugar on it, they eat it. On this particular morning, there was nobody to serve them the sugar so the elder sister scooped up a tablespoonful and dumped it onto her plate. Then the little sister did the same. For a moment the two of them looked at each other, and then the elder sister scooped another tablespoonful of sugar onto her plate. The younger one of course repeated this action. In no time, the bowl became empty. It was then that my master appeared from the bedroom and replaced the sugar the girls had taken so much trouble to scoop out.

It might be true that human beings are superior to cats in the idea of fairness but their intelligence is certainly inferior. It would have been wiser to have licked the sugar before heaping it onto their plates. They would not have understood my suggestion, though, so I only watched them from the top of the boiled-rice container.

I don't know where my master had gone with Kangestu but he returned very late that night and it was not until nine o'clock the following morning that he sat himself down to breakfast. Watching him from my position on top of the rice container, I saw him silently eating *zoni**, with pounded rice *mochi*** ' swimming ' on top of the vegetables. He had his bowl refilled time after time. Though the lumps of pounded rice were not very large, he ate six or seven of them. Leaving the last ball of *mochi* in the bowl, he put his chopsticks down to show that he had had his fill. He always gets mad when others waste food but he likes to show his authority as the master of the house and he feels proud of this privilege. He looked down at the remaining *mochi* floating

* *Zoni* is a type of soup traditionally eaten during the three-day New Year's holidays.
** *Mochi* is considered a New Year's delicacy. It is made from steamed rice pounded to produce a sticky dough-like substance, rolled and flattened into small cakes which harden after a day.

like a roasted corpse in the thick soup but he felt no shame. The Mrs. then took out the Taka-diastase from the closet and put it on the table.

" I'm not taking that medicine any more. It doesn't help at all," snorted my master.

" But, dear, it's for your own good. Take some."

" I don't care how good you think it might be, I don't want any," repeated my master firmly.

" Really! You never stay with anything long," sighed the Mrs. as if to herself.

" That's not true. It's just that it's no good."

" But only the other day you said that it was very effective."

" It was effective then, but now it's no good I tell you," said my master in an antithesis.

" If you have good medicine but don't take it, it won't do you any good. You have to be more patient. A weak stomach isn't like most sicknesses," insisted the Mrs., nervously glancing at Osan who was waiting with a tray in her hands.

" That's true," agreed Osan. " You should keep taking it a while longer to see if it is really effective or not." Osan was generally on the side of the Mrs.

" It doesn't make any difference. I'm not taking it so that's that. Women don't understand things like this so shut up!"

" Yes, I'm a woman!" shouted the Mrs. slamming the bottle of Taka-diastase on the table right in front of my master so that he would be sure to notice it.

Without saying another word, my master stood up and went into his study. Then the Mrs. and Osan looked at each other with a sly smile. At such times, it wasn't safe to sit on my master's lap, so I padded around to the veranda and peeped through a crack between the paper sliding doors.

My master took out a book by Epictetus and commenced reading it. Now if my master understood what he was reading, this would have been all right but after five or six minutes, he threw the book down on the desk again. I thought that something like this would happen but I kept on looking. Then I saw my master take out his diary. He made the following entry:

[23]

Walked around Nezu, Ueno, Ikenohata and Kanda with Kangetsu. In Ikenohata, the geisha girls were all dressed in their best kimono and were playing battledore and shuttlecock* in front of their establishments. Their kimonos were beautiful but their faces were indeed poor. They looked somewhat like my cat.

It was all right for my master to mention their faces but he didn't have to use me for comparison. If I went to the Kita barber shop and had my face shaved, I wouldn't be much different from most human beings. No sir, you can't manage them, the human race—they only think about themselves. My master continued his diary:

Turning the corner at the Hotan pharmacy, another geisha came our way. She was slim with lovely sloping shoulders. The pale purple kimono she was wearing was modest and she looked very refined. Her white teeth showed when she smiled a greeting to a passing stranger: 'Oh, Gen-chan, I was so busy last night I couldn't get away to see you.' I was astonished at her voice. It was as hoarse as a raven's. All of a sudden the beauty that had attracted me disappeared. I didn't even take the trouble to look around to see who she had spoken to. However Kangetsu seemed to have become somewhat restless. We kept walking along until we came to the main street.

I find that there is nothing as hard as trying to understand the psychology of male humans. For instance, I can't often tell whether my master is mad or joyful, or if he is trying to find consolation by reading philosophers. I am generally at a total loss to tell whether he is coolly laughing at the world, or if he is mad at something not worth being mad about; or whether he wants to be considered as a member of society or to isolate himself in another world.

Such matters are quite simple with us cats. When we are hungry we eat, when we want to sleep we do so; when we get mad we get as angry as we can; and when we cry, we do our best to make as

---

* It is the custom for little girls and women to play battledore and shuttlecock on New Year.

much noise as possible. In the first place, we don't keep such senseless and meaningless things as diaries. There's no need. A person, like my master who has two sides to his personality probably keeps a diary in order to express the feelings he cannot express to others. But with us cats, everything we do is known. There is no need to go to the trouble of jotting down what we already know. Instead of keeping a diary, I much prefer to take a nap on the veranda. The diary continued:

Had dinner at a restaurant in Kanda. Drank several cups of Masamune *sake*, the first in a long time. This morning, my stomach felt good. I believe that drinking *sake* at supper is the best medicine for weak stomachs. Of course diastase is of no use. Whatever people say, it's no good. Anything which has no effect cannot be good.

My master was now against Taka-diastase and attacked it like anything. It was as if he were carrying on a bitter argument all by himself. His irritation of that morning had begun to show itself. The significance of a diary might well lie in its being able to relieve anguish.

The other day someone told me that if I stopped eating break-fast, I could soon cure my stomach. I gave up my morning meal for several days but the only thing that happened was that my stomach emitted gurgling sounds.

Then another person told me to stop eating pickled vegetables. According to his theory, all stomach disorders come from eating pickles. My chopsticks avoided the pickles on the table for about a week but then, finding no change in my condition, I began eating them again.

According to still another person, massage is the only way to cure weak stomachs, but not in the ordinary way. He suggested that I try the Minagawa school of massaging, a very old method. If I tried this once or twice, I would be completely cured—that was what he told me. Sokken Yasui, a scholar of Confucianism, favored this method of massage and it is said that Ryuma Sakamoto, a famous swordsman, also received this treatment. Therefore, I wasted no time in going to Kami-Negishi.

When I went there, I was told that they had to massage the bones, and that they had to turn my intestines upside down before they could completely cure me. I received a terrible beating, as if my body were being pounded into pulp. I quit this ordeal after only one try.

Mr. A told me not to eat any solid food. I tried drinking only milk one day but I kept hearing a "plump, plump" in my stomach that made me think of a flood and I couldn't sleep at night.

Then Mr. B. came around and told me that if I breathed with my diaphram and exercised my stomach I would become healthy. I tried this for a while but somehow I felt a little unsteady around the belly. I'd try to remember to breathe with my diaphram but after five or six minutes, I'd completely forget. Then I'd force myself to think about nothing else. When I did this, my mind became full of pictures of diaphrams and I wouldn't be able to read or even write. A scholar of aesthetics, Meitei by name, said that I looked like a woman suffering labor pains. Having been made fun of, I quit this too.

And then a Mr. C. suggested eating buckwheat noodles. I commenced eating noodles three times a day but the only thing that happened was that I developed loose bowels. I've tried all possible means to cure my weak stomach but to no avail. But the three cups of *sake* I drank with Kangetsu last night had results! Hereafter, I'll start drinking several cups of *sake* every night.

I knew that he wouldn't keep this up either. His mind was like the pupils of my eyes—constantly changing. He wrote in his diary that his stomach was weak and that he was very worried about it, but that was funny because outwardly he tried hard to pretend he wasn't sick at all.

The other day, a learned person came to visit him and told my master that all sicknesses were due to nothing other than the sins of one's ancestors and the sins of the individual concerned. It seems that he had studied the subject to a great extent because his reasoning was clear, his explanation was comprehensive, and his theory rang true. It is only unfortunate that my master does not have either the brains or the learning to argue with such a person. Yet, even at that, he tried his best not to lose face. He answered, " Your theory is interesting but, you know, Carlyle had a weak stomach, too." He made it sound as if he were proud of his bad stomach. But his answer was way off the point.

" Yes, that's true but not everyone with a weak stomach can be a Carlyle," replied his friend. He said it so strongly that my master had nothing to say. He didn't even try to press the point.

My master was only full of vanity—he didn't actually have such a bad stomach. It was comical that he meant to drink *sake* at supper. Coming to think of it, he might have eaten so much *zoni* at breakfast that morning only because of having drunk Masamune *sake* with Kangetsu the previous night. I got the urge to eat some of the *zoni* myself.

I am a cat, but I can eat almost anything. I don't have the strength to make frequent trips to the fish dealer's alley like Kuro, nor am I in a position to expect extravagant food like the tortoise-shelled cat that used to live in the home of the two-stringed *koto* teacher down the street. I don't have many dislikes. I can eat the left-over bread of the children and I often lick the sweet candied beans of cookies. Pickled vegetables are tasteless but just out of curiosity, I have eaten some.

It's funny but you can eat almost anything if you try. To say that you dislike this or that is being extravagant, besides it would hardly be possible for a cat living in the house of a schoolteacher. According to my master, there was a French writer by the name of Balzac who was extremely extravagant—he was not extravagant only in food but also in writing novels.

My master said that this Balzac once tried to find some good names for the characters in a new novel, but he couldn't. A friend came to visit him and they went out for a walk. This friend went without knowing what was on Balzac's mind but as for Balzac himself, he was only trying to think up some good names for his characters. He walked along looking at all the signs, however there was no name to his liking. He kept walking on without even thinking about his friend, and his friend tagged along without knowing what all this was about.

On their way back Balzac noticed a sign on a tailor shop: "Marcus". Balzac clapped his hands and shouted, "This is it! It has to be this! Marcus is a good name. Just add 'Z' for the initial and you've got a good name. Z. Marcus—yes, a wonderful name! You know, when you create a name yourself it sounds so artificial that it's not interesting at all. At last, I've found a name that's to my liking." Without even considering his friend's displeasure, he was happy.

If you have to walk the whole length and breadth of Paris just to find a good name, it seems to me like too much trouble. As for me, with an oyster-like master, I don't usually have the nerve to go to such extremes. That I could satisfy myself by eating— just eating anything at that—was due, most probably, to the environment in which I lived. The reason I felt such a strong desire to eat the *zoni* was not because I wanted to be extravagant but because I wanted to eat as often as I could. I thought that some of the *zoni* which my master had left in his bowl might still be remaining in the kitchen so I took a trip to the kitchen to see for myself.

And there I saw some *mochi* that looked much like that floating in the *zoni* soup at breakfast. It was stuck to the bottom of a pot the same color as my master's. I had not, as yet, eaten any *mochi*. It looked good but then, again, it looked horrible. With my forepaw I pushed aside the greens which were floating above the pounded rice, and found that it was sticky when my claws caught at the outer surface. I found that it smelled the same as boiled rice when it was being transferred from the cooking pot to the serving container, but I could not make up my mind to eat it. I took a look around but found nobody coming. I didn't know if this was fortunate or not.

Osan, the maid, was playing shuttlecock and battledore outside. Her expression showed indifference as to whether it was the beginning of a new year or spring. In another room, the children were singing something about a race between a hare and a turtle. I would never have a better chance. If I didn't take advantage of it, I would miss the opportunity of tasting *mochi* until the following

New Year, a whole year away!

Although I am a cat, at this moment I arrived at a certain truth:
"All living creatures will do things they should not if they have the
opportunity." It was not really my desire to eat *mochi*. Actually,
the more I stared at the stuff at the bottom of the pot, the more
horrible it looked. If Osan had opened the rear door and had
come in at that very moment, or if I had heard the footsteps of the
children coming, I would have scampered away with no regret.
The fact that I wouldn't have been able to eat *mochi* for another
year would never have occurred to me again. But nobody came
in. I stood there in hesitation. On the other hand, however, there
was a whisper within telling me to go ahead and eat it. I kept
wishing that somebody would hurry up and make an appearance.
But nobody came. That only meant that I had to eat the stuff.

Wiggling my body so that my whole weight would come down
against the bottom of the pot, I sank my teeth into the sticky
mochi. What with the strength I put behind that bite, I reasoned
that I'd be able to tear almost anything off, but, try as I would, I
found to my astonishment that I couldn't pull my head away. I
tried to sink my teeth deeper into the mass but I couldn't even do
that. By the time I realized that this stuff they called *mochi* was
something for cats to avoid, it was too late.

The situation was the same as if I had fallen into a swamp. The
more I stamped around to free myself, the deeper I sank. The
more I tried to free my teeth, the heavier my jaws became. The
aesthetic Meitei had once criticized my master by telling him that
he was a man who could not be advised. With my head stuck in
the pot, I found myself admiring Meitei for his wisdom. This
mochi was the same as my master: it would not take advice. I
twisted and squirmed but it was something like trying to divide
ten by three—there was no end to it.

During my agony I arrived at another truth: "All living creatures can intuitively foresee the suitability or the unsuitability of
each action." I had discovered two truths now but having been
trapped by the *mochi*, I wasn't pleased with myself at all.

The *mochi* pulled at my teeth and it felt as if they were being pulled
out. Besides, if I didn't get loose and make my escape, the maid

would soon discover me. The children seemed to have stopped singing and it was most likely that they'd come running into the kitchen too.

Struggling against this terrible ordeal, I waved my tail around in circles but to no avail. I erected my ears and then laid them down flat but this did not have any effect either. My tail and my ears had nothing to do with this *mochi*. When I found that it was senseless to slash with my tail or to wiggle my ears, I quit. After a while, I decided that it would be best to use my forepaw in trying to get the stuff away from my mouth. First I used my right forepaw. I kept pounding at my cheeks but there was no reason why the *mochi* could be unstuck just by doing this.

Next, I used my left paw but this didn't work either. Thinking that dignity was not too important at such a time, I tried using my left and right paws alternately but whatever I did, the *mochi* still stuck to my mouth.

Getting impatient, I used both forepaws. To my astonishment, I found that I could stand on my two hind feet. In this position, I felt that I wasn't a cat any more at all. But I didn't care whether I was a cat or not at that time; I had to get free so I clawed more at my face. My right paw seemed stronger than the left so I almost lost balance. I'd shift my hind legs so I could keep standing; however I couldn't stand still long in one place but kept hopping all around the kitchen. I was surprised at my being able to remain erect so well.

It was at this time that the third truth popped into my mind: "In time of danger the impossible can become possible." I was still fighting when I heard some footsteps. Somebody was coming. I couldn't let anyone find me in this state, so I furiously went around and around the kitchen. The footsteps came nearer.

It is a shame but I seem to lack just a wee bit of the thing they called the grace of Heaven. I was, at last, discovered by one of the little girls.

" Oh, the cat's eating the *mochi* and dancing around! " she called out in a loud voice.

Osan, the maid, was the first to hear her. She came bouncing in through the rear door. Throwing aside her battledore, she

[30]

only exclaimed, "My, my!"

"What a disgusting cat!" said the Mrs. Even my master came in from his study and shouted, "You fool!" It was only the children who were shouting with joy. They seemed to think that all this was fun.

Suddenly, as if by arrangement, everyone else also commenced laughing. This made me angry but I was suffocating and I couldn't stop dancing. I was in a fix. At last, when the laughter dwindled down, the five-year-old girl said, "Oh, Mother, the cat's naughty, isn't it?" The group burst out laughing all over again. I have often experienced lack of sympathy in the human race but at no other time did I feel so humiliated.

At last, all the fight had gone out of me. I came down on my four feet, rolled my eyes and blinked. It seems that the master didn't want to see me die because he asked Osan to take the *mochi* from my mouth. Osan, with a look in her eyes as if to say that she wanted to let me keep on dancing, looked at the Mrs. The Mrs., too, seemed as if she wanted to see me continue the performance but she evidently didn't want to see me dancing to death. She said nothing.

"Hurry up and take that stuff from its mouth. Hurry up or it'll die!" My master was now giving a stronger order to the maid.

Osan had the same expression on her face as when she eats only half of a good dinner. She looked very unenthusiastic about her mission. In any case, she took hold of the *mochi* and pulled it with all her strength. Although it wasn't much like the mushroom Kangetsu had eaten, I felt as if all my teeth were being broken. It hurt like anything, and no wonder. The *mochi* was being pulled away with no consideration for my feelings whatsoever. It was then that I arrived at a fourth truth: "All comfort comes after suffering." By the time I felt well enough to look around, everybody had gone into another room.

After that mishap, I felt embarrassed whenever Osan looked at me so in order to get a change of air, I went out to call on Mikeko who lived at the house of the *koto* teacher nearby. Mikeko was famous among the other cats of this vicinity for her beauty. There is no doubt that I am a cat, but I know what it is to feel blessed.

Whenever I feel sullen because of looking at the bitter face of my master or because of a scolding from Osan, I invariably try to call on one of the opposite sex, especially Mikeko, and talk to her. I feel relieved and refreshed, and all the worries and the sufferings I had gone through are forgotten. I have the feeling of being born all over again. It is very true that females can sometimes help.

Peeking in through the fence, I saw Mikeko sitting on the veranda. She was wearing a new collar because it was New Year. The soft curve of her back was so lovely that I do not have words to express it. The graceful tail, the way she held her paws, the unconscious movements of her ears were all something I could never express with mere words. She had seated herself in a dignified position in the sunshine. Though she sat still, her fur took on the texture of velvet and gleamed in the sun. The fur seemed alive though there was no breeze. I could only stare at her in ecstacy. After a while, I recovered myself and called out in a low voice, " Oh, Mikeko, Mikeko." I waved my forepaw at her.

Mikeko cried out, " Oh, it's you, sir ! " Then she came down from the veranda ; the bell on her red collar tinkled as she walked.

" Oh, ho ! She must have received that new bell for New Year," I thought in admiration. In the meantime, she had come to my side and, curving her tail to the left, she said, " Happy New Year to you, sir."

The feline family, in greeting each other, generally stiffens the tail straight up and then curves it to the left. In our neighborhood, Mikeko was the only one who addressed me as " sir."

As I have previously said, I am still without a name but, living in the house of a schoolteacher, Mikeko showed her respect by saying " sir," to me. As for myself, this being called " sir " was not bad at all. I, in turn, replied, " I wish you a happy New Year too. By the way, your new collar is very nice."

" Yes, this is something my mistress bought me as a year-end gift. Don't you think it's lovely? " So saying, she kept tinkling the bell.

"Hmmm. It has a very nice tone. That's the prettiest bell I've ever heard."

"You don't say! Everyone's wearing one." She kept ringing it. "Don't you think it's melodic? I'm so happy," she purred. And the bell continued to tinkle.

"It seems that your mistress takes very good care of you," I sighed with envy. This was said to make her compare her situation with mine and I let it escape with good intention.

Mikeko was an innocent thing, and she answered naively, "Really, she treats me as if I were her own child."

It cannot be said that cats don't laugh. Man thinks that no creature can laugh except himself but that's a great mistake. When I laugh, the shape of my nostrils becomes triangular and my Adam's apple quivers. It would be quite impossible for a man to know that I was laughing.

"What is your mistress? How does she live?" I inquired.

"She is a teacher. A teacher of the two-stringed *koto*."

"Yes, that I know. But what is her standing—ah—her social position? I imagine she must have been highly respected once."

"Why—ah—yes."

A song came floating through the paper sliding doors. The *koto* was being played as accompaniment. "While awaiting you, a little female pine tree. . . ."

"Don't you think she has a nice voice?" asked Mikeko proudly.

"I guess so but I can't understand the song, really. What is it?"

"That? Oh, it's just a song. My mistress likes it very much. And to think that she's sixty-two! She's really very healthy for her age."

Coming to think of it, she must have been healthy to be able to live to be sixty-two.

"Yes," I agreed. I knew my answer was somewhat out of place but I couldn't think of anything else to say.

"She often talks about her former life."

"Oh, what did she do before?"

"They say that she is a daughter of the nephew of the mother, whose son married the younger sister of the secretary of the wife of the 13th Shogun, Tokugawa Iesada."

" What ? "

" She was the daughter of the nephew of the mother whose son married. . . ."

" Now, wait a minute. Let's get this straight. She was the daughter of the nephew of the mother—okay ? "

" Yes, she was the daughter of the nephew of the mother—you're right so far."

"All right now. Of the mother who married—."

" No, no. Of the mother whose son married—."

" I see, I've made a mistake. Of the mother whose secretary of the younger sister married—."

" No."

" Married the younger sister of the secretary ? "

" That's right."

"All right. Then she's a secretary's sister."

" Yes, the younger sister of the secretary."

"And this secretary got married ? "

" No, that's wrong. The younger sister of the secretary got married."

"All right. I was wrong. And this secretary was of the wife of the 13th Shogun, Tokugawa Iesada ? "

" Yes, that's right. Now do you understand ? "

" No. It's somewhat confusing and I can't get it straight. Anyway, what is your mistress in relation to the wife of the 13th Shogun or whatever he may happen to be ? "

" You don't seem to be too clever. She is the daughter of the nephew of the mother whose son married the younger sister of the secretary of the wife of the 13th Shogun, Tokugawa Iesada. I've been telling you this from the beginning."

" Sure, sure. I understand it clearly now."

" Then it's not too complicated, is it ? "

" Well, I guess not." That was the best I could manage. I gave up. At times, we have to tell lies.

The sound of the *koto* abruptly stopped and the teacher's voice was heard calling, " Here, Mi-ke, Mi-ke, Mi-ke."

" Oh, the mistress is calling me now. You don't mind my going in, do you ? " she purred happily.

I couldn't say that I did, so I kept still.

"You'll come again some time, won't you?" So saying, she ran towards the house but suddenly came back and added, "You don't look very well. I hope there's nothing wrong with you." She said this as if she were worried about me.

I couldn't confess that I had just tried eating *zoni* or that I had been dancing with a *mochi* in my mouth, so I only replied, "Oh, there's nothing wrong with me. It's just that I have a little headache. I've been thinking about something important. To tell the truth, I thought that if I could talk to you I'd get well and that's why I came today."

"Oh, I didn't know. Take good care of yourself, won't you? Goodbye." She seemed somewhat reluctant to leave, and this helped me greatly after that *mochi* affair. I was in high spirits.

I had planned to go home by way of the tea grove. I walked along, stepping on the melting ice, but when I poked my head through an opening in the bamboo fence, I found Kuro of the rickshawman's sitting on a heap of dead chrysanthemums. He was humping his back and yawning. I wasn't afraid of Kuro any more but I knew it would be troublesome if I entered into any conversation with him, so I tried to pass by as if I hadn't noticed him.

Kuro is a cat which, when he thinks that he is being slighted, won't keep quiet. He said, "Hey, you! You without a name! You seem to be getting stuck up these days. I know that you're living with a schoolteacher but that doesn't mean that you have to go around with such an arrogant look, does it? It's disgusting!"

Kuro sounded as if he hadn't known that I had become famous. I wanted to tell him about my picture on the greeting card but, on second thought, I knew that he would not understand. I made up my mind to get away from him as soon as possible. That does not mean that I didn't have to greet him so I said, "Happy New Year, Kuro. It's good to find you looking healthy as always." So saying, I erected my tail and let it curve a little to the left. Kuro lifted his rear end but did not return my greeting.

"Happy New Year? That's all foolishness! Better watch

[35]

your step, you belly-faced cat," he said.

It sounded as if he were sneering at me but I was not sure. I asked him what he meant by being belly-faced.

" You're only a New Year's bastard!"

This "New Year's bastard" was another new expression. It sounded more poetical but as for the meaning, it made less sense than a "belly-faced cat". Just for fun, I wanted to ask him to explain those terms but I knew that I wouldn't be able to get any clarifying answer, so without a word I started to leave again. It was quite an awkward situation.

Suddenly the rickshawman's wife angrily shouted. "Where's the salmon I put on the shelf? It's gone! It's that Kuro again. What a dreadful cat! Just let it come back and see what I'll do to it!" Her loud voice vibrated through the otherwise serene atmosphere and drowned out the chanting of the *koto* teacher.

Kuro assumed a bored look, as if to tell the woman that she could holler her head off if she liked. He then jutted his square jaw out at me as if to ask if I had heard his mistress. Although I had not noticed them before, I now saw some dirty salmon bones under his paws. The fish must have cost about two and a half sen. Forgetting all about what had gone on before, I blurted out, " You're as good a thief as always, aren't you?" But Kuro wasn't a cat who would change the subject just because of such an interruption.

" Who's a thief, you bastard? And only because you see a slice or two of a fish, what do you mean by saying ' as always '? Do I have to remind you that I'm Kuro of the rickshawman's?" Instead of rolling up his sleeves like a man would have done, he jerked his right paw up as high as his shoulder.

" Sure, I know you're Kuro."

" Then why did you have to say ' as always '? Come on. Tell me why." He was getting terribly worked up.

If we had been men, I would have been grabbed by the collar and shaken. I wasn't feeling any too comfortable but suddenly the rickshawman's wife was heard again: " Hey, Nishikawa. I've got an order for you. Go and get me a pound of beef, and get it quick. Do you hear? A pound of beef, and it has to be tender. Do you understand?" The voice ordering a pound of beef shattered the stillness of the whole area.

Kuro planted his four feet firmly on the ground and sneered, " Huh, just listen to that old hag. She wants to let all the neighbors know that she's ordering beef. She only gets to eat it once a year or so. What a person!"

I had nothing to assert so I said nothing.

" I won't be satisfied with only one pound of beef but that can't be helped. If the old hag puts it in the cupboard, it'll be mine to eat," said Kuro as if he were trying to make me understand that the order was really being made for his sake.

" It's going to be a real feast this time." I was hoping to get Kuro to leave as soon as possible.

" What would you know about eating beef? Shut up! You make too much noise." Kuro suddenly kicked some of the melting ice with his hind feet, showering my face with cold water. While I was shaking it off, Kuro crept through the fence and slipped away. Most probably he had gone to steal the beef which was going to be delivered to his house.

Returning home, I found a spring-like atmosphere in the sitting room. My master was laughing loudly which was, in itself, something unusual. Wondering what this could mean, I hopped up onto the veranda, through the open sliding door, and went to my master's side. There I found a guest I had never seen before.

His hair was parted neatly and he was wearing a cotton *haori* coat and a split *hakama* skirt. He looked like a serious-minded student. When I looked into the corner of my master's hand-warming brazier, I saw, lying beside a lacquered cigarette case, a card. It said, " Introducing Mr. Tofu Ochi " and it was signed by Kangetsu Mizushima. By this, I got to know the name of the guest and also to know that he was a friend of Kangetsu.

As I had entered in the middle of their conversation, I couldn't tell exactly what they had been talking about but I gathered that the subject was something about the aesthetician Meitei.

" . . . and he asked me to come along with him as there was a very interesting plot," said the guest.

" What do you mean? You were going to have a Western meal with an interesting plot? " asked my master as he poured more tea and passed a cup to his guest.

" Well, I don't exactly understand what Meitei meant by a plot but knowing him as I do, I was sure that it would be interesting."

" Did you go with him? "

" Do you know what really happened? "

My master suddenly slapped the top of my head as I sat on his lap and, I'm telling you, it hurt. This gesture was as if he meant to say, " I'm pretty sure what happened."

What escaped his mouth was : " You must have been treated to a farce. That is what usually happens." He was remembering the case of Andrea del Sarto.

" He suggested eating something unusual."

"And what did you have? "

" Well, we looked over the menu and Meitei discussed various dishes."

" Was this before you had ordered? "

" Yes, that's right."

"And then what happened? "

" Then he turned his head somewhat towards the waiter and said that there wasn't anything interesting on the menu. The waiter wasn't going to stand that so he suggested a roast duck or some pork chops. Meitei replied that he hadn't come to a restaurant just to eat common everyday food. The waiter didn't seem to understand what was meant by common everyday food so he didn't say anything."

" Quite understandable."

" Then Meitei looked at me and said, ' Do you know, my dear friend, that if you go to France or to England, you can eat a lot of dishes which have a flavor of times gone by? But here in Japan, wherever you go, you get nothing but superficial food. That's the reason I do not prefer Western-styled restaurants.' Meitei said all of this with a twinkle in his eye. Do you know if he has ever really gone abroad? "

" Meitei go abroad? Of course not. He has the money, though, so he could go any time he wants to. I'll bet he's thinking of going abroad and that he told you about his trip as if it had already happened. It was just a joke." My master said this believing he had said something funny because he looked up at his guest inviting him to laugh. The student didn't seem much impressed, however.

"Is that so? I thought that he might have gone without my knowing it and so I believed everything he said. He explained snail soup and frog stew as if he had actually seen them prepared."

"Must have heard about them from someone. You know, he's a wizard at telling lies."

"So it seems," said the guest gazing at the daffodils in a vase on the table. His expression suggested that he was somewhat disappointed.

"Then this plot you were speaking of—this was it, wasn't it?" asked my master, trying to come to the point.

"Oh, that's just the beginning. The main story is still coming."

"So?" exclaimed my master.

"Then Meitei said that it was quite impossible for that restaurant to serve snails and frogs so that we might as well settle for some *tochimenbo*. I consented somewhat reluctantly."

"What's this *tochimenbo*?—sounds a little funny."

"Yes, doesn't it? You see, Meitei said all this so seriously that I didn't realize what was behind it." The visitor was telling all this to my master as if he were apologizing.

"And then what happened?" asked my master, indifferent to his guest's feelings. He didn't show any sign of sympathy at all.

"Then he roughly called the waiter and ordered two servings of *tochimenbo*. When the waiter asked if he meant fried mincemeat, Meitei became extremely serious and corrected the waiter. He repeated that it was *tochimenbo* and not mincemeat that he wanted."

"So. Well, just what is this *tochimenbo*? Does it actually exist?"

"Though I thought it all strange at first, Meitei seemed very composed. Moreover, he understands many Western customs. I still believed that he had been abroad, so I chimed in and told the waiter that we wanted *tochimenbo*, even without knowing what it was."

"And what did the waiter do?"

"Thinking of it now, it was very comical. He stood there for a while and then told us that he was sorry but the *tochimenbo* was all sold out. He said that he could bring two servings of fried mincemeat, however. Meitei seemed extremely peeved and said it wasn't worth-while coming to this restaurant any more. He asked the waiter whether there was any way at all possible for us to have *tochimenbo* served, and he tipped him twenty sen. The waiter immediately changed his attitude and said that he'd go and ask the chef if something could be arranged."

"It seems as if Meitei wanted this *tochimenbo* very badly."

"Presently the waiter reappeared and apologetically asked if we could wait. He said it would take quite a while to prepare what we had ordered. Meitei said that as we had plenty of time, being New Year, we were willing to wait. He then took out a cigar and serenely began puffing on it. Having nothing else to do, I took out a newspaper and commenced reading. The waiter then returned to the kitchen."

"Going to a lot of trouble, wasn't it?" My master moved his seat closer and looked as intent as when he reads about the Russo-Japanese War.

"The waiter again reappeared and said that the ingredients for *tochimenbo* had become extremely scarce and that none could be purchased at the Kameya or at the Jugoban House in Yokohama so that they would not be able to serve *tochimenbo* for some time hereafter. He explained all this with a very long face. Meitei looked at me and repeatedly said that it was extremely discouraging because we had come here with the sole intention of eating *tochimenbo*. I couldn't just sit there without saying anything so I also added that it .was very regrettable."

"I should think so," agreed my master. As for myself, I couldn't find any reason why my master should agree.

"The waiter expressed deep regret but said that in case they were able to get the ingredients, he would want us to come again. Meitei then asked the waiter what materials they used in preparing *tochimenbo*. The waiter just gave a giggle for an answer. Meitei, in order to make sure, asked him if they used a bunch of Japanese

Haijin [a Nihon school of poets] to which the waiter replied that they were indispensable. So Meitei replied that now he understood why they could not be purchased in Yokohama nowadays."

"Ha, ha, ha! So that's the joke! That's a good one!" My master laughed so violently that I almost fell off his lap. Heedless of my plight, he kept on laughing. He discovered that he wasn't the only one who was caught in a joke like that of Andrea del Sarto. This made the story doubly enjoyable.

"Then the two of us stepped outside and Meitei said, 'How about that? Clever, wasn't it? Don't you think it was genius to order *tochimenbo**?' He was boasting about his exploit. I told him how much I respected his wit and said goodbye. But because of this, we missed lunch and I was famished."

"Yes, that would be inconvenient." · This was the first time that my master had shown his guest any sympathy. As for me, I had nothing to complain about. Afterwards, the conversation dwindled and the two men were in want of some subject to talk about, but my purring caught their ears.

Tofu drank his tea, which had now become cold, and said, "The reason I dropped in today was to ask you a favor."

"And what may your request be?" asked my master, somewhat aloof.

"Well—ah—as you know, I am very interested in literature and art but—"

"That's good to know," said my master encouragingly.

"Several people interested in literature and art have gotten together and now we're holding a meeting once a month. The first meeting was held in December."

"I take it that you read poems, verses and other literary works to each other. Can you tell me how you conduct these meetings?"

"Well, you see, at first we commence with old pieces and gradually work up to the newer creations of our group."

"When you say old compositions, do you mean Hakurakuten's poem *Biwako* or something similar to it?"

"No."

---

* Tochimenbo is actually a *haiku* poet.

"Then do you mean something like Buson's free styled verse *Shimpu Batei-kyoku*?"

"No."

"Then what do you mean?"

"We took Chikamatsu's drama about a double suicide."

"What? A drama by Chikamatsu? Do you mean the Chikamatsu who wrote pieces for puppet shows?"

Actually there is only one Chikamatsu. Chikamatsu is considered as the Shakespeare of Japan and no one else has the same name. That my master should ask for confirmation shows how stupid he is. He was stroking my head with great care without knowing it. In the world of today, it is said that some girls fall in love with cross-eyed men, so I guess I shouldn't have been surprised about such foolishness as this. Therefore I allowed my master to continue petting me.

"Yes, that's right," answered Tofu as he looked up into my master's face.

"How do the meetings go then? Do you have somebody read the passages out loud or do you have the members take the different parts?"

"We have each member take a part. You see, our main object is to represent the characters in the drama by expressing his or her individuality with gestures. In quoting the lines, we try to depict the individual, whether they are girls or apprentices, as they appear in the drama."

"Then it is just like a play."

"That's right. We only lack costumes and stage settings."

"Pardon my asking, but was the first performance a success?"

"Considering it our first try, I would say it was a success."

"What was the main scene?"

"It was where the boatman rows a customer to Yoshiwara."

"That must have been quite difficult," said my master cocking his head to one side. He exhaled smoke through his nostrils and it passed his ears and floated above his head.

"Not at all. The characters were only a customer, a boatman, a courtesan, a brothel attendant, a waitress, and a geisha procurer," explained Tofu calmly.

[42]

My master made a sour face. He didn't seem to have a clear picture of the characters so he inquired, " Do you suppose that the waitress is a maid in brothel? "

"Actually I haven't looked into the facts myself as yet, but I believe that the waitress is a maid of a teahouse, and that the brothel attendant is somebody who is in charge of the maids." Although Tofu tried to imitate the manner of speech of the various characters when he mentioned them, he didn't seem to know much about them himself.

" Hmmm. Then that means that the waitress works in a teahouse, and that the attendant lives in a brothel. Well, then, what is this geisha procurer? Is it a place or a person and, if a person, is it a man or a woman? "

" I'm not too sure but a procurer is generally a man, I think."

"And what's he supposed to do? "

" I still haven't looked into that either but I'll check on it pretty soon."

I myself imagined from this conversation that the play must have been a terrible farce so I stole a glance at my master. He wore, contrary to my expectation, a very serious expression.

" Who participated in the drama beside yourself? " asked my master.

" Oh, many others. For instance, there was a lawyer; he took the part of the courtesan. It was quite funny because he wore a moustache but had to speak in a sweet feminine voice. Moreover, he had to throw a fit."

My master asked in a worried tone, " Do you have to act as if you're having spasms when you're reading?"

" You see, the expressions and feelings are of great importance," replied Tofu as if he considered himself a serious artist.

" Was he able to act convincingly? " wondered my master.

" It was a bit difficult, being the first try," said Tofu.

" What part did you take, by the way? "

" Me? The boatman."

" You? A boatman? " My master's exclamation sounded as if to say that if Tofu were able to take the part of the boatman, he himself could have played the procurer. Presently, he asked frankly, " Was the part too much for you? "

Tofu didn't seem to be hurt by the question at all. He calmly explained, " To confess, the recital started out fine but ended in failure because of me. It was like this : There's a boarding house near the meeting place and four or five schoolgirls live there. I don't know how but they found out that we were going to hold a recital and they came to watch through one of the windows. In the meantime, I was reading my lines. I thought that I played my part pretty well but, probably because of my exaggerated acting, the girls burst out laughing. This flustered me. Having been interrupted, I didn't feel I could continue so we ended the meeting."

If this was what Tofu called a success, I could not imagine what he would term a failure. My Adam's apple quivered and I emitted a loud purring sound. My master stroked my head all the more lovingly. It is nice to be petted, even by the people I laugh at, yet I had a feeling of unrest at that time.

" That's a pity," said my master, extending his first consolation of the new year.

" In order to make it more successful we're going to try something different from our second meeting and that's the real reason why I'm here today. I've come to ask you to join us and help us out."

" Oh, I can't throw a fit," replied my master passively. He was trying his best to decline.

" I don't ask you to do that. I've brought a list of supporters of our group and if you would only write your name and attach your seal to it, I'd be much obliged." So saying, Tofu carefully unwrapped a small notebook from a purple handkerchief and placed it in front of my master.

Looking at it, I found the names of several professors and other people with degrees in literature neatly written in it.

" I'm not saying that I won't become a supporter, but what obligations would I have? " asked my oyster-like master. He seemed somewhat troubled.

" There's actually nothing much more for you to do. We would only like your name to show that you approve of these meetings. That's about all there is to it."

" Well, if that's the case, I'll gladly sign." My master, having been told that there was no obligation attached, seemed suddenly relieved. He would probably sign a pact for a treason if he believed there were no obligation attached. Moreover, in this way my master would have his signature listed with prominent persons. It was a great honor, something which had never happened to him before, so it is quite natural that he was eager to comply with the request.

Then my master excused himself and went into his study to get his seal. I was unceremoniously thrown onto the matted floor. It was then that Tofu took a piece of sponge cake from a plate and threw it into his mouth. He munched on it for a while but, being quite a mouthful, I was afraid he would choke. I visualized another incident like mine with the *mochi* that very morning.

By the time my master had returned with his seal, however, the sponge cake had settled in Tofu's stomach. My master did not seem to notice that one slice of the cake was missing. If he had, the first one he'd suspect would have been me.

After Tofu left, my master went into his study again and found a letter from Meitei.

" Greetings for the Happy New Year," it began. My master hesitated because Meitei's letters usually lack such seriousness. Only the other day, my master received a message which began : " There have been no ladies who have recently sent their love to me nor have I received any letters from them. But please don't worry because I've been taking good care of myself." This New Year's greeting, however, began in a surprisingly normal way. The letter continued : " I would like to call on you but, unlike you, I have planned to start this new year as actively as possible so I am extremely busy. I hope you will understand."

Meitei, being the person he is, must have been extremely busy— extremely busy enjoying the New Year's holidays—and it seems my master understood. The letter went on : " Yesterday, while enjoying a few moments with Tofu, I invited him to a dish of *tochimenbo* but, unfortunately, we could not find any owing to the present scarcity of the ingredients."

My master smiled when he recognized Meitei's usual style. The letter then said: "Tomorrow I will attend a card-playing party at the home of a baron; the day after tomorrow, a New Year's meeting held by the Association of Aesthetics; the next day, a reception for Professor Toribe; and the following. . . ." My master skipped the rest as it was tedious reading.

"And so, as I have mentioned, I shall be kept quite busy for the time being. I am also going to take part in various *no* recitations, in some epigrammatic poem parties, in a few classical ode gatherings, in some modern poetry teas, and in other affairs. You'll have to pardon my being unable to call on you. Instead, I am writing to extend my thanks for the many favors of last year."

My master only mumbled an answer to the letter, saying that there was no need for him to come.

"When you visit me the next time, I would like to enjoy a meal with you. I'm afraid that there won't be much variety during the cold winter months but I'm looking forward to eating a dish of *tochimenbo* with you."

Now, thought my master, he's coming to me with his *tochimenbo* ! He looked a little insulted.

"But owing to the scarcity of the ingredients, I'm afraid it might be impossible. Instead, we can try some peacocks' tongues."

My master read through this trick but it only made him want to read more.

"As you know, a peacock has only one tongue. It is not even half the size of your little finger, so that a man with a healthy appetite like you. . . ."

This reference distracted my weak-stomached master.

"And so we'll need about twenty or thirty peacocks. Although we can see a few in the Asakusa Hanayashiki Zoo and in Ueno, there are none at ordinary poultry stores. This might cause extreme difficulty."

My master only shook his head.

"Peacock tongues were often served during the Roman Empire, being a favored dish. They are still considered as an extravagant delicacy and I myself enjoy eating them very much."

My master was indignant that Meitei actually expected him to believe such lies.

"In the sixteenth century, peacock tongues became a necessity at all banquets. When the Earl of Leicester invited Queen Elizabeth to Kenilworth, peacock tongues were served. Rembrandt once painted a peacock on the table with its fantail spread."

My master considered that if Meitei had time to write a history of peacock tongues, he wasn't nearly as busy as he claimed.

"With all the rich dishes which I'm eating these days, I'll become, in no time, just as weak in the stomach as you, my dear friend."

That "my dear friend" could have been omitted. Moreover, he didn't have to refer to my master's weak stomach as if it were a standard to measure other people's ability to digest.

"According to historians, the Romans used to throw two or three banquets a day. In eating so much, even the person with the strongest stomach in the world would soon find himself getting eventually something like you, my dear friend."

The impudence of the man! He mentioned "my dear friend" again and once more used my master's stomach as an example.

"But the Romans, in order to enjoy so much extravagant food and still stay in good health, made a thorough research of the problem. They found it essential to consume much food but, at the same time, to keep in good condition. Thus, they hit upon an excellent idea."

My master suddenly became interested.

"After eating, the Romans would always take a bath. Afterwards, they would throw up whatever they had eaten and, in this way, they kept their stomachs clean. Having thus cleansed their stomachs, they would sit at the table again and once more enjoy the delicacies. In that way, they could consume as much as they wanted and still be able to maintain a healthy function of their internal organs. This is what you call killing two birds with one stone."

This really was killing two birds with one stone! My master looked envious.

"Today, in the twentieth century, we are witnessing a great increase in banquets and parties. Moreover, since we Japanese are sure to defeat the Russians in the present war and will have to celebrate the victory, I sincerely believe that we have arrived at a stage in which we should seriously consider this technique, the bathing-vomitting method, used by the Romans. If not, I am sincerely afraid that the Japanese will be, in the future, one and all, as weak in the stomach as you, my dear friend."

Again that "my dear friend"! That Meitei really likes to aggravate a person.

"Now that the Japanese are more acquainted with Western ways, we should study their ancient traditions and try to re-discover extinct customs that can be applied successfully to the society of the Meiji era. In that way, we might be able to prevent much misfortune and calamity. Usually, I indulge in pleasure all by myself. By carrying on such research, however, I am doing something to make up for my selfishness."

My master cocked his head to one side as if to imply that this didn't make any sense.

"In the meantime, I've been studying some literary works of Gibbon, Mommsen and Smith, but I can't find even a trace of their writing about this problem in any of their books. It is extremely unfortunate. But, as you know, I'm not one to give up easily. I always try to accomplish what I've once made up my mind to do. That's the reason I can say that the revival of the bath-vomitting method, hitherto mentioned, will eventually come into practice in the not too distant future. In any event, I'll notify you so please be waiting for word from me. As to the *tochimenbo* and peacock tongues, let's have this party after we are·sure that we can get them. I could make my own arrangements but as for you, my dear friend, because of your chronically weak stomach, I am ·ure that this will also be to your advantage. Yours truly,"

My master laughed and said to himself, " So Meitei is playing another of his pranks! He wrote so seriously that he had me reading the whole letter to the end. Well, if he can write such letters, it only means that he has a lot of free time."

During the days that followed, nothing worth mentioning happened. The daffodils in the white earthenware vase gradually withered away while the sprigs of plum branches in another vase commenced to blossom. This wasn't much fun to watch so I went out to visit Mikeko a couple of times but didn't get a chance to see her. At first I thought she had gone on a trip but I later found out that she was ill. I hid myself in the shadow of an aspidistra near the outdoor hand-washing basin and overheard the maid and the *koto* instructress talking to each other.

" Did Mi-ke eat anything today? "

" No, ma'am. She hasn't eaten a thing. I've placed a foot-warmer near her though."

It sounded as if they were talking about some other human, not at all as if they were taking care of a cat. Considering my own lack of attention at home I could not help feeling envious. But on second thought, when I considered how well the one I loved was being treated, it made me happy.

"Oh, what shall we do? If she doesn't eat she'll become weak."

" Yes, ma'am. Even with us, we wouldn't be able to work if we didn't eat," answered the maid. She sounded as if the cat were better off than she was. Actually, in this home, the cat was probably much more pampered than the maid.

" Did you take her to the doctor's? "

" Yes, but the doctor acted very queer. When I went into the

[49]

consulting room with Mi-ke in my arms, he asked me if I had a cold and began taking my pulse. I told him that it wasn't me who was the patient but this cat, and I placed Mi-ke on my lap. The doctor only smiled slyly and said that he didn't know anything about cats. He added that it would probably get well in a couple of days if we just let it alone. Isn't he awful? I got so angry that I told him that he didn't have to go to the trouble of looking her over. I also reminded him that this was a very precious cat, and so, placing Mi-ke into the bosom of my kimono, I left."

" Really ! "

The tone in which the instructress said " really ! " was of an elegance I cannot hear at my own place. She could probably use the expression so well because of her family ties with the wife of the 13th Shogun Tokugawa Iesada, et cetera, et cetera. I myself thought that it was all very elegant.

" She's sniffling a little."

" She must have caught a cold and her throat hurts her. When it becomes cold, everybody coughs, you know, ma'am," replied the maid. The language the maid used was also extremely polite, just as refined as that of the instructress who had family ties with the wife of the 13th Shogun.

" Moreover, there has been quite a bit of tuberculosis around lately."

" Yes, ma'am. Actually there is such an increase of new sicknesses that no one can feel safe."

" Nobody today is as healthy as those who were born at the time of the Shogunates so you must be very careful too."

" Do you think so, ma'am ? " said the maid. She seemed greatly impressed.

" Mi-ke hasn't been going out much lately so she shouldn't have caught cold."

" No, ma'am. But do you know that she's made some bad friends lately ? " The maid felt as proud of herself as if she were informing her employer about some confidential state secrets.

" Bad friends ? "

" That's right, ma'am. It's that dirty male cat that lives with the schoolteacher down the street."

" Do you mean that schoolteacher who emits such barbarous sounds every morning? "

" Yes, ma'am, the one that gargles and sounds like a goose being strangled to death."

Haaa! That was good! Every morning my master goes into the washroom to gargle. He practices making queer sounds by sticking his toothbrush down his throat. Yes, that was the way to describe the sound—like that of a goose being strangled to death—exactly! When he is in a bad mood, he only lets out a sound like a hoarse laugh but then in a good mood he will let go full blast. In other words, whether in a bad mood or not, he makes strange sounds every morning when gargling. According to the Mrs., my master didn't do this before they moved into the present house. He accidentally happened to make a funny noise when gargling one morning and ever since he tries out different sounds daily. He does not miss a day.

This is a very annoying habit and we cats cannot imagine why he has to keep it up with so much enthusiasm. All this about my master was well said, but that remark the maid made about the dirty cat was an entirely different matter. I continued to listen attentively.

" I wonder if there is any charm or spell behind those sounds. Before the Meiji Restoration, even lackeys and sandal carriers were careful about their manners. And in the residential quarters of a city, there wouldn't be a soul that would dream of disturbing others in such a way."

" I should think not! " agreed the maid with admiration.

" Having such a master, the cat is probably just as bad. If it happens to come around again, you have my permission to beat it."

" Yes, ma'am. That I'll be glad to do. I'm sure it's because of that tomcat that Mi-ke has become sick. I'll see to it that she's avenged."

I found that I was being falsely accused of many misdemeanors. This being the case, it wasn't healthy for me to be found and so, without seeing Mikeko, I went home.

On arriving I found my master in his study deeply absorbed in writing. If I had told him about what I had overheard at the home of the *koto* instructress, he would have been furious. But ignorance is bliss; he only continued to be engrossed in his work. He wrote as if he were a holy poet, but he emitted grunts now and then.

Meitei, whose New Year's greeting said he was too busy to visit my master, suddenly dropped in.

He began, "Are you trying to write some new type of poetry? If you've made any good verses, let me have a look."

" Here's a composition that I think is so good that I'm making a translation of it," replied my master through his heavy lips.

"A composition? Whose composition?"

" I don't know whose."

"An unknown composer's composition! You know, there's many a good work by unknown writers. You can't make fun of them all. Where did you find it?"

" In the second book," answered my master coolly.

" In the second book? What's this second book got to do with it?"

" It's only to say that the composition which I am now translating is in the second book."

" Don't joke, now. You're only trying to revenge yourself for the story about the peacock tongues I wrote you the other day. That's what you're trying to do, isn't it?"

" I want you to remember that I'm not a prankster like you are. Just remember that." My master twisted his moustache and tried to look dignified.

" Long ago, Sanyo produced a letter demanding payment of a debt. It had been written by a pack-horse driver. Sanyo considered it an excellent piece of prose. You, who have an eye for the beautiful, might have found something unexpectedly good so go ahead and read your piece. I'll do the criticizing," said Meitei, trying to sound like an authority of beauty. My master, mimicking the chant of a Zen priest reading the admonition left by Daito Kokushi, commenced : " Giant Gravity."

" Wait a minute! What do you mean by ' Giant Gravity'?"

"That's the title of the composition."

"What a strange title! I can't understand it."

"It's about a giant named Gravity."

"That's an impossible supposition but I'll let it go, being the name of the composition. Get going with the rest. You have an excellent voice so it ought to sound good."

"Don't joke with me now," warned my master before he started again.

"Kate looked out of her window. She saw some children playing with a ball, throwing it high up into the air. The ball went up, up, up into the air; then it came down towards the earth. The children threw it into the air again, and again it came down. The ball always fell towards the earth. 'Why does it fall towards the earth? Why doesn't it keep going up never to stop?' asked Kate. 'That's because a giant lives in the earth,' said her mother. 'He's Giant Gravity and he's very strong. He pulls everything towards himself. He pulls houses towards the earth. If he did not, everything would go flying around. The children would all go flying out into space. You have seen the leaves of trees fall—that's because Giant Gravity is pulling them towards the earth. At times, you might drop a book and it falls to the floor. That's because Giant Gravity is calling to it to come his way. When the ball is thrown into the air, Giant Gravity calls to it and it drops back to earth.' ".

"Is that all?" asked Meitei.

"Don't you think it's good?"

"Well, well. Can you believe it? You've got even for my *tochimenbo*, haven't you?"

"This has nothing to do with *tochimenbo*. I believe that this piece is really good and that's why I've translated it from English. Don't you really like it?" My master looked hopefully at his guest over his gold-rimmed spectacles.

"Amazing! It's amazing! Didn't know you had such talent. It's incredible how you fooled me this time. Yes, I surrender," gasped Meitei, as if he were saying all this to himself.

My master didn't seem to understand. He replied, "I wasn't trying to get you to surrender. I translated it because I think

[53]

that it is a very good piece."

" It is exceedingly interesting. Wonderful! I bow my head in surrender."

" Oh, don't be that way. You see, I've given up painting and instead I'm writing. That's all."

" Well, to tell the truth, your composition is far better than your water colors. Your paintings had no perspective and no regard for colors. Now I admire you more than ever."

" You shouldn't praise me so much. If you keep this up, I'll have to be going at it strong and hard," said my master, still not being able to understand.

It was at this moment that Kangetsu came. He seemed rather apologetic because of paying so many visits.

" Oh, it's you. Come on in. You're just in time. I've just heard a magnificent passage that surpasses even my own story about the *tochimenbo*." Meitei was making no sense at all in what he said.

" Well, well, is that so." Kangetsu's answer made no sense either. It was only my master who didn't seem to feel relieved at this interruption. He told Kangestu that Tofu Ochi had come around with the introduction Kangetsu had written.

" Oh, did he? You know, Kochi Ochi is rather serious-minded but he's a lot of fun in a way, too. I hope he didn't trouble you. He wanted me to introduce him to you very badly."

" No trouble at all, but— "

" Did he explain his name when he was here? "

" No. I don't recollect that he did."

" Is that so? He has the habit of explaining his name whenever he makes a visit for the first time."

" Well? " put in Meitei, as if waiting for the explanation himself.

" You see, his name is Kochi but the written character for Kochi can be read in a different way. He gets extremely nervous about it."

" I wonder why," said Meitei. He took some tobacco out from his gold-studded leather pouch.

" He generally tells a new acquaintance that his name is not

Tofu Ochi but Kochi Ochi."

"That's funny," laughed Meitei taking a deep drag on his pipe.

"This all comes from his enthusiasm for literature. When the name is read Kochi, it means, ' here ' as in ' here and there '. He's proud of this and insists on having his name read as Kochi and not as Tofu. He carries a grudge at those who read his name as Tofu, saying that they don't appreciate the hardship he suffered in getting the name."

"You don't say !" exclaimed Meitei with so much force that tobacco smoke exploded from his nostrils. The smoke got caught in his throat and Meitei started coughing.

"When he came here the other day, he told me how the schoolgirls had laughed at him when he was reading the part of a boatman," chuckled my master.

"That's how it is with Tofu," exclaimed Meitei striking his knee with his pipe. Finding that sitting so close was getting a little dangerous, I moved away a wee bit. "Yes, we talked about that literary meeting when we went to eat *tochimenbo* the other day. He said that he was planning to invite some prominent writers to their second meeting and told me to be sure to come. I asked him if the group was planning to take up Chikamatsu's story again but he said everyone had decided to perform *Konjiki-Yasha*. He told me he'd take the part of Omiya. Tofu taking the part of Omiya would really be interesting. I'll be there without fail so I can give him all the encouragement I can."

"That sounds like fun," said Kangetsu with a queer laugh.

"But you know something? Tofu is sincere throughout—not at all frivolous. A great difference between Tofu and Meitei, don't you think?" said my master avenging himself for the stories of Andrea del Sarto, the peacock tongues and the *tochimenbo* all in one. Meitei didn't seem to mind this one bit and retorted, "Well, we're all a class of fools and quite pertinacious besides." He laughed.

"That's about the size of it," concluded my master. Of course, he didn't understand Meitei's statement but he was good at camouflaging his ignorance. He had been a schoolteacher for a long time and knew many such tricks. It was only at such times that his experience as a teacher served him.

"What do you mean by this class of pertinacious fools?" asked Kangetsu frankly.

My master, looking towards the flowers in the alcove suddenly said, "Have you noticed those daffodils? They're the ones I bought on my way home from the bathhouse at the end of last year. Don't they last long?" He had forcibly changed the subject of conversation.

"When you mention the year end, it reminds me of an extremely strange experience I had," said Meitei, twirling his long pipe with the tips of his fingers like a juggler.

"What kind of an experience? Let's hear it," answered my master, relieved to know that the unfamiliar subject had been left far behind.

Meitei's strange experience, according to him, was:

"If I remember correctly, it happened on the 27th of December. I receive word from Tofu requesting me to be at home as he wanted to ask something about literature. I waited for him to come but he didn't show up. I ate lunch and was sitting by the stove reading a humorous story by Barry Pain when a letter from my mother arrived.

"She still treats me as if I were a little boy. This is probably due to her age. She cautioned me against going out during the cold winter evenings. She also wrote that although it was all right to take a cold-water bath, I should keep the stove going and the room warm otherwise I'd catch cold, et cetera, et cetera. I am grateful for her concern, she being my mother, but I wouldn't accept such advice from anyone else. I'm generally very carefree but her kindness impressed me a great deal that day.

"I got to thinking that it is a shame that I do nothing but fool around all day long. I began to feel that I should make a name for myself and bring honor to my family while my mother is still alive. I even inspired to make myself known as *the* Meitei of the Meiji era literary world.

"I continued reading her letter. She said that I was really a lucky boy because most of the other young men were fighting for their country in the Russo-Japanese war, while I did nothing but enjoy myself all year round as if it were always New Year. But, you know, I'm not really that lazy. My mother followed this by listing my primary-school friends who had died or had been wounded in the war. After having read the names one by one, I got the feeling that life is meaningless and that man is worthless too. In closing, she wrote that as she was getting old, this New Year's *zoni* might be her last. I became all the more wretched and wished that Tofu would hurry up and come. He never showed up.

"By then, it was suppertime. After eating, I wrote about twelve or thirteen lines to my mother. The letter she had sent covered a six-foot-long scroll. I don't have the knack of writing such long messages so I generally write only about ten lines.

"But because I hadn't had any exercise all day, my stomach felt rather bad. I made up my mind to run down to the mail box to send the letter, and then to take a little walk. I decided it would do Tofu good to wait a while himself if he came.

"Without my knowing it, my legs seemed determined to go in the direction of Dote Sanban-cho instead of going towards Fujimi-cho, a thing quite unusual. The night happened to be somewhat cloudy and a dry wind came blowing from the palace moat. It was terribly cold. Listening to the shrill whistle of a passing train, my feet took me under an embankment near a river. I immediately sensed the loneliness of this vicinity.

"The year end, death on the battlefield, old age, uncertainty—such thoughts entered my mind and went around in circles. I've often heard of people committing suicide by hanging themselves but it was not until then that I realized that people feel most enticed to kill themselves when they are in such a state of mind. I happened to tilt my head back and found myself just below those pine trees."

"Those pine trees? What pine trees?" interrupted my master.

"Those neck-hanging pines," said Meitei, pulling his neck deeper into his collar.

"Aren't the hanging pines at Konodai?" put in Kangetsu, adding a question of his own.

" No, the pine trees at Konodai are for hanging bells. Those at Dote Sanban-cho are for committing suicide. It is said that from time immemorial whoever pass beneath the pines at Dote Sanban-cho get the urge to hang themselves. On the embankment, there are a great many pine trees, and when news gets around that somebody had hanged himself somewhere, you are sure to find a body dangling from one of those at Dote Sanban-cho. There are several suicides there every year. It seems that no other trees appeal so much to suicides. When you look up, you'll see the branches stretching across the road in a most appropriate fashion.

" What nice-looking branches! It's a shame to let them spread out for nothing like that! You want to see somebody hanging from them. You look around to see if anybody is coming to fill your purpose but nobody comes. You feel frustrated at first but then you get the idea to hang yourself. You might say, ' No, if I hanged myself, that would mean taking my own life. I'd better quit.'

" But you know, long ago, the Greeks used to amuse themselves by putting on an act of hanging at banquets and they enjoyed it. One of them would stand up on a stool and put his head through a noose. Then somebody else would kick the stool out from under him. The trick was for the man on the stool to loosen the rope and jump down before he was killed. Now, if this is possible, there would be nothing to fear at Dote Sanban-cho. Thinking of trying it out myself, I touched one of the branches. It swayed in just the right way. Its curve was actually beautiful. When I thought of how it would look with somebody hanging from it, it became irresistible. I firmly decided to have a try myself. But then, on second thought, I realized that it would be impolite to have Tofu wait for me if he came, so I decided to go home first and carry out my resolution afterwards. So I returned home."

" It all had a happy ending then, didn't it? " asked my master.

" Interesting, very," said Kangetsu, with a smirk.

" Tofu was not at my home but I found a post card which said that he couldn't come because of some urgent business, but that he was looking forward to seeing me at a later date. I felt that now I was free to go and hang myself, and I was happy. So I put on my wooden sandals and hurriedly returned to the pine trees. I looked up when— "

Meitei looked at my master, and then at Kangetsu, but his face was expressionless.

"And what did you see?" asked my master impatiently.

"Now we're coming to a good part," said Kangetsu, as he twisted the string of his *haori* coat.

"In looking up, I found that somebody was there already. You know, it was most disheartening. The suicide impulse must be just as William James, the American philosopher, claims: the subconscious, which lives in the shadowy kingdom of the dead, and I, who exist in the practical everyday world, sometimes meet eye to eye due to some misfortune," continued Meitei coolly.

My master, thinking that he had again fallen victim to another trick, threw a piece of broiled *mochi* into his mouth and commenced munching it without saying anything. As for Kangetsu, he only bent over the handwarming brazier and began neatly raking the ashes. There was a smirk on his face. Presently, Kangetsu opened his mouth and commenced to speak in an exceedingly quiet tone.

"Well, your story would have been incredible to me because it is about an experience which very seldom happens, but I myself had an experience something like it just the other day. So I find no reason to doubt what you have told us."

"Did you want to hang yourself too?"

"Well, it wasn't anything like suicide in my case. It happened at the end of last year and, moreover, it was on the same day and at the same time as Meitei had his adventure. It is all the more strange because of these facts."

"This is good," said Meitei, stuffing his mouth full with *mochi*.

"On that day, I attended a year-end party at Mukojima. A little concert was to be given so I took my violin with me. There were about fifteen or sixteen young ladies present and the function was a great success.

"We had finished both the banquet and the concert, and every-body was talking excitedly. When it became quite late, I thought of leaving but the wife of a professor approached me and asked in a low voice if I knew that Miss So-and-So was sick. I had seen this young lady only a couple of days before and there seemed to be nothing wrong with her. I was taken by surprise and asked for details. The professor's wife explained that during the night after I had last seen her, the young lady was suddenly attacked by a fever and became quite delirious. I was told that she often called my name."

Meitei and my master surprised me by remaining silent. I would have expected them to make such comments as: "Look, the boy's in love!"

"When they called in the doctor, he said that he could not name the malady but that the brain was effected as the fever was very severe. He added that if the barbiturate he had given her did not take effect, her condition would become even more serious. I felt very uncomfortable when the professor's wife told me this. I felt terribly oppressed, as if I were having a nightmare in which the air around me had become so solid that it was pinning me in from all sides. While on my way home, the news of the girl's illness clung to my mind and I felt it overbearing. That the lovely, cheerful and healthy Miss So-and-So should have become—"

"Just a minute. I'm sorry to interrupt your story but you mentioned a 'Miss So-and-So' several times. We'd like to know who she is," said Meitei. My master grunted to express agreement.

"That might cause her some embarrassment so let's leave her name out. Don't laugh. I'm serious about this. In any case, this young lady's suddenly becoming sick got me all worried. I felt like a withering flower or a falling leaf—all my energy suddenly left me, as if it had gone on strike. All at once I found myself on the Azuma-bashi Bridge.

"Leaning against the rail, I looked down but couldn't tell whether it was high tide or low. Yet, the black water was there, moving along in a dark mass. A rickshaw came from the direction of Hanakawado and went rolling over the bridge. I followed the light of the lantern with my eyes. It gradually became smaller and smaller and then disappeared entirely when it reached the Sapporo Beer Company building. I turned my eyes again to the water below. It was then that I faintly heard someone calling my name from upstream. I wondered who it might be. I looked over the water but it was too dark to see anything, much less make anyone out.

"Thinking that this was probably only my imagination, I decided to be getting home. I took a step or two but again I heard my name being called, softly and far away. I stopped and listened carefully. When I heard it the third time, I had to hold on to the railing because my knees were trembling like leaves. I couldn't tell whether the voice came from far away or from the bottom of the river but, in any case, it was without mistake the voice of Miss So-and-So. Involuntarily I answered, 'Ye-es.' My voice seemed so loud when it resounded over the quiet water that I was taken aback. I looked around to see if anybody was nearby but there was not a soul, not even a dog. Even the moon remained hidden.

"It was then that I wanted to be enveloped in the darkness of the night and go to the place the voice had come from. Miss So-and-So's pleas sounded as if she were suffering, as if she were appealing to me, as if she were asking me to help her. I whispered, 'I'll be there with you right away.' I leaned over the railing and again looked down at the dark water below. The voice seemed to be coming from under the ripples of the river. I climbed onto the rail and decided to jump if the voice called again. I stared down at the water when the sad voice, even so faintly, came floating to me again. I jumped high and then commenced dropping with no feeling of regret at all. I could have been a stone."

"So you finally jumped in," breathed my master blinking his eyes.

"I didn't think it would come to this!" exclaimed Meitei, pinching his nose.

"When I was falling, I must have fainted. I don't know exactly what happened but when I came to, I felt cold but not wet at all. I thought this was extremely strange. When I looked around, however, I was surprised to find that I was in the middle of the bridge. I had made a mistake in directions and jumped backward instead of forward."

Kangetsu had a sly smile on his face but only kept fondling the string of his *haori* coat.

"Ha, ha, ha! That's wonderful!" laughed Meitei. "Your experience really was the same as mine. This is also material for James' theory. If your story were written, it would most probably surprise the whole literary world. By the way, what happened to Miss So-and-So?"

"I paid her a New Year's visit a couple of days ago and found her playing shuttlecock and battledore with the maid. She had evidently recovered."

My master had remained silent but, not to be outdone, he opened his mouth to say that he, too, had had a strange experience. "You did? Well, well, what is your story?" Meitei's eyes seemed to say that my master couldn't possibly have had any adventure of this kind.

"Mine also took place around the end of last year."

"Funny how all of our experiences happened to take place at the end of last year," laughed Kangetsu. I noticed that some of the *mochi* was sticking to Kangetsu's remaining teeth.

"Must have been at the same time and on the same date," interrupted Meitei smartly.

"No. It was around the 20th, if I remember correctly. My wife had told me that instead of my giving her a year-end present, she wanted me to take her to the theater to appreciate Settsu Daijo's performance. I promised to take her, and asked what was playing. Looking in the newspaper, she found *Unagidani* was being performed. I didn't want to see that so I put off going for that day.

"The following morning, my wife came with the newspaper and asked if it was all right to go that afternoon to see *Horikawa*. I told her that this *Horikawa* was mostly composed of samisen music and that the drama itself had no meaning at all. My wife made a face but we didn't go.

"On the next day, my wife said that they were performing *Sanju-sangen-do* and that she wanted very much to see it. It was being performed by Settsu himself. She added that though I myself may not like it, it was she who was supposed to enjoy her-

self so I could at least take her. Her request sounded more like
a demand so I said that if she wanted to go that badly, she could.
But I told her that as it was a once-in-a-lifetime performance by
Settsu, it would be so crowded that we wouldn't be able to get
seats if we had no reservations.

" In the first place, when you want to go to such a performance,
the usual routine is to go to the theater teahouse where you can
reserve a seat. But if you don't, you would be doing something
out of the ordinary and that is not right. Therefore I told my
wife that, though it was regrettable, we wouldn't go.

" With a fierce gleam in her eyes, my wife said that she was a
woman and didn't know about such complicated procedures but
that Ohara's mother and Kimiyo Suzuki had attended the theater
without going to all that trouble. She added with a sob that
I was very trying and that even if I were a schoolteacher, I didn't
have to go to so much trouble just to listen to music.

" Under this attack, I said that I'd go even though we wouldn't
be able to get seats. I told her we'd go by streetcar after supper.

"All of a sudden she became very animated and said we had
to get there by four so we didn't have much time left. She said
that Kimiyo Suzuki had told her that we had to be there by four
o'clock in order to get a good seat. I asked her again, just to make
sure, whether we could get seats or not if we arrived after four.
She answered that it would be absolutely impossible. But what
do you think? It sounds odd but just then I had a sudden attack
of chills."

" Did you say you got it or your wife? " asked Kangetsu.

" No, it wasn't my wife; she was as lively as ever. It was me.
I felt myself shriveling up like a balloon with a leak in it. Everything seemed to be twirling around and I couldn't move."

" Then it was an acute case." said Meitei, explaining more
than asking a question.

" Terribly. I was at a loss. You see, this was the only request
my wife had asked of me throughout the year, and of course I
wanted to make her happy. I had often scolded her and at times
I wouldn't even speak to her ; she endured great hardship because
of me and the children but I had done nothing to make up for all

this. But that day, we had money in our purse and time. Without any doubt, my wife wanted to go very much and I wanted to make her happy. Yes, I wanted to take her out but with the chill and the dizziness, I wouldn't have been able to get to the front door, much less to the streetcar.

" The more I pitied my wife, the worse my chill and dizziness became. I thought that if I could get the doctor to look me over and give me some medicine, I might recover before four. I consulted my wife and sent for Dr. Amaki. Unfortunately, however, he had received a call and hadn't returned home yet. We were told that he'd be back around two and that word would be left for him to call on us as soon as he returned. It was really very depressing.

" I knew that if I could take a sedative, I'd get well before four o'clock. But when one thing goes wrong, everything else also goes wrong and you can't do much about it.

" I had looked forward to seeing my wife's happy face but it seemed as if everything were going to the contrary. My wife, with a longing plea, asked me with no expectation if I would be able to make it. I told her not to worry, that I'd be able to go without fail. I assured her that I was going to get well by four o'clock. I also told her to change her kimono and to get ready. But deep down inside me, I was afraid it would be impossible to go to the theater.

" Gradually my chill became worse and so did my dizziness. If I didn't get well by four and keep my promise, there was no telling what my wife would do as she is very narrowminded. I was in a sad plight and didn't know what to do.

" I got to thinking that it would be the duty of a husband to explain, if my health became worse, the chances of mortal life and the inevitable where all living things must die. I wanted to have my wife comprehend these facts so that she'd understand and be prepared for the final moment. I hastily called her into my study. I asked her whether, as a woman, she understood the meaning of the English proverb ' many a slip 'twixt the cup and the lip '.

" ' I don't understand English ; ' she screamed and added that I shouldn't tease others knowing that they don't understand a word of the language. 'All right,' she said. She didn't understand English at all but if I liked English so much, why didn't I marry a girl who had graduated from a Christian school? She was terribly angry and called me heartless. Consequently, I forgot to tell her to be prepared for the final moment.

"But I didn't use English with any bad intention. I used English only because of my love for my wife but my intention was misinterpretèd. Because of the chill and the dizziness, I must have become confused. I had quite forgotten that my wife doesn't understand English and I rashly used it without thinking. Coming to think of it now, it was wrong of me and it was all my fault that my wife became angry.

"But because of this incident, the chill and the dizziness became worse. My wife went to the washroom just as I had told her to do, and was powdering herself and getting all ready. She took out her kimono from the chest of drawers and changed. Then she waited without any expression on her face, as if to say now she was ready so there was nothing to do but go.

"I didn't know what to do. I looked at my watch, wishing that Dr. Amaki would hurry, and found that it was three o'clock. We had only one more hour.

"'Don't you think we'd better be going?' asked my wife, opening the door of the study. I know it might sound funny saying something nice about my own wife, but this was a time when I thought that she was really very beautiful. Her skin, which she had just washed with soap, was radiant and it made a lovely contrast to the black *haori* coat she was wearing. Her face shone bright, not only because of the soap she had used but also because of the hope she had of going to the theater. One form of beauty was substantial and the other abstract.

"Seeing her looking so nice made me want to take her out very much. I lit a cigarette in order to muster up enough strength to get me to the streetcar but just then Dr. Amaki came.

"He was just in time. I told him about my condition and the doctor looked at my tongue, felt my pulse, tapped my chest, stroked my back, turned my eyelids and felt my skull. Then he sat down to think things over.

" ' I feel somewhat worried,' I told him. But the doctor calmly answered, 'Actually there's nothing much to be worried about.'

" ' I wonder if it's all right for him to go out for a while?' put in my wife.

" ' Well——,' said the doctor after thinking for a moment. ' It's perfectly all right if he doesn't feel sick.'

" ' But I feel sick,' I said.

" ' In any case I'll prepare some medicine for you.'

" ' If you believe it will help. But I think my chill is going to get worse.'

" ' There's nothing to worry about. There's no need to get nervous about this,' said the doctor, and with that he left. The time was then three-thirty.

" My wife told the maid to go to the doctor's and get the medicines. The maid ran both ways. The time was now fifteen minutes to four. Fifteen minutes until four o'clock! Though I had not felt nauseous until then, all of a sudden I felt like throwing up. In the meantime, my wife emptied some of the medicine into a cup and placed it in front of me. I picked the cup up and was just going to drink the medicine when a belch formed itself and came rushing up from my stomach. I had to put the cup down.

" My wife said, ' Don't you think you had better take it?' Her question sounded like an order. I felt that I must drink that stuff and get going so I wouldn't be breaking my promise to my wife. I decided to drink the medicine in one gulp. I brought the cup to my lips but once more I belched. This again prevented me from drinking. I tried again but again I had to put the cup down. Try as I would, the medicine remained in the cup because I felt like belching. While I was repeating my efforts, the clock in the tearoom struck four.

" It was four o'clock! I knew I couldn't waste any more time. I picked the cup up again, and what do you think? It's strange but at the stroke of four, the nauseated feeling vanished and I drank the cup of medicine without any trouble at all. At ten minutes past four I realized why Dr. Amaki is so famous. The shivers I had had in my back and the dizziness completely disappeared. Although I couldn't stand up for a while, due to the condition I had been in, I had completely recovered and I felt very happy."

"And did you go to the Kabuki-za with your wife?" asked Meitei with a puzzled look.

"Well, I wanted to go but, you see, it was past four o'clock. As my wife had said that we couldn't get in after four, it was impossible to do anything about it so we didn't go. If the doctor had come about fifteen minutes earlier I could have fulfilled my promise and my wife would have been greatly pleased. But because of a difference of fifteen minutes, we had to remain at home."

My master, upon finishing his story, seemed to be satisfied by having said his piece. Most likely he thought that he had done his share of the talking and was now on equal terms with the other two.

" That was extremely unfortunate, wasn't it?" laughed Kangetsu, showing his missing tooth.

Meitei commented with a blank expression, as if to himself, " Having such a kind and considerate husband, your wife is indeed a lucky woman."

Just then, the Mrs. coughed on the other side of the paper door.

I listened to the stories told by these three individuals but found that they were neither funny nor sad. I found that man opens his mouth only in order to consume time. Human beings laugh at that which is not funny and enjoy that which is not interesting; they have no ability to do otherwise. I had always known that my master was self-willed and narrowminded but, having heard this story, I suddenly came to despise him.

Why couldn't he simply listen quietly to the other two? What did he think he could gain by describing his unwillingness to admit defeat? Was anything written like that in the book of Epictetus? Though my master, Kangetsu and Meitei believed themselves to be of a special class—enjoying the blessings of peace, standing as aloof as a gourd being blown in the wind—actually they are greedy and share many common evils. That they love competition and the thought of winning against others can be seen in their daily conversations. If they ever take even one additional step down, they will be on the same level as the animals they denounce. This, as understood by a cat, is extremely sad. The only point in their favor is that they do not try to express simple meanings in grandiloquent phrases.

A few days later I went over to the garden of the *koto* instructress again to see how Mikeko was.

The New Year's decorations of pine and bamboo bound with a straw rope had been discarded. Ten days had already passed since the beginning of the new year. Not a streak of cloud could be seen in the deep azure sky on that serene spring-like day. The sun seemed to shine over the four oceans of the world. The small garden seemed much livelier than when it received the first rays of the sun on New Year's Day.

On the veranda I saw a cushion but not a glimpse of anyone nearby. The paper sliding door was shut. Finding no one around, I jumped up onto the veranda, dirty feet and all, and stretched myself out comfortably on the cushion. It felt so good that I forgot all about Mikeko and commenced dozing. All of a sudden I heard voices from within.

" Thank you for all the trouble. Was it ready? " The mistress was at home after all.

" ' I'm sorry for being late. The maker of Buddhist images and decorations said he had finished it just before I arrived."

" Oh, isn't this pretty? Mikeko would have been pleased, I'm sure. There's no fear of the gold paint coming off, is there? "

" No, ma'am. I made sure to ask the man himself and he told me that he had used the very best. He said that it would last longer than the monumental tablets used for most people. In writing the inscription he used the simplified form for the character ' honorable.' It looks nicer this way."

"All right, then. Let's put it in the shrine and offer incense."

I wondered what had happened to Mikeko. I sensed that something was wrong so I stood up on my hind feet on the cushion and looked. I heard the ring of a bell and the voice of the instructress murmuring her prayers, "Namu-Myoyo-Shinnyo, Namu-Amidabutsu."

"You may offer your prayer now," she told the maid.

"Ting," sounded the bell and the maid repeated the same words.

My heart suddenly began to throb like anything and I stood on the cushion without even moving my eyes—as if I had been a cat carved of wood.

"It's really a pity. She had only a little cold at first," commented the maid.

"She might have recovered if Dr. Amaki had given her some medicine."

"Yes, ma'am. Dr. Amaki was wrong. He only made fun of Mi-ke."

"Don't blame others too much. This, too, is what you call life. . . . But really, I think it was because of that tomcat of the schoolteacher's. He was with her too much."

"Yes, ma'am. That brute is the enemy of Mi-ke. Yes, indeed!"

I wanted to speak up for myself but, on second thought, I realized that this was a time to show endurance. So I swallowed hard and kept listening. Then the conversation dwindled.

"It's strange, but we cannot always have our own way. Mi-ke who was such a beautiful cat dies, and that ugly stray cat keeps on living and doing bad things."

"A cute cat like Mi-ke! You wouldn't be able to find the likes of another cat like her even if you went searching the world over."

The maid, in speaking of the cat, seemed to be referring to some person. She might have been thinking that cats and people were the same. Coming to think of it, she looked somewhat like a cat herself.

"If instead of Mi-ke—," murmured the instructress.

"Don't you think that it would serve him right if that cat of the schoolteacher died, ma'am?"

Well, well! It wouldn't be any too well for me—not for me! I hadn't experienced death as yet and I didn't know how it felt to die but it had been only a few days before that I almost did. Being extremely cold, I crawled into the pot for extinguishing live charcoal. The maid, not knowing this, shut the lid tight and I almost suffocated. It was terrible! According to Shiro, if I had stayed in there, I would have been dead by now. If I were to die for Mikeko's sake, it might not be too bad. But if I have to go through that terrible ordeal before death, I wouldn't care to die for anybody, no, not me!

" Mi-ke would have nothing to regret as for her funeral. We had the priest come to offer prayers for her, and he even changed her name according to religious rites."

" Yes, ma'am, that's true. She's a very lucky cat. The only thing that I have to complain about is that the priest's prayers were too short and too simple."

" Yes, they were short and simple. I asked Priest Gekkei-ji about it and he said he had recited the part which was most significant and that ought to be sufficient to get a cat to paradise."

" Really? But in the case of that scoundrel— "

I have many a time said that I do not have any name, but for the maid to call me a scoundrel was indeed an insult!

" —he has sinned so much that no amount of prayer would do him any good."

I don't know how many times the maid used the word " scoundrel", but I soon got tired of the endless talk. Sliding myself off the cushion, I jumped down from the veranda, fluffed all of the 88,888 hairs of my body and shook myself. I have not visited the home of the *koto* instructress since. I don't know what has happened to her but she herself might now be resting in her grave after being given short and simple prayers by Priest Gekkei-ji.

Recently, I have not had the energy to go out much. My world seems to have become too languid. I have become a lazy cat, just as lazy as my master. I have even developed the feeling that people are not at fault when they gossip about my master, saying that he is frustrated in love because he keeps himself locked up in his study all day long.

Having caught no rats as yet, Osan, the maid, brought up the subject of chasing me out of the house. But my master at last

We had the priest come to offer prayers for her.

seems to realize that I am not just an ordinary cat and he spoke up for me. I am still able to stay at his home, doing nothing.

Considering these facts, I will not hesitate to say that I am deeply grateful to my master. At the same time, I express my respect for his penetrating insight. I don't get mad at Osan any more when she treats me roughly because I now know that she acts that way without realizing it. If a second Hidari Jingoro, the famous lefthanded Japanese sculptor, appeared and carved my image on a two-storied gate, and if the Japanese brethren of the brush of Steinlen, the famous French painter, choose to portrait my likeness on their canvases, it would be then that the blind idiots I now know would feel ashamed of the way they have been treating me.

III

MIKEKO is dead, and I have absolutely nothing to do with Kuro any more. I used to find myself lonely but fortunately I have made new friends with humans so I am not as bored as I might otherwise be. The other day a man wrote to my master asking him for my picture. And then another man sent some famous *kibidango* cakes from Okayama in my name. In having someone to sympathize with me, I gradually came to forget that I am a cat. I have more contact with humans than with cats nowadays so I do not get together with my own breed any more to fight to the finish with the two-legged humans. At times, I actually believe myself to be a human being. I have no intention of despising my own kind but it goes without saying that one tries to find safety and comfort in the nearest person. It would be extremely embarrassing, however, to have this considered illogical, as being fickle or a betrayal. Those who say such things about others are generally the most unfortunate anyway.

Having broken off my ties with other cats, I do not feel attached any longer to Mikeko or Kuro. With the same pride that humans possess, I want to criticize and comment on their thoughts, speech and actions. This is not anything unusual. The only matter that upsets me is, though I have a great deal of dignity, my master still believes me to be just a plain ordinary cat. Without even a word to me, for example, he ate all the *kibidango* cakes that had been sent to me. I really did feel hurt. As for the requested picture, he hasn't taken one and sent it as yet. You may consider this a complaint, but let my master be himself and let me be myself. We cannot help it if our views differ.

Now that I consider myself as being human, it would be quite difficult for me to write more concerning cats. You'll have to excuse me but I'll have to keep writing about Meitei and Kangetsu.

It was one of those fine Sundays. My master came out of his study and laid some sheets of paper, a brush and a slab of India ink by my side. He then stretched himself out on his stomach and mumbled to himself. I suspected he was making such sounds as a prelude to his writing so I just watched him carefully. Then he took up his brush and wrote in large strokes: " Ko-isshu," the posthumous name of Tennen-koji. I thought at first that my master was going to do well for a change but then I wondered if he was going to write a verse or an ode. Just as I should have known, however, my master stopped writing the first line and switched over to the next: " I am thinking of writing something about Tennen-koji." The brush travelled to the last character and stopped. My master cocked his head to one side, as if by doing so he would encourage some new idea. It seemed that nothing came to mind because he put the tip of the brush to his mouth and commenced licking it. His lips became black with ink.

Just below the last character he had written, my master drew a round circle. Then he placed two dots for eyes, and right in the middle of the circle he drew two round nostrils, under which he drew a straight line for the mouth. This was not a sentence nor was it even a verse.

My master seemed to be disgusted with his drawing because he then smeared the design with more ink. Then he selected a new line on the paper. It seemed to my master that he could write easily only by changing over to a new blank line. Presently he wrote: " Tennen-koji was a person who studied the infinite—who read the *Analects* of Confucius—who ate baked sweet potatoes— and who had a dripping nose." This he wrote with furious strokes. It was a somewhat clumsy sentence. Then, without reserve, my master commenced reading this out loud. " Ha, ha, ha! This is great! But the part about his nose dripping— that's going a little too far so I'll just cross it out." And so saying, he drew a line through the offensive phrase.

One line would have done the job neatly but he then drew a second and then a third. Actually they made nice parallel bars. He kept drawing lines, indifferent as to whether they crossed into the other parts. Altogether he had drawn eight lines, but nothing new entered his mind. He then laid down his brush and began to twist his moustaches. He kept twisting them furiously, first up and down and then in circles, as if he were trying somehow to wring some good ideas from the growth of hairs. It was while he was twisting his moustache that his wife came in from the tearoom. She sat down right in front of him.

"Listen," she said.

"What?" My master's voice sounded as if a gong were being sounded under water. His wife did not seem satisfied with his answer.

"Listen, I say," she repeated.

"What do you want?" grumbled my master. He inserted the tip of his thumb and forefinger into his nostril and yanked out some hairs.

"We haven't got enough for this month's bills."

"That can't be so. The doctor's bill has already been paid and the bill from the bookstore was taken care of last month. We should have something left to carry over for this month." My master then stared at the hairs he had pulled out, as if they were something wondrous.

"But you won't eat rice. You insist on eating bread and jam."

"All right then, just how many cans of jam did I eat?"

"We needed eight cans this month."

"Eight? That's impossible! I don't remember eating that much."

"It's not only you. The children like it too."

"Even at that, the jam should be only about five or six yen," responded my master coolly while planting each hair carefully on his piece of writing paper. As they had tiny bits of flesh still attached to the roots, the hairs stood upright, straight and erect. My master's face suddenly took on the expression he has when he hits upon a new idea, then he merely blew at the hairs. Having stuck to the paper, they did not scatter. Commenting on how strong they were, my master continued to blow.

"It's not only the jam. I have to buy other things," pouted the wife.

"I suppose so," answered my master, yanking out some more

hairs. Among the black and red hairs, there was a white one. With wide saucer-like eyes, my master took the white hair and, placing it between two fingers, he brought it right up in front of his wife's face.

" That's horrible! " The Mrs. shrank back and pushed her husband's hand away.

" Just look, a white nostril hair! " ejected my master. At this, the Mrs. ran into the tearoom laughing. It seemed as if she had given up hope concerning the household economic problem. Again alone, my master tried to continue with Tennen-koji.

Having thus chased his wife away, he happily pulled out more hairs while, at the same time, thinking of what to write. The more he concentrated, the more stubborn his brush grew.

" Eating baked sweet potatoes is superfluous—I'll cross this out, too." This he did and then decided, " Ko-isshu's not good either so out it goes." He crossed this out without a bit of hesitation. That left only: " Tennen-koji was a person who studied the infinite—who read the *Analects* of Confucious." My master thought that this would be too simple so he decided to cancel the whole thing altogether and make up a new sentence. He took his brush and drew a picture of an orchid on the paper. All the trouble he took was for nothing. The orchid also looked terrible. Then he turned the paper over and wrote on the back, " Born in nothingness, having studied the infinite, he dies in the infinite. Nothingness and abstraction, Oh, Tennen-koji! " This of course didn't make any sense at all.

It was just when my master had finished writing that line that Meitei came in. Most probably Meitei considers other people's home his own, for he had come in without being announced. Sometimes he even comes in from the back door. He is a man who discarded worries, restraint, anxieties and hardship as soon as he was born.

" Writing about 'Giant Gravity' again? " he asked, still standing.

" Do you expect me to write only about Giant Gravity? No, I'm trying to select an epitaph for Tennen-koji's tomb," said my master with pomp.

"So? Is this Tennen-koji any relation to Guzen-doji, may I ask?" hazarded Meitei, saying something at random as always.

"What do you mean by Guzen-doji?"

"Well, nothing. I only thought most probably there would be some connection," replied Meitei.

"I don't know Guzen-doji but you know this Tennen-koji."

"Who would call himself Tennen-koji and still let it be known?"

"He's Sorosaki. After graduating, he entered the post-graduate school and studied about the infinite. He worked so hard that eventually he died of peritonitis. Even at that, Sorosaki was my friend."

"It's all right to be his friend—I didn't say that that was bad, did I? But who changed his name from Sorosaki to Tennen-koji?"

"I did. I gave him that name. You know, there's nothing simple about giving someone a posthumous name," answered my master as if to imply that Tennen-koji was an elegant name and that he was proud of it.

Meitei laughed, "Well, well. Let me see the scripture you intend to put on his tombstone." He picked up the draft. "What's this? 'Born in nothingness, having studied the infinite, he dies in the infinite. Nothingness and abstraction. Oh, Tennen-koji!'" Meitei read this in a resounding voice. "Just right. It suits the name."

My master happily asked, "Don't you think it's good?"

"Why don't you carve this on a stone and leave it in the rear of the main temple hall to be used by weightlifters? It would be nice. Tennen-koji would have liked that."

"I thought of doing just that," replied my master quite seriously. Then he continued, "You'll have to excuse me for a while. I'll be back soon, so, in the meantime, play with the cat." Without waiting for Meitei's answer, he left.

And therefore, without any forewarning, it fell my lot to take care of Meitei. As I could not keep aloof, I meowed to make myself more hospitable and jumped on his lap. Meitei then seemed to notice me for the first time and said, "We-ll, you've become quite fat. Now, let's see." He roughly picked me up by the scruff of my neck and held me in midair.

" If a cat dangles its hind legs like this, it can't catch rats. How about it, Mrs. Kushami, does this cat catch any rats?" As if he wasn't satisfied by just looking at me, he had to call to the Mrs. who was in the next room.

" Nothing of the kind! Instead of catching rats it tries to eat *mochi* and dances," answered the Mrs., recalling a sore spot when least expected. Hanging in space I felt terribly embarrassed. Meitei would not put me down.

" Hmmm? So? It seems to have the face of a dancing cat. You know, it has a cunning face. It looks like Nekomata, the cat in the old fairy tale," shouted Meitei, again making up something at random even when addressing the Mrs. Because of this, the Mrs. stopped sewing and, making a face as if to say that Meitei was a nuisance, she came into the room.

" I'm sorry you have to wait so long. My husband should be back any minute now," she apologized while pouring tea for Meitei.

" I wonder where he's gone."

" I wouldn't know. He's not one to tell others where he's going. Most probably he's gone to see the doctor."

" Do you mean Dr. Amaki? Well, the doctor will have a nuisance on his hands."

" Yes," commented the Mrs. making her reply short and brief. She was at a loss for another answer.

Meitei, without noticing, continued, "And how has his stomach been recently?"

" Well, I don't know. If he's going to eat so much jam, there's nothing to be surprised about if his stomach doesn't get well." The Mrs. was letting Meitei know about the complaint she had had a little while before.

" Well, well. Does he eat much jam? He's like a baby."

" It's not all jam. The other day he started eating grated radishes because he said it was good for the stomach."

" That's something!" exclaimed Meitei.

" You see, the other day the newspaper reported that there was diastase in grated radish."

"So he's trying to make up for all the jam he eats. He's been doing some thinking," chuckled Meitei, amused at the Mrs.'s complaints.

"And just the other day he tried to get one of the babies to eat some."

"Jam?"

"No, grated radish. I thought he was taking care of the child for a change, but he was only doing something foolish. A couple of days ago he picked another of his daughters up and put her on top of a chest of drawers."

"But why?" Meitei always wants to know why.

"He was trying to make the child jump down! She's only three or four years old. She wouldn't jump and no wonder!"

"He's got no head at all. But then he's good inside."

"If he were a bad man besides being what he is, I couldn't endure all this." sighed the Mrs.

"Well, you can't complain too much if you can get along with him every day. Mr. Kushami has nothing that interests him long. He doesn't care about his looks. I guess he's just a family man," said Meitei preaching to the Mrs. This was not like him at all.

"But there's something else."

"What? Did he do something on the sly? You know, you can't relax for a moment," said Meitei casually.

"There's nothing that interests him long but he wants to buy a lot of books—books he doesn't read. It would be all right if he could afford them but he charges them at the Maruzen bookstore. Come the end of the month, and he says nothing about them to me. The books he buys accumulate and I'm terribly embarrassed at the end of the year."

"That's all right. As a matter of fact, tell your husband to buy all he can. And when the bill collector comes, just insist that you'll pay up later and keep repeating this. He'll stop bothering you pretty soon."

"But I can't keep stalling always, can I?" sulked the Mrs. gloomily.

"Then how about explaining your budget to Mr. Kushami."

"He wouldn't understand. The other day he said that I wasn't like the wife of a scholar at all, and that I didn't know the value of books. ' There's an old story which you should know for later reference ' was what he answered."

" Is that so? And what was this story? " Meitei seemed anxious to hear the tale. It was more out of curiosity than of sympathy that he asked.

" Well, he said that at one time there was a king of Rome by the name of Tarukin or something," the Mrs. commenced.

" Tarukin? That sounds a little funny."

" Well, you see, I'm not good at remembering European names. But in any case he was the seventh king."

" Is that so? The seventh king—Tarukin? That's funny. What about this seventh king? "

" Why, you're making fun of me, too. If you know, tell me his name," pleaded the Mrs.

" Make fun of you? No, no, I'm not as bad as that. I only thought that the name of Tarukin was good, that's all. Now, wait a minute—you said the seventh king of Rome. I don't know for sure but you might mean Tarquinius Superbus. But it doesn't make any difference. What did he do? "

" Well, anyway, a girl once went to this king with nine books and asked him if he would buy them."

" Yes? "

" The king asked how much they were but the girl quoted a very high price. When the king asked for a reduction, the girl took three of the nine books and threw them into a fire."

" What a shame! "

" It's said that the books contained prophecies or something that no one could find except in these books."

" Is that so? "

" The king, finding that there were only six books instead of the original nine, believed that the price would be smaller, but the girl said that they would cost the same as all nine. Not a sen cheaper! The king thought that that was outrageous, and said so. The girl, on hearing this, threw three more of the books into the fire. But it seemed as if the king wanted them badly. He asked the girl how much the remaining three would be but was told that they were priced the same as the original nine. If he asked for a reduction again, the remaining books might be thrown into the fire so the king reluctantly bought the three at a high price. My husband then asked me if I had realized the value of books through this story. He kept asking this but *I* wouldn't know the value of books, no, not a woman," said the Mrs. with some dignity as if she were challenging Meitei to contradict her.

Meitei himself was at a loss so he only took out a handkerchief from the sleeve of his kimono and began playing with me. " But, you know, ma'am," he suddenly boomed, as if he had hit upon a good idea, " it is only because he buys books and keeps piling them up that people call him a scholar. The other day I happened to read a criticism of one of Mr. Kushami's poems in one of the literary magazines."

" Oh, really? " The Mrs. immediately changed her attitude. That she is interested in everything that has to do with her husband shows that the two are surely a married couple. "What did it say? "

" Oh, it was only a couple of lines. It said that Mr. Kushami's writing was like passing clouds and flowing water."

Smiling, the Mrs. urged, " Was that all? "

" Then it had: ' He appears only to vanish again; and dead he would forever forget to return '."

The Mrs. had a queer expression on her face. She asked Meitei, " Was this praising my husband's work? "

" Well, I would say it was somewhat in praise, yes," responded Meitei. Then he again dangled his handkerchief in front of me.

" Books are material for his work but, you must understand, he's awfully eccentric."

Meitei realized that the Mrs. had not been completely satisfied with his answer so he added, " Well, it's just as you say. He's eccentric. But you must remember that all scholars are eccentric." His answer was meant to relieve the strain and, at the same time, to say something favorable about my master.

The Mrs. then changed the topic a little. " The other day he came home from school but said he had to go out again soon. He decided it was too troublesome to change clothes. What do you think? He sat down on top of the desk without taking off his overcoat and, putting the table on top of the foot warmer, he ate his dinner there. I just sat with the rice container in my lap staring at him, it was so comical."

"It seems as if he's always trying out something new. But that's because Mr. Kushami is himself and nobody else. In any case, no matter how you look at it, he's not a common person." Meitei praised him but not too eagerly.

"I don't know if he's common or not, being a woman myself, but his conduct is often outrageous."

"Still that's better than being common." The more Meitei defended her husband, the more it seemed that the Mrs. had a right to complain.

"By the way, what do you mean by a common person?" The Mrs. again somewhat changed the subject.

"What? Well, it's a little difficult to explain," fidgeted Meitei.

"Well, if it's difficult, then there should be nothing wrong with being common," retorted the Mrs. with feminine logic.

"I don't mean to be evasive, nor do I mean that it is difficult to explain; I know what being common is but I just can't find the right words, that's all."

"Isn't it that anything you don't like you call common? Isn't that so?" asked the Mrs. without being able to check herself. Meitei was now forced to give an explanation.

"You see, when you say common, it's like this. You'd call a man common if he longed for a beautiful girl—say, about 16 or 18 years old—without doing more than lying in a room thinking about how she would be. If it happened to be a nice clear day, he might buy a bottle of *sake* and go strolling along the river Sumida but—as a common man—he would not try to satisfy his longings by actually finding a girl."

"I wonder if there really are such people," mumbled the Mrs., not out of curiosity but just for the sake of something to say. "It all sounds somewhat complicated and difficult," she continued, giving up.

"Well, how about this example, then. Just hang the head of Major Pendennis around the waist of Bakin and let it be shrouded in European air for a year or two."

" Will that produce what you call a common man? "

Meitei, instead of answering, just laughed. " But you needn't go to all this trouble to find one. All you have to do is to put a middle-school student and a clerk of the Shirokiya store together, and divide them by two. Then you'll get someone you can call common."

" Is that so? " The Mrs. tilted her head, unable to grasp all this nonsense.

" You still here? " My master had come back.

" What do you mean ' still here'? You told me to wait, didn't you? "

" That's just what I was saying," sighed the Mrs. looking towards Meitei.

" While you were out, I heard everything about you," bragged Meitei.

" Women talk too much. If everyone were as silent as this cat, everything would be much better," said my master, stroking my head.

" I understand you tried to feed your child some grated radish."

" Hmmm," smiled my master. " Children are clever. When I asked her where it felt hot, she stuck her tongue out to show me. Isn't that cute? "

" You don't understand children. That's just like trying to teach a dog how to do tricks. By the way, it's about time Kangetsu came."

" Is Kangetsu coming? " asked my master.

" Yes. I sent him a post card telling him to come to the home of Mr. Kushami at one o'clock."

" You always take things into your own hands, don't you? Calling Kangetsu here! What do you have in mind? "

" This was Kangetsu's idea. He was saying something about making a lecture at a scientific meeting and he asked me to listen to him rehearse; I told him that it would be a good chance to have you listen too, so that's why I am having him come. As you have a lot of free time, I knew it would be all right. I know that you don't have many engagements." Meitei had made all the arrangements himself.

" I can't understand physics," complained my master.

" Oh, it's not one of those dry stories where a nozzle is magnet-ized. It's a lecture about the dynamics of death by hanging. You can probably benefit a great deal by listening to it."

" *You're* the one who almost hanged himself. You will pro-bably find it of great interest, but as for me—."

" You don't have to tell me again that you had chills just because you once planned on going to the theater. You'll have to hear this lecture, though," interrupted Meitei in his usual light manner. The Mrs. just laughed and, looking at her husband, went into the adjoining room. My master kept stroking my head in silence. For some reason he was petting me very softly.

About seven minutes after this, Kangetsu in person made his appearance. As he was going to make a lecture that evening, he wore a fine frock coat. Besides, his shirt and collar had been freshly laundered, a thing quite unusual. It made him look twenty per cent better than he really is. " Sorry I'm so late," he murmured, serenely addressing us.

" We've been waiting for some time now. Let's hear your lecture right away. What do you say? " Meitei asked my master.

Not ever being able to express concrete opinions, my master just made a grunt: " Ummm."

Kangetsu did not seem to be in a hurry. He asked for a glass of water.

" You're going at lecturing in the regular way. Good! Next you'll be asking us to clap our hands," said Meitei, greatly enjoy-ing himself.

Kangetsu took his manuscript from his pocket and then slowly told us that this was only a tryout and that he would welcome criticisms. Then he began his lecture:

" Death by hanging as capital punishment is a method first used by the Anglo-Saxon race. Before they devised it, hanging took place for the sole purpose of self-destruction. Among the Hebrews there was the custom of stoning a criminal to death. According to the Old Testament, hanging meant to hang the corpse after death to be devoured by beasts and birds of prey. According to Herodotus, the Hebrews—even before they left Egypt—greatly disliked having corpses hung at night. The Egyptians decapitated their criminals and nailed the corpse, minus the head, to a cross and left it out during the night. As for the Persians—"

" Look, Kangetsu, you're getting too far away from the hanging business," cautioned Meitei.

" I'm getting to the main part of the lecture, so please be patient. And as for the Persians, it seems that they sentenced criminals to the cross. It is not clear whether they were nailed to the cross while still alive or after they had been killed."

" We don't have to know such details," yawned my master. He was getting impatient.

" I've prepared a rather detailed oration. But if it's going to be of inconvenience to you—"

" Don't call it an oration. Say 'lecture'. It's nicer form. Don't you think so, Mr. Kushami?" broke in Meitei for the second time.

" It doesn't make any difference," said my master flatly.

"All right then, I'll continue reciting my lecture."

" Wait. Don't say you are going to recite it. That's a word storytellers use. A speaker should use more elegant language," interrupted Meitei again.

" If 'reciting' is vulgar, what should I use?" asked Kangetsu somewhat angered.

" You know, you can never tell whether Meitei is serious or only trying to confuse his friends. Don't pay any attention to him. Go ahead with your story," said my master. He was trying to get Kangetsu to finish as soon as possible.

" Oh, the gentle willow soothes the long speech angrily delivered," said Meitei as serenely as ever. Then Kangetsu burst out laughing.

"Actually, capital punishment by hanging, according to my research, was mentioned in the 22nd volume of the *Odyssey*. There was the case of Telemachus who hanged twelve of

Penelope's maid servants. I could read this passage in Greek but it might sound as if I were bragging. If you read lines 465 to 473, you'll see that I am right."

" You'd better not start talking Greek; it would sound as if you really understood what you were talking about. Isn't that true, Kushami?"

" I'm of the same opinion. It would sound too elegant," replied my master. He agreed with Meitei instantly, a thing which seldom happens. Neither Meitei nor my master understand Greek.

" Then I'll omit that part and—ah—continue with the rest.

" Considering the methods of hanging the maidservants, there were two. At first Telemachus, with the help of Eumaois and Philoitios, tied one end of the rope to a pillar. He then made knots at a couple of places in the rope but did not pull them tight. A girl's head was inserted through a knot, one to each, and then the loose end of the rope was yanked tight. In this way Telemachus had a string of girls hanging from one rope."

Meitei again interrupted, " Then it's somewhat similar to shirts hanging from a clothesline like in Western countries."

" That's it. Now, the other method was to have one end of the rope tied to a pillar just as mentioned before. But the other end was tied to the ceiling. To this, several other ropes were tied. The ends were looped and a girl's head was inserted into each noose. At the crucial moment, the stools on which the girls stood were taken away."

" In other words, visualize lanterns dangling from shop curtains made of rope, then you've got the general idea, isn't that so?" Meitei could never stay quiet long.

" I've never seen a lantern hung in that way so I wouldn't be able to say for sure, but that's just about it. Now, I'd like to prove that the first method is not practical as far as dynamics is concerned."

" This is wonderful!" exclaimed Meitei and my master grunted his affirmation.

" All right then, the girls are now strangled at certain distances from one another. But let us consider that the rope between the two girls nearest the floor is horizontal. That means that the angle of the rope, in relation to the horizon, is a_1 a_2 to a_6. The weight which the respective parts of the rope receive can be considered as T_1 T_2 to T_6. The load received by the lowest part of the rope can be said to be $T_7 = X$. W will naturally stand for the weight of each woman. Now, do you see what I mean?"

Meitei and my master looked at each other and said, "Yes, almost." The way they said "almost" was spontaneous so it could not have been rehearsed. Their intonations were exactly alike, however.

"Now, according to the theory of equilibrium pertaining to a polygon, which I believe you know, we have arrived at twelve equations: $T_1 \cos a_1 = T_2 \cos a_2 \ldots$ (1) $T_2 \cos a_2 = T_3 \cos a_3 \ldots$ (2) $\ldots$"

"That's enough of equations," snorted my master.

"But these equations are the whole backbone of my speech," pleaded Kangetsu.

"Then how about giving the backbone, as you say, later on?" suggested Meitei somewhat obligingly.

"If we leave that out, my research on dynamics would not make any sense."

"You don't have to be so modest. Just omit that part and get on with your speech," insisted my master without any concern.

"Then I'll continue, though it'll be difficult if I omit that part."

"Don't worry. Go ahead," said Meitei while clapping his hands, an odd moment to do any applauding.

"All right then. Now for England.

"We find the word 'galga' in *Beowulf*—that means gallows, so there is no doubt that the hanging of criminals took place at that time. According to Blackstone, if a criminal did not die, due to some defect in the noose, the ordeal would be repeated over again. But, strange as it may seem, in *Piers the Plowman*, the author insists that the person did not have to be hanged twice if the first execution proved unsuccessful.

"Well, actually I don't know which of the two theories is true but there were probably many times when a person was hanged more than once. In 1786, for example, a famous criminal by the name of Fitzgerald was hanged. When he jumped from the stool, the rope broke. The second time the rope was too long and his feet touched the ground. Some onlookers during the third attempt helped and finally Fitzgerald was sent to eternity."

" Well, well. That's very interesting," breathed Meitei, becoming more enthusiastic.

"Almost escaped death, didn't he? " My master was also somewhat excited.

" There is a great deal of scientific interest in this, too. Did you know that a person becomes about one inch taller when hanged? The doctors measure the condemned before and after their execution so there's no mistake about it."

" That's a good idea! How about it, Kushami? If you added another inch to your height you might look more human," laughed Meitei looking towards my master.

My master seriously asked Kangetsu if one might ever be revived after adding an inch to his height.

" Of course not. The reason for this is that the spine stretches or, better explained, the spine snaps."

" Well, if that's the case, I'll refrain," shrugged my master.

The speech was really much longer. Kangetsu afterwards tried to talk about the physiological affects of hanging but Meitei kept interrupting and my master kept yawning all the time, so Kangetsu finally stopped and left. Unfortunately, I cannot tell you how Kangetsu did with his speech that evening because it took place too far away.

Nothing happened for the next couple of days. About two o'clock one afternoon soon after, however, Meitei again suddenly dropped in. After being seated, he burst out, " Have you heard about the Takanawa case of Tofu Ochi? " His voice had the enthusiasm of someone relating news of the downfall of Port Arthur.

" No, haven't met him recently," replied my master.

"Though I'm rather busy today, I dropped in to tell you about Tofu."

"Why do you have to exaggerate so much? You're impossible, really!"

"You don't mean impossible, you mean improbable, ha, ha, ha! Just remember that you are speaking about my honor."

"It's all the same," roared my master. His sudden vehemence made me think that Tennen-koji's soul had entered my master's body for a moment.

"Last Sunday, Tofu visited the Takanawa Sengaku-ji Temple. He shouldn't have gone, being so cold. Going there at this time of the year shows that he doesn't know much about Tokyo. He is still terribly countryfied at times."

"That's Tofu's business, not yours."

"But that's not the point. That temple is the head quarters of the Association for the Preserving of the Forty-seven *Ronin*. You know that, don't you?"

"No, I didn't know it."

"No? But you've gone to the Sengaku-ji Temple, haven't you?"

"Never."

"No? It's amazing. No wonder you are speaking up for Tofu. It's terrible for a man born in Tokyo not to know the Sengaku-ji."

"Even so, I can still be a teacher," said my master with great dignity.

"Never mind that. Getting back to the story, Tofu entered an exhibition room on the temple grounds and saw a German

---

* The term *ronin* implies a samurai or warrior who is without a master. The forty-seven *ronin* were samurai of the house of the Lord Asano Takumi-no-kami who was compelled to commit harakiri for having violated a regulation regarding swords within the Shogunate palace in Edo (present Tokyo), after having been continuously insulted by another lord, Kira Kozuke-no-suke. The forty-seven *ronin* pledged secret revenge of their master and after two years they were able to accomplish their ultimate object by finally beheading Kira. Thereafter, they surrendered themselves to the authorities and committed harakiri at the Sengaku-ji Temple where even today people pay their respects to their fidelity and devotion.

couple. The couple spoke to Tofu in Japanese but you know how Tofu is—he wanted to speak German. He tried a couple of words and was able to make himself understood."

"And then what happened?" asked my master. He now found himself interested in the story.

" The Germans pointed to a small lacquered medicine case once used by Gengo Otaka and asked Tofu whether it was for sale. Tofu's answer was really good! He said that as the Japanese were virtuous and of great integrity, it could not be bought. He was doing fine but, as the German couple believed him an authority, they kept asking more questions."

" What questions? "

" Well, there would have been nothing to worry about if all the questions were understood, but, as they were spoken quite rapidly and one right after the other, Tofu wasn't of much help. Tofu understood them to be talking about fireman's hooks and mallets. He was at a complete loss."

" Poor Tofu! " sighed my master, sympathizing with him from a language teacher's point of view.

" Other people felt curious and began to gather around. Tofu became flushed and bewildered. Contrary to the confidence he had had at first, he was now withering."

" So what did he do? "

" Finally Tofu, unable to endure the situation any longer, just said ' sainara ' and left. ' Sainara ' sounded funny so I asked him if people in his home town used that for goodbye instead of ' sayonara '. He explained that though his people use ' sayonara ', he had said ' sainara ' to give the word harmony as he was speaking to Westerners. Tofu, even in a tight spot, doesn't forget about harmony. I admire him for that."

" Never mind about the ' sainara ' part. What became of the Germans? "

" The couple was taken so much by surprise that they just stood there in wonder. Ha, ha, ha! Don't you think that's good? "

" I don't see anything funny about that. I don't understand why it was so important for you to come and tell me about it either. That in itself is much funnier," said my master, dropping his cigarette into an ashtray.

Just at that moment, the front doorbell suddenly rang. This was followed with an " Excuse me " in a sharp feminine voice. Meitei and my master glanced at each other in surprise and became silent.

It is not often that visitors of the fair sex come to visit my master. I noticed that when the owner of the sharp voice came into the room her crepe kimono was dragging on the floor because it was so long. She wore two coats, one over the other, and looked somewhat over forty years of age. She wore her hair high over her brow. It stood up, like some kind of a dike construction, and this gave the effect of doubling the length of her face. Her eyes had a slant similar to that of the slope leading from Hongo to Yushima. The eyes looked out of straight slits, thinner than the eyes of a whale. The nose was extraordinary! It seemed as if she had stolen somebody else's and had placed it in the middle of her own face. It was like a large stone lantern in a little garden. It completely dominated the face and did not seem to be at home at all. Besides, the nose was hooked, like the beak of an eagle. It had evidently commenced to grow straight out but then, thinking that this might be going too far, it had become more modest and began to droop. Finally it ended up by hanging down to tickle the lips. It was such a phenomenon that it made one believe that the nose, not the mouth, was doing the talking. In order to show my respect to this wonder, I shall, hereafter, call its proud owner Hanako, " Mrs. Nose."

Having completed with the formalities of her greeting, Hanako exclaimed, " What a wonderful place you have here." Her eyes were busy wandering around the room.

My master was not impressed by this false compliment and only continued puffing at his cigarette.

" By the way, is that a leak in the ceiling or is it the grain of the wood showing? It's a funny pattern," hinted Meitei, trying to induce my master to say something.

" It's a leak, of course," retorted my master.

" Interesting, isn't it? " murmured Meitei serenely.

Hanako was confused at finding the two so unsocial, and the three of them just sat in silence for a while.

" Oh, by the way, I dropped in to ask you a favor," gushed Hanako, opening the conversation again.

" Yes? " replied my master.

Hanako seemed flustered by the cold response but continued. " Well, I happen to live right near you. As a matter of fact, in that large house on the corner across the street."

" That large Western-styled house with a warehouse? I've noticed your name plate above the door." My master had often passed by the Kanedas' elegant house but the construction did not impress him much.

" To tell the truth, my husband should have come but he is busy at the company." She began again with a gleam in her eyes, but my master remained indifferent. For one thing, my master did not like Hanako's unlady-like brusqueness when speaking to a person for the first time.

" My husband doesn't belong to just one company, you know, but to several. He is the director of them all though I believe you already know this." This time she was being more direct, as if to say now that my master knew who she was, he could be more civil.

The master of this house, however, only became obliging to those who possessed a doctorate or who were professors of universities. Queer as it may sound, he showed very little respect for businessmen. He believed that a junior-high-school teacher was much more important than a man of business. Besides, he had absolutely no hope of ever receiving favors from businessmen or millionaires. Once he realizes that he can expect nothing from the other party, he becomes extremely indifferent to their interests. He knows nothing outside of education and is especially ignorant of business circles. Even when he comes into contact with businessmen, he cannot bring himself to show even the slightest respect for them.

As for Hanako, she did not have the slightest idea that such a freakish person could exist. She met many people and there had been no occasion when a person did not change his attitude once she told him that she was the wife of Kaneda. She had naturally believed that just by telling this schoolteacher, confined to his tiny home and enduring a gloomy life, that she lived across the street in that big house on the corner would have been sufficient to bewilder him.

"Do you happen to know Kaneda?" my master asked Meitei off hand.

"Sure, I do. Mr. Kaneda is a friend of my uncle's. The other day he attended a garden party held at my uncle's home," replied Meitei seriously.

"Your uncle? Oh, who's he?"

"Baron Makiyama," answered Meitei even more seriously.

My master was about to say something else but before he could, Hanako quickly changed her position so she could face Meitei. Meitei just sat there serenely in his pongee kimono.

"Oh, you are Baron Makiyama's—well, what is your relation to him? I didn't know this at all. My husband often tells me how indebted he is to Baron Makiyama. We often talk about him," said Hanako, commencing to use more polite expressions all of a sudden. She even bowed.

Meitei just murmured with a chuckle, "Not at all, not at all."

My master was so surprised that he could only stare at the other two.

"I understand he has gone to a great deal of trouble about my daughter's marriage."

"Oh, is that so?" It seemed as if Meitei had lost a little of his assurance because his reply sounded rather weak.

"To tell the truth, many men have come to ask for her hand but, as we must consider our position, we have to be very careful about whom we give our daughter to."

"That's certainly true," beamed Meitei, assured of himself now.

"And I've come to see you about this," said Hanako to my master. Her voice suddenly became rough again. "I understand that a man by the name of Kangetsu Mizushima often comes here to visit you. What kind of a man is he?"

"Why are you asking about Kangetsu?" returned my master

with a trace of disgust.

" It must be about her daughter's marriage. I think she wants to know something about Kangetsu's character," put in Meitei.

" I'd appreciate it very much if I could get some information about him."

" Does that mean you would want to give your daughter to Kangetsu in marriage? "

" Who said anything about marriage? " quickly responded Hanako. This stopped my master.

"As she has many other suitors, we won't be inconvenienced in the least if he doesn't ask her to marry him."

" In that case, I don't see any reason for your asking questions about Kangetsu," replied my master rather heatedly.

" But there's nothing to hide, is there? " retaliated Hanako. Her tone suggested that she was ready for an argument.

Meitei was sitting between the two contestants, holding his silver pipe as if it were a warfan.*

" Has Kangetsu asked to marry your daughter? " inquired my master head on.

" No, not exactly."

" Then has he hinted that he would like to have your daughter? " My master believed that it was best to ask abrupt questions when dealing with this woman.

" Well, you see, the negotiations haven't progressed that far. Nevertheless, Mr. Mizushima is of course interested." The lady was now desperate because of the constant thrusts.

" But is there any sign at all that Kangetsu loves your daughter? " repeated my master, throwing out his chest as if challenging her to reply.

" Well, it's something like that," said the lady. This time my master's tactics seemed to have failed.

Meitei, who believed that he was in a position somewhat like that of an umpire, was arrested by the last comment made by the lady. His curiosity roused, he put aside his tobacco pipe,

---

* A warfan is similar in shape to the fan called *gunbai* used by referees in present-day *sumo* (Japanese wrestling) matches.

leaned forward and said, " Did Kangetsu write a letter to your daughter? Well, isn't this good ! " He was the only one who seemed to be enjoying the situation.

" No, it's not a letter—it's something much more personal. Both of you know about it, don't you? " asked Hanako, getting her ideas strangely entangled.

" Do you know anything about this? " my master asked Meitei.

" Not me. You're the one who should know," Meitei replied with a blank face.

" Why, both of you know, I'm sure," Hanako insisted haughtily.

" So-o-o? " said the two men.

" Well then, if you have forgotten, I'll explain the story. There was a concert last year in the home of Mr. Abe of Mukojima. Mr. Mizushima was there. Don't you remember? He told you that something happened on the Azuma-bashi Bridge when he was returning home that evening. I won't repeat the story because it would be quite embarrassing for Mr. Mizushima, but I know he has related this experience to you. What do you say now? " Hanako sat upright with her hands on her lap. The diamond ring on her finger gleamed menacingly. Her enormous nose somehow made its presence known all the more and made the noses of my master and Meitei seem smaller.

Meitei, as well as my master, seemed greatly surprised. They looked as if they had just been relieved of the tortures of ague. They just sat there. By the time they had recovered from their bewilderment, they were suddenly attacked by a fit of laughter. Both of the men commenced simultaneously and laughed until tears streamed down their faces.

Hanako was not getting the result she had anticipated and she thought that this was all very rude. She glared at both of them.

" Was that your daughter? Well, well, this is good ! Yes, it happened just as you said. How about it, Mr. Kushami? Do you think that Kangetsu has really fallen for her? I don't see any sense in hiding anything now. How about telling Mrs. Kaneda that story? "

" By all means," was the only answer my master could manage.

" There's no use hiding anything because I have evidence,"

announced Hanako proudly.

"Well, I guess there's nothing to do but tell everything we know. Look, Mr. Kushami, we'll get nowhere if you keep smirking like that. And you the master of this house at that! Secrets are bewildering. Even when you try to keep them, the truth is bound to come out sooner or later. But this secret is funny—really funny. And Mrs. Kaneda knows about everything. It's amazing!" rambled Meitei, as if talking to himself.

"I'm not a person to be often kept in the dark, you know," said Hanako triumphantly.

"But you seem to know everything already. Who told you this in the first place, may I ask?"

"The wife of the rickshawman around the alley."

"The rickshawman who owns that black cat?" asked my master wide-eyed.

"Yes, I've spent a lot of money to get facts about Mr. Mizushima. Every time he comes here, I have the wife of the rickshawman eavesdrop and then tell me what he has said."

"That's going a little too far!" shouted my master.

"What you yourself did or what you said is of no concern. What I want to know is only about Mr. Mizushima."

"I don't care. That rickshawman's wife gets on my nerves," said my master, getting angrier all the time.

"But there's nothing wrong in her coming and standing near your fence. If you don't like it, why didn't you speak quieter? Or better still, you could move into a larger house." Hanako wasn't embarrassed a bit. She continued, "And my information isn't only from the rickshawman's wife. I've heard plenty from the *koto* instructress, too."

"Do you mean about Kangetsu?"

"No, not only about him," she said.

I thought this would stop my master but he continued. "That instructress thinks that she's so elegant and that she's the only respectable person around here. She's a terrible old hag."

"I beg your pardon! She's a real lady. She's hardly what you'd call a hag!" Hanako's language had now attained a coarseness which showed her whole mediocre upbringing. It was beginning to look as if she had come here to pick a fight. Meitei was just as Meitei always is—listening to the conversation with sharp interest. He somehow looked like Tekkai, one of the Chinese genii, enjoying a cockfight.

My master finally discovered that he was not Hanako's equal in discourtesy so he became mute. But presently he spoke as if he had remembered something: "According to your story, it's Kangetsu who is in love with your daughter. Well, I've heard differently. Isn't that so, Meitei?" My master needed his help.

"Well, according to the story we've heard, it seems that your daughter became sick and said something when delirious."

"That cannot be," shot back Hanako with confidence.

"But Kangetsu told us that he heard this directly from a doctor's wife."

"That was only a trick. I myself asked the doctor's wife to do me this favor to see what she could find out."

"And do you mean to say the doctor's wife willingly did this?"

"Of course. But you have to understand that a favor like this cannot be expected just by asking. I've given her presents from time to time, you know."

"You certainly are a determined woman. I suppose that now you will not leave until you've found out all about Kangetsu one way or the other." Meitei now felt somewhat indignant so he was far from polite, a thing rare in Meitei. But he continued, " Mr. Kushami, there's nothing to lose so let's tell her everything. Now we're willing to tell you what we know."

Hanako then began her interrogation. Though her voice was generally rather rough, when she turned to Meitei she politely asked, " I understand that Mr. Mizushima is a bachelor of science but what does he specialize in?"

"He's studying the force of the earth's gravity in the post-graduate school of the university," replied my master seriously. But, unfortunately, Hanako did not understand.

"What—?" she commenced. But in an instant her face reflected doubt and she asked, " And do you think that he can acquire a doctorate by studying that?"

"Are you implying that you will not give your daughter to him unless he has a degree?" asked my master with a sneer.

"Well, yes. You must understand that there are so many college graduates that I really couldn't give my daughter to just a plain bachelor of science." Hanako didn't turn a hair in saying this. My master stole a glance at Meitei and his face registered an even more unpleasant expression.

"Actually, we're in no position to guarantee that Kangetsu will receive his doctor's degree. How about asking some other question?" Meitei was not in too good a mood himself.

"Is he still studying the earth's—whatever he's studying about?"

"A couple of days ago, he made a lecture at the Scientist's Hall about the results of his studies concerning the dynamics of death by hanging," my master mentioned without noticing anything strange about the subject.

"Oh, how terrible! Hanging! He must be indeed a strange man. Most probably he will never be able to become a professor if he is studying hanging and whatever that other thing is."

"It's somewhat debatable if he hung himself. But it's not impossible if his study were the dynamics of hanging."

"Do you think so?" asked Hanako, this time looking at my master for some sign. She did not understand the term dynamics and that kept her unsteady on the subject. She believed that she would lose face as Mrs. Kaneda if she asked the meaning so she just looked at the speaker's face to find some hint, if any. My master's face looked grim.

"Do you know if he's studying anything more simple than that?"

"Well, the other day he wrote a thesis on the 'Stability of the Acorn and the Movement of the Heavenly Bodies'."

"Do you study about acorns at universities?"

"I didn't myself but if Kangetsu studied acorns, there must be something worth studying about them," replied Meitei coolly, and partly out of fun.

Hanako found that she could not cope with the conversation covering studies so she changed the subject, "By the way, I heard that on New Year's Day he ate some mushrooms and broke two of his front teeth. Is that right?"

" Yes, and, you know, particles of food now stick to the gums where his teeth used to be," said Meitei, suddenly becoming more his usual self. Such subjects were more within his ability.

" He doesn't seem to be a very nice man. Why doesn't he use a toothpick?"

" I'll tell him to do so the next time we meet, ma'am," giggled my master.

" His teeth can't be very strong if they can be broken by mushrooms."

" I myself don't know how strong they are. Do you, Meitei?"

" Well, they're not very strong but Kangetsu looks kind of cute without them. He hasn't had them replaced yet, either. It's still a *mochi*-catching place."

" Doesn't he have the money for a dentist, or is it that he just likes being seen with two front teeth missing?"

" Please don't worry. I'm sure he doesn't expect to make a name for himself as being the ' man with two front teeth missing '." Meitei was gradually becoming even more like himself. Hanako again changed the subject.

" Do you happen to have something here he wrote himself? If so, I would like to see it."

" Oh, yes. There's a lot of post cards here." My master then brought out thirty or forty cards from his study.

" Oh, I don't have to look at all of them. A couple will do."

" Let's see. I'll find some good ones for you," offered Meitei, and he selected an illustrated card from the pile and handed it to the visitor. " Don't you think this is interesting?"

" Why, he draws, too! He really must be clever. Now, let's see." Once Hanako had the card in her hands, she exclaimed, " Why, it's a badger. Why did he draw a badger, of all things? But it's not bad. It at least looks like a badger."

" Read what's written on it," said my master with a laugh.

As a maid would read a newspaper, Hanako had difficulty in deciphering the characters.

" On New Year's Eve, a badger attended a garden party. While he danced he sang, ' Come, come here on New Year's Eve; come! No mountain folk will be here—suppoko pon-no-pon.' What in the world does this mean? He's making fun of people!" Hanako was still finding fault with everything.

"How about this one?" suggested Meitei, producing another card. It was a picture of an angel wearing a robe of feathers, and playing a lute.

"I think the angel's nose is a little too small."

"That's the size of most people's noses. Go ahead, read what's written on it."

The inscription was: "Once upon a time, there was an astronomer. One wintry night, as usual, he climbed high to the top of his tower, and was studiously looking at the stars. Suddenly a beautiful angel appeared in the sky and began to play heavenly music. The astronomer was so fascinated with the enchanting melody that he forgot all about the bitter cold. On the following morning, the astronomer was found dead, his body covered with frost. This is a true story, so said an old storyteller."

"This card doesn't mean anything, either. And he calls himself a bachelor of science! It would be much better for him to read the *Bungei Club* magazine for a time." Hanako was not at all impressed by Kangetsu. Meitei then produced a third card just for fun. "How about this one, ma'am?" There was a picture of a sailboat on it and again there was something written at the bottom of the card: "The little prostitute with whom I slept last night was a girl of sixteen; she wept when she saw a plover in flight in the early morning, thinking of her father who now lies at the bottom of the blue sea."

"Oh, this one is beautiful. It's wonderful! He might have some talent after all."

"Do you really think so?"

"And you could accompany this on the samisen, too."

"Well, if that's possible, it must be good. How about this example?" said Meitei producing still another card.

"I think I've seen enough, thank you. I've discovered that he's not altogether worthless," answered Hanako, making all the decisions herself. Hanako seemed to be through with asking questions about Kangetsu because she now said, "I'm sorry for having dropped in on you so suddenly today, but I would like to ask you one more favor. The truth is, I wish you would keep my visit here a secret." She evidently did not want Kangetsu to know that she had been here. Meitei and my master automatically replied, " Of course." Hanako continued, " I'll be back presently with some gifts for you." After impressing the two men with her generosity, she left.

When Meitei and my master returned to the room after seeing her off, they looked at each other and exclaimed simultaneously, " It's unbelievable ! "

The Mrs. couldn't hold back her giggles any longer, and she could be heard laughing in the inner room. Meitei shouted to her, " Ma'am, a good example of a common individual was just here. Perhaps now you will understand what I was trying to explain. There's nothing to hide any longer so you can laugh as much as you like."

My master mumbled the general opinion in a mean voice, " I didn't like her face in the first place."

Meitei followed, " But her nose is right in the middle of her face."

" But it's crooked."

" A little humpbacked. Queer, isn't it ? A humpbacked nose ! " laughed Meitei.

" One that pecks the husband, too," added my master still vexed.

" That face could have been carried over from the 19th century only to be put on the inventory for the 20th century." Meitei is always saying such queer things. It was at this moment that the Mrs. came into the room and, being a woman herself, she warned, " If you keep saying such bad things, the wife of the rickshawman will go and tattle everything."

" But that would serve Mrs. Kaneda right, ma'am."

" You really shouldn't criticize a face. Nobody would have asked for a nose like that and, besides, the person you're speaking of is a woman. You're being too hard." She was both defending Hanako and, at the same time, speaking up for her own imperfect features.

" Who's being hard? She's not a woman—she's a fool, isn't she, Meitei ? "

" She might be a fool but she can certainly take care of any situation. She certainly gave you quite a rough time, didn't she? "

" What does she think a schoolteacher is in the first place? "

" The same as the rickshawman around the corner, that's all. You have to have a doctorate to be respected by such people, isn't that so, ma'am? " Meitei again turned towards the Mrs.

"A doctorate? My husband couldn't make it no matter how hard he tried." Even my master's wife had forsaken him.

" Oh, I don't know. I might still make it some day. Maybe you don't know it but Isokrates did some of his best writing at the age of ninety-four. Sophocles was almost one hundred at the time he produced his world-shaking masterpiece. Simonides was eighty when he wrote his best poem. Even I— "

" Nonsense! How do you expect to live that long with your bad stomach? " The Mrs. had the life span of her husband all planned.

" Why, you— Go and ask Dr. Amaki about it. That woman! Making fun of me! You know why? It's only because you keep me wearing this crumpled cotton *haori* coat and these other patched things. All right, from tomorrow I'm going to wear as elegant clothes as Meitei here has on, so get them out."

" Get them out? You don't have any such clothes. Besides, the reason Mrs. Kaneda was so polite to Meitei was that he mentioned his uncle. The clothing had nothing to do with it." The Mrs. made her explanation strategically, freeing herself from all responsibility.

My master suddenly seemed to remember something and said to Meitei, " You mentioned an uncle this afternoon but this was the first time I've heard of him. Do you really have an uncle? "

Meitei answered with enthusiasm, as if he had been waiting for this question. " Yes, but he's a blockhead, a leftover from the 19th century." While talking, he studied his audience carefully.

" You say such remarkable things! And where does he live now? "

" In Shizuoka. He still wears a topknot—quite embarrassing —and when I told him he should wear a hat, he merely countered that he would never wear one. He boasted that he was not old enough to feel the cold yet. I tell him to stay in bed when it's cold but he insists that four hours' sleep is plenty. He believes that those who sleep more than four hours are extravagant. He gets up so early in the morning that it is still dark. Of course it's not strange that a person can't sleep much at the age of sixty-seven, but the old man thinks that he formed the habit only because of great self-control. And when he goes outside, he always carries an iron fan with him."

" What for? "

" I wouldn't know, but probably he uses it for a cane. By the way, a funny thing happened the other day." Meitei was addressing the Mrs.

" Yes? " replied the Mrs. automatically, without any attentiveness.

" Last spring he suddenly wrote asking me to send him a frockcoat and a derby. I was surprised but wrote back to inquire when the old man was going to wear them. It seemed he needed the clothing immediately as he was going to attend a party in Shizuoka. But, there was something funny about his request. He asked me to buy the frockcoat and a derby of moderate size at the Daimaru Department Store."

" Have they begun selling suits at the Daimaru? "

" He must have meant the Shirokiya Department Store."

" How did you manage to order them without knowing your uncle's size? That must have been difficult."

" That's the way my uncle is."

" Well, what did you do? "

" I ordered a suit I thought would fit and sent it to him."

"And did it fit?"

" In one way or another. I later found an article in my home-town paper which mentioned that old Mr. Makiyama had shown up at the party in frockcoat, a spectacular sight, and with his usual iron fan."

" It seems he never lets go of his iron fan."

" When he dies, we're going to put it in the coffin with him."

" It was good that the derby and the frockcoat fit him."

"But they didn't. I myself had believed that everything had gone well, but some days later I received a little bundle from him. I thought it must be some present but it only contained the derby hat. My uncle wrote that the derby was a little too large and he wanted me to take it back to the store for shrinking. He added that he would remit the expenses involved by money order."

My master felt a glow of satisfaction to find that there were others who were as careless about such details as he. He murmured, "What happened after that?"

"What could I do? I used the hat myself."

"That's the hat, then?" smirked my master.

"He's the baron, isn't he?" asked the wife somewhat doubtfully.

"Who? Who is the baron?"

"Your uncle, the one who always carries the iron fan."

"No, he's only a scholar of Chinese classics. When he was a young man he studied Confucianism at the Holy Hall, a shrine dedicated to Confucius at Hongo Yushima, and became extremely engrossed in his studies. That's the reason he so reverently still continues to wear his topknot in this modern generation of electricity. Nothing you can do about it," said Meitei furiously stroking his chin with his hand.

"But you told Mrs. Kaneda that he was Baron Makiyama, didn't you?"

"I heard you say so from the tearoom," insisted the Mrs., agreeing with her husband on this subject.

"Did I? Ha, ha ha." Meitei laughed loudly. "If I had an uncle who's a baron, I'd be chief of some office by now." His confession was made without any embarrassment at all.

"It's amazing how coolly you can lie! I must say, you're very good at it," exclaimed the Mrs. with wonder.

"Oh, I don't know. Mrs. Kaneda is much better."

"You needn't fear being beaten by her."

"You know, ma'am, my stories are innocent but that woman's lies have thorns in them; they're lies with a catch. They hurt. They are a result of craftiness. If they should ever be confused with jokes, the god of humor would cry."

My master dropped his eyes and mumbled, "I wonder!" It was the Mrs. who laughed and said that it all amounted to the same thing.

Until then I had never crossed the street. The residence of Kaneda, located on the corner, I still had not seen. This was the first time I had ever even heard of it. No conversation pertaining to any businessman had taken place within the home of my master so that I, one who partook of the food in this house, not only had little concern about such people but was very cool to them. But, as it perchanced, Hanako dropped in and, unwittingly, I had listened to the conversation.

When I tried to visualize the beauty of the daughter, and the wealth and the influence of the family, even as a cat I could not lie stretched out on the veranda with satisfaction. Besides, I felt great sympathy for Kangetsu. All the while, the Kanedas had been bribing the doctor's wife, the wife of the rickshawman, and the instructress of the two-stringed *koto* to get facts about him, and hearing such details as about his having broken two front teeth. Kangetsu, on the other hand, was probably just as usual— smiling and twirling the strings of his *haori* coat. Even though he will probably become a doctor of science soon, he is still worse than brainless. Even in such a case as this, my master would remain indifferent. As for Meitei, he did not have to worry about money but, being so casual, he would not help Kangetsu much. So the most unfortunate was the person who had lectured on the Dynamics of Hanging. It would not have been fair not to muster up enough spirit to find my way into the enemy's castle and get some information. I am only a cat but I am a cat that lives in the same home with a scholar who can slam a book by Epictetus hard on his desk after reading it. Being a woman with such a big nose in the middle of her face, there would hardly be many others dropping in to see Mrs. Kaneda.

I have always possessed a spirit of adventure hidden, not up my sleeve, but in the tip of my tail. This does not mean that I felt indebted to Kangetsu in any way whatsoever, nor that this visit was going to be any hot-headed action to save him. Broadly speaking, this was only going to be a commendable action to prove that God favors impartiality and moderation. It is disgraceful for people, without receiving permission, to go around telling others about the Azuma-bashi Bridge incident, or for them to spy under the eaves of a house and then brag about the information acquired. Such people should reflect on how they are employing the otherwise useful talent of the nation when they use rickshawmen, grooms, thugs, good-for-nothing students, old day workers, midwives, vampires and massagists to accomplish their ends. Cats would never be so wasteful.

Fortunately, the weather was fine; the melting frost would be somewhat of a hindrance but as it was for the sake of righteousness, I went ahead and risked my life. Getting my feet wet and leaving the plum-blossom marks of my paws on the porch would be troublesome for Osan, the maid, but that was not my concern.

Not wanting to wait, I decided to take action right away so I hopped toward the kitchen. But an inner voice told me to wait. I know that I am a perfect cat. At the same time, I also realize that I am more intellectually developed than a third-year student of a junior high school. But, unfortunately, the construction of my throat is that of all cats and I cannot speak the language of humans.

Even if I were able to sneak into the home of Kaneda and observe the entire situation with my own eyes, I would not be able to tell Kangetsu. I would not even be able to tell Meitei or my master. I was a fool for thinking that I could help. I just stood by the door thinking of quitting altogether.

But to quit something once decided is as difficult as to wait for a summer shower to pass while watching the black clouds pass by. Some kind of action is almost impossible to resist. The matter would have been different if I had been in the wrong, but the desire to serve justice and humanity is strong in cats and admired by humans. To waste energy only to walk around might be fit for other cats but not for me.

I have no ability to speak the human tongue or to exchange my thoughts with Kangetsu, Meitei or my master but, being a cat, I am more talented in the art of sneaking around. Having the ability to accomplish something which others cannot do so well is a pleasant thought. That I would be the only one to know the inside story of Kaneda would be even more satisfying. Though I might not be able to tell the story to others, it would be sweet to know that the others knew I knew. Finding myself extremely impatient, I could not put off my adventure.

Crossing the street, I found a Western-styled house on the corner dominating the intersection—just as I had heard. Thinking that the master of this house might be just as arrogant as the construction itself, I went inside the gate and gazed at the building. It looked very oppressive and its two stories seemed to be there without meaning. Was this what Meitei had implied when he defined commonness?

I passed through the shrubbery and went to the back door. The rear garden was amazingly large, about ten times as big as that of Mr. Kushami's, my master. It was nicely arranged and as beautiful as the garden of Count Okuma described in detail in the *Nihon* newspaper the other day. Thinking that it must also have a model kitchen, I went inside and found a large lacquered floor. The wife of the rickshawman was there, prattling away to her husband and to the kitchen maid.

Finding the position risky, I went around behind a water barrel and hid myself. The maid was saying "That schoolteacher! It doesn't seem possible that he didn't even know the name of my employer!"

"He must be a freak without eyes or ears." This was the voice of the rickshawman.

"When it comes to that teacher, he's a queer man who knows nothing outside his books. If he knew even a little bit about Mr. Kaneda, it would scare him some. But no! He doesn't even know the ages of his own children," said the woman.

"Hmmm. Not scared of Kaneda? That teacher is a trouble-some blockhead. What about getting together and giving him a scare?"

"That's a good idea! Do you know what he was saying about the madam's nose? He said it was too large and that he didn't like her face at all. He repeated terrible things about her. And to think that he himself has a face like that of a clay badger! It's disgusting to think that he believes he's grown to be a man."

"It's not only his face. Did you ever see him going to the public bath with the towel hanging from his hand, wearing that arrogant look he has? He thinks there's nobody greater than himself.". Even the maid did not speak well of my master.

"How about all of us going to his fence and shouting at him?"

"That ought to put him in his place."

"But it won't be fun if we let him see us. The madam was saying a little while ago that we should disturb his studies because that would get him as mad an anything else."

"That's the best way," said the rickshawman's wife in a tone that hinted she was willing to do at least one third of the mischief. Now that I understood that these people were going to Mr. Kushami's place to make fun of him, I sneaked passed them and went inside.

Cats have feet but we use them as if we were floating. We never make any clumsy noise. It is like stepping on air, like riding the clouds, like tapping temple bells under water, or like playing the harp inside a cave. It is like the ecstasy one receives after drinking water in silence—recognizing its coolness or warmth without being able to define the pleasure. With such feet, there was no common-placed Western-styled house, there was no model kitchen, no wife of the rickshawman, no male servant, no kitchen maid, no daughter, no houseman, no Madame Hanako, no Kaneda. I can go wherever I want and listen to any talk I like; I can stick my tongue out, wag my tail, prick up my whiskers and walk home. In this respect I am the No. I Cat of all Japan. I have often wondered if I am a descendant of the legendary Nekomata. It is said that there is a shining pearl on the forehead of a legendary toad, but in my tail there is sometimes so much magic that I often feel I can enchant not only God, Buddha, love, and death, but all the people in the entire world.

My walking across the veranda of the home of Kaneda was much easier for me than treading jelly would be for the giants which protect each temple entrance. Though this concerns myself only, I am often greatly impressed by the power I possess. I feel that this is also due to the fact that I take great care of my magic tail. I sometimes bow my head low to show respect to the God of Tails—and pray for a long life, besides. But I find the process difficult. I have to look towards my tail and bow three times, but in turning, the tail naturally goes around with the rest of my body. I turn my head to catch up with the tail but it still goes around, keeping the same distance. Being a spirited thing of three inches, all this cannot be easily managed. After chasing it about seven and a half times, I usually get tired and quit.

I became somewhat dizzy after this attempt in Kaneda's house and felt lost. I only walked at random, not caring where I was going. But suddenly I heard the voice of Hanako from behind a paper sliding door. I realized I was in a favorable spot, so I held my ears at an angle and stopped my breath.

" Don't you think he's impudent for a schoolteacher? " she was saying in her high-pitched voice.

" He certainly is. We should try to put him in his place. There are a couple of students from my home town in that school."

" Oh? "

" There's Pinsuke Tsuki and Kishago Fukuchi. I'll have them make trouble for him."

I don't know where Kaneda came from, but I was surprised at the funny names of the people he mentioned.

Mr. Kaneda continued, " He's an English teacher, you say? "

" Yes. According to the wife of the rickshawman, he's a teacher of some English reader."

" Most probably a very bad teacher."

I was most impressed by the way he said this.

" The other day I met Pinsuke and he told me that there was a funny teacher at his school. The teacher had told his students in earnest that wild tea was ' savage tea '. Now even the other teachers are making fun of him. Pinsuke said that it's impossible to learn English from such a teacher. Most probably it's Kushami."

" No mistake about it. He has a face that makes him look that stupid. And the way he wears his moustache! "

" Outrageous ! "

Well, if it is bad to wear a moustache, then all of us cats are outrageous.

"And that individual who calls himself Meitei! What a harum-scarum person he is! He had the audacity to tell me that his uncle was Baron Makiyama. To tell the truth, I don't believe that a man that looks like him could have a baron for an uncle."

" You were wrong to have believed a man you didn't know."

" That's easy to say now. But really he was impertinent to say what he did," snorted Hanako, still unable to get over the affair.

The funny thing about the conversation was that there was nothing said, not a word, about Kangetsu. Of course they might have talked about him before I got within earshot, or perhaps they had already decided against him as their daughter's suitor and had dropped him altogether from their minds.

Crouching as low as possible, I listened for some time but suddenly I heard a bell ringing in the parlor on the other side of the house. In order not to miss anything, I made my way there.

On this side of the house, I heard a girl, all alone, talking loudly. Her voice sounded just like Hanako's so I realized that this must be the daughter of the house and the girl Kangetsu had tried to save from drowning. It is a pity but because of the paper sliding doors, I was not to be honored by seeing her beautiful features. Therefore I won't say here that she has a large nose right in the middle of her face, but, gathering from the sound of her breathing, I figured that hers would not go unnoticed in a crowd. The fact that I could not hear another person indicated that she must have been talking into one of those things they call a telephone.

" Is this Yamato, the theater restaurant? Yes? Now listen, I'm going there tomorrow so please reserve box No. 3 in the lower gallery for me, all right? Do you understand? You don't? Nonsense! You're to reserve box No. 3 in the lower gallery. What's that? You can't? But of course you can! Do you think I'm joking? Now, why should I joke about a thing like this? Who is this speaking? Chokichi? Well, Chokichi, you don't seem to understand. Get me the proprietress on the phone quick. What? What's that? How impudent! Do you know who I am? I'm

Miss Kaneda. Aha, you say you know me very well. What's that? What? You thank me for being a good customer? You don't have to be so thankful—just reserve that box for tomorrow. Why, you're laughing again! Really! What? What? Don't make fun of me now or I'll hang up. Speak up. Say something." It seemed as if Chokichi had hung up for there was no response. The girl was all worked up and she kept jingling the phone. A dog in the room commenced barking so I knew that I would have to be careful. I leaped down from the veranda and scooted under the house.

Just then I heard footsteps and the sound of the sliding doors being opened.

" Oh, Miss, your mother and father are asking for you." The voice was that of the maid.

" I don't care," shouted the girl angrily.

" They asked me to call you."

" I said I don't care."

" Well it's something about Kangetsu Mizushima," teased the maid, tactfully trying to calm her.

" I don't care if it's Kangetsu or a Suigetsu. I don't like him. His face looks like a gourd! " She rebuked the maid for the third time though her tantrum was actually meant for poor Kangetsu who was not even present.

" By the way, when did you have your hair arranged? "

The maid gulped and then answered, " Today, Miss." It was a very short reply.

" You're getting awfully elegant for a maid. And you're wearing a new collar, too." The girl's fourth scolding came from a different angle.

" It's the one you gave me some time ago. It is so pretty I hated to use it so I kept it in my trunk. But my other collar became so old that I got the new one out."

" When did I give you that collar? "

" You bought it in January when you went to the Shirokiya Department Store. It's the light green one showing the ranks of *sumo* wrestlers. You said it didn't become you."

" Well, it becomes you. I envy you."

" Thank you."

" I didn't mean it that way. I said I envied you."

" Yes, Miss."

" Why did you take it without permission? "

" But—"

" If it becomes you, there is no reason why it shouldn't become me, is there? "

" I believe it would become you very much."

" Then why stand there saying nothing when you know all the time I want it back? That's right, just stand there wearing it. You beast ! " The lashing words were ceaseless.

I was anxious about the outcome but just then, from another room, I heard " Tomiko, Tomiko." This was the master, Kaneda himself, calling to his daughter.

The girl had no alternative but to leave the telephone room. " Ye—s." Following her was a lap dog, just a little bigger than me. The eyes and mouth were all clustered in the center of its ugly mug.

As for myself, cat-walking as softly as usual, I made my way to the rear door, went out into the street, and quickly returned to my master's house. My exploration had netted good results.

Arriving home was like coming down from the sunny top of a mountain because the place I had been was so beautiful. I felt as if I were now entering a dark grotto, the change was so acute. During my exploration, I had been bent on one subject only so I did not have much time to look carefully at the decoration of the rooms, the windows or the paper doors ; but in coming home I realized what a lowly place I live in. I found I was a little envious of the things they call " common ". Perhaps a businessman is actually greater than a teacher. I found this somewhat confusing so I asked my tail, which, in such cases, is my habit. The tip answered that that was true.

Entering the house, I was surprised to find that Meitei was still there. There were so many cigarette butts sticking in the ashes of the hand-warming brazier that it looked like a beehive. Meitei was sitting with his legs crossed and was talking loudly. Kangetsu was there, too, though I don't know when he had come. My master was lying on his back with his hands folded under his head, gazing earnestly at the water-stained ceiling. Without mistake, this was a gathering of pacifists.

" Kangetsu, you once told us of a lady who called to you while she was delirious. You kept her name a secret but don't you think it's time to let us know who she is?" Meitei was teasing him.

" If it concerned only myself I would tell you but, you see, it might cause the girl embarrassment."

" Then you won't tell us?"

" Besides, I promised the doctor's wife that I wouldn't."

" Then you won't tell anybody her name?"

" No," emphasized Kangestsu, twisting the string of his *haori* coat as usual. . The purple string was of a color impossible to find in any store—so faded it was.

" That string on your coat looks as if it were a relic of the Tempo Era (1830–1843 A.D.)," said my master from his lying position. He was still indifferent to the Kaneda case.

" It might look all right on a uniform, though, complete with a crest of hollyhocks. It is said that when Oda Nobunaga was married, he wore his hair like a tea stirrer because he had to adopt his wife's family name. That string must have been used by him in those days," rambled Meitei, as usual taking a long time to make his explanation.

" To tell the truth, this was worn by my grandfather at the time the Shogun defeated the Choshu clan," Kangetsu replied seriously.

" Don't you think it's about time it was donated to a museum? To think that Kangetsu Mizushima, Bachelor of Science and Lecturer on the Dynamics of Hanging, wearing such an old string, should look like a masterless warrior!"

" I could buy another string for my *haori* but there are some people who say that this one becomes me."

" Who, for instance?" asked my master loudly as he turned over.

" Oh, you wouldn't know."

" That doesn't make any difference. Who was it?"

" Well, a certain girl."

" Ha, ha, ha! You must be quite a ladies' man. Want me to guess? It must be that girl who called you from the bottom of the river Sumida. Why not put that *haori* coat on and try drowning yourself again? " said Meitei out of turn.

" Ha, ha, ha! She's not calling me from the bottom of the river now. Northwest of here, in a world ever so pure— "

" It's not as pure as you think—don't forget that fiendish nose! "

" What's that? " asked Kangetsu with an anxious face.

" That ' Nose' came here, yes, here. She gave us quite a surprise, isn't that right, Kushami? "

" Uhuh, " grunted my master, drinking tea still in a lying position.

" Who do you mean by that ' Nose'? "

" The mother of the eternal female you so dearly love, of course.'"

" Why! "

" A woman who said that she was the wife of Kaneda came and asked a lot of questions about you." My master told this to Kangetsu in a surprisingly serious tone.

I looked toward Kangetsu to see if he would be shocked, or if he would be glad or whether he would be embarrassed, but I found his face expressionless. Kangetsu, continuing to finger his string, murmured as softly as always, " Must have been asking if I would marry the girl."

" On the contrary. You know, the possessor of that large, enormous nose— " Meitei was going to continue, but my master interrupted " I've been trying to think up a poem about that nose of hers." My master was changing the subject entirely, like trying to graft a bamboo on a tree. The Mrs. commenced laughing softly from the adjoining room.

" You're not being very serious. Well, have you composed the poem? "

"A little. The first line begins: ' On this face is enshrined a nose'."

"And then? "

" The second line goes: ' To which one offers wine'."

"And what's the next line? "

" That's as far as I've got."

" Sounds good," smiled Kangetsu.

" Now, the next should go like this: ' There are two holes, dim and faint.' How's that? " attempted Meitei, adding this part of the poem immediately.

Then Kangetsu joined in. " Would it be all right to add this: ' Deep inside, no hairs can be seen'? "

Each was saying whatever came into his mind when from the street, on the other side of the fence, were heard several voices: " Pottery badger! Pottery badger! "

Meitei and my master were somewhat surprised. They looked through the slits in the fence and saw people laughing. Suddenly the sound of feet running away could be heard.

" What in the world would a pottery badger be? " Meitei asked my master, not being able to make anything out of the commotion.

" How would I know? " shrugged my master.

"Quite original," murmured Kangetsu, adding his own criticism.

It is always difficult to understand what is going on in Meitei's mind but suddenly he stood up and said seriously, as if he were going to make a speech, " Hitherto, I have been studying noses from the point of aesthetics, and now I would like to announce part of my discoveries. Please give me your kind attention." This happened so suddenly that my master was complete taken by surprise. Kangetsu said in a very low voice, " Hear, hear."

" Even after much research, the origin of the nose is still not altogether clear. The first question that arises is whether the nose should be considered as practical; a person only needs two nostrils, nothing more. There is absolutely no need for it to protrude in the middle of the face. Though no reason can be given, it definitely protrudes as you can very well see for yourselves." Meitei pinched his own nose to illustrate this phenomenon.

" Yours does not protrude much," interjected my master without restraint.

" Well in any case, it's not imbedded, is it? In order to avert any misunderstanding, I would like to point out that two holes, the nostrils, run parallel to each other in the middle of the face. According to my opinion, the evolution of the protruding nose came about due to the delicate action of man blowing his nose."

" That's a good opinion," said my master.

"As you know, when a person blows his nose, he holds it between the two hands. In doing so we stimulate the growth. According to the laws of evolution, if one section of the body is stimulated, that part develops more than the unstimulated areas. The flesh gradually becomes tougher until it finally hardens into bone."

"You can't tell me that flesh hardens as easily as that," interrupted Kangetsu, speaking as a bachelor of science. Meitei continued as if he had heard no objection to his theory.

" Proof is better than argument. You can't help agreeing because the bone is there. Yes, the bone is there, but even so the nose continues to run. When it runs, you have to blow your nose. Because of this action, the bone has became more rigid through the centuries and now protrudes. It is incredible! Drops of water eventually drill through rock! A bald head emits light all by itself! Just as the proverb says, ' Wonderful fragrance, wonderful stink ! ' The ridge was thus made and hardened into a protruding nose ! "

" But look at yours. It's plumpy."

" It is not for the lecturer to discuss his own nose. But the nose of Mrs. Kaneda is one which shows extraordinary development. It must be considered as a masterpiece and it is with admiration that I am explaining it to you." At this point Kangetsu again cried out, " Hear, hear ! " He had become even more enthusiastic about Meitei's lecture. " But when a nose becomes overdeveloped, though it might still possess admirable qualities, it becomes so big and terrible that it is difficult to approach. There's no doubt that Mrs. Kaneda's nose is great but it is also somewhat rugged. For instance, the construction of the noses of Socrates, Goldsmith and Thackeray might have lacked ' something ', but this lack made them all the more charming. ' Be not arrogant because of possessing a long nose but be respected because of its individuality,' as the saying goes. Among the common people, there is a proverb : 'A dumpling is better than a nosegay '. But no, it would be better 'A dumpling is better than a nose.' As far as beauty is concerned, the type which I, Meitei, possess is just about right."

Kangetsu and my master commenced chuckling and Meitei himself heartily laughed at his own foolishness.

" Now, the facts I have just stated— "

" Just a minute. That word ' stated ' sounds too much like a lecturer. I don't want you to use it," mimicked Kangetsu, taking revenge for the time Meitei had said the same thing to him.

"All right, if that's the case, I guess I'll have to wash my face and begin all over again. Ahem—I would now like to enter upon a discussion concerning the relation of the nose to the rest of the face. If I could discuss the nose alone, completely divorced from the other parts of the face, that of Mrs. Kaneda's would have no comparison in this world. If it were displayed in a contest at Mt. Kurama where many long-nosed demons live, it would still win first prize. That's how great a nose she has. It is only a pity that her nose developed without consulting the other parts of her face—the mouth, the eyes, etc. The nose of Julius Caesar was, without doubt, one of the greatest in history. But if it had been cut off and planted in the middle of this cat's face, what would you get? It would be like taking the Great Buddha of Nara and placing it on a chessboard. It would be more than out of proportion and of no value as far as beauty is concerned. The nose of Mrs. Kaneda is, like that of Caesar's, an extraordinary specimen. But what is its environment? Of course, it is not as inferior as the nose of this cat, but Mrs. Kaneda has a round face so she looks, like an epileptic maidservant. The slits of her eyes slant up under her eyebrows which slant down—that's a fact. So now, gentlemen, I can but conclude it is a pity that to this face is attached such a nose! "

During this pause in Meitei's oration, a voice was heard from the rear of the house: " Still talking about the nose. How unoriginal! "

" That's the wife of the rickshawman," explained my master to Meitei. So Meitei again continued to talk:

" The speaker has been greatly honored to discover that there is still another audience listening at the rear of this house. It gladdens his heart that one with so charming a voice should be listening to such a dry lecture. It gives me great pleasure, more than she might know. I would like to make my lecture as simple as possible but, unfortunately, we will now go into the subject of dynamics. I'm afraid this might be somewhat difficult for ladies to understand. I ask you your forgiveness." Kangetsu, upon hearing the word "dynamics", commenced to smile slyly.

"What I want to prove here is that her nose and her face are not harmonized. The combination goes against Zeising's rule of the Golden Cut. I would like to explain this strictly according to the formula of dynamics. Let us consider that H is the height of the nose and a is the angle made by the nose coming in contact with the surface of the face. W is the weight of the nose itself. I believe that you understand everything now."

"How could we?" sighed my master.

"How about you, Kangetsu?"

"It's somewhat difficult even for me to understand."

"That's a shame. I'm not surprised about Kushami but as for you, a bachelor of science, I was sure you'd understand. This formula is the whole backbone of my lecture so I cannot omit it—it would have no significance if I did. Well, I guess there's nothing else I can do but leave out the formula and come to the conclusion of my theory."

"Do you have a conclusion?" asked my master doubtfully.

"Of course. A theory without a conclusion is like a Western dinner without dessert. Now listen, both of you. Here's the conclusion of the story. In reference to the formula, borrowing the theories of Virchow and Wiseman, allowance must be given to take into consideration the heredity of such forms. Even though there are powerful theories which claim that heredity is not important, the condition of the mind affected by these forms has considerable influence. Therefore, it can be said that the possessor of such an uncomely nose will, upon having children, pass the same unsightly nose on to her offspring. You are still young, Kangetsu, so perhaps you have not paid special attention to the shape of Mr. Kaneda's daughter's nose, but the period of incubation of such hereditary effects is sometimes quite long. There's no telling when the nose might suddenly inflate with a change of climate to become just like her mother's. Therefore, as a friend offering scientific proof, I advise you to give up any thought of marriage while you can; that would be playing it safe. In regard to this, I believe that the master of this house and the honorable cat which lies asleep here have nothing to say against such a suggestion."

My master slowly rose from his lying position and agreed: "That's right. Who'd marry the daughter of such a woman! Don't do it, Kangetsu!" My master was unusually enthusiastic about pressing the point. In order to voice my own approval, I meowed twice.

Kangetsu didn't seem to be much excited. He only commented, "If the master of this house says so, it's all right with me. But if the girl should become ill because of this decision, that would constitute a crime."

"Ha, ha, ha! A crime in sex!"

My master was the only one who remained serious. "She couldn't be affected enough to become ill, not she. The daughter of that woman is worthless. You know, that woman came here and questioned me and—the long-nosed witch!" my master was grunting his dissatisfaction all by himself when, suddenly, several laughing voices were heard again from the other side of the fence.

One of them shouted, "Stupid braggart!" while another cried out, "You want to move into a better house, don't you?" Then another voice was heard: "I'm sorry for you scholars. You hold your heads high, but you're only a lot of good-for-nothings!"

My master, not to be outdone, ran to the veranda and shouted back, "Shut up! What's the big idea of coming up to the fence and making all this noise?"

"Ha, ha, ha! Savage tea! Savage tea!" They were now chanting their abuses in unison. My master, like a ruffled cock, grabbed his cane and rushed outside. Meitei, clapped his hands and encouraged him. "This is great! Go to it!" Kangetsu just sat there fingering his *haori* string with a smirk on his face. I followed my master and found him standing in the middle of the street holding his cane awkwardly. There was nobody else around.

He had only made a fool of himself again.

IV

AS BEFORE, I often went sneaking into the Kaneda estate.
I do not believe I have to explain "often". It only
means that I went there many times. You do something once
and you want to do it the second time. After the second time,
you dream about doing it the third time. The feeling of curiosity is not limited only to humans; even we cats are full of psychological whims and we wish they were respected more. After
the third time, an act becomes a habit, a necessity in our daily
lives. There is no difference in this respect between humans and
cats. You might wonder why I went to the Kaneda estate so
often. Very well—but before giving you an explanation, I would
like to ask a question myself. Why is it that you humans like
to inhale cigarette smoke through your mouth and exhale it
through your nostrils? Cigarette smoke does not fill the stomach,
nor does it act in any way as medicine for the blood; yet humans
insist on smoking. You who smoke don't have to criticize my
sneaking into the Kaneda estate because, to me, such trips act in
the same way as cigarette smoking does to humans.

By the way, the phrase "sneak into" is apt to bring about a misunderstanding. It sounds like the actions of a thief or a clandestine
lover, and is not adequate. Although no invitation was ever sent
to me, I went to the Kaneda estate not to steal bonito fish or to
have secret meetings with the pug with the shrinkled face—the
eyes and nose all clustered in the center—oh, no! Investigating?
Nonsense! There are no occupations so low as those of detectives
and money lenders. It is true that, in a spirit of chivalry, I first
went to the Kaneda house with the object of helping Kangetsu.
It was unbecoming behavior for a cat, but that was only the first
time. Since then, I have done nothing to put cats to shame. Then,
you'll ask, why did I use such incriminating words as " sneaking

in ". Well, to tell the truth, there's a good reason.

Great Heaven was made to shelter all creation, and the Good Earth a place to put creation on. Even those who like arguing cannot deny this fact. When we ask to what extent human beings helped with the creation of heaven and earth, we must admit that they did nothing. There is no rule which says that you can possess something you did not make. It may be permissible to claim possession of a place, but that is no reason to prohibit others from entering it. Still, many people stake poles and build fences around an area and call it So-and-So's land, as if claiming not only that part of the earth but also that part of heaven, and registering it as their own. If it is possible to divide plots of land into small areas and sell the land per lot, then the air around it must also be available to be divided into cubic feet and sold. But if the air which we breathe cannot be divided and if heaven cannot be restricted, then does it stand to reason that only the earth can be divided? I have firm faith in such a doctrine, so I feel free to go wherever I desire. Of course, I would not go just *any* place, but I am unperturbed about going anywhere I *want* to go—north, south, east or west. As for Kaneda's place, there is no reason why I should restrain myself from entering it.

Unfortunately, however, when it comes to using force, we cats are no match for humans. They say that strength is power. As long as we live in this fleeting world, we cats cannot hope to uphold our opinions no matter how wrong humans might be. If we tried to guarantee our rights, we would only meet the same fate as Kuro of the rickshawman's, getting hit on the head with a pole for carrying loads.

When reasoning is with us but strength with the other party, what would be the wisest action? To yield while perverting our own reasoning, or to steal past the powerful eyes of the authorities and take action according to reason? It goes without saying that I select the latter method. In order to avoid a blow from a carrying pole, one must " sneak in " without being seen. Therefore, as there was no reason not to go into the estate of Kaneda, I went. Now you understand why I use the term " sneak in ".

As my experiences of sneaking in accumulated, the situation

at the Kaneda family slowly became clearer though I did not really try to eavesdrop. I had no intention of doing any detective work but such proved inevitable. I could not help noticing that when Hanako, the Mrs., washed her face, she would wipe her nose with special care; that the daughter, Tomiko, ate many rice cakes between meals; and that Mr. Kaneda himself had an extremely flat nose, quite unlike that of his wife's and daughter's. It was not only his nose that was flat—his whole face seemed leveled off. It is most likely that when he was a boy he had had a fight. A bully had probably grabbed him by the neck and pushed his face against an earthen wall with all his might and this, after forty years, had produced a face as flat as a pond—or so I guessed. It was an extremely mild face with no dangerous traits, but one which lacked variation. Mad as he might get, it was still a flat face. I also got to know that when Mr. Kaneda ate slices of raw tuna, he would slap his bald head with his hand. Not only was his face flat but he was short in height. For that reason he would wear a high-crowned hat and high wooden sandals. The rickshawman, finding this comical, would tell this to the house boy who, in turn, would praise the rickshawman for this deep observation. There would be no end of telling everything about them all.

I generally passed through the garden by the rear entrance and took a look around from behind the man-made hill. If the paper sliding doors were closed and everything calm and still, I would go quietly into the house. But, on the other hand, if I heard cheerful voices, or if I could be seen from the house, I'd go around the east fringe of the pond, pass the water closet and station myself under the veranda as quickly as I could.

I never did anything wrong so there was really no need to hide or to be afraid, but I have learned to resign myself to the illogic of most humans. If more people were like Kumasaka Chohan, a noted burglar of the Kamakura period (1192–1333 A.D.), every virtuous man would take the same action.

As Mr. Kaneda was a dignified businessman, there was no need for him to swing a five-foot-three-inch-long sword like Kumasaka Chohan but, according to my understanding, it seemed as if he did not think of men as men. And if he did not believe men to be men, he would certainly not consider a cat a cat. That would mean that no matter how virtuous a cat might be, a cat could not be overly cautious within Kaneda's estate. Perhaps that was why I liked coming ; I wanted to challenge this risk. I will leave the explanation of this to a later time when we have a better chance to diagnose the mind of a cat in more detail.

One day, after I had climbed the man-made hill, I laid my chin on the grass and looked the situation over. I found that the largest room of the house was opened to the early spring air, and Mr. and Mrs. Kaneda were in conversation with a guest. Unfortunately, Hanako was facing me and her nose pointed directly at my forehead across the pond. This was the first time in my life that I had ever been glared at by a nose. Mr. Kaneda was facing the guest so I could see only a portion of his face. From my positon I could not recognize the flatness of his face but then neither could I see the whereabouts of his nose. A growth of gray hair, which happened to be a moustache, could be seen; so imagining the two nostrils that must be right above it, I could easily estimate the approximate location of the nose. The wind would have no trouble at all in blowing against a face as flat as his. The guest was the only one of the three with normal features. Being an ordinary face, it had nothing characteristic to describe. Some might like being so normal, but it is a pity to be so common. And who was this person with the ordinary face living in the peaceful years of the Meiji era? I would never have known if I had not been able to scamper under the veranda to listen to their conversation.

". . . and my wife took the trouble to go to the man's house and ask about him." Mr. Kaneda was talking with an arrogance which did not sound convincing at all. His speech, like his face, was flat and prosaic.

" Is that so? That man taught Mizushima? Is that so? That was a very good thought. Is that so? " repeated the " is-that-so " guest.

" But, I still can't understand him."

" No, you wouldn't understand Kushami. Even when we were

boarding together, he could never make up his mind. Yes, you must have had quite a time with him," said the guest, to Hanako.

"Quite a time is right! In all these years, that was the first time I have ever been treated in such a way when making a visit," snorted Hanako.

"Did he say something insulting? He's terribly obstinate. As a teacher of the English reader, you immediately understand what kind of a man he is," commented the guest keeping in the spirit of the conversation.

"He was absolutely unreasonable. To whatever question my wife asked, he answered rudely."

"That's a shame. It's a fact, however, that with a little education one becomes arrogant. If one is poor, besides, one becomes impossibly stubborn. Yes, there are, in this world, many strange individuals. They don't realize their own incompetence; they only pick on the wealthy, as if their own wealth had been taken away by the rich. Yes, it's unbelievable but true. Ha, ha, ha!" The guest seemed to be in an extremely jolly mood.

"It's unspeakable! This is evidently an example of selfishness born from a misunderstanding about the world. That's why I have thought of disciplining him. I've already taken some action."

"Is that so? It would indeed do him good," agreed the guest even before knowing what action had been taken.

"But, Mr. Suzuki, he's awfully stubborn. At school, he won't even talk to Mr. Fukuchi or to Mr. Tsuki. They thought at first that he was silent because he felt ashamed of his ability. But no! The other day he chased our house boy with a cane. Just think, a man over thirty years old! It's outrageous—just outrageous— that he acts so foolishly. He must be out of his mind."

The guest seemed somewhat startled because he asked, "But why did he become so violent?"

"Well, you see, the house boy was saying something as he passed him. All of a sudden, Kushami kicked off his sandals and came after him with a cane in his hand. Even if the house boy had said something bad, the man's not a child. He's a grownup with a moustache, and a teacher at that!"

It seemed that the conclusion reached by the three of them was that if a person happened to be a teacher, he should accept insults as quietly as a wooden statue.

"And moreover, that man Meitei is really an eccentric! A man who likes to tell useless lies! Actually, that was the first time I had ever met such a queer personality."

"Meitei? Is he still telling lies? Did you meet him at the home of Mr. Kushami, too? Well, you can't get the better of him. Yes, he was also one of my group. We used to do our own cooking but he always made fun of us and I had many a fight with him."

"He would make anybody angry. At times, of course, it's perfectly all right to lie—for instance, when you're thanking someone or when it is the fashion. At such times, everybody says something or other they don't necessarily mean. But that man Meitei lies only with the intention of lying, even when there is no need for it. Why does he do it? It's a wonder how he rattles them off."

"You're right, ma'am. Actually he lies from habit. It's a bad custom."

"I went there only with the object of asking about Mizushima but everything went badly. I was terribly offended. But still, an obligation is an obligation—I couldn't go there and ask a favor without repaying it in some way, so I had the rickshawman take a dozen bottles of beer to the house. But what do you think? It was sent back! The rickshawman told them that it was a gesture of appreciation, but that man said that he prefers jam! That beer was too bitter. Then he closed the door without even excusing himself!"

"That was rude," interjected the guest, this time sounding as if he really meant it.

After a short silence, Mr. Kaneda was heard to say "And that's why I asked you to come today. It might be amusing to make fun of him behind his back but then it wouldn't serve our purpose for the moment." Mr. Kaneda again slapped his bald head just as when he eats raw tuna. Of course I was under the veranda so I didn't actually see him slap his head, but as a priestess would know the sound of a wooden altar bell, I recognized the slap on a bald head because recently I had become quite familiar with that sound.

"So I thought I might ask you a little favor."

" If it is within my power, I would be delighted to help. My transfer to Tokyo was due entirely to your kindness." It seems that Mr. Suzuki was under an obligation to Kaneda.

The case was getting more interesting all the time. The weather being so good, I had come with no special intention—I had not expected to get such good information as this. It was like going to a temple during the equinox and then being unexpectedly treated to some cakes in the priest's sitting room. I cocked my ears carefully to hear the plan Kaneda had for his guest.

" That Kushami! He keeps giving funny ideas to Mizushima. He even kind of hinted to him not to marry my daughter. Isn't that what the rickshawman's wife told us ? "

" Hinting's no term for it. ' Who in the world would marry the daughter of that bloodsucker. Kangetsu, don't ever marry her.' That was what he said."

" The insulting fellow! Did he really say ' that bloodsucker ' ? "

" He did. The wife of the rickshawman told me all about it."

" Well, Mr. Suzuki, it's just as you've heard. The case is very annoying."

" Yes, very. Actually, there shouldn't be so many people involved. Even Kushami should have the sense to know better than to interfere."

" Now, the thing is this—I understand you boarded with Kushami during your schooldays and, though it might be quite different now, you were once on very good terms with him. That's the reason I am asking you this favor. Go and see him and talk with him. He might be uncooperative but if he is, it will only be to his disadvantage. If he's understanding, I'll see that he is repaid and I'll do nothing to hurt his feelings. But if he's going to act like he did before, then I will have my own way of dealing with the situation. In any case, if he remains stubborn, it will only be to his disadvantage."

" Just as you say. Resistance is to his disadvantage—all right I'll try to make him understand."

"By the way, as there are many others asking for the hand of my daughter, I can't promise that I'll give my daughter to Mizushima. I've found out that as an individual and as a student, however, he's not so bad. If he's willing to work hard enough to earn his doctorate in the near future, I might give my daughter to him. I won't mind if you say something to that effect to Kushami."

" If I tell him that, it might work as an incentive. Kangetsu might begin to study in earnest. All right, I'll go."

" And here's something else. It's an odd way to put it, but I think it's unbecoming for Mizushima to be calling that freakish Kushami ' Sir, sir,' and doing exactly what he tells him to do. That's very annoying. Moreover, though this does not only concern Mizushima, whatever Kushami might say to cause trouble will not be taken into consideration."

" Because it wouldn't be fair to Mr. Mizushima," added Hanako.

" I haven't met Mizushima as yet but, in any case, if he marries your daughter, he is sure to be very happy. He couldn't possibly have anything to say against my helping."

" Yes, Mr. Mizushima wants to marry my daughter but he's stalling because of those queer characters, Kushami and Meitei."

" It doesn't suit a person of considerable education to be influenced like that. I'll go and have a good talk with Kushami."

" I'd be much obliged though I'm afraid I'm causing you a great deal of trouble. But Kushami knows Mizushima quite well. When my wife went there, it ended as we've just told you. If you could see Kushami and ask about Mizushima's conduct, and see how he manages his studies, I'd be much obliged."

" I'll do that. Today is Saturday, so he should be home now. Where does he live? "

" Go straight down this road until you come to a dead end. Then go to the left for about a block. It's the house with the crumbling black fence," directed Hanako.

" Then it's quite close by. It should be easy if he has a name plate by his door. I'll drop in on my way back."

"At times you'll find his name on the door and at other times you won't. He pastes his calling card on the gate with a grain of boiled rice. When it rains, it comes off and he has to paste another on. It would be much easier to have a name plate made of wood. He's a difficult man to understand."

" But, in any case, if it has a crumbling black fence, I

should be able to find the house."

"Of course. It's simple because there's no other house less well cared for in this neighborhood. Oh, yes, if you have difficulty, here's another detail; you can't miss it if you find a house with grass growing on the roof."

"It must be quite a house! Ha, ha, ha!"

If I didn't get back home before the honorable Suzuki arrived, all wouldn't go well. The conversation up to this point was all I needed to know so I crawled out from under the veranda, traversed the west side of the water closet, and made for the street. I quickly arrived at "the house with grass growing on its roof" and hopped onto the veranda as if nothing had happened.

My master had spread a white blanket out on the veranda and was lying on his belly, his back soaking in the warm spring sunshine. Believe it or not, the day was fair. The sun shone on the grass that grew on the roof and into the room, making it just as nice and warm as the guest room in the Kaneda home. But, unfortunately, the blanket indicated little of spring. The manufacturers must have meant the blanket to be white and the store must have sold it as a white blanket; my master probably purchased a white blanket, but all this had taken place twelve or thirteen years ago. Its period of whiteness was far past. Now it was passing through a period of a dark grayish color. It might eventually change to a dark black, but it is very doubtful whether the life of the blanket itself will last that long. It was worn out evenly so the warps and wefts could easily be counted. Calling it a blanket now was too good a name for it; a better term would have been just " - - - - ket." As for my master, he seemed to believe that in having possessed an object for one year, two years, five years and then for ten years, that he should possess it for a lifetime.

My master, as I have explained, was stretched out on the blanket he so intimately had relations with. Lying on his belly, he had his chin cupped in his hands and a cigarette tucked between the fingers of his right hand. Under the dandruff and inside his head, universal truths might have been twirling around like a pinwheel but, from outside appearances, no one could have imagined such a phenomenon happening within.

The cigarette slowly burned and the ashes, about an inch long, fell onto the blanket. My master, without noticing this, kept staring at the smoke which rose and vanished in the air. The smoke floated in the spring breeze in slow waves and a moving circle of smoke was drawn towards the dark hair of the Mrs. But I should have mentioned the Mrs. before.

She was seated on the floor, her posterior facing my master. You say that's impolite? Well, there's really nothing wrong about that. Courtesy depends on the parties concerned. My master's chin calmly pointed at the large and sublime rear end. There was nothing discourteous about it whatsoever. The couple, after their first year of married life, did away with any pretense of etiquette —in other words, they are a super-married couple.

As the day was fine, the Mrs., with her rear end facing my master, had just washed her long tresses with a substance like glue mixed in raw egg. She had her hair flowing down over her shoulders, as if showing it off, and was sewing a child's dress silently. She had brought her sewing box to the veranda and, sitting on a crepe silk cushion, was drying her hair in the sun. Her posterior just happened to be facing my master. Or perhaps my master had turned so that he would be facing the rear end. As I said before, the cigarette smoke rose and mingled with the black locks of freshly washed hair. This produced a halo. My master gazed at it, lost in thought. But smoke does not stay at one definite place forever. The nature of smoke is to rise higher and higher so after my master had studied the intermingling of the smoke with his wife's hair, his eyes followed it higher and higher. My master's gaze started from the location of the Mrs.'s hips and then gradually went up her back, and then from her shoulders to the back of her neck.

Once when his stare reached the head, he let out a sudden yell of surprise. He noticed that the Mrs., with whom he had promised mutual fidelity till death, had, right in the middle of her head, a large round bald spot! The naked shape, reflecting the soft spring light, shone brightly as if boasting of its existence. The eyes of my master, which had made this great discovery when least expected, showed great astonishment. Indifferent to the bright glare reflecting from the bald spot, he opened his eyes wide and concentrated on it in fascination. The naked patch first reminded my master of an old-fashioned saucer for candles placed in the family altar. My master belongs to the Shinshu sect of Buddhism whose custom it is to spend more than one can afford on family altars.

When my master was still a child, he had seen a small dirty shrine covered with thick gold leaf in a warehouse. He had noticed a brass saucer hanging inside and also that it reflected a dull light. Memories of the saucer suddenly came back to him when he saw the bald spot on his wife's head, or so it seemed. But soon his reverie was shattered.

All at once, it reminded him of the pigeons around the Goddess Kwannon at Asakusa. It would seem that his wife's baldness and the pigeons of Kwannon could have little connection yet for my master, there was an intimate association between the two. During his childhood, he would often buy some peas to feed the pigeons whenever he went to Asakusa. A saucer of peas cost only three rin.* All the saucers were made of red clay. Now, the size of the saucer and its color were exactly the same as the bald patch on his wife's head.

" It sure looks like one of those saucers," mumbled my master. Therefore the Mrs. asked, without looking back, ": What does? "

" Do you know that you have a bald spot on your head? "

" Yes," sighed the Mrs. without stopping her work. It seemed she wasn't embarrassed in the least at having her baldness discovered. She is a model wife!

" Did you have it before we married, or did it happen afterwards? " asked my master. Although he didn't say it, he was thinking that if she had had it before they were married, he had been deceived.

" I don't know when it began. It doesn't make any difference anyway, does it? " Her logic sounded convincing.

" What do you mean ' it doesn't make any difference'? It's your own head," barked my master, somewhat irritated.

" That's right. It's my own head, so it doesn't make any dif-

---

* *Rin* is one tenth of a sen.

ference," she replied. But she seemed to have become more self-conscious of the spot. She placed her right hand on it and caressed it. " Why, it's getting bigger! I didn't know it was this size." Considering her tone, she seemed to acknowledge the fact that the bald spot was larger than it should have been at her age.

" When a woman wears her hair in a *marumage* style*, the part in the center is so strained that all of us get bald there," she said, now on the defensive.

" If all women got bald so early in life, no women over forty would have hair. It must be some kind of a disease and it might be contagious. You'd better go to Dr. Amaki and have him look it over," suggested my master, feeling his own head.

" You say such things about me, but just look at yourself— you have white hairs in your nostrils. If baldness is catching, white nostril hairs might be contagious, too." The Mrs. was somewhat grumbling now.

" There's no harm in having white hairs in the nostrils because you can't see them. But when it comes to a bald spot on top of your head—especially the head of a young woman—it's not nice to look at. It's abnormal."

" All right! If I'm abnormal, why did you marry me? You married me because you loved me, and now you say I'm abnormal."

" That's because I didn't know. I didn't know about it until today. Why didn't you show this to me before we were married?"

" Nonsense! There's no country in. the world where a girl must show her head before getting married."

" I'll drop the subject of the bald spot. But you're shorter than average. It's unsightly."

" You knew that I was short when you married me, didn't you? "

" Sure, I knew it. I knew that you were short but I thought you'd grow taller."

"Do you think that a person grows after the age of twenty? You certainly like to make fun of me! " She put down her sewing and twisted her body to face my master. Her countenance now showed that, depending on his reply, she might really get worked up.

---

* The *marumage* coiffure is worn only by married women.

"There's no law that says you can't grow after the age of twenty. I thought that after marrying you, if I fed you good nutritious food, you'd grow a bit taller." My master was explaining this very seriously. This queer reasoning was interrupted, however, by the bell at the front door. This was followed by a voice asking for entrance. Suzuki had finally reached the house with grass on the roof, the house of Mr. Kushami, the forlorn teacher.

The Mrs., postponing the quarrel to some later date, hurriedly picked up her sewing box and dress, and ran into the tearoom. My master then rolled up the gray blanket and threw it into the study. Upon looking at the calling card the maid had brought, my master gave a slightly surprised look but asked the guest to be shown into the room. He then went into the toilet, with the calling card in his hand. Why he went into the toilet so suddenly I can find no reason. And why he went there with the calling card of Tojuro Suzuki is another thing I am at a loss to explain. In any case, it must have been an annoying surprise that compelled my master to go to that evil-smelling place.

The maid took out a printed cotton cushion, placed it in front of the alcove, and ushered the guest in. Suzuki took a look around the room after the maid left. A scroll written by Mokuan, a well-known master penman, was hanging in the alcove. It was an imitation but read: "Flowers in bloom. Spring has come to all countries". There was also an arrangement of pre-seasonal cherry blossoms in a cheap pottery vase made in Kyoto. After inspecting these items by turn, Suzuki's gaze fell on the cushion the maid had brought for him. He found a cat serenely sitting on it. There is no need to mention that the cat was me—The Cat—and nobody else!

The moment Suzuki saw me there, he felt a slight annoyance and it showed a little on his face. He knew that the cushion had been placed there for him but, before he could sit down, he found a strange animal curled on it. This was the first episode of that day to put Suzuki off balance. Even if the cushion had been left as the maid had placed it, Suzuki would have sat on the hard straw mats anyway, showing his modesty until my master came and urged him to use the cushion. But what had already occupied the cushion that he would eventually use? He might have offered his cushion to another person, but a cat! This was disgusting. That a mere cat was on his cushion gave him even more displeasure. This was the second thing that put Suzuki off balance.

Last, but not least, he found the attitude of the cat itself an irritation. The animal did not show any sign of pity at all for the guest. Though it had no right to be on the cushion in the first place, it assumed a haughty attitude. It looked up at Suzuki with wide round belligerent eyes, as if asking what right the man had to invade this home. This was the third factor that put Suzuki off balance. Of course he could have grabbed me by the neck and pulled me off the cushion but no! Suzuki just looked down at me. A dignified man would not be afraid of a cat. The reason Suzuki did nothing to satisfy his rage was simply because he wanted, as a man, to show more self-respect. Or so I believe. When it comes to using force, a child three feet tall is free to do what he likes with me. But this was Tojuro Suzuki, the right-hand man of Kaneda! He would not stoop to touch the cat, the Supreme God that had established itself in the middle of the two-foot-square cushion! Even though nobody was looking, it would have been beneath his dignity to fight with a cat over a cushion. It wouldn't be manly to fight. It was comical. In order to avert dishonor, he had to experience the discomfort of the floor. But the more he endured it, the more he hated the cat. Occasionally, Suzuki would look at me and make a face. I, on the other hand, felt great pleasure in seeing him complain. Trying to ignore the ridiculousness of the situation, I attempted to maintain an unconcerned air.

While this pantomime was being acted between Suzuki and me, my master came out from the toilet. He was now wearing his crested *haori* coat. He said " Well " to Suzuki and sat down. As I did not notice Suzuki's calling card in his hand, I believe that he disposed of it forever in the ill-smelling hole. As I was considering the fate of the innocent card, my master grabbed me by the neck and threw me onto the veranda with a curse.

" Here, take this," mumbled my master, offering his old friend

Suzuki the cushion. " When did you come to Tokyo? " Suzuki turned the cushion over and sat on it.

" Well, as I have been quite busy I had no time to notify you, but I have been working in the main office here in Tokyo since quite a while back."

" That's nice. Haven't seen you for a long time. Ever since you first went out to the country, isn't it? "

" Uhuh. About ten years now. I came to Tokyo several times but as I was always busy I couldn't drop in. Unlike your occupation, the business I'm in always keeps me busy."

" Ten years make a great difference," murmured my master, looking Suzuki up and down. Suzuki had his hair parted neatly and wore a suit of English tweed. He also wore a gaudy tie. The golden chain across his vest shone brightly. No matter how you looked at these two, it was difficult to realize that they were old friends.

" In my present position, I have to wear these things," said Suzuki, fingering the golden chain.

" Is it real gold? " asked my master without restraint.

" Eighteen karats," smiled Suzuki. " You've aged quite a bit. I'm sure you have children. One? "

" No."

" Two? "

" No."

" Still more? Three, then."

" Yes, three. But I don't know how many more might be coming."

" Still joking! How old is the biggest? "

" Don't remember exactly but around six or seven."

" Ha, ha, ha! It's good to be a teacher. Wish I had become one."

" Be one and you'll want to quit after three days."

" I wonder. It looks like a nice job. You have no worries, you have plenty of time, you can continue to study what you like, and—well, it must be good. Being a businessman isn't all bad but in my position, it's rotten. If you're going to be a happy businessman, you have to be the top man. If you're down the ladder, you have to say things you don't feel and drink *sake* with clients even when you don't want to. It's all very foolish."

" I have never liked businessmen. They'd do anything for money. In the olden days they were looked down on, and rightly so." My master, with a businesman sitting right before him, was being indiscreet.

" You can't say that they're all bad, but it is true that some of them are lacking in taste. In any case, a person has to resolve to die rich in order to be successful. Money is important. I've just come from the home of a businessman and he told me that in order to make money, you have to use three techniques— forget obligations, forget sentiment, and forget shame. Don't you think that's interesting? Ha, ha ha!"

" Who's that fool?"

" He's not a fool at all. He's really a very clever man. He's made a name for himself in business circles. Wonder if you'd know him—he lives just around the corner."

" Kaneda? What a person!"

" You're mad now. Or maybe you're joking. But actually you have to be very clever or else you can't make money. You take these things too seriously."

" The three techniques you just mentioned can be laughed at but take a look at Kaneda's wife's nose. You've been there so you must have seen it."

" His wife? She seems to be a very understanding woman."

" The nose, man, the nose! I'm speaking about her big nose. The other day I composed a poem about it."

"A poem? What do you mean?"

" You don't know what a poem is? You don't seem to know much."

" When you're kept as busy as I am, you don't have much time for literature. Besides I was never very interested in poetry."

" Do you know the shape of Charlemagne's nose?"

" Ha, ha, ha! You're joking again. No, I don't."

" Wellington was nicknamed ' The Nose ' by his men. Did you know that?"

" What's gotten into you—talking only about noses? What

difference does it make if a nose is round or pointed?"

"Plenty. Do you know what Pascal said?"

"What? Another question? It seems I'm here to take an exam. What about Pascal?"

"Pascal said—"

"All right now, what did he say?"

"If Cleopatra's nose had been a wee bit shorter, it would have effected a great change in the world."

"Is that so?"

"There, you see. You shouldn't underestimate the importance of a nose."

"Well, never mind. I'll take better care of mine in the future. By the way, the reason I dropped in today was to ask you about —what was his name?—Mizushima. Yes, that's right, Mizushima something. Do you remember him? The one you said you taught, the one who comes here so often."

"You mean Kangetsu?"

"That's him, yes. Kangetsu. I want to ask you something about him."

"You mean about marriage?"

"Something along that line, I guess. Today when I visited the Kanedas—"

"The other day the 'Nose' herself came here."

"Is that so? Oh, yes, she said she did. She mentioned that she had come to ask some questions but that, unfortunately, Meitei was here and he kept interrupting the conversation."

"She shouldn't have come. And with such a nose!"

"Meitei was here, therefore Mrs. Kaneda couldn't ask very personal questions. So she asked me to ask you. This is the first time for me to do such a favor, but if the two persons concerned wish to be together, I don't think it would be a bad idea to try to help them."

"Thanks for the trouble," said my master coldly. But way down deep inside, he seemed to be moved by the sentiment— "If the two persons concerned wish to be together." As to why this should affect him, I don't have the slightest idea but my master's sentimentalism made him feel as refreshed as if a cool breeze had passed through his sleeves on a hot, stifling summer night.

My master generally expresses his thoughts without restraint. He is stubborn and without tact. But then he is not a product of modern times, a man entirely without sympathy. His nonconformity makes it easy to understand why he gets angry and flares up so often. When he had his dispute with the " Nose ", he became angry because he didn't like the Nose herself—but he had nothing against the daughter. He does not like businessmen so therefore he dislikes Kaneda. But again, this did not reflect on the daughter. He did not have any grudge against the girl, yet Kangetsu was his favorite disciple. He loved Kangetsu even more than he would love a real brother. So if the situation was as Suzuki had stated—that if the boy and girl loved each other —it would not be gentlemanly to hinder it even indirectly. Most probably Kushami, the teacher, believed that he was a true gentleman. If the two loved each other—Ah! this was a big problem. In order to know how to proceed, it was essential for my master to get all the facts.

" Listen, Suzuki. Does the girl really want to marry Kangetsu? I don't care anything about Kaneda or Hanako, but how about the girl herself "

" Well—you see—ah—that is—in any case—ah—perhaps she wants to." Suzuki's explanation was rather vague. He had been requested to ask about Kangetsu but he had come without knowing what the girl herself thought about the matter. The usually dextrous Suzuki was thrown into confusion.

" What do you mean by that? " My master almost always tackles his problems head on.

" Well, perhaps I didn't make myself clear. Of course the girl wants to marry him. Absolutely! Mrs. Kaneda told me so, though at times it seems she speaks ill of him."

" Do you mean the girl? "

" Ye-s."

" That's bad. Speaking badly of Kangetsu! That might mean that she doesn't think much of him."

" But you don't understand. That's the most delicate part of love. There are times when people say especially bad things about those they like best."

"Are there really such foolish people?" My master was quite ignorant about matters concerning human feelings.

"It can't be helped. Even Kaneda's wife interprets the situation as such. At times the daughter says that Kangetsu looks like a long overly ripe gourd; that certainly goes to show how much she loves him."

My master, upon hearing this queer interpretation of affection, was so astounded that he could only stare wide-eyed at Suzuki. He looked like a fortuneteller studying a client. Because of my master's expression, Suzuki thought that he might have gone a little too far. He therefore changed his mode of speech so that my master could grasp the full significance of what he had said.

"Just look at it this way: the Kanedas are wealthy and the girl is a beauty; it would be easy to marry her to a family of means. Kangetsu might be a great man but consider his position —ah—I'd better not use the word "position" because it might sound insulting. But let's consider it from the point of wealth. Anybody can see that he is not her equal. But the fact that I was asked to go out of my way to come and ask questions about him certainly shows how anxious the parents are. The girl thinks highly of Kangetsu." Suzuki was in good form now, adding adequate reasoning. He was sure that my master understood him this time. But if he stopped talking, he was apt to be interrupted again. He believed it wiser to go ahead and get his mission over with as quickly as possible:

"So you see, it's just as I have explained. They are not asking for money or wealth; all they ask is for his qualifications, that is, his title. They're not threatening when they say that they will not give their daughter to Kangetsu only after he gets his doctorate. Don't get me wrong. When Kaneda's wife came here the other day, Meitei said all kinds of queer things. No, you didn't do anything wrong. As a matter of fact, Mrs. Kaneda spoke highly of you. She said that you were the kind of person who speaks his mind without worrying about compliments. I think it was Meitei who did so much harm that day. Now, if Kangetsu should get his doctorate, the Kanedas would be able to hold their heads high and maintain their reputation. What do you say? Can you arrange it so that Kangetsu will complete his thesis soon in order to obtain his doctorate? If only the Kanedas were concerned, there'd be no need for Kangetsu to hurry. But you have to consider what other people would think so—"

When thought about in such a way, there would be no harm in my master's asking Kangetsu to try for his degree. It was all logical enough. There could be no reason why my master shouldn't do just as Suzuki had requested. My master's final decision was now in Suzuki's power. Yes, my master is a simple but honest man!

"All right, then. The next time Kangetsu comes, I'll tell him to finish his thesis as soon as possible. But first, I'll have to ask him whether he really wants to marry Kaneda's daughter or not."

"Why do you have to ask? If you're going to be so particular, you'll never be able to convince him. The best way is simply to sound his mind casually in ordinary conversation."

"You mean I should sound his mind?"

"Perhaps you misunderstood. Listen, there's a better way. You don't have to do that, exactly. If you talk things over with him, its importance will naturally be noticed."

"You might be that subtle, but as for me I like to ask outright."

"All right, all right. But don't ruin everything like Meitei would. Of course, you can't hasten Kangetsu to marry; such a thing is up to him to decide. When Kangetsu comes the next time, try not to distract him—no, I'm sorry I said that, I was thinking of Meitei. If Meitei caught you with Kangetsu, he'd ruin the whole affair."

While I was listening to Suzuki talk against Meitei—opinions really meant for my master—Meitei himself came in from the back door, riding on the spring breeze, true to the old saying "Speak of the devil and he will appear."

"Oh, you already have a guest—someone I haven't seen for a long time. Don't pay any attention to me. A good friend of Kushami like me needs no formality . . . You know, it's nice to call on him at least once every ten years. Well, these refreshments are better than the ones he usually serves," boomed Meitei, stuffing a piece of sweet bean-paste cake into his mouth. Suzuki looked uneasy but my master was smiling slyly. Meitei was busy tackling the cake inside his mouth. As seen from the veranda, the spectacle inside could have been a play in pantomime. If a speechless question-and-answer act performed at a Zen temple was dramatic, this speechless play could also be called high drama. Though extremely short of duration it was good theater.

"I thought you had become a nomad, Suzuki, but I see you've come back. The longer I live, the more surprised I am at the people I meet," went on Meitei. In speaking to Suzuki, Meitei was not at all reserved. It was as if he were speaking to my master. Even if they had lived together as students, there should have been a certain amount of reserve after ten years. But not so with Meitei; that he did not stand on ceremony only meant that he was either great or a fool—you couldn't tell which.

"Isn't it a fact! It doesn't generally make much difference to me, though," retorted Suzuki. This reply was inoffensive, but somehow he did not seem to be at ease. He kept fingering his chain nervously.

"Have you ever ridden an electric streetcar?" my master suddenly asked Suzuki.

"You must be joking. It looks as though I've come to be made fun of. I might look rustic, but I have sixty shares of the Tokyo Streetcar Company."

"You can't brag about sixty shares," answered Meitei. I once had 888-1/2 stocks of the same company but most of them were eaten by worms. Now I have only about half a share. If you had come to Tokyo a little earlier—before the worms got to them—I could have given you ten shares."

"I see you still have a nasty tongue. That must be a joke but if you possess such stocks you are sure of making a profit. Year after year they go higher."

"That's right. Even half a share will, after one thousand years, enable you to build three warehouses. In regard to such things, you and I are clever but when it comes to Kushami here, it's a pity. If you talked to him about stock, he'd think you meant cattle." So saying, Meitei flung another piece of the beanpaste cake into his mouth and looked at my master. Meitei's eating habits seemed to be contagious because my master stretched out his hand and took one of the cakes, too. Among humans, everything done aggressively has the right to be copied.

"I don't care anything about shares but I really wanted to see Sorosaki ride a streetcar," said my master, disheartenedly looking at the teeth marks in his bean paste cake.

"Sorosaki would have gone as far as the Shinagawa terminal every time. I still think it would be safer simply for him to be carved on the stone weight in the name of Tennen-koji, the 'Man of Nature'."

"Speaking of Sorosaki, he died, didn't he? What a pity! He was very clever, too—it's a shame," said Suzuki. Meitei followed this by remarking, "He had a clear head but he was a terrible cook. When it was his turn to prepare the meals I always went out to eat *soba** noodles."

"That's true. The rice Sorosaki cooked was always burnt and it was too hard. Moreover, he'd always serve uncooked bean curd. You couldn't eat it because it was so cold," mumbled Suzuki, remembering his complaint of ten years before.

"Kushami was Sorosaki's best friend. They went out every evening to eat bean soup. And now, because of that, Kushami is cursed with a weak stomach. Actually, Kushami ate more of the soup than Sorosaki so he ought to have been the first one to die."

"That's not very logical. But enough about me and my bean soup. Remember the time, you used to go out with a bamboo sword to the graveyard to fence with the tombstones? The priest was furious when he saw you." My master seemed to enjoy talking about Meitei's past wrongs.

"Ha, ha, ha! That's right. The priest said that striking the head of a Buddha would prevent everyone from getting a restful sleep, and he made me stop. I used a bamboo sword but General

* *Soba*, buckwheat noodles.

Suzuki here was much more violent. He used to wrestle with tombstones and he overturned three of them, large and small, once. Remember?"

"And wasn't the priest mad! He told me to put them back the way they had been but I insisted that I needed help. I asked him to wait until I could hire a laborer. But he said that laborers were no good and that I had to replace them myself in order to show repentance, otherwise it would be a grave offence to Buddha."

"And how you looked, tugging at the gravestones! You were wearing only a shirt and a loincloth. It had just rained and you were covered with mud."

"And you tried to sketch me while I was working. I don't get mad often but that was one time I thought you were insulting. I still remember what you said when you were sketching me. Do you remember?"

"Who remembers what was said ten years before? But I do remember the inscription on one tombstone: 'Kisen-inden Kwo-kaku Daikoji, January in the Year of the Dragon, the fifth year of An-ei'. The tombstone was old and refined. It was so elegant that I wanted to steal it and keep it always. It was really beautiful. A stone carved in Gothic taste at that!" sighed Meitei, as usual saying something vague about aesthetics.

"Never mind about that. What you said was this: 'As I am going to major in aesthetics, I should sketch everything of interest between the heaven and earth for future reference. I am so dutiful in my studies that I must not allow my sentiments to sway me or to take pity.' That's what you said. I got so angry that I grabbed your sketch book and tore it to pieces."

"My great talent for drawing was obliterated because of that. You took all hope from me. I'm still peeved."

"Don't be a fool. I'm the one that should be peeved, not you."

"Meitei loved to boast even then," reminisced my master who had now finished eating his bean-paste cake. "He never kept a promise nor would he apologize. He would only say this, that or the other and talk himself out of all responsibility. Once when the crepe myrtle was in bloom in the compounds of the temple, he said that he'd finish writing a thesis about aesthetics by the time those blossoms died. Well, I told him he couldn't. To this, Meitei replied, ' I'm a man of great will power though I may not look it. If you're in any doubt about my completing the thesis, we ought to make a bet.' I'm pretty sure we decided that the loser would treat the winner to a Western-styled dinner at a restaurant in Kanda. I felt quite sure that I would win but way down inside, I was a little worried because I didn't have any money at the time. But Meitei didn't do any writing. Seven days passed and then twenty days, but he didn't finish even one page. Finally all the blossoms were gone and I was looking forward to the Western-styled dinner. When I demanded that he make good the wager, he did not even consider the case."

" Well, did he do any explaining? " asked Suzuki.

" Of course, but how illogical! He said that even though he had nothing to show, his will power was still as strong as mine."

"After not writing even one page? " Meitei himself asked this.

" You said that as far as will power is concerned, you had nothing to be ashamed of. You blamed it all on your poor memory. You argued that although you had enough will power to write your paper on aesthetics, you had forgotten all about it the following day. The reason for not writing your thesis, then, was not due to your lack of will power but due to your forgetfulness. You insisted that as it was not because of your will power, so you refused to treat me to the Western-styled dinner."

" Is that so? Well, that's interesting. Meitei making his own rules! " interrupted Suzuki. I don't know why he was so interested but his mode of conversation differed greatly from that of before Meitei's arrival. This change might be characteristic of a clever man.

" What's so interesting? " grumbled my master, still angry at not being able to collect his bet.

" But don't you remember that I tried to make up for it? We went around trying to find peacock tongues. You don't have to stay angry. By the way, I've come here with wonderful news."

" With your kind of wonderful news we can't be too careful."

" But today's news is wonderful, really wonderful! Do you

know that Kangetsu has begun to write his thesis? I hadn't believed Kangetsu was that interested in a degree, but love does great wonders. Suzuki, you'd better tell the ' Nose ' about this. Most probably Kangetsu's dreaming of becoming a doctor of acorns now."

Suzuki, on hearing Kangetsu mentioned, made signs with his eyes to my master, trying to tell him not to talk any more about Kangetsu. But my master did not understand. When my master had first talked with Suzuki, he began to sympathize with Kaneda's daughter. Now, however, hearing Meitei mention Hanako and Hanako over and over again, he began thinking once more about the dispute he had had with her a few days before. But the fact that Kangetsu had begun to write his thesis was better than any gift. It was, just as Meitei had stated, the best news of recent times. It was not only wonderful, it was truly exciting. It didn't make any difference any more if Kangetsu was going to marry Kaneda's daughter or not. The most important was that Kangetsu was going to try for his degree. My master himself was like an imperfect wooden statue standing in one corner of the sculptor's studio. But he wanted another statue, a successful work of art to be covered with gold leaf as quickly as possible.

" Has he really commenced writing? " asked my master earnestly, taking no heed of Suzuki's frantic signals.

" You never seem to believe me. Actually I don't know if his thesis is on the dynamics of hanging or on the stability of an acorn, but in any case it will be enough to oblige the ' Nose '."

Every time Meitei repeated ' Nose ', Suzuki showed signs of anxiety. But Meitei did not notice this, so he continued referring to Mrs. Kaneda as such.

" The other day, I had an opportunity to study more about the nose and I found several passages concerning its function in *Tristram Shandy*. If Mrs. Kaneda's nose could have been shown to Stern, it would have helped him greatly in his work. A pity! Since Mrs. Kaneda's nose has sufficient qualifications to name even its owner, it's a shame to let it go to waste. The next time she comes here, I'll make a sketch of it as reference for aesthetics," rattled away Meitei.

" It seems as though the girl really likes Kangetsu," interjected my master, repeating what he had just heard from Suzuki. Suzuki, on the other hand, made more faces and signs with his eyes to tell my master that this was embarrassing. But my master seemed insulated against this kind of electricity.

"A lucky boy, eh? That the daughter of such a rich person should fall in love with him! It can't be much of a love, though. Most probably ' nose love '."

" Even if it is only ' nose love ', it is all right as long as Kangetsu wants to marry her, isn't it? "

"As long as they get married? Why, you were against it the other day. You've softened quite a bit, haven't you? "

" It's not a question of softening. I never soften, but— "

" But what? Listen, Suzuki," said Meitei facing the third person, " you now consider yourself a businessman although of not much status. I'd like to tell you this, just for reference. It's about that person Kaneda—Kaneda and his daughter. If Kaneda's girl became the wife of talented Kangetsu, it would be like hanging a lantern next to a bell, so different would the combination be. We, as friends of Kangetsu, cannot allow this to happen without saying anything. A businessman like you probably has nothing to say against this, or have you? "

"As usual, you're full of interest about other people's affairs. You haven't changed in all these years," murmured Suzuki, trying to evade the question.

" If you think I'm interested in everybody, I might as well show you something more of my extensive learning. In days of old, the Greeks admired physical training to a great extent. They awarded precious prizes at all games and devised many means to encourage sports. But a funny thing is that there is no record that they ever gave prizes to learned men."

" That's interesting, isn't it? " replied Suzuki, as always in tune with the speaker.

" Only a few days ago, however, while I was experimenting on aesthetics, I happened to find a reason for this. It instantly cleared up the doubts I had all these years. This bit of enlightment drew me away from worldly desires; I was in the realm of heavenly and earthly happiness."

Meitei's enthusiasm was so exaggerated that Suzuki, who was also good at talking, adopted an expression to show that he was not Meitei's equal. My master only looked down at the cake plate, drumming on it with his ivory chopsticks, as if to imply that Meitei had now begun another of his roles. Meitei, with much pride, was the only one doing the talking.

" When trying to understand this contradicting phenomenon, who do you think saved me from the dark doubts I had had for so many years? It was Aristotle, the father of the peripatetic school, who was the most learned of all learned men in the history of education. According to his theory—oh, stop tapping the plate, will you, and listen carefully—, the prizes the Greeks won at games were to be of equal value to the skill they had performed. In that way, they were given encouragement. But how about knowledge? If something were to be awarded for learning, that prize would also have to be of equal value to the knowledge displayed. But is there anything as valuable as knowledge? Naturally the answer is negative. If something of less value were given, it would only debase knowledge. They once piled boxes of gold as high as Mount Olympus and relieved Croesus of his wealth in order to reward knowledge. Finally they realized, however, that they could not meet the demand so they decided against giving anything at all. By this, you should understand that gold, silver, and copper coins are not the equal of knowledge. Having understood this principle, let us now consider Kaneda's daughter and Kangetsu.

" What's Kaneda? He's a hundred-yen note, with the eyes and nose of a man attached to it. In using a more original and figurative expression, you could say that he's only a walking currency. And if he's a walking currency, his daughter must be a walking cheque.

" On the other hand, what can we say about Kangetsu? Not to be put to shame, he graduated from one of the best schools in Japan at the head of his class, and with no signs of weariness or fatigue. Now, wearing a string on his *haori* coat that dates back to the time of the Choshu invasion, he still continues to study—day and night—the stability of the acorn. Not finding enough satisfaction even in this, he is now going to publish a great thesis, one that would outdo even Lord Kelvin.

"It is true that once when he was crossing the Azuma-bashi Bridge, he threw himself over the side in a suicide attempt. But such ideas attack many zealous young men. Such rashness does not detract from the vast knowledge he possesses. If I, Meitei, were allowed to personify Kangetsu in my own simile, I would say that he is a walking library. He is like a projectile made of knowledge and molded to fit a .28 caliber gun. And should this projectile, finding the time ripe, burst into the intellectual circles —just imagine how that projectile would burst! Most probably it would be—"

By the time Meitei had reached this part of his eulogy, he found himself at a loss for the right adjective to carry on. This adjective must have been used secretly because he didn't bother to finish the sentence. The speech soared like a rocket but got stuck in midflight. But he continued, "The millions of walking cheques will eventually become nothing more than powdered dust. That's why I say that the daughter of Kaneda is not the girl for Kangetsu. I do not consent. It would be like marrying an elephant, the wisest of all animals, to a pig, the most greedy. What do you think, Kushami?" Meitei had terminated his long discourse.

My master remained silent but commenced tapping the cake plate with his chopsticks again. Suzuki looked somewhat exhausted.

Suzuki only mumbled, at a loss for another answer, "I don't think so." He had been speaking against Meitei just a short while before so if much more were said on the subject, there was no telling how my master would take it, unpredictable as he is. The cleverest way to handle Meitei's speech would be as lightly as possible, merely to get it over with. Suzuki was a wise man. He meant to avert as much resistance as possible. He believed that all unnecessary dispute was a thing of the feudalistic past.

The object of life was, in his opinion, not in talking but in practical action. Suzuki felt that to advance one's thoughts only in the practical field would be sufficient to attain success; and if this could be done without any trouble, anxiety or dispute, it would be best accomplished. Suzuki himself had succeeded in this way. He was now in the possession of a gold watch, and he found himself in the favor of the Kanedas. By this same principle Suzuki had met with Kushami and had, he felt sure, succeeded in making him understand the situation. Now, however, he found himself interrupted by Meitei, a vagabond who could not be judged by ordinary standards. Meitei possessed a psychology altogether different and Suzuki felt confused by all that had happened in so short a time. Those who created the principle of practical action were the gentlemen of the Meiji era, but the one who most sincerely put it to use was Tojuro Suzuki. It should be pointed out, though, that the one who was most confused by this principle was also none other than this same Tojuro Suzuki. It was Meitei who again broke the silence.

" You just sit there serenely saying ' I don't think so.' That's because you don't realize the importance of what I'm trying to explain. You say little and this is usually not the case at all. If you had seen the ' Nose ' when she came here the other day, even you, my good friend—and a friend of businessmen—would have been disgusted. Isn't that right, Kushami?

" But it seems that my reputation is better than yours as far as the Kanedas are concerned," retorted my master.

" Ha, ha, ha! What self-confidence! Of course you have to be that way, otherwise you couldn't attend school with all the pupils and teachers making fun of you, nicknaming you ' Savage Tea.' My will power is not in the least inferior to others, but, by God, I'm not as audacious as you. I have to bow my head humbly to you in that respect."

" What's there to be afraid of? I don't care if the pupils and other teachers complain. Sainte-Beuve was a great critic but when he was lecturing at the Academy of Paris, he was extremely unpopular. In order to defend himself against the students, he'd always carry a dagger up his sleeve when he went out. Besides, when Brunetiere attacked Zola's novel at the university in Paris— "

" Now, wait a minute," interrupted Meitei. " You're not a university professor, so you don't have anything to worry about. You're only a teacher of the English reader. If you keep on talking so much about such learned people, your students will only laugh at you all the more. It's like a minnow talking like a whale."

"That's only your opinion. I feel that I'm equal to Sainte-Beuve as far as learning is concerned."

"A great opinion! But you don't carry a dagger because you're too timid. If a university professor can use a dagger, it might suit a teacher of the reader to carry a penknife. On second thought, anything with a blade would be dangerous, so it might be better to go to the stalls along Nakamise in Asakusa and buy a toy popgun. You could sling it over your shoulder. You'd look cute. Don't you think so, Suzuki?"

Suzuki, relieved that the conversation had switched from the Kaneda case, replied, "As always, your talk is harmless and enjoyable. Meeting you both after ten long years, I feel as if I had suddenly come to a large field after walking through a narrow alley. With the people I usually go around with, I have to be very careful about what I say. It's wonderful to be with old school friends because I don't have to be reserved. I enjoyed today very much —having seen you again, too, Meitei—but I'll have to be running along now as I have other things to attend to."

As Suzuki was about to rise, Meitei said, "I'll go with you. I have to go to a meeting at Nihon-bashi anyway, so I'll tag along."

"That's nice. Let's leave together then."

And so the two of them departed from the house of my master.

V

IF I WROTE DOWN everything that happened during a twenty-four hour period in full detail, it would take at least another twenty-four hours to read it. The new style of writing, originated by Shiki Masaoka, which describes minute observations in prose form, is a feat which a cat can by no means perform. Though my master may spend twelve active hours each day I do not possess the ability or the perseverance to introduce all of his eccentricities to others. Though regrettable, it cannot be helped. Rest, even for a cat, is necessary.

After Suzuki and Meitei had left, it became as quiet as a night when the wind suddenly stops blowing and the snow begins to fall. My master, as was his habit, forted himself in his study; the children, with their pillows lined up in a row, slept in the six-mat room. In the south room, divided from the children's by a paper sliding door, the Mrs. lay nursing Menko her three-year-old daughter.

The sun seemed in a hurry to sink into the hazy horizon, and the sound of wooden sandals could be heard from the street. Strains of a Chinese flute came floating through the windows from a boarding house nearby to dull the sleepy ears. Having emptied my abalone shell of soup, I also felt tired.

I've heard much about cats who are unable to sleep. According to my understanding, we often go out at night, especially in the spring, in search of romance. As for myself, however, I do not seem to be much affected by the changing of seasons. Love is a universal motivation. All creatures, from Jupiter in Heaven to the lowly earthworm and cricket, indulge in it. It is therefore reasonable to believe that we cats often enjoy the pursuit of love. I myself used to think about Mikeko a great deal. It was rumored that even Tomiko had fallen in love with Kangetsu.

I have no intention of scorning those cats who go mad because of this torment in the spring, a season worth a thousand gold pieces; but try as I might, I myself just cannot get into the mood. At the moment, my only desire was for rest. I was so sleepy that I couldn't even think about love, so I stretched myself out at the foot of the children's bedding and slept to my heart's content.

After a while, I happened to open my eyes and found that my master had come out from his study and had crawled into the bed spread next to the Mrs. As was his habit, he had brought a book in English with him. He seldom read the book. He would usually leave the book near his pillow without touching it. Since he doesn't read even a line from the book, it would be more logical not to bring it at all, but that is how my master is. Even though the Mrs. laughs at him, he comes to bed with a book every night. At times, avariciously, he brings several books. The other evening, he brought one of those enormous *Webster's* dictionaries.

This was my master's trick to induce sleep, much like the extravagants who claim that they cannot sleep unless they can hear the singing of an iron kettle. My master cannot go to sleep unless he has a book by his pillow. In other words, the book is a sleeping pill in print.

On that evening, I sensed something would happen so I took a peep around. My master was in bed holding a thin red book just in front of his moustache. From the fact that he had the thumb of his left hand between two pages, it meant that he had actually read a few lines. As usual, his nickel pocket watch was by the bed. Its dull, cold reflection seemed a contradiction to the warm spring night.

The Mrs. was asleep, her suckling child a few inches from her. The Mrs.'s mouth was open and she was snoring. Her head had slipped off the pillow. Of all the unsightly humans, I think a person sleeping with his mouth open is the most ugly. Cats never suffer such shame. The mouth serves to make noise and the nose to inhale and exhale air. However in the north of Japan, the people are indolent and, to be thrifty, they try to save themselves the trouble of speaking with their mouths so they use their noses for speaking. This sounds awkward, but when it comes to closing the nose and opening the mouth for breathing, it is worse than awkward—it's unsightly. Besides, if the droppings of a mouse came falling down from the ceiling, it would be dangerous.

Looking toward the children, I saw they were not to be outdone by their parents. Tonko, the eldest, had stretched out her right arm and held it over the ear of her sister, as if to show that as the eldest child she was free to do whatever she liked. But Sunko, the other little girl, stuck one of her legs over her elder sister in revenge. Both of them had circled the bed by about ninety degrees since they had first fallen asleep. They were in a deep slumber, however, in spite of maintaining such unnatural positions.

Though this scene was not very elegant, there was something wonderful about this spring night—something inspiring. I looked around the room, wondering what time it was, but everything was quiet except for the ticking of the clock, the snoring of the Mrs., and the gritting of the maid's teeth which could be heard from the distance. The maid refuses to believe that she grits her teeth when asleep. Osan is stubborn. She will never promise to try and break herself of the habit nor will she apologize about the noise. She just stresses the point that she has never in her life gritted her teeth. I suppose it's only natural that a person knows nothing about what he does in his sleep but though he might not know it himself, the fact remains. There are many people who do wrong but claim they are right. They convince themselves that they are innocent. But however amiable they may otherwise be, habits that cause a nuisance to others should be broken. The night was far gone while I was considering this point.

Suddenly there was a thump, thump. I heard it twice on the outer sliding door. Somebody had bumped against it. No one would be calling at this time of the night. I thought that most probably it was a rat. By the way, as far as rats are concerned, I had resolved not to try and catch them, so they were free to roam and ramble about the place at will. But again, there was the thump, thump. It didn't sound like a rat at all. If it *was* a rat, it was being more cautious than usual. The rats in my master's house, like the pupils at his school, believe in being outrageous. They seem to think that it is their privilege to disturb, with sudden surprise, my troubled master. They are not usually as hesitant as this one. I was pretty sure that it was not a rat.

The other night a rat came into the bedroom of my master and left victoriously after taking a nibble at my master's already short nose. This one sounded cowardly. No, it wasn't a rat at all.

The next sound was a creak. The outer sliding door was being lifted from its groove and, at the same time, I heard another partition being quietly slid open. This was certainly not a rat. It had to be a human being!

Coming in the middle of the night without being asked and removing sliding doors was something that could be expected from neither Meitei nor Suzuki. I decided it was one of those honorable thieves that I had heard so much about. I wanted to take a look at his face as soon as possible.

The thief had placed his large muddy feet on the kitchen floor. His third step must have been placed on one of the removable floor boards because there was a sharp crack that broke the silence of the night. I felt as if a shoe brush had been pushed the wrong way along my back. There was only silence for a while after this. The Mrs. still had her mouth open and was furiously inhaling and exhaling. My master only looked as if he were dreaming about the book he had been reading. Presently I heard a match being struck in the kitchen. It seems that the honorable thief cannot see as well in the dark as I can. As the kitchen was always cluttered, it must have been extremely inconvenient for him to proceed.

I brought myself to a crouching position, but then began to wonder whether the thief would enter the tearoom from the kitchen, or go left to the study after passing through the entrance hall. A sliding door of shoji paper was opened and then footsteps were heard making their way toward the veranda. The thief had entered the study. After that there was again only silence.

I found myself wishing that my master and the Mrs. would wake up and I wondered how I might rouse them from their sleep. Thoughts which got me nowhere were twirling in my mind. Ideas spun as furiously as a well-greased waterwheel, but they didn't result in any plan. I tried grabbing the corner of the quilt with my teeth; I shook it a couple of times, but with no effect. I then tried rubbing my cold nose against my master's cheek but he merely stretched out his arm in his sleep and soundly hit the tip of my nose. It hurt like anything! The nose of a cat is its Achilles' heel and the pain was terrible. Afterwards I tried meowing. I don't know why, but something seemed to be stuck in my throat and I couldn't meow as I wanted to. Finally, I was able to emit a harsh low meow, but the sound frightened me so much I couldn't continue. There was no indication that my master would wake up. And suddenly I heard the footsteps again.

They were coming closer, slowly but surely, crunching along the veranda. "It's finally come," I thought. I was in a hopeless situation, so I went around behind a clothes trunk and hid myself.

The footsteps came along the veranda but suddenly stopped when they reached the *shoji* paper door leading to the bedroom. I killed my breath and waited for the thief's next move. If I could stay this quiet more often, I'd have no trouble catching rats. I felt as if my soul were about to spring out from my eyes. I was glad I was able to attain such immobility. It was really the only time in my life.

Presently, the third square of *shoji* paper on the door became discolored, as if a raindrop had fallen on it. Something pinkish was soon seen on the other side and then the paper parted to reveal a red tongue. The tongue then disappeared into the darkness beyond. In its place, I saw a terrible gleam on the other side of the hole. Without doubt, this was an eye of the thief. It seems strange now but the eye did not appear to look around the room but gave the impression that it was centering only on me as I hid behind the clothes trunk. It might have been only a fleeting moment but when stared at like that, it shortens one's life. I felt I couldn't endure it any longer, but just as I had made up my mind to jump out from behind the trunk and run away, the door slid open and the thief stood before me.

But now permit me to introduce the thief who had made this sudden intrusion. Even before that, however, I would like to explain something else. It is usually believed that God is omniscient and omnipotent. The God of the Christians, until the twentieth century, seemed especially omniscient and omnipotent. But He possessed an omniscience and omnipotence which the ordinary person generally interpretes as dullness and ignorance. This is clearly a paradox. That I am the one to refute this pradox for the first time gives me a feeling of vanity and also of not being a cat at all. Therefore I would like to warn haughty men that cats do not like to be made fun of.

God made all creation so man must also be a creation of God. This, it seems, is stated in a book they call the Bible. Now, in regard to human beings, they pride themselves in knowing what has happened during the past several thousand years. Though they hold God in deep wonder, it is a fact that they also seem to possess the tendency of recognizing Him as Omniscient and Omnipotent. This is not beside the question because in this crowded world, there is not one person who has exactly the same face as another. It's true that the faces of most humans are composed of the same ingredients and the size of each part is almost the same. In other words, it may be stated that the makings of the face are all the same but that the effect is never identical. It's amazing that so many different faces can be made with such simple materials. You cannot but wonder at the Creator's great technique. So many different faces could never be made unless a large creative imagination were responsible. A painter, during his lifetime, could complete only about twelve or thirteen different masterpieces. When we consider this, the skill of the Creator, who alone undertook the task of making human beings, is a greater wonder than words can express. Such inventiveness cannot be seen in human society so it must be considered omnipotential.

Perhaps for this reason, man seems to fear God. And when considered from man's point of view, it is naturally something to be feared. But when considered from a cat's point of view, this same variety might possibly be interpreted as proof of God's incompetence. Though you might not dismiss Him as completely incompetent, it can be concluded, I'm pretty sure, that He is really not much better qualified than man.

God, as we have seen, made all people with different faces. But did he, in the first place, have this planned? How can we be sure He had not tried to make all faces the same? If so, he failed miserably and therefore brought about the present confusion. You might still argue that the creation of so many different faces is proof of God's great success, but it could also stand as proof of his failure. You may call God omnipotent if you wish but that is hardly a reason for me to consider Him as anything but incompetent.

Man's eyes are placed side by side on the front of his face so, unfortunately, he cannot look both to the left and the right at the same time. Only half an object comes into view. Much is occurring around him day and night that he remains unaware of. By not being favored by God, humans have no way of finding out much that goes on even in their own community.

If variation is difficult, it is also difficult to produce identical copies. Asking Raphael to draw two identical pictures of the Virgin Mary would be like asking him to paint two pictures of the Madonna showing opposites in character. Besides, this would be embarrassing to Raphael. No, it might be even more difficult to draw two identical pictures. It would be much easier for Kobodaishi, one of the three most excellent penmen in Japan, to write in two different hands than to have him find two identical meanings to the same written character.

The language that man uses is based principally on practice. Man has language handed down to him by his mother, his nurse, and by others; he has no thought of learning it except through repetition. Humans try hard to imitate others but the language, established through imitation, naturally changes after every ten or twenty years. This proves that man does not even have the ability to imitate correctly. A simpler explanation would be difficult to find.

Therefore if God could have made each human face so much alike that it would be impossible to tell them apart—faces as identical as mass-produced masks—it would prove his omnipotence much better. His making each face so differently is merely instrumental, therefore, to prove his incompetence.

Now I forgot why I entered into such a discourse. You'll have to forgive me but, as you know, humans also forget so this happening to a cat is understandable. In any case, when I saw the thief standing at the threshhold of the bedroom, the thought of God's omnipotence just naturally entered my mind. And why did ideas concerning human faces come to my mind? I must do a little more thinking to reply but the reason is this:

When I saw the thief calmly standing in front of me, I noticed that his face was so familiar that it was enough to contradict the doubts I previously mentioned concerning God's incompetence. The eyes and the eyebrows of this man were identical to those of my dear friend Kangetsu Mizushima! Of course I don't have many acquaintances among thieves, but yet I had secretly imagined what they would look like. I was sure that they would have eyes as big and as round as one-sen coins on either side of their nose, and, without a doubt, they would have their hair cropped short. But there's as much difference between heaven and earth as between imagining and actually seeing. One should never give too much importance to imagination.

This thief was a slender, dark-complexioned man with straight even eyebrows. He seemed high spirited and an expert at his profession. He must have been around twenty-six or -seven. That description would also be close to that of Kangetsu. If God has the knack of creating such identical faces, perhaps it is wrong to consider him completely incompetent.

The man looked so much like Kangetsu that I stood aghast, wondering what had happened to Kangetsu to make him visit us in the middle of the night. It was not until I noticed he was not wearing a moustache that I realized the intruder was not Kangetsu.

Kangetsu is awe-inspiring as far as his good-looking features are concerned. That he is an excellent product can be seen by the fact that Tomiko Kaneda, called by Meitei a " moving cheque ", had become interested in him. This thief probably had the power to fascinate women, too. Because of his eyes and the shape of his mouth, Kaneda's daughter might have fallen for this thief as she had fallen for Kangetsu. If this thief were to be taken to Kaneda's daughter, she would probably give him both her body and soul happily. If Kangetsu were to be moved by Meitei's sermon and the match were ruptured, it would make no difference to the girl as long as this thief were available.

I had worried about the future developments in this case, but now I felt assured concerning Tomiko's happiness.

The thief was holding something under his arm. Taking a good look, I found that he had the old blanket my master had flung into his study a little while before. The thief wore a short taffeta coat tied with a grayish-blue *obi*. His white legs were bare from the knee down. He placed one of his feet on a mat in the bedroom. My master, still dreaming with his thumb between the pages of his red book, turned heavily and said in a loud voice, " It's Kangetsu !"

The thief dropped the blanket and quickly withdrew his foot. I could see the shadows of his two legs silhouetted on the paper door and they were trembling a little. My master let out another groan, grumbled in his sleep awhile, and then flung the red book aside. Afterwards, he began to scratch his dark arm, as if he were suffering from a skin disease. After this, all was quiet and my master again fell into deep slumber. His head slipped off the pillow. He had called Kangetsu's name in his sleep but he didn't know he had spoken.

The thief stood on the veranda listening. Finding the couple had gone to sleep again, he once more placed a foot inside the room. This time there was no calling out so he placed his other foot inside. The flickering night lamp in the six-mat bedroom glowed on the body of the thief and cast his shadow on the clothes trunk and on part of the wall. The shadow of the thief's face moved about two thirds of the wall. The good-looking man's silhouette looked awkward—like the ghost of a taro. For a while, the thief stared at the Mrs. from above and smirked. For what reason, I am at a loss to know. I was surprised that even his smile was exactly like Kangetsu's.

There was a wooden box about four inches high and one-and-a half feet long by the pillow of the Mrs. Its lid was closed tight and looked as if something precious might be inside.   Actually the box only contained some yams, a present from Sampei Tatara whose home town was Karatsu in the Province of Hizen.   He had brought it as a gift after a recent visit.   It is very seldom that a person places yams by the pillow, but then the Mrs. has a poor conception about storing articles.   She even put sugar in her wardrobe. - The Mrs. would not have objected to having pickled radishes in her bedroom, I am sure, much less a box of yams.

But the thief was no God so he had no way of knowing that the Mrs. was this kind of woman.   That he had supposed the box full of jewels was not without reason.   He lifted the box and felt its weight.   He seemed extremely satisfied.   I knew he was going to take it but when I thought of this good-looking man stealing a box of yams, it made me want to laugh.   But as it would have been dangerous, I suppressed the urge.

The thief commenced to wrap the box of yams in the old blanket very respectfully.   Then he looked around the room to see if he could find something to tie the bundle up with.   His eyes fell on the silk crepe *obi* my master had taken off before he went to bed. With this and the blanket, the thief formed a sack and lightly flung it over his shoulder.   Women would have been less attracted to him if they had seen him like this.

He then took the children's coats and shoved them into my master's knitted underwear.   The drawers bulged as much as a cobra after swallowing a pig.   No—a better expression might be to compare the underwear with a pregnant snake.   In any case, it looked terribly awkward.   If you think I'm joking, just push a couple of coats into your own winter underpants and see.

After the thief had tied this around his neck, I watched him proceed.   He spread open the pongee coat of my master and put inside the Mrs.'s *obi*, my master's *haori* coat, the underwear, and other loose garments lying around.   He then folded the pack up neatly.   I was amazed at his skill.

He tied this bundle with a kimono string of the Mrs., and then picked it up in his left hand.   He looked around once more, hoping to find something more to take, and noticed a packet of Asahi cigarettes by my master's pillow.   He picked up the pack and threw it into his sleeve pocket. As if on second thought he took one out and lit it by the flame of the night lamp. He inhaled deeply, enjoying it, and blew the smoke out. The smoke hesitated for a moment around the milky glass chimney of the lamp, but before it had disappeared, the footsteps of the thief along the veranda could be heard no more. My master and the Mrs. had slept through it all. Humans are, contrary to many people's opinion, rather stupid.

As for myself, I felt exhausted. If the thief had stayed much longer, I wouldn't have been able to stand it. So after a deep sleep, I awoke to find my master and the Mrs. talking to a policeman at the rear entrance of their home.

" Then the thief entered from here and went around to the bedroom, but you didn't notice because you were asleep. Is that right? "

" Yes, that's right," answered my master in a somewhat embarrassed tone.

" All right, then. At what time were you robbed?" questioned the policeman. He was asking something impossible to answer. If my master had known the time, he wouldn't have been robbed in the first place. But my master and the Mrs. didn't consider the question from this angle so they commenced consulting each other in order to make some kind of reply.

" Now what time was it? "

" Let me see, now," muttered the Mrs., as if thinking would net the answer. " What time did you go to bed last night? "

" I went to bed after you did."

" Yes, and I went to bed before you did. That's right."

" Then, what time did you get up? "

" Must have been around 7 : 30."

" But at what time could the thief have broken in? "

" I'm sure it must have still been dark."

" I know that it was during the night, but at about what time? "

" We won't be able to say for sure unless you give us a chance to talk it over," replied the Mrs., still sure that thinking about the problem would eventually solve it. The policeman had asked only as a formality—any hour given would have filled the purpose.

He had expected the couple to state a given hour, though it might not have been the exact time of the robbery, but the teacher and his wife were anxious to please. The policeman became somewhat irritated.

"All right then. You don't know at what time the robbery took place, is that it?"

My master answered in his usual way: "Well, I guess so."

The policeman, without laughing, continued, "Then you'll have to submit a report—not a report—an accusation in writing, stating that a thief entered your home after removing the door from such-and-such a place after you had locked your house and had gone to bed on such-and-such a date and that you had been robbed of so many items of the below-listed articles. It's better not to address the report to anyone in particular."

"Do we have to list each individual item?"

"Make it out in list form stating so many *haori* coats were stolen valued at so much, et cetera. No, there's no need for me to go inside the house now. The things have been stolen already, haven't they?" Then the policeman calmly left.

My master got out his brush and inkstone and placed them in the middle of the room. Afterwards he called his wife and grumbled as if he were picking a fight, "I'm going to start writing the accusation now so tell me one by one which articles were stolen. I'm ready so go ahead."

"Why! You don't have to be so belligerent with me. Who'd want to tell you anything when you give orders like that." The Mrs. then sat down squarely in front of him. She had tied her kimono closed with a length of string.

"Look at yourself! You almost look like a prostitute of a post town. Why aren't you wearing an *obi*?"

"If you object so much to how I look why don't you buy me an *obi*? Not even a prostitute of a post town could wear an *obi* if the only one she had were stolen."

"Did the thief take your *obi*? That's terrible! All right, I'll begin with your *obi*. What kind was it?"

"What do you mean, 'What kind'? I only had one. It was a double black *obi* made of satin and silk crepe."

" One double black *obi* of satin and silk crepe. Now, about how much did it cost? "

" About six yen. "

" How is it you had such an expensive *obi*? You'll have to buy a new one but don't pay more than one yen fifty sen. "

" Where do you think you can buy an *obi* at that price? You're awful! You don't care how your wife is dressed—all you can think of is yourself, isn't that so? "

" Forget it. What's next? "

" A woolen *haori* coat. My Aunt Kono gave it to me as a keepsake. It's different from the ones you see nowadays. "

" I don't have to know all that. How much? "

" Fifteen yen. "

" You had a coat worth fifteen yen? "

" Why worry? You didn't buy it. "

" What's next? "

" A pair of black stockings. "

" Yours? "

" No. They were yours. Twenty-seven sen. "

" Next? "

" A box of yams. "

" Did he steal the yams, too? Wonder if he's going to eat them cold or heat them first. "

" I don't know what he's going to do. Why don't you ask him? "

" How much were they? "

" I don't know the price of yams. "

" All right, I'll put them down as twelve yen and fifty sen. "

" Don't be absurd! They couldn't have cost twelve yen fifty sen, even if they *were* from Karatsu. "

" But you said you didn't know how much they were. "

" I don't know. I don't know, but twelve yen fifty sen is absurd. "

" You don't know but yet you say that twelve yen and fifty sen is absured. That doesn't make sense. That's the reason I call you Otanchin Paleologus. "

Perhaps I had better let you readers in on this. " Otanchin " means a stupid person and the word is ordinarily used by adults as an abusive term. My master, however, added the family name of Constantin Paleologus, the last emperor of the Eastern Roman Empire, so the Mrs. would not be able to understand.

" What was that? "

" I said Otanchin Paleologus."

" What do you mean by Otanchin Paleologus? "

" What's next? I haven't heard any of my things mentioned yet."

" Never mind about the list. Tell me what Otanchin Paleologus means."

" There's no meaning to it at all."

" What's wrong in telling me? You're making fun of me again, aren't you? You call me a lot of bad names just because I don't know English."

" Nonsense! Better get on with the list. I'll have to submit the accusation soon or else we won't be able to get our things back."

" We won't see those stolen articles for a long time. Oh, please tell me the meaning of Otanchin Paleologus."

" You're very insistent, aren't you? I tell you, there's no meaning."

" Well, if that's your attitude, there's nothing more for the list."

" Stubborn woman! Then do as you wish. We just won't work on the list any more."

" And I won't tell you what else was stolen. You're the one who should make out the accusation. You already know what was taken from me."

" All right then, I quit." Then my master stood up and entered his study. The Mrs. went into the sewing room and sat in front of her sewing box. Both sat in silence for about ten minutes, staring at the *shoji* paper sliding door separating them.

Suddenly the entrance door opened with a bang, and Sampei Tatara who had given the Kushamis the yams entered. Sampei Tatara had formerly been my master's house boy but he was now working in a mining department of a certain trading company.

Since his graduation from a law college, he had become a budding businessman, much like Tojuro Suzuki. Sampei often came on Sundays to visit my master and sometimes he spent the whole day there. With this family, he felt completely at home.

"Nice day, is it not?" Sampei still spoke with a strong Karatsu accent. He sat on the floor on one leg with the other knee in the air.

"Oh! Is that you, Tatara?"

"Is the teacher here?"

"Yes, he's in his study."

"Ma'am, it's not good for his health to study so hard. Especially on a Sunday."

"You'd better tell the teacher yourself."

"I think I will," agreed Sampei, looking around the room. "Where are the children today?" He had just finished asking this question when Tonko and Sunko came running in from the next room.

"Oh, Tatara, did you bring any rice balls today?" The elder, Tonko, had not forgotten the promise he had made during his previous visit.

Tatara scratched his head and confessed. "You have a good memory, have you not? I have forgotten it today but I'll bring some the next time. It's a promise."

"Oh, I'm disappointed!" said Tonko. Sunko, the younger sister, immediately imitated the older girl and repeated, "Oh, I'm disappointed!" The Mrs. seemed to have returned more to her usual self because she smiled a little.

"I didn't bring any rice balls but I gave you some yams the last time I came. Did you like them?"

"Yams? What's that?" asked Tonko. Sunko again imitated her sister: "What's that?"

"So you haven't eaten them yet? You had better have your mother cook them for you. They are different from the ones you get here in Tokyo and they are delicious," explained Sampei, proud of his home town.

The Mrs. seemed to remember the present and said, "Thank you, Tatara, for bringing so many."

The thief had placed his large muddy feet on
the kitchen floor.

"How were they? I had them packed firmly so they would not bend. They were preserved in their long state, were they not?"

"Unfortunately, the yams you were so kind to bring were stolen last night."

"By a burglar? What a foolish thief! He must like yams a lot!" Sampei seemed amazed.

"Mother, did a thief really come into our house last night?" asked the elder sister.

"Yes," replied the Mrs. lightly.

"There was a thief—a thief! What did he look like?" The younger sister was speaking this time but the Mrs. was puzzled as to how to answer this question.

"He had a terrible face," said the Mrs. looking toward Tatara.

"A terrible face? Do you mean like Tatara's?" asked the elder sister, without hesitation.

"What are you saying? Don't be so rude!"

"Ha, ha, ha! So you think my face is terrible? That's a shame!" chuckled Tatara while scratching a bald spot on his head about one inch in diameter. He had developed a skin infection about a month before and though he had gone to the doctor's, it was slow in getting well. Tonko was the first to notice this spot.

"Look, Tatara's head is shining just like Mother's!" she exclaimed.

"I told you to be quiet!"

"Was the thief's head shiny too, Mother?" This came from the younger girl. The Mrs. and Tatara both burst out laughing. The children were so annoying that the grown-ups could not talk.

"Now, now. Go out to the yard and play. Mother will make you some cookies pretty soon." Then the Mrs. asked Tatara seriously. "What really happened to your head, Tatara?"

"It became infected and it's hard to cure. Do you have a skin infection, too, ma'am?"

"How awful! An infection? No, not I. All women who wear a *marumage* coiffure get a little bald."

"All bald spots are caused by bacteria."

" But mine's not due to any germs."

" Now, ma'am, you're being stubborn."

" I don't care, but it's not bacteria. By the way, how do you say ' bald ' in English?

" ' Bald ' is spelled b-a-l-d—bald."

" That's not it. There must be another name for it—a longer name."

"Ask the teacher. He should know."

" He won't tell me so that's why I'm asking you."

" I only know the word ' bald '."

" The word is Otanchin Paleologus. ' Otanchin ' means bald and ' Paleologus ' means head, isn't that so? "

" That might be so. I'll go into the study later and look it up in *Webster's* dictionary. By the way, the teacher sure is a queer man—staying in the house on such a fine day. Ma'am, you can't expect his stomach to get better if he goes on like this. You had better tell him to take a walk some time. The cherry blossoms at Ueno are beautiful now."

" No, you tell him. He won't listen to anything a woman says."

" Does he still like jam? "

" Yes, as always."

" When I came here the other day, the teacher told me he was annoyed because you keep saying he eats too much jam. He said that there must be some mistake. I pointed out that you and the children might be eating a lot of jam, too."

" Tatara! Why did you say such a thing? "

" But you have a face that looks as if you liked jam."

" How can you tell by a face? "

" I can't exactly, ma'am, but are you telling me that you don't like it at all? "

" Well, I do eat some—just a little. But what's wrong with that? The jam is ours, isn't it? "

" Ha, ha, ha! I thought so. But, by the way, it's a pity, really—I mean about the robbery. Did he take anything besides the yams? "

[167]

" I wouldn't worry if he had taken only that. He stole all of our everyday clothes."

" I suppose you'll have to borrow some money, then. It's a shame this cat here isn't a dog. Ma'am, why don't you keep a dog, a big one. Cats are no good. All they do is to eat. By the way, does this one catch rats?"

" It hasn't caught one yet. It is a terribly lazy cat."

" Why don't you give it to me? I'll take it home and eat it."

" Tatara! Do you eat cats?"

" Sure, I do. They're good."

" You must have a strong stomach."

I have heard that among the lower class of house boys there are some who eat cats—savages!—but I had not imagined, even in my dreams, that Tatara would do such a thing. Besides, he was not a house boy any more. Although he had only graduated recently, he was now a dignified bachelor of law and a member of the Mutsui Trading Company. My surprise was even more great.

There is a proverb that says " When you meet a man, consider him a thief." This was proven correct by the actions of Kangetsu II. Now, because of Tatara, I invented a new proverb: " When you meet a man, consider him a savage."

Living in this world, one gets to know a lot. It's good to have this knowledge, but day by day one learns he has to be more cautious. Becoming crafty and mean, and learning how to defend oneself—all comes from knowing more about life. The hardest part of growing up is realizing the effects of what we have learned. While thinking that I might one day be cooked with onions in a cauldron by Tatara and thus become a spirit, I made myself small in a corner. Soon, however, my master, who had forted himself up in his study after quarreling with the Mrs., came out into the tearoom.

" Sir, I just heard you've been robbed. How foolish!" Tatara exclaimed head on.

" The thief who entered was the fool," replied my master, always esteeming himself to be more clever than others.

" He might be a fool, but it's even more foolish to be robbed."

"A person like you, Tatara, who has nothing to be robbed of, might be the cleverest of all," commented the Mrs., taking sides with her husband.

" But the most foolish is this cat. I wonder what it's thinking about? It doesn't catch any rats and doesn't do anything to prevent a thief from entering the house. Sir, will you give me this cat? It doesn't do any good around here."

" Sure, I can give it to you. But what would you do with it? "

" Cook it and eat it."

When my master heard this, an eerie sound escaped from his weak stomach. But he did not give any answer and as Tatara did not press his desire to eat me, I felt more fortunate than I could have expected.

Eventually my master changed the subject: " Never mind about the cat. All my clothes have been stolen and it's cold." He was full of self-pity—but no wonder! Until yesterday he had worn two cotton-lined kimonos, whereas he was now only wearing a short-sleeved shirt and a single kimono. Moreover, he had been sitting still all morning without taking any exercise. His already thin blood was all being used up by his weak stomach so it didn't have a chance to circulate to the rest of his body.

"Actually, sir, it's miserable to be a teacher. You get robbed so now you're suffering even more. How about changing your mind and becoming a businessman? "

" My husband doesn't like businessmen so it's useless to make such a suggestion," said the Mrs. She would have liked him going into some business, however.

" How many years is it now since you graduated, sir? "

"About nine, I guess," answered the wife, turning to her husband. My master didn't either confirm or deny the figure.

" Just think. Nine years and you still haven't got a raise. Besides, you still aren't recognized—even though you study hard. ' Lonely is my young man, all by himself.' " Tatara was reciting a line from a Chinese poem he had memorized in junior high school. The Mrs., not understanding, didn't answer.

" Of course, I do not like being a teacher but I would hate being a businessman even more." My master himself seemed to have been wondering about his future lately.

" My husband doesn't like anything."

" What he likes best is his wife," giggled Tatara jokingly, something quite unusual.

" I hate being married most." My master's response was simple and direct. The Mrs. looked the other way for a moment, but turning to her husband again she said, " Most probably you hate even to live." She believed she had revenged herself with this statement.

" I don't like it very much," was the husband's carefree answer. He was hard to manage.

" Sir, how about taking a walk for a change. You'll ruin your health staying indoors all the time. Be a businessman. It's simple to make money that way."

" You're not making much yourself."

" Oh, but I've just started. Still, I have saved more than you."

" How much do you have? " asked the Mrs. seriously.

" Fifty yen."

"And how much do you make? " The Mrs. was anxious to know more.

" Thirty yen. But five yen is put aside every month by the company; in case of an emergency, I can use it. Ma'am, why don't you buy some shares of the Sotobori Railway Line with your small change? In three or four months you'll double your investment."

" If we had enough money for investments, we wouldn't worry about being robbed."

" That's why I'm telling you that it's best to become a businessman. Sir, if you had studied law or some practical subject, you could have been working in a company or a bank. By now you would be making three hundred or four hundred yen a month. By the way, do you know a former engineering student by the name of Tojuro Suzuki? "

" Umm? He came here yesterday."

" Is that so? When I met him at a party the other day, I told him about you. He was surprised to find out that I had been your house boy, and he told me that he had lived with you at a temple in Koishikawa when you were cooking your own meals. He asked me to give you his best regards, and also to tell you that he would drop in to see you soon."

" It seems he's been transferred to Tokyo."

" That's right. He had been working at a mine in Kyushu, but was transferred to Tokyo the other day. He's very clever. He speaks to me as if I were an old friend. Sir, do you know how much he makes? Well, he gets two hundred and fifty yen besides two allowances every year—during the *Bon* season* and at the end of the year. He must average about four-hundred or five-hundred yen a month. But you, sir, have only been teaching the reader for the last ten years, wearing the same old suit. It's senseless ! "

" Yes, it's senseless—exactly ! " My master, when it comes to the conception of money, is no different from anyone else. Perhaps he might want money even more than anybody else. Tatara seemed finished with his discourse on the advantages of going into business because he asked the Mrs., " Does a man named Kangetsu Mizushima come here sometime "

" Yes, fairly often."

" What kind of a person is he ? "

" He's well educated."

" Is he good-looking ? "

" Ho, ho, ho ! He looks something like you."

" Is that so ? Like me ? " He repeated this seriously.

" How do you know his name ? " queried my master.

" Someone requested me to ask you about him. Is he worth the trouble ? " Tatara somehow looked even more elegant than Kangetsu when asking.

" He's better educated than you."

" Is that so ? Better educated ? " He didn't laugh, nor was he angry. This was characteristic of Tatara.

" Will he get his doctor's degree soon ? "

" He's writing his thesis now."

---

* The *Bon* Festival: the Buddhist All Souls' Day.

[171]

" Writing a thesis? I thought of him as being more practical and intelligent."

"As usual, you don't have a very high opinion of higher education," laughed the Mrs.

" I've heard that somebody is going to give him his daughter when he gets his doctorate. It seems foolish to become a doctor just because of a girl. Instead of giving the girl to such a fool, I said that it would be better to give me the girl."

" Who did you say this to? "

" To the person who asked me to inquire about Mizushima."

" Could that be Suzuki? "

" No. I'm in no position to talk about such things with him yet. He's one of my bosses, you know."

" You're a strange boy, aren't you, Tatara? You can talk while you're here but you make yourself small in front of Suzuki, isn't that true? "

" Yes. Otherwise I would be without a job."

Suddenly my master said, " Tatara, how about taking a walk? " He was only wearing a thin kimono and, as it was quite cold, the thought of some exercise occurred to him. This was quite extraordinary. Of course Tatara agreed.

" Yes, let's. Is it to Ueno? Let's go to Imozaka and eat some of those famous dumplings. Sir, have you ever tried them? Ma'am, you'll have to go and taste them some time. They're soft, and cheap besides. They serve drinks there, too." As usual Tatara made his explanations unsystematically. In the meantime, my master had put on his hat and stood waiting at the front door.

I myself felt some rest was necessary. There was no need for me to find out what my master and Tatara did at Ueno Park or how many dumplings they would eat at Imozaka. Nor did I have the courage to go with them. All creatures need rest from time to time. We who must live in this world must move around, and we all require rest in order to accomplish that obligation. If God claims that we are born to work, I must insist that we should also be given rest in order to work. Even my master, a hardheaded man, must rest every day besides Sunday. With many regrets, I myself exert both body and soul day and night. Though I am a cat, it goes without saying that I require more rest than my master. Tatara said that I was worthless because I did nothing but sleep. That worried me. Such people are only influenced by outside appearances. They have not learned to use their five senses to advantage because they only judge others from their appearance. They believe that unless you sweat yourself at some task, you aren't working.

It is said that a priest by the name of Dharma sat in religious meditation until his legs rotted. Even if a vine had crept through a crack in the wall and encircled his eyes and mouth, he would not have moved. But he was not asleep, nor was he dead. Within his mind, he was always active; he was thinking about some secret principles of the Zen doctrine, perhaps about why there is no difference between a saint and a mediocrity. There are many followers of Confucius who sit in religious meditation, but that does not mean they shut themselves up in a room and simply practice sitting like cripples. Their minds are working hard even though, from all outside appearances, they seem to personify tranquility and quietness. A common person would probably believe these masters of knowledge were in a state of unconsciousness, or of being half dead; he would abuse them and condemn them as good-for-nothings or idlers. Most people with ordinary eyes are born with abnormal sight in that they see only outside appearances but not the soul. But that Tatara was the worst of all. It would not surprise me if he considered me no more important than a wash pail. What made me most angry was that my master, who reads modern books as well as the classics and who somewhat understands such human errors, agreed with everything the shallow-minded Tatara said. He might even learn to relish a dish of broiled cats himself some day!

But thinking of this problem from another angle, perhaps it is only natural that they despise me. Proverbs say " Loud voices remain in the ear shortest " and " Overly refined music gathers a small audience." It is senseless to ask those who can see only the superficial to understand the brilliancy of one's spirit. It would be like asking a bald-pated priest to fix himself an elaborate hairdo, or to ask a tuna fish to make a speech, or to have an electric train derail itself, or to ask my master to resign his post as a school-teacher, or to ask Sampei not to think about money. It would be a request for the impossible.

But even cats are members of the community and no matter how high we may esteem ourselves, we must learn to adapt ourselves to some extent, to society. It is regrettable, but understandable, that my master, the Mrs., the maid, and Sampei consider me worthless. To be slaughtered due to their ignorance, to have my skin sold to the samisen makers, to have my flesh chopped up and served on Tatara's table would be a terrible end. I am a cat with a mission. I keep active here on earth by using my head, so I consider my existence of great importance. There is a proverb that says " Even a child of wealth should not sit idly ". No one can succeed merely by boasting of his superiority. This would not only be asking for trouble but would also be a crime against society. If a magnificent tiger let itself be captured and taken to a zoo, it might be put next to a smelly pig; or if a stork were caught by a poulterer, it might meet the same fate as a mere chicken— on the chopping board !

I myself am destined to be among only common people. So to be better understood I decided to pretend to be a common cat. And in order to be considered a common cat, I would be expected to catch rats—and this I finally made up my mind to do.

I understand that Japan has been fighting a big war with Russia for some time. As I am a Japanese cat, I am, of course, on the side of Japan. If I could do so, I'd have organized a Mixed Cat Corps to go and scratch some of the Russians. Being in such high spirits and feeling so energetic, I felt I could catch a few rats with ease, even in my sleep. At one time, long ago, a man asked a famous priest of the Zen sect how he could perceive truth. The priest told him to watch a rat as a cat does. By this he meant that cats have no fear of failure. There's another proverb which says " Shrewd be the woman, she often fails to sell her cow ". But yet, I'm pretty sure there's no proverb which says that shrewd be a cat, it often fails to catch a rat ! It is not that I cannot catch rats. There is no doubt that I can. The only reason I had not caught any as yet was that I had just not felt like it.

This spring day came to an end, the same as the day before. A storm of falling cherry blossom, riding an occasional spring gust, would come blowing in through a hole in the paper door. The petals settled on the surface of the water in a barrel in the kitchen and floated there, white under the dim light of the lamp.

Since I had resolved to accomplish a meritorious feat and surprise everybody in the family, I decided to inspect the layout of the battlefield. The battle line was not very large: only the size of a four-mat room. The kitchen has a sink on one side, and the other half was left open for delivery boys from the wine shop and the vegetable store to stand when receiving orders. The stove was splendid, quite out of place in this poor kitchen, and the copper pots were polished and shining brightly. Near the stove was a space about two square feet covered with removable floor boards where my food was placed in an empty abalone shell. There was also a cupboard, six feet long, near the tearoom where trays, wooden bowls, saucers and other small dishes were kept. This big piece of furniture made the small kitchen even smaller. Above was a shelf which stuck out at about the same height as the cupboard. Underneath was an earthenware mortar vessel. Inside was a small pail placed upside down. Beside the hanging radish grater and the pestle for the mortar stood a dejected looking pot for extinguishing live charcoal. Where two blackened rafter beams crossed, hung a basket from a hook and the basket waved gently with the wind. When I first came to this house, I didn't know why the basket was there, but I soon found that food was placed in the high-hanging receptacle so stray cats could not get at it. It was then that I began to understand how ill-natured man is.

As to my strategy, I decided to do battle with the rats at the place or places they would most likely appear. If I just waited in any corner, the quick-moving rats wouldn't give me a chance. So I stood in the middle of the kitchen and took a look around, studying the location of rat holes. I felt somewhat like Admiral Togo!

The maid was at the public bath; the children had gone to bed long ago; my master, who had returned from Ueno Park, was now in his study; and the Mrs.—I wondered where she could be. She was most probably dozing away, dreaming about the stolen yams. Occasionally the stillness would be broken by a rickshaw passing in front of the gate. After each carriage had rolled by, the silence could be felt all the more.

My resolution was firm, my spirits were high, the kitchen was engulfed in the silence of the night—the whole atmosphere was perfect for my mission. I again felt like an Admiral Togo, at least of the cat family.

In every such situation, there is, within all its terribleness, a spark of joy. Everybody must feel the same. But behind this joy, I had one great worry. I wasn't afraid of the rats coming out in great numbers, but what bothered me most was that I didn't know from what direction they would come. After a long detailed search, however, I found three likely routes the rats might take.

Gutter rats would most likely come by way of the earthenware drain pipe under the sink, and then go around to the rear of the stove. In this case, I could hide myself behind the pot for live charcoals and intercept the rat on its return trip. If it made a detour through the drain of the wash basin, it would suddenly pop out into the kitchen from the washroom. Therefore, I stationed myself on top of the rice cooker so I could pounce on my enemy as it passed under my eyes. Upon looking around the room, I also found a half-moon-shaped hole at the lower right corner of the closet door that would be of great convenience to rats. It smelled a little ratty. If a rodent came charging out from there, I'd let it pass by the pillar, which it would probably use as a shield, and then make a pass at it with my claws.

Thinking that they might possibly come by way of the ceiling, I looked up and saw the blackened surface shining brightly in the lamplight. It resembled hell hung upside down. I knew that rats wouldn't come from such a high place so I disregarded this direction altogether. Even at that, there was a liability of being attacked from three different directions. If rats came from two directions only, I felt I could manage them with only one eye open; if they came from three directions, however, even I, who was born with the instinct for catching rats, would have quite a time of it. To ask Kuro, the cat of the rickshawman, to help me would only bring me shame. I didn't know what to do.

Now, when you don't know what to do and cannot think of any good plan to solve a problem, the best thing to do is to pretend that such a problem will not occur. Just forget it. That's the quickest solution of all. For instance, take a look at what happens every day in the world. It would be impossible to say that the bride of today will not die tomorrow. But the bridegroom thinks about nothing except his present happiness—"We will live as long as an olive tree and we will be bound together everlastingly in bliss " —and shows no worry at all. That he does not worry is not because there is nothing to worry about—no! It is only because worrying does not solve the problem.

As for me, I had no way of knowing definitely that the rats would not charge from three directions simultaneously, but to think that this would not happen was extremely convenient and gave me a feeling of security. Security and contentment are necessities for the happiness of all creatures. I, too, needed security and contentment, so I decided that a charge from all three directions would not occur.

Even so, I couldn't help worrying about which would be the best of my three strategic plans. My strategy was ready to meet the charge from the closet, from the washroom and from the sink. But I was greatly at a loss as to which of these plans I should choose. Admiral Togo himself must have also worried about whether the Baltic Fleet woud pass the Strait of Tsushima, the Strait of Tsugaru or the Strait of Soya. I can now easily understand how he must have felt. Not only was I like Admiral Togo, but I felt my anxieties were also the same as his.

While I was feverishly trying to decide which plan I should use, the old and torn paper door suddenly slid open and Osan's face came into view. By saying that the face came into view does not mean that she was without hands or feet, but the rest of her body was obscured by the dark night and only her face came clearly to my vision. Osan, her red cheeks redder than ever, had returned from her bath. She commenced locking up the kitchen earlier than usual, most probably because of what had happened the previous night. From the study came the voice of my master asking that his cane be placed by his pillow. I was at a loss to know as to why my master wanted to decorate the side of his pillow with his cane. He isn't as eccentric as to want to pretend to be a Ching Ho, who, with a sword under his sleeve, crossed the river I in an attempt to assassinate the first emperor of Ch'in. But in any case, beside the pillow the previous evening was a box of yams; that night it was to be a cane. I wondered what it would be the following night.

The evening was still young; there was much waiting to be done before the rats would appear and I required rest before the coming battle.

There was no window in the kitchen of my master's home but there was a transom about one foot in width cut above the door through which the wind blew, summer and winter alike.

I was awakened by the wind which seemed to bring the fragrance of falling cherry blossoms. I opened my eyes to find that the hazy moon had come out. The stove was slanting its shadow onto the removable floor boards. Fearing that I might have overslept, I twitched my ears a couple of times and took a look around. It was deadly quiet and, like during the previous night, the clock could be heard. It was time the rats should make their appearance —but from where?

Sounds came from inside the closet. It seemed as if a rat were holding on to the edge of a saucer and nibbling at what was on it. I was pretty sure a rat would come out from a hole nearby, so I crouched down beside it. Soon the noise on the saucer stopped but then there was a scratching on a bowl or something. At intervals there was a thumping on the closet door. The noise was not more than three inches from the tip of my nose! At times tiny footsteps were heard coming near the hole but no rat showed its face. The enemy was causing great havoc and I could only sit still and wait! Osan should have left this door open a little so I could enter the closet—that stupid woman!

Suddenly, from behind the stove, I heard my abalone shell being rocked. The enemy was coming from that direction, too! I crept very softly toward my shell but I only caught a glimpse of the end of a tail as it slid into the sink.

Then the cup used for gargling clinked against the metal basin. The enemy was behind me now. Just as I turned around, a big rat about five inches long dropped a bag of tooth powder and disappeared under the flooring. I tried to catch it but when I jumped down, it was nowhere to be seen. It was much harder to grab hold of a rat than I had thought. I wondered whether I really had *áprióri* the ability to catch rats.

When I crossed to the bath, the enemy popped out from the closet; and when I was on guard by the closet, another would jump out from the sink. I stationed myself in the middle of the kitchen, but then they all became wildly active every place else. Should I consider them intelligent or cowardly? They did not prove themselves sporting enough, in any case, to be played with by a gentleman. I lunged around the kitchen this way and that, about fifteen times, doing my best to engage them in combat. But alas! I did not succeed in catching even one of them. Though regrettable, in dealing with such small adversaries, even Admiral Togo would have had no method.

At first, I had had courage—a gallant and spirit-stirring feeling —but now I found this game troublesome and foolish. Moreover, I was getting somewhat sleepy. I sat down right in the middle of the kitchen to take a long rest. Though I didn't move, I sat glaring all around me so the enemy, terrified of my great size, could do but little damage. My enemies proved themselves, contrary to my belief, cowards. My dreams of winning honor in battle disappeared and left me only with dislike of the rats. With this feeling of dislike, my enthusiasm disappeared, and I felt exhausted. I became indifferent to the rats and began to slumber. Even among enemies, one must rest.

Through the transom above the door, a handful of cherry petals were again blown in by the strong wind and they swirled around me. Then from a hole in the closet, a rat came charging out. Although I had time to escape the attack, it came toward me at full speed and bit my left ear. Just then another dark shadow came around to the rear and suddenly began to gnaw at my tail. This all happened in a flash. Mechanically, without thinking at all, I leaped up, and with all my strength I tried to shake these monsters off. The rat with his teeth in my ear lost his balance and hung limp across my face. The tip of its tail felt as soft as a rubber tube. Taking a strong hold of this tail, only thinking about ridding myself of these pests, I shook myself to the left and right. The body of my assailant hit an old newspaper that had been pasted on the wall and bounced back on the floor. Its tail was still between my front teeth. Without giving the rat a chance to recover, I pounced on it but it was like a rubber ball. It darted away right in front of my nose and then sat on its haunches on the edge of a shelf. It looked down at me while I could only look up at it from the floor. The shelf must have been about five feet tall. Between us, the moonlight cast its beams along the floor like a white *obi*.

After gathering strength, I jumped high into the air. I was able to grab hold of the shelf with my forepaws but my hind legs could only tread air. Moreover, the rat that had attached itself to my tail wouldn't let go. I was in danger! I tried to get a better grip on the shelf but when I moved my paws, the weight on my tail pulled me down. My claws scratched noisily along the shelf.

Knowing that I couldn't go on like this, I made a swing with my left paw to get a stronger grip but missed the shelf so I was now hanging only by my right paw. My body began to swing back and forth. The monster on the shelf had stayed still until now, watching and waiting the outcome. Suddenly, however, it aimed at my forehead and charged at me like a rock thrown from the shelf. I lost my hold and all three bodies, as if one, fell vertically, cutting through the moonbeams. The earthenware mortar, the pail and the empty jam can that were on the shelf fell too and clattered on the pot for live charcoal. All this took place in the dead of night so the racket we made was enough to freeze the blood.

" Thief, thief! " screamed my master hoarsely as he came rushing out from the bedroom. A lamp was hanging from his left hand and the cane was in his right. From his sleepy eyes shone a brightness that was appropriate in such a case. I myself quickly curled up beside my abalone shell and the two monsters disappeared into the closet. My master, feeling somewhat awkward, shouted in anger, " Who's there? Who's making all this noise? " There was no one to hear him.

The moon slanted farther west and the shaft of light that fell across the kitchen became narrower and narrower.

VI

IT IS DIFFICULT even for a cat to endure the heat. There's a story about an Englishman by the name of Sidney Smith who once said he would like to take off his skin and flesh, and become just bones to keep cool. I wasn't exactly asking to become just bones, but at least I would have liked to take this grayish spotted fur coat of mine off in order to have it washed, or to leave it in a pawnshop for a while. We cats might look as if we were enjoying our frugal life, wearing the same face throughout the year and wearing the same clothes spring, summer, autumn and winter. But just the same, cats do feel the heat and the cold. It is not that I don't like to take showers—no!—but it's extremely inconvenient to dry this fur of mine once it becomes wet. That is why I endure smelling sweaty. And that is also the reason I have never been honored with a bath all through these years! I wish I could use a fan in the summer but, unfortunately, I am not able to grip one so this is out of the question.

When compared with cats, humans pamper themselves too much. They boil or broil what they could eat raw; they soak their food in vinegar or preserve it in bean paste. They go to all this trouble just to eat. It's the same when it comes to clothes. It would be asking too much to suggest that they wear the same clothing throughout the year like we cats do. Although humans are born abnormally bare, they don't have to wear as much as they do. They have to feel indebted to sheep, silkworms and even to the cotton plant. It can be definitely said that such extravagance is a result of their being so incompetent.

I will drop this food and clothing subject, but I cannot understand why they go about changing what hardly affects them at all. Let's take an example: the hair on their heads. It grows a little every day so it would be simple just to let it grow. They have hair for their own protection.   But instead of using it as such, they go about devising various means of decorating or snarling it into many shapes.   And they're proud of it!   Look at the humans who are called priests; they have their heads shaved blue-black all the time.   When it's hot, they use a parasol and when it's cold, they cover their bald heads with a hood.   Since they must go to all this trouble, it's difficult to understand why they have their heads shaved in the first place.   Then there are the people who use an object called a comb—a worthless tool that looks like a saw.   They part their hair straight down the middle and seem happy about the results.   Others part their hair on one side, making a man-made boundary along their skulls.   Some even make this boundary reach all the way down to the back of their necks, making them look like counterfeit banana leaves.

Then there are those who cut their hair short on top, and long on the sides.   They look as if their round heads had been put into a square frame, much like a hedge of small cryptomeria trees trimmed square by a gardener.   There are also the half-inch, one-third-inch and the close-cropped styles.   As such people grow older and balder, all this might end up in their having a minus-half-inch or a minus-one-third-inch style—a new mode.   But in any case, I don't know what humans are trying to do with their sorry selves by de-voting so much time to fashion.

They're extravagant in other ways, too.   They only use two of their four feet, for example.   They'd be able to walk quicker if all four were used, but they only let the remaining two hang awkwardly, like a couple of dried codfish.   Isn't that foolish? Because of such time-consuming customs, it seems that humans have much more free time than we cats do.   Cats don't go around invent-ing such schemes or pretending to enjoy them.   But perhaps the funniest human custom is that whenever people get together, they commence telling each other how busy they are.   Indeed most of them actually look as if they really were busy.   They make such a fuss that you'd think they are killing themselves with overwork.

Some humans express the wish to be as easy-going as I am.   But if they want to be easy-going, all they have to do is to try—that's all.   Nobody asked them to be so fussy.   Inventing so many needless customs is like building a big fire and then complaining of the heat.

If the day ever comes that we cats begin to trim our hair in twenty different styles, then we won't be as easy-going as we are now. If you wish to be more carefree, simply practice being like me—wear a fur coat during the summer. But, I must confess, it's somewhat hot. Actually, it is a little too hot.

In such heat, I am not able to enjoy my naps, my sole pleasure. For want of something better to do one hot summer day, I decided to observe humans, something I had not done for quite some time. It's curious to see how fussy they are. My master, considered from this angle and regrettable as it is to say, has a character much like that of a cat. He naps just as much as I do and, especially during the summer vacation, he does nothing that most people consider human. It was extremely depressing to observe only him that day. I kept wishing that Meitei would appear because Meitei sometimes causes some reaction in my master's weak stomach and makes him less cat-like—at least for a while.

It really was about time Meitei came again. Suddenly from the washroom, I heard water being splashed. Someone was taking a shower. Occasionally this individual could be heard saying, "It's just right. What a fine feeling!" and "One more pailful, please." The voice was so loud that it vibrated through the whole house. A person who would come to my master's home and talk in so loud a voice could be none other than Meitei himself.

Haaa, he's come! Now I knew that half the day would be occupied.

Meitei soon unceremoniously entered the room, wiping away perspiration and tucking his clothing into place. "Ma'am, what's become of Kushami?" he began as he threw his hat on the straw-matted floor.

The Mrs. who had been taking a nap beside her sewing box in the adjoining room, woke up in surprise. She came to the parlor, trying hard to open her sleepy eyes wide. Meitei, in a fine hemp kimono, had sat down and was furiously trying to cool himself with a fan.

"Oh, it's nice to see you," the Mrs. mumbled a little shyly. "I didn't know you were here." Then she bowed, and some perspiration dripped off her nose.

"I just came but I had the maid pour some water on me. Now I feel like myself again. Isn't it hot!"

"Yes, isn't it? These last two or three days! Even when I sit still, I perspire. And how are you?" asked the Mrs. The sweat was still dripping from her nose.

"Thank you, ma'am. I'm not generally much affected by the heat but it's especially hot today, isn't it? I feel kind of heavy."

"I don't usually take naps either but when it's as hot as today—"

"You take naps? Why, that's good! If you can sleep in the daytime and again at night, there's nothing better." Meitei was as easy-going as usual but, for want of something more to say, he added, "You know, I don't need much sleep. I envy Kushami. He's sleeping every time I come here. Of course, the heat would affect a weak stomach, I suppose. On a day like this, even a strong man feels tired of holding his head up. As long as you have your head between your shoulders, though, you can't very well have it picked off, can you?" Unlike his usual self, Meitei seemed to have difficulty in disposing of the head. "As for yourself, ma'am, you are wearing so much on your head that it must be difficult just to keep yourself seated upright. With the weight of your long hair, it's no wonder you want to lie down."

The Mrs. put her hand to her head, believing that Meitei was talking about her disordered hair, and answered with a laugh. "Ho, ho, ho! You're being sarcastic."

Meitei remained indifferent. "Ma'am, I tried frying an egg on the tile roof yesterday." This seemed very odd.

"What did you say about frying?"

"The roof was so hot that I decided it a shame to waste this opportunity. I buttered a tile and dropped an egg on it."

"Oh?"

"But it didn't work. The egg didn't even begin to fry, so I went down to read the paper. In the meantime, a friend dropped in to see me and I forgot all about the egg. I remembered my experiment suddenly this morning and, thinking that the egg would be cooked, I went up to take a look."

" And how did you find it ? "

" It was gone. Instead of cooking, it had run down the side of the house."

" Oh ! " exclaimed the Mrs., knitting her brows.

" It's strange that it was so cool during July but so hot now."

" It really is. I was comfortable even in a kimono until recently but since the day before yesterday it's become hot."

"A crab walks sidewards but this year's weather is going backwards. Well, it might be saying to itself, ' Somehow I'm going backwards but what's wrong with that ? ' "

" What ? What was that ? "

" Oh, nothing. The way the seasons seem to be going backwards, it's like Hercules' bull." Meitei was getting bolder and beginning to make queer statements again. But unfortunately, the Mrs. could not understand him and only answered, " Yes." She didn't bother to ask Meitei about his last remark but Meitei was fishing for a response so he tried again. " Ma'am, do you know about Hercules' bull ? "

" No, I'm afraid I don't know anything about bulls."

" Let me tell you about it, then."

The Mrs. couldn't very well say that he needn't, so she just sat and listened.

" Long, long ago, Hercules was leading a bull along a road."

" Is this man Hercules a cowherd ? "

" No. Nor was he the proprietor of a sukiyaki restaurant. In his time there were no butchers in Greece."

" Then this is a Greek story ? You should have said so in the first place," cautioned the Mrs. She at least knew what Greece was.

"But I said Hercules."

" Then does Hercules mean Greece ? "

" Well, Hercules is a Greek hero."

" No wonder I didn't know about him. And what did this man do ? "

" Well, ma'am, Hercules fell into a deep sleep, just like you."

" You don't say ! "

" And while he slept, the son of Vulcan appeared."

"What's this Vulcan?"

"Vulcan was a blacksmith—and the son of this blacksmith stole the bull. But he led the animal away by pulling it backwards by its tail so when Hercules woke up he couldn't trace the bull. And no wonder! The son of that blacksmith had done a good job," explained Meitei, already forgetting about the heat. "By the way, what's become of your husband. Is he sleeping again? Naps in Chinese poems sound elegant, but when they become a daily habit like Kushami's, napping becomes common. It's like being dead for a short time every day. I'm sorry but would you mind waking him up for me?" asked Meitei.

The Mrs. seemed to agree with Meitei's definition of naps because she immediately said, "Not at all. It's bad, in the first place, for the health. And he just ate lunch at that!"

She was about to stand when Meitei commented, "When you mention lunch, ma'am, I remember that I haven't eaten mine yet." He was extremely cool in making such unexpected hints.

"Why, how forgetful of me! It's lunchtime and I didn't even notice it. There's nothing much I can offer you but how about some tea poured over rice?"

"If that's all there is, I don't think I want any."

"Well then, since we don't have anything else—," scowled the Mrs. disagreeably.

Meitei, realizing that he had said the wrong thing, quickly interrupted, "It's all right, ma'am. Please don't worry. On my way to your house I ordered a lunch to eat here."

The Mrs.'s only reply was "Oh!" But the way she said "Oh!" showed surprise, expressed her hurt feelings and also indicated that she was happy that she needn't go to any trouble. The word "Oh!" implied all three sentiments.

It was just then that my master came out from his study. He walked unsteadily, as if he had been disturbed by the noise just as he was about to go to sleep, something that seldom happens in this house.

"You're as noisy as ever, aren't you? I was just dozing off." This complaint was accompanied with a yawn.

"I'm sorry I interrupted your precious sleep but it might be better for your health that I did. Come, take a seat." It was difficult to tell who was the guest and who was the host. My master, without a word, sat down, extracted an Asahi cigarette from his wooden cigarette case, and began to smoke furiously. His eyes suddenly fell on Meitei's straw hat which had been thrown in the corner. "So you've bought yourself a new hat."

Meitei right away picked it up and showed it proudly to my master and to the Mrs.

"How soft! It's woven so closely, too," said the Mrs., stroking the hat again and again.

"You know, ma'am, it's very convenient. Look, you can do whatever you want to it." Meitei clenched his fist and gave the Panama hat a blow on the crown. He made a dent as big as his fist, but when the Mrs. screamed in distress, Meitei put his hand inside and shoved it, and the hat flopped back into position. Afterwards he gripped the brim with both hands and crushed it. The crumpled hat looked like a noodle flattened by a rolling pin. Then he rolled it up, as if it were a straw mat.

"What do you say now?" asked Meitei shoving his new purchase into his bosom.

"It's wonderful!" exclaimed the Mrs., as if she had just seen the best tricks of the magician Shoichi Kitensai. Meitei, almost like the magician himself, pulled the hat from his bosom, out through his left kimono sleeve and boasted, "There's not a scratch on it." After restoring it to its proper shape, he twirled it around and around on his forefinger. I thought he had finished with his tricks, but no! He ended his act by throwing it on the floor and then sitting squarely on it.

"Are you sure you know what you're doing?" asked my master nervously. The Mrs. also worried. "I think you'd better stop now." She was trying to save the precious hat.

But the owner wanted to show off even more. "It can't be damaged. That's the wonderful part of it." Meitei took the crushed hat out from under him and put it on his head. All of a sudden it regained it's regular shape.

"Really, it's a wonderful hat! I wonder how it is made," sighed the Mrs. with admiration.

" It always stays this way," explained Meitei to the Mrs. with the hat still on his head.

" You should buy that kind of a hat," suggested the Mrs. to my master.

" But Kushami already has a nice straw hat, doesn't he? "

" The other day the children stepped on it."

" What a pity! "

" So I think it would be nice if you bought a hat just as strong and nice as this one," she continued.   She had no idea how much Panama hats cost.   " I really think you should."

Meitei then produced a pair of scissors wrapped in a red sheath from his right sleeve pocket and showed them to the Mrs. " Let's forget the hat for a while, ma'am.   Now take a look at these scissors.   They're precious too, because you can use them in fourteen different ways."

If the scissors had not made their appearance, I'm afraid my master would have been pestered more to buy a Panama hat. Because the Mrs. is a woman and possesses the curiosity of all women, my master was able to avoid further trouble.   His luck was due, according to my estimation, not to Meitei's wit but to his being uncommonly fortunate for once.

The Mrs. of course asked how these scissors could be used in so many different ways and Meitei was ready with his explanation: " I'll tell you about them one at a time, so please listen.   Are you ready?   You see this crescent shape.   You can insert the end of a cigar here and cut it off.   This gadget cuts wire.   You can also use the scissors as a ruler if you place them flat on a piece of paper like this.   Notice the backside of this blade shows divisions so you can use it for measuring as well.   On the other blade, there's a fingernail file.   Now look carefully.   You can use this flattened tip as a screwdriver.   You can force open the lids of almost all wooden boxes, too.   The tip of this blade is sharpened so you can punch holes with it like an awl.   And this can be used to scratch out misspelled words or mistakes.   You take the scissors apart and you have a knife.   Last, but not least, is the best of all: there's a ball the size of a fly's eye here in the handle.   Just take a look."

"I don't want to. I'm sure you're going to make fun of me again."

"Don't be so suspicious. Come, take a look making believe you know you'll be fooled. Come on, just a tiny peek." Meitei passed the scissors to the Mrs. while insisting. She accepted them with uncertainty but placed an eye to the place indicated by Meitei.

"What do you find?"

"Nothing. It's only dark."

"That can't be. Hold it more towards the paper doors where it's lighter. Don't hold the scissors so flat. Now, how's that?"

"Oh, it's a picture, isn't it? I wonder how they fit a picture into such a small place."

"That's the most marvellous part." The Mrs. and Meitei were the only ones talking.

My master had kept silent until now but he wanted to see the picture, too. "Let me have a look."

The Mrs., holding on to the scissors, wouldn't let go. "Oh, how lovely! What a beautiful nude!"

"Let me look, I tell you!"

"Just wait. Oh, what lovely hair, all the way down to her hips! She's awfully tall, but how beautiful!"

"I said I want to see it. You don't have to be so greedy, do you?" insisted my master impatiently.

Finally the Mrs. handed the scissors to my master and told him to look to his heart's content. Just then, Osan appeared from the kitchen bringing the two round wooden lacquered receptacles of cold buckwheat noodles that Meitei had ordered.

"Ma'am, this is my lunch, paid for by myself. Kindly allow me to eat it here," said Meitei with extreme politeness. Meitei seemed so serious that it was as if he were joking again. The Mrs. was at a loss how to answer so she lightly replied, "Please."

My master, finally taking his eye away from the picture snarled, "Eating buckwheat noodles in such hot weather is bad for the health."

"Aha, but don't worry. Nobody gets sick eating what he likes." Meitei then took the lid off one of the receptacles and sniffed. "Good! It's fresh. Day-old noodles and thick-bearded men are two things I never welcome." Meitei put grated horse-radish into some sauce and commenced stirring vigorously.

"You put too much horseradish in the sauce. It's going to be too hot," warned my master a little worried.

"But noodles are supposed to be eaten with sauce and horse-radish. You don't like buckwheat noodles much, do you?"

"I like the ordinary kind better.

"That's what pack-horse drivers eat. I feel sorry for anyone who doesn't appreciate the delicacy of cold buckwheat noodles." Meitei then drove his wooden chopsticks into the receptacle and pulled up as much as he could.

"Ma'am, there are many ways to eat noodles. You'll find that a novice dips his into the sauce indiscriminately before eating. You lose the flavor of the noodles that way." Meitei lifted up his load but the long noodles hung about a foot from his chop-sticks. Meitei, thinking that he had lifted his hand high enough, looked down and found that twelve or thirteen strands were still coiled in the receptacle.

"My, they're long.' Don't you think they're very long?" asked Meitei, and in such a way that the Mrs. had to answer.

"They certainly are!" replied the Mrs. as if with admiration.

"Now, you're supposed to dip only one third of them into the sauce, and then swallow them all in one gulp. Don't chew them, though. That would spoil the taste. The best way is to swallow the noodles whole in one breath." Meitei lifted his noodles still higher until he was finally able to get the longest strand out of the receptacle. He maneuvered the dangling strings into the small cup containing sauce in his left hand, and then slowly lowered the noodles inside. The sauce filled about eight tenths of the cup and, in accordance with the theory of Archimedes, the sauce gradually rose as the noodles were lowered into it. When about a fourth of the noodles had been immersed, the sauce had reached the brim. The chopsticks abruptly stopped about five inches above the cup. Any further movement would have caused the sauce to overflow.

Meitei now hesitated a little but then with a sudden movement, like that of a jack rabbit, he brought his mouth to the chopsticks, and the noodles slid inside with a swish. His Adam's apple jumped up and down a couple of times but by then the noodles on the chopsticks had completely disappeared.

I saw one or two tears flow from the corners of Meitei's eyes and trickle down his cheeks. Could it have been because the horse-radish was so hot, or did he have such a hard time swallowing so many noodles in one gulp? I don't know even as of today.

"That was quite a feat, swallowing all the noodles like that," murmured my master with great respect.

"Wonderful!" agreed the Mrs., applauding Meitei for his skill.

Meitei put his chopsticks down and stroke his chest a couple of times with the palm of his hand. As he took out a handkerchief to wipe his face, he said, "You know, everyone should learn to finish a receptacle of noodles in less than three-and-a-half or four mouthfuls. You don't enjoy them if it takes more." Meitei needed a rest after explaining this.

And to this scene, Kangetsu suddenly appeared. I don't know why he was wearing his winter hat or why he had so much dust on his trousers, however.

"Enter the most distinguished handsome friend! But you'll have to excuse me. I just started eating and am not quite through," Meitei told him without any hesitation or embarrassment. He finished his second receptacle soon afterwards. Though he didn't do it in such a fancy way, and though he didn't need his handkerchief after eating or take a rest between mouthfuls, he cleaned the two receptacles in no time.

"Kangetsu, are you planning to finish your thesis soon?" asked my master. Meitei followed, "Kaneda's daughter is waiting, my boy. You'd better submit it as soon as you can."

Kangetsu wore his usual mysterious smile. "It's a crime to keep her waiting. I'm doing my best to finish it but, as you know, the subject of my thesis is terribly difficult." He was telling them something that wasn't quite true but he tried to sound sincere.

"That's right. The subject is hardly what the 'Nose' would choose. But remember, that 'Nose' is worth listening to."

Meitei was again talking more like himself. Of the three, my master seemed the most serious.

" By the way, what's the title of your thesis? "

" It's called ' The Effects of Ultra-Violet Rays on the Electro-Movement Action of the Frog's Eyeball '."

" Extraordinary ! That sounds like a subject Kangetsu would do best. Frog's eyeballs—that's a good one ! What do you say, Kushami? Should we relay this title on to the Kanedas before the thesis is completed? "

But my master ignored Meitei's suggestion. He asked Kangetsu, " Is that such a difficult subject? "

" It's terribly complicated. In the first place, the construction of the frog's eye isn't very well understood so it requires much research. I've planned to make a round crystal ball for this purpose and start from there."

" It's easy to procure crystal balls in glass shops, isn't it? "

Kangetsu puffed out his chest a little and replied, " In the first place, lines and circles are problems of geometry. There's not a crystal ball to be found in the world that would serve as a model for a frog's eyeball."

" If it is so difficult, why don't you change your subject? " asked Meitei.

" I wouldn't think of it," responded Kangetsu. " But it's very difficult. Finding one radius longer than another, I grind the ball down a bit. But then the other radius is too long. Keeping up this process, I only find that I make off-center crystal balls. I begin with a ball the size of an apple but end up with an object that looks like a strawberry. I try to correct it but eventually the ball becomes the size of a bean and still not uniform. I've worked hard—ever since New Year's Day. I've ground down six balls all told." His explanation didn't ring true but on the other hand it didn't sound as if he were lying either.

"And where have you been doing all this grinding? "

"At the school laboratory. After lunch, I rest a little and then commence grinding until dark. It's a terrible job."

" Do you mean to say that you've been grinding glass every day, even on Sundays? "

" Indeed. I've been doing nothing but grinding from morning till night."

" Then you'll probably become a professor on glass grinding. But if the 'Nose' knew how enthusiastic you are, she'd be impressed, I'm sure. The other day, I went to the school library and happened to meet Robai at the entrance. I thought it strange because Robai has already graduated. He told me that he hadn't gone there to read but, as he was passing the gate, he found he wanted to use the toilet. That was his only reason for entering the library. We had a big laugh over this. Robai and you make good examples for comparison. I'd like to write about you two in a book of morals," chuckled Meitei, as always adding too many details to his explanation.

My master, a little seriously, tried, " But when do you expect to finish all this grinding? "

"At this rate, it's bound to take about ten years," replied Kangetsu. He seemed much less worried than my master.

" Ten years! Can't you manage it sooner? "

" That was a conservative estimate. It might take twenty for all I know."

" That's terrible! Then you won't become a doctor after all! "

" Well, I'd like to receive my degree and put Tomiko at ease. But whatever the case, I'll have to go on grinding glass or I can't even begin my main experiment." Kangetsu paused, but continued triumphantly, " Don't worry so much about me. Tomiko understands what I'm doing. When I visited her a couple of days ago I explained the situation."

The Mrs. who had been absent-mindedly listening to the conversation suddenly commented suspiciously, " But the Kaneda family has been in Oiso since last month! "

Kangetsu looked somewhat bewildered but managed to stammer, " That's funny. I wonder what happened? " On such occasions, the presence of Meitei is invaluable. When conversation dwindles, or when one is in an embarrassing situation, or when one becomes sleepy or troubled, Meitei almost always comes to the rescue:

" To see Tomiko in Tokyo when she was in Oiso is both mysterious and interesting indeed. It must have been an exchange of spirits. At times, when sentiment becomes overly strong, a phenomenon like this can happen. It is like a dream but more authentic than usual dreams. This might sound extremely rare to those who don't know the true meaning of love. You, for instance, ma'am, are married to Kushami but you still don't know if he thinks of you or—"

"What right do you have to say such a thing?" The Mrs.'s sharp attack cut short Meitei's discourse.

"I don't remember of you, Meitei, ever being in love yourself," added my master, backing the Mrs. all the way.

"All my love affairs have lapsed more than seventy-five days so you might have forgotten them. As a result of frustrated love, however, I've remained single all these years." Meitei then looked into each face impartially after this confession.

"Ho, ho, ho! I don't believe you!" This came from the Mrs.

"Hmm." This came from my master who turned his face towards the window. It was Kangetsu who, with his eerie smile, urged, "I'd like to hear more for further reference."

"My favorite recollection is about a mysterious experience. Lafcadio Hearn should be here; he would have like it very much but, unfortunately, he has passed away. Besides, there's no significance in my telling it to others. As you've asked me to relate it, though, I guess I'll have to. But promise you'll listen to the very end of the story." After making this point clear, he commenced.

"Well, reflecting back, it must have been—let me see, how long ago was it?—oh, bother! Let's make it fifteen or sixteen years ago."

"Nonsense!" snorted my master.

The Mrs. made fun of him: "You have an excellent memory, don't you?"

Kangetsu was the only one who kept his promise. He didn't say a word, and his expression indicated that he wanted to hear more.

"Well, in any case, it happened during the winter. I was in the Aizu District near the Octopus Trap Pass. I had just passed through Bamboo Shoot Valley in the Province of Echigo."

" That's a funny place," interrupted my master.

" Quiet, now, quiet. This is going to be interesting!" scolded the Mrs.

" The sun had set and I had lost my way. I was also hungry so I knocked at the door of a lonely hut in the middle of the pass and asked for a night's lodging. A voice asked me in. When I opened the door and saw the girl who held a candle to my face, I began to tremble. It was the first time for me to know how formidable the power of love is."

"Amazing! I wonder if there are many beautiful women living in the mountains?"

" Be it in the mountains or on the sea, ma'am, I would have liked to show this girl to you once. And she had her hair set in a gorgeous *shimada** coiffure."

" Is it possible?" The Mrs. was taken completely by surprise.

" Upon entering, I found a fire blazing in a hole cut in the middle of the large room. The four of us—the girl, her old father and mother and I—sat around the flames. I told them that I was famished, and that I could eat anything. I asked them to serve me right away. The old man said that as I was a special guest, they should prepare some snake rice. Now this is the beginning of my frustrated love so listen carefully."

" Sure, we'll listen. But any way you look at it, there are no snakes in the Province of Echigo in winter."

" Right you are. But when it comes to such a romantic story, you can't always insist on its logic. In a novel by Kyoka Izumi, for example, there's a place where crabs crawl out from snow. Don't you remember?"

Kangetsu simply replied " I see." He then assumed the expression of an interested listener.

"At that time I loved to eat strange foods. I was tired of eating locusts, dew snails, frogs and whatnot, so snake rice sounded just perfect. The old man placed a pot over the fire, put rice into it, and commenced boiling it. I noticed about ten variously

---

* The *shimada* is an elegant coiffure that used to be worn by fashionable women of marriageable age.

[196]

shaped holes on the lid and steam puffed out of them at intervals. I was amazed to find how ingenious these country folk were. The old man, without a word, left the room but presently returned with a large basket under his arm. After he had placed it by the fireplace, I took a look inside. And there they were! Several long snakes had entwined themselves into one big ball because of the cold."

"Oh, stop! It's terrible," grimaced the Mrs. bringing her brows together.

"I can't stop here. This is only the beginning. Then the old man took the lid off the rice pot with his left hand, nonchalantly picked up the snakes in his right and threw them quickly into the pot before closing the lid. And let me tell you, it was then that I thought I'd choke."

"Please stop. It's frightening," pleaded the Mrs.

"Just a little more and I'll come to my frustration, so please wait. Now then—after a couple of minutes I was surprised to see a snake stick its head out from one of the holes. While I was watching this, another head appeared from another hole. Soon heads were coming out from all the other holes until the whole surface of the lid was covered with snakes' heads."

"Why did they stick their heads out?"

"It was hot inside and they wanted to escape, that's why. Then the old man said that it was just about ready. The old woman answered "Ha-a," and the girl "Ai". The woman then took hold of the snakes' heads and pulled strongly. The bones were neatly drawn through the holes while the flesh remained inside the pot."

"That was a wonderful way to debone the snakes, wasn't it?" laughed Kangetsu.

"Actually it was very clever. Then the girl took off the lid, ladled the rice and snakes out, and served me."

"Did you really eat it?" asked my master coldly. The Mrs. again made a sour face and once more pleaded, "Let's stop it now. I feel sick and won't be able to eat for days."

"That's because you haven't ever tasted snake rice yet. Eat it once and you'll never forget the wonderful flavor."

" Nasty !   Who'd eat snakes ? "

" Well, anyway, I ate my fill.   I soon forgot the cold and found myself gazing at the girl.   I was thinking that I had nothing else to ask for but then the family bid me good night.   I thanked them and, being tired myself, I laid down and immediately fell into a sound sleep."

"And then what ? "   It was the Mrs. now asking to hear more of the story.

" I woke up the next morning and lost my love."

" Did anything happen ? "

" Nothing in particular.   After getting up, I looked out of the window and happened to see somebody with a bald head by a bamboo water pipe."

" Was it the old man or the old woman ? " asked my master.

" I was too far away to see at first but when the person faced my way, I was shocked to discover that the bald head belonged to the girl I had fallen in love with the previous night."

" But you said that the girl had an elaborate *shimada* coiffure, didn't you ? "

" The night before, yes, and beautiful at that.   But the following morning the girl was bald-headed."

" Impossible ! " grunted my master, staring at the ceiling.

" It was quite mystifying.   I felt a little afraid, yet I kept on looking.   The girl, after washing her face, picked up a wig from a rock beside her and nonchalantly put it on her head.   She then entered the house.   So I said to myself, ' Indeed ! '   But though I snorted ' Indeed ' to myself, it was from that time that I have been destined to suffer one frustrated love affair after another."

" Lost love !   Meitei is always jolly and full of energy.   Do you think it's because he so often loses his love ? "   My master was making fun of Meitei's frustration.

Kangetsu suggested, " But if this girl had not been bald and if Meitei had come back to Tokyo with her, no doubt he would have been even more energetic.   In any case, it must be like a curse of a thousand autumns for a pretty girl to be bald.   How could all of her hair have fallen out like that ? "

" I've been thinking about that myself, and I've come to the conclusion that it must have been because of eating too much snake rice. Snake rice causes the blood to rush to the head."

"It was fortunate that you were not affected by it."

"No, I didn't become bald, but I've been nearsighted ever since." Meitei then took off his gold-rimmed glasses and wiped them carefully.

After a few moments, my master commented, as if he had remembered a forgotten question, "What's so mysterious about the story in the first place?"

"How would a girl living in the mountains buy herself a wig like that? Or did she pick it up some place? That's the mysterious part of the story," answered Meitei, replacing his glasses on his nose.

The impression the Mrs. received from Meitei's story was: "It's just like listening to a storyteller."

Meitei had concluded his story so I thought he wouldn't talk any more. But he is the kind that keeps on talking until he's gagged. He continued, "My frustrated love was a bitter experience, yes. But suppose I had married the girl without my knowing about her bald head. My eyes would have been offended for the rest of my life. Any marriage is risky unless you give it a lot of thought."

"In many marriages, one finds hidden scars so, Kangetsu, don't become too infatuated or so bewildered that you forget to be careful. It might be best just to keep on grinding your glass balls." Meitei's conclusion sounded like good advice.

"I wouldn't mind grinding glass balls but the Kanedas won't let me," complained Kangetsu.

"In your case, it's the other party that's getting worked up. There are many funny experiences concerning love. For instance, take Robai, my friend who uses the library only because it has a toilet."

"What did he do?" My master was becoming interested already.

"Once he stayed for one night at the Tozai-kan Hotel in Shizuoka—remember now, for one night only—and on that very night he proposed to a maid working there. I'm care-free myself, but not to that extent! You see, there was a good-looking maid there by the name of Onatsu. Robai's room was in her charge, so he couldn't help seeing her."

" I think he must have gone out of his way to see her. It's probably exactly the same as your So-and-So Pass incident."

" When you say so—well—yes, somewhat. There's no big difference between Robai and myself. Anyway, he proposed to this Onatsu but, before he received her answer, he felt a great urge to eat some watermelon."

" What was that? " exploded my master with astonishment. It wasn't only my master; the Mrs. and Kangetsu both pondered over this, slanting their heads to one side. But Meitei continued without paying any attention to their bewilderment.

" So he asked Onatsu if they had any watermelons in Shizuoka. Onatsu replied sarcastically that even in Shizuoka they had watermelons, and brought a tray full of sliced watermelon to his room. It seems as though Robai ate them all—the whole trayful—and then waited for Onatsu's reply to his proposal. Soon, however, his stomach commenced to ache. He began to groan but that didn't bring much relief. He then asked Onatsu if they had any doctors in Shizuoka and Onatsu answered sarcastically again that even in Shizuoka they had good doctors. She called in a doctor by the name of Genko Tenchi or something like that. Anyway, the name made me think that the doctor had stolen it from the book *One Thousand Chinese Characters*.

" The following morning the pain had gone. Fifteen minutes before he was to leave the hotel, Robai called Onatsu to his room and asked for her answer to his proposal of marriage. To this she replied that in Shizuoka they had watermelons and they had doctors, but that they did not produce brides overnight. She then walked out of the room and didn't show her face again. Robai, like myself, has been disappointed in love and thereafter goes to the library only to use the toilet. Coming to think of it, most women are deceitful."

My master followed this up with, " That's really the truth! In a drama by Musset I was reading the other day, a character referred to a Roman poet who once wrote: ' What is lighter than a feather is dust; what is lighter than dust is the wind; what is lighter than the wind is a woman; and what is lighter than a woman is nothing at all.' Isn't that profound? Women are no good." He had an odd way of emphasizing his point.

But the Mrs., of course, did not agree. " You say that women, being light, are bad; but men, who are heavy, are not good, isn't that so?"

"What do you mean by heavy?"

"Heavy means heavy—something like you."

"What do you mean by saying I'm heavy?"

"Because you are, that's why."

And thus, a queer dispute began. Meitei at first listened with much interest, but presently he opened his mouth and said, " That a couple can attack each other so freely implies that they are truly man and wife. Married couples in former days were less lucky." I couldn't tell if he were making fun of the man and wife or whether he was praising them, so vague was his statement. Another person would have stopped then and there, but Meitei always had to give an explanation.

"In olden times, no woman would even dream of talking back to her husband. But I myself wouldn't like having such a cowed woman as my wife. I'd prefer to be accused of being heavy— just as you are saying to Kushami now, ma'am. It would be tiresome for married couples not to have a few quarrels.

" My mother, for instance, would say nothing but ' Yes, yes, ' when talking to my father. They lived more than twenty years together, but in all that time my mother never left the house except to visit a temple. But because of this, she was able to memorize all the posthumous Buddhist names of our ancestors.

"And boys and girls were as separated as man and wife. In those days, it would have been absolutely impossible for a boy to be seen walking with a girl. No one could talk about his sentiments as freely as Kangetsu does now."

" It must have been awful," said Kangetsu, bowing to Meitei.

" It *was* horrible. But, ma'am, this doesn't mean that the girls of those days conducted themselves any better than the girls of today, even though people claim that modern schoolgirls have become terribly degraded. The girls of olden times were much worse."

" I wonder," mused the Mrs.

" That's the truth. No, I'm not joking. I have proof. Kushami, you must remember that when you and I were five or six years old, girls were often placed in baskets like pumpkins, carried around on ends of a wooden pole over the father's shoulder, and sold. Isn't that so? "

" I don't remember."

" Of course I don't know about your home town, but in Shizuoka they did it—I'm certain."

" Is that really true? " asked Kangetsu, doubting the authenticity of Meitei's story.

" It's true all right. Once even my own father priced a little girl. I guess I was about six at the time. My father and I were taking a walk along Tori-cho from Abura-machi. A man came toward us from the opposite direction shouting loudly that he had some girls to sell. The man passed us at the corner of 2-chome, in front of the Isegen textile store. This store is sixty feet wide at the front and has five warehouses; it is the biggest textile store in Shizuoka. When you go there the next time, take a look at it. Even today it is imposing. The chief clerk of this store was called Jimbei and he sat at the counter with an expression that seemed to say that his mother had died only three days before. Beside Jimbei sat Hatsu, a young man about twenty-four or -five. He was so pale that he always looked as if he were at the end of a twenty-one-day fast, during which period he had eaten nothing more than watery noodle soup to show penitence to the famous priest Unsho Risshi. Chodon sat next to Hatsu. He usually looked as if he had just lost his home in a fire. He would lean on his abacus, using it as an arm rest, with a sorrowful face. And next to Chodon sat— "

" Now wait a minute. Are you going to tell us about the store or about selling girls? "

" Oh, that's right. Well, there's a good story about this Isegen, too, but I'll save it for some other time. Now, as to my girl-selling story— "

" How about quitting altogether while you're at it ? "

" This has a great deal to do with the conduct of the girls of the present as compared to the behavior of the girls in the early days of the Meiji era, so how can I quit now? And so when we were in front of the Isegen store, the man asked my father if he wouldn't buy the last girls he had for sale. He said that he'd let them go at a good price. While talking, he unshouldered his wooden pole and wiped his sweaty face. I took a look and found a little girl about two years old in each of the baskets. My father said that he would buy them if they were cheap enough. He also inquired if those two were the only ones left. The vendor replied that the others had been sold that very day.

" The man picked up the two little tots as if they were pumpkins or some other vegetable and shoved them right under my father's nose. My father tapped each of their heads lightly and agreed that they sounded solid. Then the two men began bargaining. After my father had brought the price down, he agreed to buy both girls if they could be guaranteed.

" The man said that he could easily guarantee the one in the forward basket because he could see her while he carried them; there was nothing wrong with her. But as for the one in the rear basket, he could not guarantee her since he had no eyes in the back of his head, so he couldn't tell if there was a crack in her or not. He promised to make the price even lower in order to make up for this possibility.

" I still remember that conversation and, even as a child, I realized that one can't be off his guard when it comes to girls. But today, in the thirty-eighth year of the reign of Emperor Meiji, you don't find people going around selling girls; nor do you hear such arguments concerning the guarantee of one girl because the guardian couldn't keep his eye on her. Therefore, it can be said that the conduct of girls has greatly improved since we started adopting Western customs. What do you say to this, Kangetsu ? "

Kangetsu, before replying, noisily cleared his throat and then expressed his own observations in a purposely self-possessed voice.

" When going home from school, or at concerts, charity meetings and at garden parties, the girls of today will often approach a man and ask, of their own accord, if he would like to 'buy' her. 'No?' Therefore, there's no need to feel sorry for the girls who were sold as if they were left-over vegetables. That they now sell themselves is, I suppose, natural because of their new ideas concerning independence. The old folks become anxious and are apt to criticize them but this is the trend of civilization. Therefore we should congratulate ourselves on being able to take advantage of this welcome phenomenon. There's now no need to tap a girl's head or ask if she is guaranteed before buying one. If we had to go to all that trouble, there would be no limit. But when such girls become fifty or sixty years old, they probably wouldn't be able to find husbands or get married." Kangetsu, being a young man of the twentieth century, had now expressed his own ideas concerning his generation. After talking, he blew the smoke of his Shikishima cigarette into Meitei's face.

Meitei was hardly the kind of a person to be bothered by mere smoke. "As you say, schoolgirls nowadays are more independent. It's admirable the way they won't let themselves be treated as inferiors. Take, for instance, the schoolgirls in my neighborhood. They practice gymnastics on a bar every day. It's really beautiful the way they do it. Every time I see them going through their exercises from my upstairs window they remind me of the Greek women who—"

"There's that word 'Greek' again," burst my master with a cold laugh.

"Well, I can't help it. In most cases, anything concerned with beauty has its source in Greece. You can't separate aesthetics from the Greeks. Especially when I see that tanned girl, exercising with her whole body and soul, I recollect the anecdote of Agnodice," continued Meitei with an "I-know-everything" face.

"You found a difficult name for this story too," smirked Kangetsu.

"Agnodice was a great woman, and I admired her. At one time in Athens, there was a law prohibiting women from practicing midwifery. Even Agnodice found this regulation irksome."

"Who's this? What's this you're talking about?"

"It's a name—the name of a woman. This Agnodice lamented

the fact that women could not become midwives. She herself wanted to become one so she pondered on the problem for three days and three nights. At dawn on the third day, upon hearing a baby next door cry, she cut her long hair with sudden determination, put on men's clothes, and went to Hierophilus' lectures on childbirth. After she had learned all she needed to know, she commenced practicing as a midwife.

"And she was in a good business. A lot of babies were being born and Agnodice made a great deal of money. But the lives of all humans are full of misfortune as well as joy. Finally Agnodice was found out. Having violated the law of the land, it was decided that she should be severely punished."

"This sounds just like a storyteller again."

"Don't you think I'm good at it?—But the women of Athens got together and signed a petition for her release. The authorities were at a loss what to do when faced with so much opposition, so Agnodice was found innocent and set free. Thereafter, the law was changed so even women could become midwives. And everybody lived happily ever after."

"You know something about everything. It's a wonder!"

"Yes, ma'am, I know pretty nearly everything. The only thing that I don't know, I guess, is how much of a fool I am. But I might have even a slight idea concerning that, too."

The Mrs. suddenly became convulsed with laughter. And as she was laughing, the front doorbell rang. Its tone had not changed since it had first been installed.

"Oh, we seem to have another guest," said the Mrs., and she retreated to the tearoom. I wondered who this person would be, but it only turned out to be Tofu Ochi whom you already know.

Now, with Tofu here, you readers might believe that I'm going a little too far in describing all these eccentrics who come to visit my master. At least enough of them come to keep me amused. It would not be true to say that they are lacking in number.

If I had been brought up in a different home, I might have lived all my life without knowing that such excellent scholars existed among the human race. But I am fortunate to belong to Mr. Kushami, the teacher. Being with my master from morning till night, I can witness for myself the scholarly activities of my heroes—Meitei, Kangetsu and Tofu, not to forget my master—each of whom possesses an invaluable character extremely scarce even in such a large city as Tokyo. To live here is an honor, an honor which might only be expected once in a thousand years. I was especially grateful to these four. Because of them, I forgot that I am clothed in fur on that hot day so I was able to enjoy myself.

With these three visitors, I was pretty sure that something interesting would take place soon, so I respectfully looked in from behind the sliding door.

" I've neglected calling on you for a long time. How are you? " murmured Tofu while bowing. I noticed that his hair was as neatly parted as before and he looked like a subordinate actor. But my criticisms are not centered only on his head. The way Tofu wore his coarse white *hakama* skirt made him look like a pupil of Kenkichi Sakakibara, the famous swordsman. In other words, Tofu only looked like an ordinary person between his shoulders and his waist.

" It's kind of you to call in such hot weather. Please come in," greeted Meitei, as if he were ushering a guest into his own home.

" I haven't seen you for quite a long time."

" That's right. The last we met was, I'm pretty sure, at the recitation gathering last spring. Speaking of recitations, are you still practicing? And have you performed the part of Omiya again? The last time I saw you, you were very good. I applauded quite loudly. Did you notice me? "

" Thank you. You encouraged me a great deal."

" When will you have your next recitation," put in my master.

" I intend to rest until the end of this month but I will be prepared for a lively performance some time in September. I wonder if you could suggest some good subject."

" I wonder," replied my master without enthusiasm.

" Tofu, how about using my composition? " This was Kangetsu addressing him.

" If it's your composition, I'm sure it would be interesting. What is it? "

"A play write-up," answered Kangetsu, trying to give a favorable impression. As expected, the other three looked surprised. They all stared at him, as if by arrangement.

"A play write-up? That's wonderful! Is it a comedy or a tragedy?" queried Tofu.

Kangetsu calmly replied, "No, it's neither a comedy nor a tragedy. Nowadays, people are very particular about dramas, so I invented a new type and have named it a poem-play."

"A poem-play?"

"It's a play along poetic lines. I myself call it a poem-play," said Kangetsu. Neither Meitei nor my master seemed to grasp the meaning of his explanation.

"What's the plot?" Tofu was interested in all the details.

"As the play is based fundamentally on poetic lines, I decided not to make it long or too heavy. It takes place in one scene only."

"I see."

"I suggest that the stage settings be as simple as possible. The only set is a big willow tree in the middle of the stage. A branch is sticking out to the right from the trunk and a raven is sitting on it."

"Let's hope the raven stays put," interrupted my master, as if he were talking to himself.

"That's no problem. All you have to do is to tie the raven's feet to the branch with a piece of string. And below the raven you place a wooden bathtub. In it, there'll be a beautiful girl, her head turned sideways, washing herself with a cotton towel."

"That's slightly indecent. Who do you think you can find to play the girl?" asked Meitei.

"Quite easy. We can hire one of those models from an art school."

"But the police board is very strict about these matters," winced my master, again worried.

"What's the difference? It doesn't matter if she doesn't act. If all naked girls were objectionable, there wouldn't be any nudes at art schools."

"But students there are studying. It's somewhat different on the stage."

"If you scholars take all such matters so seriously, you're going to hinder all progress in Japan. Whether it's a drawing or a play, it's art, isn't it?" Kangetsu was in high spirit.

"All right. We'll forget that argument, but what happens now?" Tofu seemed as if he really wanted to use the play.

"So then the poet Kyoshi Takahama appears on the ramp leading to the stage. He has a cane in his hand and wears a white helmet. His *haori* coat is of silk crepe while his kimono is of a splashed pattern. The skirt of the kimono is tucked inside his *obi*, and he is wearing a pair of low shoes. He looks like a pro-vision supplier for the army but actually, being a poet, he should look more independent. Kyoshi should walk down the ramp in such a way as to show that he's always thinking about poetry. When he steps onto the main stage, he suddenly notices the big willow tree and the white-skinned girl taking her bath under it. He also sees the raven on the branch just above the girl. The poet should then hesitate for about fifty seconds to show that he is greatly inspired by the scene. Then in a loud voice he recites, 'A raven, in love with a bathing girl'. Right after he finishes this line, the wood clapper off-stage commences signalling the end of the play, and the curtain falls.

"Well, what do you think? You don't like it? I'd say it's a lot better to play Kyoshi than Omiya."

Tofu, his face showing he felt that something was lacking, just said, "It's too short. Too short, I think. I'd like to have some-thing with more human sentiment in it." He was still speaking seriously.

Meitei had kept comparatively quiet until now, but he was not to stay silent forever.

"Is that all there is to a poem-play? It's terrible. According to Bin Ueda's theory, all poems and comics should be abolished because they can ruin a nation. Just try presenting one of those overly artistic plays and you'll only be laughed at. In the first place, the audience can't tell whether it's a short play or a burlesque. Sorry, Kangetsu, but it would be better for you to continue grinding glass balls. If you wrote one or two hundred of those plays, you could ruin Japan as a nation and that wouldn't do."

Kangetsu seemed a little irritated and shot back, " Do you really believe it's that bad? I think it's extremely original." He tried to give a clearer explanation of his piece, but it still didn't make much sense. " This Kyoshi—the way he tries to impress us that the raven is in love with the girl, 'A raven, in love with a bathing girl'—that's definitely original!"

" Considering the play as a bachelor of science, it does not stand to reason that a raven should fall in love with a girl."

" Exactly."

" But this fantasy does not sound awkward."

" I wonder." My master sounded doubtful, but Kangetsu remained defiant.

" I'll tell you why it isn't awkward. After explaining it psychologically, you'll understand much better. Actually, the raven has nothing whatsoever to do with love—it's the poet himself who longs for the girl. He says that the raven has fallen in love, but he is speaking for himself. When Kyoshi sees the beautiful girl taking her bath, he is surprised and, at the same time, fails in love with her. With his eyes filled with nothing but love, he happens to see the raven sitting on a branch above, looking down at the girl. He decides that the bird is also in love with the girl. There's no doubt that he makes a mistake, but that's why the play is so original. He gives to the raven what he himself most desires. How about that?"

" I see your point and your reasoning is good," answered Meitei. " If Kyoshi had heard this explanation, however, he'd have been greatly surprised, I'm sure. The motive is now clear but if you present this play, the audience will still be confused. Do you agree, Tofu?"

" I'm afraid, it's a little too original for me," replied Tofu seriously.

My master seemed anxious to change the subject of conversation, so attempted, " How about it, Tofu. Have you written any masterpieces recently?"

" I haven't done much, but the other day I decided to try publishing a collection of poems. Fortunately, I have the manuscript with me so I'd like you to criticize it for me." Tofu then produced a small notebook wrapped in a purple crepe material from his bosom. The notebook contained fifty or sixty pages, and Tofu placed it in front of my master.

My master glanced at the first page and saw the two lines written on it:

"Dedicated to Tomiko,
Whose milky complexion is unlike any other."

My master assumed a mysterious expression and kept staring at the first page. Meitei sitting beside him asked, "What is it? A new kind of poem?" While asking, he also caught sight of the dedication and exclaimed, "So you've already dedicated it, Tofu! And to a Miss Tomiko!"

My master, still looking doubtful, asked, "Tofu, does this Tomiko actually exist?"

"Of course. She's one of the girls that Meitei and I took to the recitation party the other day. And she happens to live right near here. To tell the truth, I dropped in on my way to show her this collection but, unfortunately, she has been in Oiso since last month." Tofu seemed very enthusiastic about the girl.

"Kushami! This is the twentieth century so you don't have to make a face like that. Go ahead and read the masterpiece. By the way, Tofu, this dedication isn't very good. Your wording could be better. Do you know what 'milky,' implies?"

"I take it to mean white or lustrous."

"Well, yes. You could interpret it in that sense but it could also be interpreted as sticky. If I were you, I wouldn't write the dedication that way."

"Then how should it read?"

"Write it like this:

Dedicated to the nose of Tomiko.
It is unlike any other.

It's only a matter of interpretation but without 'to the nose' it sounds weak and insincere."

"I see," answered Tofu. His eyes showed that he was trying

hard to digest something he could not comprehend very well.

My master had remained quiet but he finally turned the first page over and commenced reading Part I:

> " Through the hazy cigarette smoke
> Perfuming the air,
> I am at leisure.
> And your image appears to me—
> The figure
> Of my most beloved one.
> Ah! Poor me! Could I but have
> Your sweet kisses
> To sweeten this bitter world ! "

" This is a little difficult for me," sighed my master, so he handed the script to Meitei.

" This is extraordinary ! " commented Meitei, passing the book on to Kangetsu.

" Hmmm—I see," murmured Kangetsu who then returned it to Tofu.

" It's not terribly strange that you don't understand it. Poetic styles have greatly changed in the last ten years so you have nothing to compare this with. You can't understand modern poems by reading them lying down or while waiting for a street-car. Even the writer himself has a difficult time answering questions about his own compositions. They're written only when the poet feels inspired, so even the poet himself has little responsibility for the outcome. Notes and explanations are later attemped by critics but that's no concern of the poet.

" The other day, a friend of mine, Soseki by name, wrote a short story entitled 'One Night'. Everyone found it vague; there didn't seem to be any point to the plot. When I last met him, I asked about the parts I did not understand. He insisted that he himself didn't know either. This might be characteristic of all poets."

" He might be a poet but I think he's a little crazy," commented my master.

" He's a fool ! " boomed Meitei, condemning Soseki entirely.

Tofu was not at all satisfied with the reaction so he continued, " Of course Sōseki is an exception. But I'd like you to consider my poems like Sōseki considers his own writings. Pay special attention, for example, to the part: ' the bitter world ' and ' sweet kisses '. I had to rack my brains to compose this contrast."

" You must have worked hard on it."

" The contrast between ' sweet ' and ' bitter ' is especially interesting in that it has the tang of seventeen spices mixed with pepper. I pay great respect to the special technique of Tofu. It is due you," rattled on Meitei, only too happy to continue confusing this honest man.

My master suddenly stood up and went into his study—for what reason, I couldn't tell. Presently, however, he returned with a sheet of paper. " We've seen Tofu's masterpiece so now I'll read mine and ask for your criticisms." My master seemed determined.

" If it's about Tennen-Koji and the inscription on his gravestone, I've already heard it several times."

" Keep quiet. Now, Tofu, this is not one of my favorites, but I want you to listen to it."

" I would like to hear it very much."

" Kangetsu, you might as well listen too."

" It's not a long one, is it? "

" It only consists of a few words," said my master, and he commenced reading his home-made masterpiece:

" Long live the Japanese Spirit! " shout the people,
But coughing as if they were consumptive."

" You've started it very well. It rises like a peak, doesn't it? "

" ' The Japanese Spirit! ' cry the papers.
' The Japanese Spirit! ' screams the pickpocket.
And in one great leap, the Japanese Spirit
Crosses the ocean
And is lectured on in England;
A play concerning the Japanese Spirit
Is shown in Germany! "

" I see this is much better than your poem on Tennen-Koji,"
said Meitei, sticking out his chest.

> "Admiral Togo has the Japanese Spirit;
> The fishmonger, Gin, also possesses it;
> Swindlers, cheats and murderers as well
> Cling to the Japanese Spirit."

" Sir, please add that Kangetsu has the Japanese Spirit, too."

> " In asking what the Japanese Spirit is,
> The answer is only that it is the Japanese Spirit.
> The answerer walks about ten yards or so away
> And then, 'Ahem.'
> That is the answerer clearing his throat."

" That sentence is the best.   You're a literary genius.   What's
next ? "

> " Is the Japanese Spirit a triangle
> Or is it a square?
> No! As the words indicate,
> It is a spirit.
> And being a spirit,
> It is without measure."

" This is all very interesting but don't you think you repeat the
phrase ' the Japanese Spirit ' a little too often? " cautioned Tofu.
" I agree! " It was, of course, Meitei who shouted this.

> " There's no one in Japan
> Who has not used the phrase,
> But no one has practiced its principles.
> Everybody has heard of it,
> But nobody has experienced it.
> *Yamato-damashii*, the Japanese Spirit—
> Is it, then, like Tengu,
> The long-nosed goblin? "

My master finished reading with a trailing note but, as there
was no special point, his audience believed there was more coming.
They waited but not a sound followed.   Finally Kangetsu

broke the silence, "Is that all?" My master lightly answered, "Uhuh." His answer was perhaps too light-hearted.

It is a wonder that Meitei had not harassed my master more during the reading of this excellent example of his poetry. But now, readjusting his seat, he suggested, "How about collecting your poems and dedicating them to somebody, too?"

My master casually responded, "I'll dedicate them to you. How about that?"

"No thanks," replied Meitei, nervously clipping his fingernails with the scissors he had shown the Mrs. a little while back. Kangetsu turned to Tofu and asked, "Do you really know the daughter of Kaneda?"

"After taking her to the recitation party last spring, I've continued to see her from time to time. When I find myself before her, I'm overcome by her charm. And when composing poems or writing odes, that feeling of happiness and warmth returns to me. There are many love poems in this collection because I have received so much inspiration from her. Since I am so indebted to her, I want to express my sincere appreciation— from the bottom of my heart. Now, taking this opportunity, I am dedicating this collection of poems to her. It is said that even in olden times no poet could compose excellent poetry unless inspired by a woman."

"I wonder," mused Kangetsu seriously. But he was laughing behind that mask of solemnity.

Even though this had turned out to be a gathering of braggarts, they could not keep on talking forever. Gradually the flames of enthusiasm smoldered and commenced to die. Since I had no obligation to listen any more, I excused myself and went out to the yard to hunt mantises.

The rays of the setting sun in the western sky filtered through the green paulownia leaves and threw splashes of light around the garden. Up on the trunk of a tree was a cicada singing as loudly as it could: " *Tsukutsuku-boshi, tsukutsuku-boshi.*"

It looked like we could expect rain that evening.

VII

A T ONE TIME, I went in for sports. Some of you, upon hearing this, will surely laugh at me because even some of you humans don't enjoy them. Many of you think that your only mission in life is to eat and sleep. There was once a time when noblemen, with their hands folded at their bosoms and their buttocks rotting on cushions, claimed that they were in a state of ecstacy; they felt they were assuming the honors and the wealth of their superiors. Only recently have we heard that we should take exercise, drink milk, dash cold water over ourselves, dive into the sea, seclude ourselves in the mountains, and eat mist for the good of our health. These are all recent maladies which have infected this divine land from Western countries, and these suggestions should be classified as being as dangerous as the pest, tuberculosis and neurasthenia. I myself was born only last year so I am only one year old now. Therefore, I did not witness the time that men were first infected by this sickness but it must have been before I began floating around in the wind of this world. But we may say that a year of a cat's life is equal to ten years of a man's. The span of my life is only a fraction of a human's, but during that short interval, I will manage to accomplish what all cats should do. It would be wrong to calculate the days of cats as the same as the days of humans.

You might consider me as proof of this theory. Though I am only one year and a few months old, I have very worldly views. Compare me with my master's youngest daughter. They say that she's already in her third year, but when it comes to knowledge —my dear!—she's really quite thick. She knows only how to cry, soil her bed and to cuddle her mother's breast for milk. When making a comparison of this child and me, she's definitely stupid. In my short life, for example, I have managed to study the complete history of exercising, sea bathing, and treatment by change of air. If anybody is surprised at this, that " anybody " must certainly be a human—the two-legged slowpoke.

Man was made to be slow right from the very beginning. That's why humans have only recently commenced to understand the virtues of exercise and the advantages of sea bathing. They seem to think they have made a great discovery. In regard to such matters, I knew about these benefits almost as soon as I was born.

When considering the medicinal value of sea water, it can be easily recognized simply by visiting the seashore. I don't know exactly how many fish there are in that wide span of water but, in any case, no fish ever becomes sick enough to go and see the doctor. They're all there, swimming about in the best of health. When fish are sick, their movements become impeded; and when they die, they float. That's why we Japanese term fish that have died as floating or, in other words, as having risen. As for birds, they're considered as falling or fallen; but for humans, they only pass away or simply croak.

Ask any person who has crossed the Indian Ocean if he has ever seen a dead fish. He would be sure to give you a negative answer—and no wonder. Nobody has ever seen a fish breathing its last (well, no—a fish could not be breathing its last so perhaps I'd better say gulping its last water) or seen one come floating to the surface. Considering the difficulty of finding even one poor fish that has risen, even after continuously searching by day and by night in the vast and boundless sea, we must arrive at the conclusion that fish are extraordinarily healthy and strong.

And why is it that fish are so healthy? The answer is so simple that even humans should easily guess—that is, if people weren't so human. The reason for such health in fish lies in the fact that they continuously gulp water and bathe themselves in the sea. Obviously, bathing is of great importance to fish. And if it is so advantageous for fish, it must also be of great importance to humans as well.

You can laugh and point out that this theory is not new at all. It is true that in 1750 Dr. Richard Russell claimed that if a person took a dip in the ocean at Brighton, it would cure him of four hundred and four illnesses instantaneously. His claim, however, proved greatly exaggerated.

I know that sooner or later most of us cats will have the opportunity to go swimming at Kamakura, but, as of the moment, that time has not as yet come. As I have already pointed out, the Japanese people lived and died until as late as the Meiji Era without realizing the benefits they could receive from sea bathing; and so it is with us cats today—we have just not had the chance to take a dip in the ocean in our naked state. But, as the saying goes, " Haste makes waste." I don't believe that we cats should go blindly diving into the sea at present. The cats, for example, who have been taken to the Tsukiji canal to be thrown away still cannot find their way back home safely. We cats simply cannot go sea bathing until the laws of evolution prepare us to resist the mad and angry waves—in other words, until people say a cat has " risen " instead of saying that a cat has " died ".

Although I don't mean to go sea bathing until a much later date, I still feel that I should get some exercise. If you don't take exercise in the twentieth century, people are likely to consider you as being poor. They seem to believe that your remaining inactive is not because you don't want to exercise but because you can't afford it. In olden days, those who exercised were despised but now if you don't strain your muscles, you're considered as being inferior. Opinions are continually changing. The pupils of my eyes become small or big according to the time of day, but the changing appraisals of humans seem completely without reason.

But there are two sides to everything. Perhaps this illogic shows how well humans can adapt themselves to opposite conditions without much suffering.

Take, for instance, the written character for " ho-sun " (square inch; one's mind). When inverted, we read " sun-po " (measure; dimension). This is quite interesting as well as amusing. Again, look at the Amano Hashidate.* By peering at it upside down

---

* Amano Hashidate, literally the " Bridge of Heaven ", is one of the scenic wonders of Japan. A sandbar, 2 miles long and some 200 feet wide, it stretches across an inlet.

through parted legs, it produces a lovely picture which is altogether different from what is seen when standing in a normal position.

In the same way, it is not necessarily wise to always present Shakespeare's plays only as Shakespeare originally wrote them. At times, it might be a good idea to watch *Hamlet* while standing on our heads. Perhaps we would learn to criticize it better and there would be more progress in the literary world.

But humans are very adaptable to change so maybe that is why the people who talk most strongly against exercise suddenly begin to be the most enthusiastic about sports. My only hope is that no one will laugh at me for taking exercise or criticize me for being saucy. You might be wondering what exercise I take, but first let me do some explaining. Unfortunately, as you know, I cannot grasp anything heavy in my paws so it is impossible to pick up balls or to grip bats. Besides, I have no money so I cannot buy any equipment.

You might now be thinking that I go on long walks or that I run around with slices of tuna fish in my mouth—but no. That would be too simple and so not interesting at all. It wouldn't be much fun just to move my four legs on walks while letting them obey the force of gravity. This would belittle the sacredness of exercise, like my master generally does.

Of course there's no rule which definitely says that you have to have competition in sports. Dried-bonito races and salmon-hunting competitions are all splendid but those games can only be arranged after assembling the essential articles. Games that do not include competition usually demand greater skill.

I myself thought up many games. One was trying to leap from the edge of the kitchen eaves to the roof of the main house; another was to stand on all four legs on the plum-blossom-shaped tile ends of the roof. I also tried to walk along the bamboo laundry pole (this I could not do because it is so slippery), and to

---

Groves of pine trees bent into fantastic shapes by many wintry storms grow there. When seen from a mountain nearby, while bending over and looking at the spectacle upside down through the legs, the blue sea seems to become the sky and the sky the water. Japanese mythology relates that Izanagi and Izanami, the first male and female gods, stood there while they created the islands. of Japan.

jump suddenly up on a child's back from behind. This last-mentioned game was more fun than any other sport but I usually received a terrible scolding so I try it only about three times a month at the most. At times, a paper bag is put over my head but this game is only agonizing for me. Moreover, as it requires human participation, it isn't much of a success.

Ranking next as my favorite sport is to claw at book covers. This has the disadvantage of being too risky, because when my master catches me in the act he beats me unmercifully. Besides, it only offers exercise for my paws and does not benefit the rest of my body. I like to classify such a sport as old-fashioned.

Of my new sports, the first on the list is to hunt praying mantises. Mantis hunting is not as strenuous as rat hunting, but neither does it involve so many hazards. The best season for this game is from middle summer till early autumn.

As to the method of this game, first of all I go out to the yard and find a mantis. Although it depends on the weather, it's generally quite simple to find one or two. After seeing one, I rush it as fast as the wind. The mantis, sensing danger, will raise its head and get ready to protect itself. Mantises are rather bold, even when they don't know the strength of their foe. They're harmless but they put up a good fight so it's great fun.

After catching one, I place my right paw on its head. The head is soft and is generally cocked to one side. The mantis wears an especially interesting expression of surprise at this time. Then I jump around behind it and lightly claw its wings. The wings of a mantis are usually folded with great care so if I am too rough, they immediately become dishevelled and look like the yellowish transparent material used in making underwear. Even in the summertime, indifferent to the heat, the mantis neatly folds its wings around itself. It is like wearing a winter undershirt and long underpants in the hottest season.

With me behind, the head and long neck of the mantis usually turns toward me. At times, it attacks but generally it just holds this stance and waits for me to make the first move. If I maintained this position too long, it wouldn't give me any exercise, so I soon give the insect a swap. Any mantis that's intelligent would try to escape, but there are many highly uneducated and barbarous types that will now attack. If it happens to be one of the savage kind, I take a swing at it and knock it two or three feet away.

But if my playmate happens to have a milder nature and only retreats a couple of steps, I usually take pity on it and let it rest while I run up and around the other trees in the yard several times. The insect realizes that it has no chance in a fight and flutters to the left and to the right but I'm always right behind it. Sometimes a mantis will spread its wings in agony.

The wings of a mantis are like its neck in that they are extremely narrow. According to my understanding, the wings are only there for ornamental purposes—in other words, like the study of English, French and German for humans. They are not at all practical. When a mantis spreads its good-for-nothing wings, it is doing no good as far as its escape is concerned. Having wings sounds wonderful but actually those of the mantis only drag the owner along the ground as it walks. I often feel sorry for my prey but as it is essential for my exercise, I simply beg its pardon and run after it all the more.

The mantis cannot turn around easily so it usually keeps going straight ahead in its attempt to escape. I give it a tap on its nose, and the mantis spreads its wings and lies prostrate. Then I hold it flat against the ground with my forepaws and take a little rest. Suddenly I let go again, but not for long. I'm quick to press it flat once more. This is the strategy employed by the Chinese warlord K'ungming who let his foe escape seven times but then captured his adversary seven times.

After about thirty minutes of this, the mantis is exhausted so I pick it up in my mouth and shake it. After I let go, it lies on the ground unable to move. I give it a shove with my paw, and as it again tries to fly, I pounce on it once more. Being a little bored by the game by now, I simply commence to eat it. For those of you who haven't eaten mantises yet, I may as well admit that they're not very tasty. Nor are they especially nutritious, either.

Beside mantises, there are also cicadas to hunt. Not all the cicadas are the same. Just as there are the greasy, the arrogant, and the loud types among humans, you find the same peculiarities among cicadas. The greasy cicadas are literally very rich in oil. The arrogant cicadas are too proud and haughty, and are therefore a nuisance. The species that's most fun to catch is the *oshii-tsuku-tsuku* cicadas, the noisy kind.

I have to wait until late summer before they arrive. When the autumn wind begins to steal through your kimono sleeves and makes you start sneezing, that is the time these insects commence to sing by moving their tails up and down. And when it comes to singing, they really make a lot of noise! They seem to have no other object in life than to sing and to be caught by cats.

So in early autumn, I go about catching cicadas. It is here that I should explain that you won't find cicadas lying around on the ground. The only ones not in trees are those that ants have attacked. But the cicada that is the object of my game is certainly not the kind lying within the jurisdiction of ants! My prey is the cicada that clings to a branch of a high tree, singing out for all it is worth " *Oshii-tsuku-tsuku!* " By the way, I would like to ask you learned humans this question: how do cicadas really sing? Is it " *Oshii-tsuku-tsuku* " or " *Tsuku-tsuku-oshii* "? I believe there is still much research to be done on this insect. The reason humans consider themselves so superior to cats may lie in the fact that man supposedly knows all about such matters. But if you can give no immediate reply to this question, you'd better begin worrying more about your superiority. Considering cicadas as insects to be hunted, however, it really doesn't make much difference how they happen to sing. The trick is to climb a tree, track the cicada down by its song, and to catch one when it is in the middle of a shrill chorus. This may sound easy but actually it's quite difficult to accomplish.

I use all my four feet when traversing the good earth, so I do not feel inferior to any other animal. Considering the number of legs I possess, I know that I'm better off than humans—they have only two. But when it comes to climbing trees, there are many animals better equipped than I am. Monkeys are professional tree climbers but there are many descendants of monkeys and apes—humans—who still retain this skill. As climbing is against the law of gravity, not to be able to accomplish it should not cause anyone shame. But cicada hunting, even considered as an exercise, does have its inconveniences.

Fortunately, I have been given those sharp implements called claws so I can climb trees, one way or the other. But frankly speaking, it's not as easy as it may look and, besides, cicadas can fly. Different from mantises, once cicadas take wing, they make it impossible for me to follow. I often find myself in a sad plight, thinking that it would have been better if I hadn't bothered to climb the tree in the first place. Then, last but not least, there is the danger of being urinated on, and it almost seems that cicadas aim at my eyes. Of course, I understand their wanting to fly away, but I'd like to ask them not to make water when doing so. What is the psychological factor that effects a cicada's physiological organs and induces it to urinate when flying away? It is, most probably, caused by some pain. Or is it a way of gaining time, surprising its foes before its flight? If that is so, it would be the same as a squid which squirts black ink when in danger, or as a quick-tempered bully showing off his tattoos before coming to blows, or the same as my master who speaks in Latin when angered. This again, is another problem for researchers to deal with when studying the cicada. It might even win somebody a doctor's degree. But now let's get back to the main subject.

Cicadas concentrate—if you think my use of the word " concentrate " sounds funny, I could say " gather " but " gather " doesn't seem right so I'll stick to my first term—cicadas concentrate mostly on green paulownia trees. This might be a little technical but the green paulownia tree is called *wu t'ung* in Chinese. Its many leaves are as large as fans. When the leaves are thick, it's impossible to see the branches of the tree. This is naturally a great obstacle in cicada hunting. There's a song now popular that goes " Though the voice is heard, the figure doesn't appear." It is as if this had been especially written for cicadas, I'm afraid. Therefore, I can only track the insect by listening to its song.

All paulownia trees have a crotch in the main trunk, about six feet above the ground. After climbing this far, I generally rest and then commence searching. I must be careful because if one cicada takes flight, I am out of luck. The rest also fly away.

When it comes to imitating others, cicadas are not inferior to humans—they love to play "follow the leader." Sometimes when I've established myself in the crotch of a tree, I often find the entire paulownia enveloped in silence; and hard as I may look and listen, I don't find a single cicada around. I hardly ever feel like going down to repeat the whole performance after climbing this far, so I generally decide to stay where I am and wait for a second chance. Eventually I become sleepy and take a nap then and there. But, upon waking up, I usually find myself on a stepping stone at the base of the tree.

Yet I must average at least one cicada to each climb. The reason I prefer mantis hunting is that I have to grasp a cicada between my teeth in the tree, so by the time I reach the ground to play with the insect, it is dead.

But cicada hunting is not without its exciting moments. I stealthily creep up to one as it feverishly sings by drawing its tail in and out, and just as I pounce on it, the *tsuku-tsuku* cicada lets out a squeal and flutters its thin transparent wings in all directions. The speed at which all this happens is incredible, something that must be experienced to appreciate. The moribund flutter is indeed the most beautiful sight in the cicada world; and every time I trap one of these *tsuku-tsuku* cicadas, I thrill at this aesthetic performance. After witnessing this spectacle, I ask forgiveness and throw the insect into my mouth. At times, some of them continue to perform this aesthetic act even after they are inside.

The game that I like best next to cicada hunting is pine sliding. There's no need to make a lengthy explanation of this so I'll make it as simple as possible. When I say "pine sliding", you'll naturally presume I take slides down a pine tree, but actually it's more like tree "climbing". In cicada hunting, I climb trees mainly to catch insects but in pine sliding I climb trees with no other purpose beyond the ascent. This is the main difference between the two sports. It is said that Genzaemon Tsuneyo Sano once prepared a meal for a lay priest by the name of Sai-myoji in the days of Tokiyori Hojo (1226–1263). He cooked it using a treasured pine tree as fuel so it is said that this evergreen tree became extremely knotty. There's no tree that is so rough surfaced as a pine, and, therefore, there's no tree that's more clawable. In other words, there's no tree easier to climb.

In this game, I dash straight up the trunk and then come dashing down again. In descending, there are two methods. One is to return headfirst, facing the ground; the other is to go down in the same position as climbing up, or backwards.

Now I'd like to ask you humans another question: which do you think would be the most difficult of the two? Like most shallow-brained humans, you will probably say that it would be much easier to descend headfirst. Well, that's where you're wrong. You're probably thinking of Yoshitsune instead of cats. Yoshitsune was the famous warrior who drove his horse over Hiyodorigoe Cliff to win a battle. Do you really think that it would be proper for cats to go headfirst, too? Nothing could be more insulting!

You may already know how the claws of a cat grow, but I'll tell you anyway: they grow with the points curving backwards. That's why we can pull objects towards us so easily, like using a fireman's hook; but when it comes to pushing, we are often quite clumsy.

Let's imagine now that I've just dashed up the trunk of a pine tree. As a cat is an animal born to walk on the ground, it is only natural that I cannot maintain my perch long. If I don't take any action, I will begin to slide down. If I didn't try to break the fall, I would be sure to get hurt. Therefore I must do something to reach the ground safely.

There is a great difference between falling down and going down, but not always as great as it may sound at first. If the descent is slow; it's " going down ", but if the " going down " is too fast, it's "falling" The difference lies in a wee bit of reasoning. As I don't like falling down from a pine tree, I try to descend by slackening my speed. In other words, I try to do something to check the downward motion.

As I have already mentioned, all of my claws turn backwards so when I place my paws skyward and stick the claws out, I can slacken the speed. And thus " falling " becomes " going down ". This is comprehensive reasoning.

But if I took the opposite position and tried going down the trunk in the Yoshitsune style, or headfirst, the claws would be useless. I'd slip with nothing to check the speed of my heavy body. In any case, I sometimes go down headfirst intentionally so therefore I am literally falling down. It is quite difficult to go down headfirst, as Yoshitsune must have found out on Hiyodori-goe Cliff. I believe that of all cats, I'm the only one that can accomplish this feat. I have therefore named this sport as I please: pine sliding.

I'd also like to say a few words about " going around the fence ", one more form of taking exercise. The fence all around my master's house is made of bamboo and it forms a rectangle. The sides parallel to the veranda are probably between forty-eight and fifty-four feet long, while the other sides only measure about twenty-one feet. What I term as the " going-around-the-fence " sport is to circle the whole fence without falling off. It is true that I often fall off, but when I'm able to make a complete trek, I feel satisfied to the utmost.

There are several cryptomeria stakes supporting the bamboo lattice work of the fence. The lower halves of the poles have been burnt so as to prevent their rotting, but on top they are convenient places to take rests.

The other day I was in exceptionally good form so I was able to repeat my trek three times before noon. The more I practiced, the better I became. And the better I got, the more interesting I found the sport. I was halfway around on my fourth trip when three crows came flying from the roof of the neighboring house and settled in a neat row about three yards ahead of me.

Rather unexpected visitors, and great obstacles to my game! They had no right to come perching on somebody else's fence, so I hissed at them: " I'm coming. You'd better get out of my way."

The crow nearest me just looked my way and grinned; the one in the middle simply stared into my master's yard; and the third bird only continued to sharpen its beak on the bamboo fence. It most probably had some food in its mouth.

I gave them three minutes to leave and stood there waiting. I have always known that crows possess very bad memories, but this was the first time to find this theory true. They had no memory at all! I waited for a long time but the crows didn't speak to me or fly away. So I started walking ahead again.

The crow right in front of me spread its wings just a little. "Haa! Now he's afraid and is going to fly!" Or so I thought. Instead, it just hopped up and round-about-faced itself.

Stupid! If this had happened on the ground, I wouldn't have let it get away with such impudence. Unfortunately, however, just plain walking on a fence is difficult enough—chasing birds would be almost impossible. Still, I didn't feel like waiting until the three crows decided to take flight. In the first place, my legs wouldn't have lasted much longer. The three creatures in front of me, however, had wings so they are used to perching on such places and can stay put as long as they want.

As this was my fourth trip around the fence I felt pretty nearly all in. I was doing something similar to tightrope walking besides exercising. It was difficult to stay on the fence even with nothing hindering me, so having these three black-cloaked feathered idiots come to obstruct my path was too much. I was afraid I'd have to quit exercising and get down from the fence.

To avoid trouble, I wondered if it might be better to simply give up. The enemy had me outnumbered and, moreover, they do not come here often. The beak of a crow is rather pointed so these birds seemed as if they had been sent by Tengu, the goblin with a long nose. They would naturally be dangerous in a fight.

Retreat was the wisest action to take. To start a fight and then accidentally fall off would be terribly embarrassing. While I was pondering on what I should do, the one nearest me burst out: "Aho!"* The next one imitated the first, repeating, "Aho!" The other crow even took the trouble to shriek two times: "Aho, aho!"

---

* "Aho", the cry of a crow, means "fool" in Japanese.

The force of the wind from their wings suddenly caught me
in the face and a moment later I lost my foothold
and fell to the ground.

Even a gentle cat such as I could not stand this! To be insulted by these crows in my own yard was unforgivable and it affected my very honor. You might say that this couldn't hurt me since I don't have any other name in the first place. But my honor and dignity were involved. Now I would never retreat!

When my master talks about " a flock of crows ", he is referring to " a disorderly crowd " or " mere rabble ", so I decided these three birds might be less dangerous than I had thought. Determined to protect my good name, I commenced walking slowly forward. It seemed as if the crows were talking among themselves because they didn't even glance at me. It was extremely irritating. If the fence had only been five or six inches wider, I'd have been able to give them a good fight. Unfortunately, however, I could only creep along at a slow pace no matter how angry I was. When I was about five or six inches from them, all the crows suddenly flapped their wings and flew up one or two feet in the air, as if by previous arrangement.

The force of the wind from their wings suddenly caught me in the face and a moment later I lost my foothold and fell to the ground. Looking up from the foot of the fence, I saw the three crows still on their perch looking down at me with their beaks in a neat row.

The brutes! I glared at them but it did not have any effect. I bristled my back and snarled, but that didn't work either. Just as symbolical poems are not understood by laymen, neither were my gestures of anger understood by the crows—they showed no reaction.

Well, perhaps it was my own fault. I had been thinking of them as cats but that was wrong. If they had been cats, the crows would have naturally understood—but they were only crows. It was like a businessman trying to impress my master, Mr. Kushami, or like Shogun Yoritomo presenting Bonze Saigyo with a silver cat. It was also like crows letting their droppings fall on the statue of Takamori Saigo. I at last realized that it was to my disadvantage to persist so without more ado, I retreated to the veranda.

It was almost suppertime. Exercise is good but it shouldn't be overdone. I now felt weak and anxious to rest. Besides, my encounter with the crows took place in early autumn and, as I had been in the sun for a long time, my fur coat had absorbed too much heat from the westbound sun. It was unbearably hot. I kept wishing that the sweat that came out of my pores would run, but no! It only stuck to the roots of my fur like grease. My back felt itchy. This itchiness is quite different from the irritation I have when fleas are crawling around. I can bite at the parts that can be reached with my mouth and I can scratch the places I can reach with my paws, but when the center of my spine becomes itchy, it is beyond the limits of my power to do much about it myself. When it becomes unbearable, I seek out a human and furiously rub myself against him, or I go to a pine tree and give myself a good rubdown; if I don't find relief, I feel uncomfortable and cannot sleep.

Humans are fools. When I purr—now wait, this is the expression humans use. I prefer to say that they are being purred at. In any case, humans are such fools that when they are purred at by me, they mistakenly think that I love them dearly and they do whatever I want them to do. At times, they stroke my head.

But last summer, those little pests called fleas began to inhabit me. They multiplied in my fur so much that when I went close to a human, I was generally grabbed by the neck and flung away. I was avoided only because of these fleas, so little that they can hardly be seen. By this, it would not be altogether wrong to say that the sentiments of humans are only skin deep and tend to change abruptly according to the circumstances. Though there were just a measly one or two thousand of these fleas on my back, it was amazing how calculating humans acted. The first article in the law of love as practiced by them is: love others only when it brings personal benefit.

My appeal to humans, having suddenly changed, made it impossible for me to utilize them any more when the itching became unbearable so I had no choice but to take up the pine-bark massage method. That day, thinking that I might as well try rubbing myself against a pine tree, I was about to descend from the veranda but stopped. I suddenly realized that the disadvantages out-weighed the benefits I would receive.

There is resin in pine trees. This resin is extremely sticky and once it attaches itself to my fur it will never come off—even if it thundered or even if the whole Russian Baltic Fleet were com-pletely annihilated. Once the resin glues five strands of fur together, it soon spreads to ten and then thirty. I am a cat of fine tastes, and I detest feeling sticky. I would dislike the prettiest cat in the world if she were sticky. I hate to be tangled up in resin. It would be terrible for me to ruin this light-gray fur coat of mine with resin which is just like mucus running from the eyes of Kuro, the black cat of the rickshawman, when the north wind blows.

It would be a disgrace to even consider being so indiscreet with my fur. Though I found myself itching like anything, I was afraid I would have to endure it.

It was exceedingly disheartening. If the irritation didn't stop, I might become ill. I bent my hind legs and began to think of a solution and all at once a plan occurred to me.

There are times when my master leaves the house with a towel and a cake of soap. When he returns thirty or forty minutes later, his hazy face is tinged with vigor and seems to beam. If a bath can affect my dirty master so favorably, it was bound to have its effects on me, too. As I am quite good looking without the help of make-up, there is no need for me to go to further pains as far as my appearance is concerned. But if I became sick and died at the tender age of one year and a few months, I would be committing an unexcusable crime to the populace of the world.

I learned that the place my master visited was called a public bathhouse and that it was devised by humans to while away their time also—or so it seems. As the bath was made by humans, I felt it was bound to be quite worthless but I could think of no other way to stop the itching on this occasion. If it didn't have any beneficial effects, all I had to do was to quit. But I wondered if the humans would let a cat, a specimen quite different from themselves, into a place made for their own pleasure. This was a grave question. But if my master could enter the place easily, there was no reason why I should be refused. If I were to be thrown out, however, it would be bad for my reputation. Therefore I thought it best to go and look the place over first. If it seemed permissible, I would later take a towel in my mouth and go for a dip in the bath myself.

Turning left from the back alley, I had often seen an object that looked like a big bamboo drain pipe. It stood upright and some light smoke poured out. This was, I decided, the public bath.

I first sneaked into the back alley. Some of you readers might say that entering a place through the rear is cowardly or unmanly but it might possibly be an act envied by those who cannot enter other than from the front entrance. It is said that a wise man enters unexpectedly from the rear, and this is stated on page 5 of Chapter I of the second volume of *Gentlemen Training*. On the other side of this page, it mentions that the wise gentleman in training should even leave a note behind stating that entering the back door is a way to gain virtue. As I am a cat living in the twentieth century, I naturally possess knowledge about such matters so you needn't eye me with contempt.

Having sneaked into the place, I found, on the left side, a mountain of split pine wood, each stick about eight inches long. A hill of coal was next to it. Some of you might wonder why I use "mountain" to describe a pile of wood and "hill" for a heap of coal, but actually it is only to show off my command of the language. Humans need rice, birds, fish and other animals in order to stay alive. It seemed now that they had become so degraded as to even graft coal. How miserable!

Toward the rear of the blind alley, I saw an open door. Peeping in, I found an empty room as quiet as a graveyard. From the opposite side, however, I detected an incessant buzzing of human voices. I concluded that the bath must be where the voices originated, so I turned left, passed through the valley between the wood and coal, and found a glass window to my right. Below it, I saw some small round wooden tubs piled up to form a pyramid. That the round wash tubs should be stacked in a triangle must have been much against the will of the small pails; I sympathized with them. To the south of this triangular pile

[231]

was a boarded floor, four or five feet square, which seemed to exist only to make it easier for me to enter. The platform was about one meter above the ground, just right for me to hop onto.

I jumped lightly up on the boards and was then surprised to find the bath right in front of my nose—right under my eyes. Now what's most interesting is to taste what you haven't as yet tasted, and to see what you haven't as yet seen. The view might not be so fascinating for those of you who, like my master, go to the public bathhouse three times a week to soak yourselves for thirty or forty minutes but if you have never seen a public bath, I advise you to go as soon as you can. Even if you can't find it possible to be at your parents' deathbed, you should, by all means, visit the public bath at least once. Wide is the world, but a spectacular sight like this is without comparison.

What's so special about it? Well, that's somewhat embarrassing to explain. The noisy humans I saw through the windowpane were crowded together and, one and all, were stark naked. They might have been aborigines of Formosa, the Adams of the twentieth century. It would take too long to pursue the history of clothing so I'll leave that to Teufelsdröckh. I'll omit it here, but it's a fact that humans maintain their right to be called human mostly because of their clothing. During the eighteenth century, Beau Nash proclaimed a strict regulation for those soaking themselves in the spa of Bath in Great Britain: all men and women had to cover themselves from their shoulders to their feet while in the water.

Sixty years ago in another city in England, an art school was being planned. Sketches of nudes and models of nude statues were purchased and placed here and there. This was all very natural but just before the opening·ceremony, the staff members found this embarrassing because the ladies of the city were of course invited. In those days, ladies believed that man was primarily a being to be clothed and did not consider him as a descendant of furred-skin monkeys. They felt that a man without his clothing was like an elephant minus his trunk, a school without pupils or a soldier lacking courage. In other words, clothing was definitely an essential part of man. Once deprived of this necessary wrapping, man was not accepted as a human being, but as a beast. Even if the exhibits were only copies and models, humans shown as beasts was too much and the ladies refused to attend the inaugural ceremony of the new school.

Though the school authorities thought them a trying lot, women in the West, like in the East, are a necessary decoration at such functions. Women cannot always become good workers to refine rice by pounding nor can they become soldiers, but they are necessary ornaments at opening ceremonies of schools. Therefore, thirty-six bolts of black cloth were purchased and all the models of human beasts were draped with it. So that the ladies would not be insulted in the least, even the faces were covered. And after this, the ceremony was held without mishap.

So, as you can see, clothes are important to humans. Nowadays, there are some art teachers who go about repeatingly stressing the value of nude pictures, but that's evidently a mistake.

As for myself, I have never been naked, not even once since I was born so, if you ask me, I'll say that nudity is wrong. Nakedness became a fad in Greece and Rome soon after the Renaissance. The Greeks and Romans were accustomed to naked bodies and no question regarding public morals ever arose. But northern Europe is a cold place. You cannot walk outdoors in a naked state even in Japan, and you'd freeze to death in Germany or England. As it's senseless to die, what do you do?—you put on clothes. And if all humans wear clothing then man becomes a being of clothes. As a being of clothes, you wouldn't consider a naked person as human—you'd think of him as a beast. Therefore it is understandable that nude pictures and statues of Europeans, especially those of northern Europe, used to be considered as of beasts. Yes, they might have acknowledged these beasts as being inferior even to cats.

Beautiful? Did you say beautiful? Never mind—consider them as beautiful but still as beasts. When I say this, some of you might ask whether I've ever seen a European lady in a formal evening dress. Well, being a Japanese cat, I've never actually seen one; but I understand that they have their bosoms uncovered, their shoulders bare and their arms naked. And they call this a formal dress! It's outrageous! Up till the fourteenth century, human attire was not so comical; clothing was simply worn for protection. I won't take the trouble here to explain how fashionable clothes became as vulgar as those of an acrobat, but those who know will understand—and those who don't needn't worry.

Leaving history out, women today dress themselves up in extremely odd fashions, especially during the evening. They seem to have some queer human ideas because when the sun rises and it becomes light, not only do those same ladies cover their shoulders, hide their bosoms, put a wrap over their arms and conceal all parts of their bodies but they also consider it awful to show even a toenail to others. It can therefore be understood that this regulation concerning dresses was decided on by a group of fools. If any fashionable people are mortified by my saying this, they can go about with their shoulders, bosoms and arms bare during the day for all I care. If they like to be naked so much, they might also have their daughters become nudists and take them for walks in Ueno Park.

What? You say you can't do that? No, it's not possible but probably only because Westerners haven't walked around naked in Ueno Park as yet. But just look at yourselves at present; you ladies dream of wearing this extremely absurd evening dress and pompously going to the Imperial Hotel. In seeking a logical reason for this, there is none whatsoever. It's only that you want to wear such clothes because Western ladies do. Because the Westerners are powerful, I guess you can't stand it unless you imitate them, whether it's beyond your income or not. But maybe it's only because of being stupid. Yield to the powerful and yield to the rich—sure, but it's not sensible to be always yielding. If you can't help being so foolish, I can forgive you; but this should prove that the Japanese people are really not superbly smart. This imitation is the same even in scholastic studies, but as it does not concern clothing, I'll omit the explanation.

Clothes have become so important to humans that it is difficult to tell whether it's a case of humans and their clothing or clothing and its humans. It seems as if the history of mankind lies not so much in the history of their flesh, their bones, or in their blood, but in the history of their clothing. When I see a person without his clothes, he does not impress me as being human. It gives me the feeling of having met a goblin. If everybody decided to become a goblin, it would be all right with me because goblins are creatures that are vanishing. But then, of course, that would be of great inconvenience to humans.

Right from the beginning, Nature creates humans as equals and throws them out into the world. Every one of them is born stark naked. If mankind were truly content with equality, it would be proper, and perfectly suitable, to continue living in this naked state.

But once one of these naked individuals probably appeared and said, " Hmmm. If everybody is the same, it is worthless to live." So he began thinking of how he could make himself noticed, of how he could make others recognize him as an individual. He wanted to do something startling to attract attention.

And so, after a decade of hard thinking, he probably hit upon an idea—a pair of shorts. He put them on, and look! Everyone else was greatly awed as he proudly walked around in his new drawers. Such an individual might have been the ancestor of rickshawmen who today wear tight shorts. That it took ten long years to design a simple pair of shorts might sound somewhat queer, but we should imagine ourselves as being in those dark ages so we can understand the difficulties of such a creation. In those days, there was probably no discovery greater than this. They say that it took Descartes more than ten years to conceive his theory of " *Je pense, donc je suis* "—" I think therefore I am " —a truth that even a three-year-old child can understand.

Inventions involve a great deal of hard work so if ten years were spent in designing a pair of shorts, they are much too good for mere rickshawmen. Afterwards, other goblins, roused by a spirit of competition and envious of the rickshawmen who haughtily stalked the universal roads in their shorts, most likely spent another six years to devise the *haori* coat, an article of clothing worse than useless. Soon the vogue of shorts suddenly decreased and we entered into the golden age of *haori* coats.

Clerks in vegetable stalls, in drug stores and in dry goods stores were all enthusiastic about this big discovery of *haori* coats; but then came the period of the *hakama*, the divided skirt worn over a kimono for formal men's wear. This invention must have been made in a fit of passion by those who were enraged at the popularity of the *haori* coats. Warriors of old and government officials of today belong to this group. Other goblins, trying to be different by competing in even newer creations, finally arrived at the freakish swallowtail.

In considering the reason for these changes in fashion, they were not made under pressure; nor did they simply happen. All of them were made with the definite aim of showing that the owners were better than anyone else. These absurd costumes are now worn to show what and who the possessor is. In this way an individual does not have to go around boasting about his own importance. We can arrive at an interesting theory from this pyschological phenomenon.

Just as nature abhors a vacuum, man dislikes equality. Avoiding equality, humans now cover their bodies as if their clothing were their very bones and flesh. So important are clothes today that only a madman would discard them and return to impartial nudity. Those who try to return are considered eccentrics by civilized people. Even if it were decided that the many hundreds of millions of people of the world were equal and that their clothes should be discarded, it still wouldn't work: the day after everybody refrained from covering the body, competition would again begin. If they could not compete in clothes, then humans would compete as eccentrics. Stark naked humans would continue forever to point out admirable traits in their bodies, even in their nakedness. So, considering the problem from this aspect, clothing and fashions are things indispensable.

But now, in the public bath, right before my eyes, there was a group of humans who had taken off their shorts, *haori* coats and *hakama* skirts and had placed them on a shelf. And with no embarrassment at all of their original shameful appearances, they were nonchalantly indulging in pleasant chats. This is what I meant a little while ago by a spectacular sight. It is here that

I have the honor to introduce to you civilized readers a part of what I saw.

Everything was in such a topsy-turvy state that I don't know how to begin explaining it. As eccentrics are not very systematic, it will take a great deal of hard work to describe the scene. I'll start with the bath tank first. To tell the truth, I don't know for sure if it's called a tank or not, but it's the only word I can think of. The width was about three feet and the length about nine. It was divided in the middle by a vertical board. One half was full of milky hot water, claimed to be medicinal. It was as if lime has been dissolved in it. The liquid looked not only dirty but oily and thick. And no wonder! According to what I've heard, the water is only changed once a week.

The other half contained ordinary hot water but I cannot swear that it was pure either. Judging from the color, it was about as clear as a barrel of churned rain water.

Yes, let me tell you, it's really hard work to describe it all. In this tank, two young eccentrics were standing up, facing each other and splashing water on each other's belly. Maybe it was a game. The fact that both of them were sunburned almost black is something I am at a loss to understand, but they looked rather robust. One of them, wiping his chest with a cotton towel, said to the other, "Kin, this side here hurts a little. I wonder what it is." His friend, Kin, answered, "That's your stomach. Be careful. Sometimes a bad stomach can ruin your life." He was giving this advice very seriously.

"Oh? But it's here, on the left," said the first fellow, pointing to his left lung.

"Sure, that's your stomach; the stomach's on the left and the lung's on the right."

"Hmmm. I thought the stomach was somewhere around here." And so saying, he patted his abdomen.

At this Kin suggested, "Then maybe it's lumbago."

Just then a young man about twenty-five or -six with a thin moustache jumped into the tank with a splash. The soap suds which had covered his body came floating to the surface of the water together with the dirt. The water glittered like some metallic liquid. Next to him was a baldheaded man talking with a fellow who wore a half-inch haircut. They had only their heads above the water.

"You know, it's a shame to grow old. Once you're spent, you don't stand a chance against the young people. But whatever the case, as far as baths are concerned, I don't like them unless they're hot."

"You look as if you're still strong and healthy."

"I'm not young any more but I don't often get sick. If we take care of ourselves, we can live to be a hundred and twenty."

"Do you mean to live that long?"

"Of course! At least a hundred and twenty. Before the Meiji era, a retainer of a shogun, called Magaribuchi, lived in Ushigome. And one of his servants reached the age of a hundred and thirty, I hear."

"That's a long time!"

"Uhuh. He lived so long that he even forgot his exact age. He said he had remembered how old he was until his hundredth birthday but couldn't keep track of the rest. I knew him when he was a hundred and thirty but, mind you, he didn't die at that age. I don't know what has become of him; as a matter of fact, he might still be alive." With this, the baldheaded man pulled himself out of the tank. The fellow with the moustache stayed in the hot water, scattering glittering foam and grinning to himself.

The next eccentric to enter the tank had, unlike the others, tattoos all over his back. The pattern showed Jutaro Iwami, a warrior with uplifted sword, about to slay a python. But unfortunately, the picture was incomplete for the python could nowhere be seen. Lord Jutaro seemed a little disheartened. This person, as soon as he jumped in, complained, "Oh, it's only lukewarm!"

A younger man came into the tank right after him and also exclaimed, "This ought to be a little hotter!" But he had an expression that said it was already too hot. He then looked up into the face of "Jutaro" and said, "Oh, hello, boss."

"Jutaro" returned the greeting and then asked, "Whatever

became of Tami?"

"You know, that Tami is terribly rude."

"Yes, I know."

"He doesn't even try to be nice. I don't know why, but people just don't like him. I don't know why, but nobody trusts him. Workingmen shouldn't be that way really."

"Tami's not the obliging kind. He's too proud. That's why people don't trust him."

"That's right. He thinks he's better than anyone else."

"All the old folks around Shirokane-cho have died. You and I and Moto, the bathtub maker, and that fellow who owns the brick plant are the only ones left who were born here. Take Tami for instance. Who knows where he came from?"

"That's true. It's surprising the way he's come as far as he has.

"But nobody likes him. Nobody even talks with him. Did you know that?"

But let's forget these attacks on Tami so I can finish my explanation. The tank with the milky water was packed so tightly that instead of saying that people were in the bath, it would be more appropriate to say that hot water was added to a tank of individuals. Everyone seemed self-composed and relaxed, however. Though there were more and more eccentrics getting into the tank, no one seemed to leave. Since the water is not changed for a week running, it is no wonder that it was dirty. The spectacle filled me with awe. Looking around, I discovered Mr. Kushami, red as a boiled octopus, tight against the left corner of the tank.

Poor thing! I couldn't help wishing that someone would move and give him a little more room so he could get out. But no one did. My master didn't seem to object, however, but he kept getting redder than ever. This must have been a terrible ordeal. Maybe he was trying to get the most out of the two-and-a-half-sen bath fee, but even so I felt worried about him as I looked from the shelf by the window. If he didn't get out of the tank soon, he'd become sick.

A fellow in the tank next to my master was saying while knitting his brows, " It seems to be a little too hot, don't you think? The hot water is pouring out right behind me." He was trying to obtain the sympathy of the other eccentrics around him.

" But this is just about the right temperature," explained one of his follow bathers. " Medicinal baths should be this hot or they don't have any effect. Why, back in my home town, the baths are twice as hot as this."

" What's this medicine good for, anyway? " asked a man who had covered his unevenly shaped head with a cotton towel.

" It's good for various illnesses. They say it's effective against all diseases." This was uttered by a fellow who had the complexion and the shape of a slender cucumber. It seemed to me at the time that if the medicinal bath was effective, he himself should have been much more healthy.

" It seems the chemicals in the water are most effective three or four days after they're first put into the bath. Today it should be just about right," commented a fat individual as if he knew everything.

Perhaps he was fat due to his layers of dirt.

A whining voice was then heard asking, " Is it effective to drink it? "

" When it's especially cold, drink a cupful before you go to bed. You'll be amazed! You won't even have to get up and go to the toilet at night. Try it once." I couldn't find the face of the person that made this reply.

I guess I have told you enough about the medicinal bath but now let me describe the part of the room where the bathers scrubbed themselves before entering the tubs. The group of Adams squatting on the slats did not make a very good picture but there they were washing their bodies, all in different positions. The most amazing was the Adam who lay flat on his back looking up at the high skylight. Another eccentric nearby was on his stomach looking down between the slats of the floor boards. Both of them must have been Adams with a great deal of leisure. There was also a baldhead who sat facing the stone wall with a little, baldheaded apprentice standing behind him, fervently pounding his back. There seemed to be a relation of master and pupil between them, the younger acting the part of a bathhouse attendant.

A true bathhouse attendant was there, however, going around massaging people on request and looking after them in general. He must have had a cold that day for he was wearing a padded vest though it was terribly hot in the place. Right now he was dashing hot water from an oval tub, exclusively used by him, on one of the patrons. He held a camlet washrag in the big toe of his right foot. Nearby was a fellow who greedily monopolized three small tubs while carrying on a lengthy conversation with the person next to him. He would occasionally stop his story to urge his friend to use his cake of soap. Wondering what he was talking about, I listened:

"Yes, guns were brought to Japan from abroad. In my day, it was all sword fighting. You see, foreigners are cowards so they invented a way to fight from a distance. I don't believe that guns came from China—it must have been from some other country. They didn't have them in Watonai's period. After all, Watonai was one of the Seiwa Genjis, a family of vigorous warriors. Many years ago, when Yoshitsune crossed over to Manchuria from Ezo, he took a learned man, a native of Ezo, with him. Yoshitsune's son attacked the Great Ming of China. The Great Ming was invincible so according to the learned man's advice, he dispatched a delegate to the Third Shogunate asking for a loan of three thousand warriors. The Third Shogunate wouldn't permit the messenger to return—can't remember his name—well, anyway, he was held prisoner for a couple of years. He married a courtesan in Nagasaki and the child born from this wedlock was Watonai. After returning to his own country, the delegate found that the Great Ming had been overthrown by the rebels." I couldn't understand what he was talking about at all so I turned my attention elsewhere.

Right behind him was a man of about twenty-five or -six, with a melancholy face. He was gently massaging his lower parts with the milky hot water. He might have been suffering from a tumor or some such sickness. Beside him were two young eccentrics about seventeen or eighteen who talked very fast in the latest slang. They must have been students of the school in the neighborhood. Beyond them, I saw a queer looking back. The bones along the spine showed distinctly, and looked as if a bamboo pole had been rammed up the owner's posterior. On each side of the backbone were four spots, in neat parallel rows, like stones laid out for a game of *juroku musashi*. The spots were inflamed and some had pus around them. It would be impossible to write about everything I saw; it is not in my ability to explain even a small part.

I was beginning to feel somewhat disgusted for having even started such an adventure when, from the door of the bath, a baldheaded gentleman of about seventy suddenly entered. He was wearing a light yellow kimono and he kept bowing reverently to the naked eccentrics: "Thank you, everyone, for patronizing my bath. It is a little cold today, so I hope you'll take advantage of the medicinal water to warm yourselves. You, bath attendant! See whether the water is hot enough." To this, the bath attendant breathed a long sigh of assent.

"He's very kind, isn't he? Of course you have to be obliging to carry on a business successfully," said the Watonai individual, praising the old proprietor.

I was greatly surprised by the sudden appearance of this queer old man. Though I would like to pause a little to tell you more about the bath, it might be better to describe this old man exclusively for a while.

The old gentleman happened to see a little boy about four years old who had just come out from the hot water tank. He put his hands out and cooed, "Come, baby. Come here." The child was probably frightened at seeing the old man whose face was like a squashed rice cake stuffed with bean paste, so the infant commenced to cry. The old gentleman murmured with some reluctance, "Oh, so you have to cry! Afraid of an old man, are you? Well, well!" As the child was now out of control, he switched his attention to the father of the baby: "Hello. A little cold today, isn't it? Don't you think the robber who entered Omiya's house last night was stupid? He cut a square hole in the side door but left without taking anything. He must have seen a policeman or a night watchman." He was smiling with pity at the foolishness of the reckless intruder. But suddenly he addressed another customer. "It's cold, isn't it? Being so young, you probably don't feel it." The bathhouse owner, so old himself, was really the only one who felt the cold.

I was so absorbed in this old man that I not only forgot about the other eccentrics but even about my master who I believed to be still agonizing in his cramped position. All at once, however, I heard a shout. It came, without a doubt, from none other than Mr. Kushami himself. My master has an extremely loud voice and it is so hoarse that it is always awful to hear. Hearing it in these strange surroundings, however, came as a terrible shock.

For an instant, I believed that my master had stayed too long in the tank and had gone mad. If it were madness, there would have been nothing to criticize, but I soon found that he still had his usual possession of his senses. Acting unlike most grown-ups, my master had picked a quarrel with a little schoolboy sitting next to him on the slat-covered floor.

"Move! Move over a little! Your water is splashing into my wash tub." The person doing the yelling was, of course, my master. You can interpret the situation in any way you wish. Perhaps one man in ten thousand would compare this incident with Hikokuro Takayama's reprimanding a bandit. My master might have actually acted with that intention; but as the schoolboy was not a bandit, it was difficult for my master to achieve the anticipated results.

Turning his head, the schoolboy quietly insisted, "I was here before you came." This was a plain, honest answer which implied that the schoolboy had no intention of moving away. But this was not what my master had anticipated. The quiet courtesy and the speech of this schoolboy was admirable. Even if my master had gone mad, he should have acknowledged this.

Actually my master had not yelled at the schoolboy because of the splashed water. No—the real reason was that my master had been listening to the somewhat arrogant conversation of the two boys. He considered such talk unbecoming to juveniles and he felt extremely offended. He was taking his wrath out on these boys.

"Idiot! Do you always go around splashing dirty water into other people's tubs?" shouted my master again. As I detest these young imps myself, I felt like shouting in delight. But still, my master's tone was provocative enough, especially for a schoolteacher.

My master has always been too rigid. He is as crusty as coke and terribly intolerant besides. Long, long ago, when Hannibal was crossing the Alps, he found a big rock which blocked the progress of his army. Hannibal poured vinegar over the stone, built a fire under it, and made the rock soft. He then had this boulder sawed into sections, as if cutting boiled fish-paste, and, in this way, allowed his army to pass without mishap. People like my master could soak themselves in a medicinal bath forever but still not become softened. Perhaps vinegar should be poured over him and then burned. I'm afraid, however, my master could never be cured of his rashness.

People who soak themselves in hot baths and those who lounge about in the steam make up a special type of eccentrics. After taking off their clothes, things essential to civilized men, they cannot be fairly judged by established and universal rules. It doesn't make much difference what they do. It doesn't make any difference whether the stomach is where the lung should be, or whether Watonai is a Seiwa Genji or if Tami is untrustworthy. But once they emerge from the washroom and enter the dressing room, they are goblins no longer. They step into the world where ordinary humans live. They now wear clothes and therefore have to conduct themselves like other humans again.

My master was now standing at the threshold between the washroom and the dressing room. In other words, he was standing on the brink of the common world—a place where he would have to express his feelings without harshness. That my master remained unchanged even at such a boundary, is proof of the fact that he is a prisoner of his own stubborness. He is incurable. According to my humble theory, there is only one way of helping my master recover from this illness: have the principal of the school fire him. Once discharged he would begin to drift. He is not a versatile person so drifting along, he would eventually die. My master enjoys being sick but he greatly dislikes the thought of dying. He wants the luxury of being an invalid but not of being sick enough to die. If he were told that his illness were fatal, he, being timid, would most probably tremble. And, I believe, while trembling, his illness would completely disappear. If I am mistaken, then that's the end of Mr. Kushami.

Though he may be an idiot and an invalid, he is still my master. There was once a poet who wrote a long poem praising a lord who had entertained him one day. Likewise, a cat sometimes feels sentimental about its master. As sympathy for my master filled my heart, I was unconsciously drawn toward him. I was so attracted that I neglected to observe the bath but, all of a sudden, abusive voices were heard from the water tank. Thinking that it might be a fight, I looked and found so many eccentrics inside that there was no room left for another person. Hairy shins and hairless thighs pressed firmly against each other.

It was early evening and the washroom was filled with steam all the way up to the ceiling. The eccentrics could only be dimly seen crowding against each other. "It's too hot! It's too hot!" The shouts pierced my ears and crisscrossed my mind. Some of the voices whined, some sulked, some screamed and others demanded. They blended together to produce a sound difficult to express. It was a noise possible only in the confusion of the public bath—one which would never be heard outside. I felt dazed and hypnotized to the spot.

When the confused shouting had reached its peak, a great big fellow suddenly stood up from within the swarm of goblins swaying pell-mell. He was at least three inches taller than the rest and, besides, he had an enormous beard. It was difficult to tell whether he had grown whiskers on his face or if his face was only a secondary feature of his whiskers. With a voice like midday thunder, he shouted, "Hey! It's too hot! Pour some cold water in!" The room all at once became silent, as if everyone there had become a part of this giant. A superman! Nietzsche's superman? He's a king of goblins, the leader of the eccentrics! As I was lost in admiration, another voice came from the rear of the hot water tank, answering, "All right." The room was so full of steam that at first I couldn't distinguish the owner of the voice. But then, I saw the bath attendant, still in his padded vest, throw another lump of coal into the furnace as if he meant to crack it asunder.

This lump of coal commenced crackling in the fire and lit up the bath attendant's face. At the same time, the brick wall behind him showed in the dark as if it were on fire. I became a little afraid, so I hastily jumped down from the window and returned home. On my way, I thought about my adventure. From among the naked eccentrics who had taken off their *haori* coats, their shorts and their split *hakama* skirts in an endeavor to become equal, a naked hero appeared and overwhelmed all the others. Equality cannot be obtained even in a state of nudity.

Arriving home, I found everything peaceful. My master, his face still lustrous from his bath, was eating supper. Upon seeing me jump up onto the veranda, he grunted, " What a lucky cat! I wonder where it's been."

I saw two or three different side dishes on the table, though I do not know how they had the money to buy so many. One of the servings was of broiled fish. I didn't know what kind of a fish it was, but it had probably met its fate some time yesterday near Odaiba in Shinagawa Bay. I once mentioned that fish are healthy but when they're cooked, they invite pity. It would be much better to fall ill and die a natural death. I took my place beside the table, sat down, and pretended not to look at the fish though I was actually waiting for a chance to snatch it. If I didn't have this technique, I would have to give up hope of ever receiving anything good to eat.

My master poked the fish with his chopsticks, tasted it, and made a face. He put his chopsticks down. The Mrs. who sat opposite him silently surveyed with interest how her husband maneuvered his chopsticks and the opening and closing of his jaws.

" Hit the cat on the head," my master suddenly demanded.

" What will happen if I do? "

"That doesn't make any difference. Go ahead and hit it."

The Mrs. then struck my head with her palm. "Like this?" It didn't hurt a bit.

"It doesn't cry out."

"No."

"Hit it again."

"It won't make any difference, no matter how many times I hit it," argued the Mrs., striking me with her palm again. As it didn't do me any harm I kept quiet. Even though I am an intelligent cat, I was at a loss to understand the reason for all this. The Mrs., who had to hit me, seemed as perplexed as I was annoyed. My master, failing to get his desired reaction, became a little irritated. "Hit the cat so it'll meow."

The Mrs. asked, with a troubled expression, "Are you only going to make it meow?" And I received another slap on my head. Now that I understood the rules, there was nothing to it. All I had to do was to meow and my master would be satisfied. It's a shame my master is such an idiot. If he wanted to make me meow, he should have simply said so from the beginning and I wouldn't have been slapped so many times. If an order is given to hit another creature, it should be given with no other object than of hitting. Though the Mrs. had to strike me, it was I who was supposed to meow. This was absolutely disrespectful. My master was making fools out of us cats! This is something that Kaneda, whom my master detests like poison, might do; but coming from my own master, who is proud of his honesty, it was exceedingly base.

But my master isn't always as bad as this. The order was not given with any maliciousness. It only resulted from a brain that is as lacking in wisdom as the brain of a mosquito larva.

If you eat a lot, you're bound to become full; if you cut yourself, you're sure to bleed; if you stab a person in the heart, he's certain to die. My master had simply arrived at a rash conclusion; he thought that if a cat was hit, it was bound to meow. According to such rules, you'd surely drown if you fell into a river; you'd invariably develop diarrhoea after eating deep-fried fish; you'd definitely work if you received a good salary; and you'd

certainly become successful if you read a lot. It would sometimes be embarrassing if the results were always the same. If
I had to meow every time I was hit, it would be very troublesome.
It would be worthless to be a cat if I were thought of as being
only like the bell in Mejiro which sounds the hour. I finally let
out a meow and fulfilled the order of my master.

My master looked at the Mrs. and snorted, " It meowed! Do
you know if ' meow ' is an exclamation or an adverb? "

Being asked so suddenly, the Mrs. didn't say anything. I
myself thought that my master's question was due to his having
gone mad in the bathhouse, but my master is a queer character.
In the immediate neighborhood, some people have gone so far
as to accuse him of being mentally disturbed. But my master's
self-confidence can't be beat—he maintains that he alone is sane
and that everyone else is crazy. And when the neighbors call
him a dog, my master calls them pigs. It seems as though my
master is always trying to defend himself. Really, it is cause for
alarm. Being as he is, it was not out of the ordinary for him
to ask such an odd question to the Mrs. Looking at it from
another angle, however, it was definitely something only a de-
mented person would want to know. The Mrs., unable to answer,
said nothing. Even I could find no reply to the question.

Then my master suddenly shouted, " Hey! "

Surprised, the Mrs. asked, " Yes? "

" Your ' yes '—is that an exclamation or an adverb? Which is
it? "

" Well, I wonder—! But what difference does it make? Who
cares? "

" It makes a great difference. This is the type of problem
that continually occupies the authorities of the Japanese language."

" Do you mean to say that a ' meow ' worries the authorities?
What absurdity! Why, a cat's ' meow ' isn't even Japanese at
all! "

" That's why it's such a difficult problem. This is what you
call comparative study."

" Is that so? " The Mrs. was wise through experience so she
tried not to get herself involved in such a foolish discussion.

"And do *you* know which part of speech 'meow' is?"

"Being such a diffiult problem, it's impossible to arrive at a quick answer," responded my master, who then commenced to munch his broiled fish. He also helped himself to some of the boiled meat and the potatoes. "This is pork, isn't it?"

"Yes, it's pork."

With a face showing disdain, he swallowed it. "I'll have another cup of *sake*," said my master, thrusting his cup out for the Mrs. to fill.

"You're drinking quite a bit this evening, aren't you? You're quite red in the face already."

"Do you happen to know the longest word in the world?"

"Isn't it 'Saki no Kwampaku Dajo Daijin so-and-so?"

"That's the name of a person. I said the longest word."

"Do you mean in English?"

"Uhuh."

"No, I don't. Now you've had enough to drink for this evening. Why don't you eat your rice now?"

"No. I want to drink! Do you want me to tell you the longest word?"

"Yes—and you'll have your rice after that, won't you?"

"The longest word is 'Archaiomelesidonophrunicherata'."

"Oh, that's impossible."

"No, it's not. It's Greek."

"Well, then, what does it mean?"

"I don't know the meaning but I can spell it. When I write it out, it comes to a little more than six inches."

It is a wonder how my master can make such statements in his normal state. Most people could only do so under the influence of liquor. But then he had drunk rather freely that evening. He usually drinks only two little cups of *sake* at dinner, but that evening he had drunk four. He gets red in the face after only two cups but having had twice that amount, he was as scarlet as a pair of red hot tongs. He seemed to be suffering but he wouldn't quit drinking. "Another cup of *sake*," he repeated.

The Mrs., knowing he had drunk enough, answered sourly, "I think it's better to stop now. You'll become upset."

" I'm going to practice drinking a little tonight. Keigetsu Omachi said that drink is good for the health."

"And who is this Keigetsu?" Even Keigetsu couldn't awe the Mrs.

" Keigetsu is the best critic living today. He said to drink, so knowing how to drink must be important."

" Don't try to be funny. Keigetsu or Baigetsu, it's none of his business to tell others to drink—especially if they have a bad stomach."

" He didn't only recommend drinking; he also said we should associate more with others, play the prodigal and travel."

" Do you mean to say that a first-class critic made those suggestions? Outrageous! Just think of encouraging a man with a wife and children like that!"

" But it's good to play the prodigal. Even if Keigetsu hadn't said so, I would do it often if I had enough money."

" It's a good thing you don't have. It would be dreadful if you started living a fast life at your age."

" If you say it's dreadful, I'll give up my plans. But then you'll have to take better care of your husband and serve him better food for supper."

" This is the best I can manage."

" Well, if that's the case, I'll begin to pursue a fast life as soon as I make some money. I'd better stop drinking for this evening, eh?" He then passed his empty rice bowl to the Mrs.

My master ate about three bowls of rice with hot tea poured over it. After that I received three pieces of pork and the head of the fish. It had been broiled with salt.

VIII

WHEN explaining my fence-walking exercise, I mentioned the bamboo enclosure that encircles my master's yard. On the other side of this fence is another house, but don't get the idea that the southern neighbors are anybody important. Although the rent is cheap, my master, Mr. Kushami, is indeed a respectable man. Yes, even with only a thin fence in between, he does not associate with his less educated neighbors. On the south side is a lot on which five or six cypress trees grow close together in a row. From the veranda, it looks like a dense wood; and it seems as if my master were living in a lonely house in the middle of a field with a nameless cat, while leading an ordinary life with no thoughts of fame or wealth. Perhaps the branches of the cypresses are not really as dense as you might have guessed from my description because the roof of a cheap boarding house can be distinctly seen through them. The boarding house has the splendid name of " Gunkaku-kan ", *House of Many Storks*. It might be difficult to imagine a respectable teacher living in such an environment.

Since the boarding house was the " Gunkaku-kan ", then it might be proper to call the home of my master the " Garyo-kutsu ", *Den of Sleeping Dragons*. There are no taxes levied on names so I am free to select any name I like. The bamboo fence runs from east to west for about twenty yards. It is this north end that is often a site of disturbance.

The vacant lot is so large that it borders two sides of the house so I ordinarily have to pass through it in order to return home. My master, as well as his spirited cat—none other than myself—are often at our wit's end when it comes to dealing with the lot toward the north.

As the cypresses have control of the south side, seven or eight paulownia trees dominate the north. The wood of the paulownia tree is used to make wooden sandals. Since these trees have grown to a circumference of about one foot, we could ask a good price for them from a sandal maker. Unfortunately, however, we are living in a rented house so we can't put this into effect, even though we are often tempted. I am continually feeling sorry for my master. The other day, the janitor of the school nearby came and sawed off a branch from one of the trees. The next time he came around, he was wearing a new pair of sandals and boasting that he had made them from the branch he had cut off. The sly fellow!

Though there are paulownia trees growing nearby, they don't bring a sen to my master or to his family—or to me, either. There's an old saying that goes, " Opportunity makes a thief." Well, in this case, it is " Raising paulownia trees makes no cash." They offer potential wealth but remain like a miser's gold buried in the ground. But the person who leaves this wealth untouched is not my master, nor myself—but Dembei, the landlord. These trees are repeatedly calling out for the sandal maker to come, but the landlord, heedless of their plea, comes around only to collect the rent. As I have nothing against Dembei, I won't say anything more against him, but will go back to my main subject and tell you why this north lot is such a source of disturbance. Promise you won't tell my master about it, though. Well, it's like this :

The worst part of this vacant lot is that it has never had a fence around it. It has been a short-cut, a free-for-all-to-pass-through lot. It might sound strange to use the present perfect tense " has been ", but actually it always has been such a lot. You'd have to look into the past in order to understand the cause of this neglect. Even doctors would be at a loss to make out a prescription if they didn't know the reason for the patients' sickness. However, I'll take my time and begin by telling you in detail about this piece of land.

During the summer, it's nice to have an open space around the house. There's no need to worry about it being unsafe either for no thief would enter a place he cannot expect to find any cash.

That is why there is really no need for any kind of a wall or fence around my master's home. But the fact that there *is* a fence between the north lot and my master's garden was decided upon by the refined people living on the far side of the lot. You might consider me a little hasty to refer to them as being " refined " but by flattering others, you're generally on safe ground. The world we live in today is such a strange place that a thief hiding in the rafters might be called refined. But the refined people to whom I am referring are not the type hunted by the police. And though they may not be criminals, they make up for this by their great number. There are hundreds of the little neighbors.

They inhabit the Raku-unkan Junior High School, an institution which consists of eight hundred refined people—students who pay a monthly fee of two yen so they can become even more refined. As Raku-unkan means the Descending Cloud School, you might think that the students are exceptionally elegant. But that would be a serious mistake. The name has about as much relation to descending clouds as storks do to the Many Storks Boarding House—or to the cat living in the *Den of Sleeping Dragons*. As long as there are madmen like my master who can be called Bachelors of Something-or-other in this world, it is not difficult to understand why the refined students of this Descending Cloud School are not all elegant. If you still cannot understand this explanation, come and stop over at my master's home for a few days and see for yourself.

As I mentioned before, there has never been a fence around this lot, so the students of the Descending Cloud Junior High School, just like Kuro, the cat of the rickshawman, can always come striding into the grove of paulownia trees.

When my master first moved into this house, the students would talk over their affairs there while eating their lunches. They would lay down on the bamboo grass and do almost anything they wanted. The remains of their bamboo-sheath lunch wrappers, old newspapers, old sandals—straw as well as wooden—and almost anything else that can be termed as " old " was brought there and disposed of.

My master does not usually pay much attention to others so

at first he let things stand as they were without any complaints, although this might be difficult to believe. To tell the truth, I don't know if he actually ignored the boys or whether he knew about them but did no complaining. But ,the students, as they continued their studies, seemed to have become more and more refined, because gradually they commenced encroaching upon the lot from the north and then took possession of the south side as well. If you think the word "encroach" is not befitting refined students, I might retract it; but, truly, there's no other verb I can think of to explain their action. They were like nomads of the desert who seek water and grass; but the students' object, once they had infiltrated through the paulownia trees, seemed to be cypresses. The cypress trees grow directly facing the veranda of my master's home so only the very brave students came this far at first. After the first few days, however, their very brave spirit added another "very"—and they became very, very brave. Really, there's nothing as terrifying as education.

Not only did they come close to the house but they also commenced singing in loud voices. I don't remember how their songs went, but I can tell you that they were not inspired by any of the thirty-one syllabled poems recited in the classics. The songs were much more lively and very much more vulgar. It was not only my master who was surprised; I was also awed by the talent of the students, and I couldn't help wanting to listen to more. However I'm sure that you readers must understand that that which most awes can at times be disturbing as well. It is regrettable but these two feelings often coincide and become one. My master must have regretted this conflict of emotions too, but, out of necessity, he would fly from his study and, I believe, reprimand the noisy students. He must have told them each time that the vacant lot was not a public park and asked them to leave.

But as the students had received quite a bit of education, they would not simply listen meekly. After being chased out, they'd immediately return and again commence singing their lively songs. Besides, they would talk in high-pitched voices and—being such refined students—their language was of a special kind. It went something like this: "Yeh, dammit. Sure as hell!" and "Nah, don'cha know that whacha-ma-call-it?" Before the Meiji era, such language was used exclusively by flunkeys, coolies and bathhouse attendants, but in the twentieth century it seems to be the only language that refined students ever study. This phenomenon can be compared with sports which were once scorned by the majority but later became extremely popular. My master would run out of his study each time and ask the student whose speech was especially refined why he had entered the vacant lot. The student, however, would generally forget to use his most refined mode of speech and would answer more humbly: "I thought that this was the botanical garden belonging to my school." My master would reprimand him and then turn him out.

Turning a group of students away is like releasing a swarm of baby turtles, so funny they look when scattering away. My master must have at first believed that talking was sufficient to keep them away but, as has been said from the days of the Empress Nue Kuashih of ancient China, reality is different from anticipation. My master continually failed to get rid of these pests.

The students then made a short cut from the schoolyard through the front gate of my master's home. Whenever the gate squeaked open, we'd think it was some visiting guest. Then we'd hear laughing voices from the paulownia grove and know that we had made a mistake. The situation became quite alarming. The consequences of education became more prominent as far as bravery was concerned, and this was getting too much for my poor master. He once holed himself up in his study and wrote a courteous letter to the principal of the Descending Cloud Junior High School, pleading with him to exercise more authority over his students. The principal replied in an equally polite letter begging my master to be patient as he intended to build a fence. Presently two or three workmen came and, after half a day's work, they had constructed a rough bamboo fence about three feet high between my master's estate and the school. My master of course expected more quiet, but he is a fool. The behavior of students cannot be curbed by a three-foot-high fence.

It's fun to tease humans. Even I, a cat, sometimes go around teasing the little girls of the house. It must have also been fun for the refined students of the Descending Cloud Junior High School to tease a slow-witted person like Mr. Kushami.

When analyzing the psychology of teasing, there are two important factors. The first demands that the one being teased should not be indifferent; and the second is that the teaser should be bigger, either in strength or in number, than the teased. The other day, my master went to the zoo and saw something he admired very much. It seems he had seen a fight between a small dog and a camel. The little dog would run around the camel like a whirlwind, barking at it all the time, but the camel kept serene. Without even seeming to notice the dog, the camel just stood there hunching the hump on its back. The little dog found that it was not causing any reaction so finally, disgusted, it gave up. My master laughed, saying that the camel was insensible, but this is a good illustration for the situation now at hand. No matter how good the teaser may be with his tricks, if the teased happens to be a camel, nothing happens. Yet if the animal being teased were a lion or a tiger, they'd be so strong that the joker wouldn't have a chance. He might even end up being torn to pieces for his trouble.

When a person is teased, he shows his teeth and gets mad. He may get angry but when he is harmless and you know you're safe, it's a lot of fun. There are various reasons why teasing is such fun. First, it's a good way to kill time, especially when you are so bored you feel like counting the hairs of your moustache. Long ago, there was a prisoner who was so bored that he spent his days drawing triangles, one over the other, on the walls of his cell. There's nothing in the world that's worse than boredom; when there's nothing to stimulate you, it's pretty hard to enjoy living. Teasing is one amusement to create stimulation, but only when the other person can be made a little angry or irritated— otherwise it wouldn't be stimulating. Such amusement used to be most popular with the bored feudal lords who did not understand others. Today, teasing is especially enjoyable for the boys whose brains are so underdeveloped that they think about nothing but their own diversion, and who are at a loss how to use up their energy in other ways. Teasing is also an extremely simple method of trying to prove one's superiority. Killing, injuring, and imprisoning others are also methods employed for this object but such rash actions should only be taken when killing, injury, and imprisonment are the desired ends. Most people want to show their strength but, on the other hand, they are reluctant to cause physical harm. Teasing, therefore, is a most handy alternative. Actually, there is no rule which says that you must harm another person to prove that you are the greater. Though you might realize your own self-importance, the pleasure of this knowledge is only slight unless you can show off your superiority. Humans like to consider themselves as being self-reliant but only when other people are around to admire that self-reliance.

The people with the least amount of reasoning and those who most lack true self-reliance seem to be especially anxious to display their certificates of prowess. This can often be seen among judo enthusiasts. Many of them, still inexperienced in the sport, go around looking for someone even less skilled so they can throw him even once. Of course, there are many other reasons for a person wanting to prove himself but as it would take too long to explain, I won't discuss it here; but if you would like to hear my opinion, visit me some day with a box of dried bonito and I'll go into as much detail as you might want.

In taking the above into consideration, I believe the best way to get the most fun out of showing off one's superiority is to tease the monkeys in the Asakusa Zoo and—schoolteachers. I hope that no monkey will object to the comparison but, actually, they are in many ways similar to schoolteachers. As you know, the monkeys at Asakusa are in cages so even when they bare their teeth and shriek, there's no fear of getting scratched. Though a teacher is not in any cage, he is tied down by his meager salary so the students can tease him as much as they want. There's no fear that the teacher will resign or resort to physical violence because a person with enough courage to resign for this sole purpose would not have become a teacher in the first place.

My master is a teacher, yes, but not of the Descending Cloud

Junior High School—still, there is no mistake, he is a teacher. He is just the right type to be tormented. The students of the Descending Cloud are boys who believe that they have the right to annoy teachers as a part of their education. Moreover, if they did not tease others, they would not know how to spend their accumulated energy during the ten-minute recesses. Considering this from all angles, it is not at all unreasonable to believe that my master *ought* to be teased by the students. It is true that my master should have been too refined to get so angry but that's the kind of man he is. And now, I will explain how the students teased my master, and how he had made a fool out of himself again.

I hope you will remember the description I made of the bamboo fence. It's only a simple construction made of bamboo poles tied together horizontally and vertically to form rather large squares. I can easily pass in and out. To me, it is the same as if it weren't there. The principal of the Descending Cloud did not, of course, build this fence for cats; he went to the trouble of hiring workmen to build it so the refined students he was culturing would not go astray. Yes, the wind can pass through it easily but not humans. Even the magician Chang Shihi-Tsun of China might have found it difficult to pass through the four-inch square openings. As a fence for humans, it looks quite effective so it was no wonder that my master felt completely satisfied when he first saw it.

But there was still a big opening for trespassers—bigger than the whole fence, so large that a fish big enough to swallow a boat could have passed through. My master's logic had not considered that fences are also constructions to climb over. He believed that a fence clearly designated a boundary and that, since no one could pass through it, there was no fear. But it remains an easy matter to climb over or to jump over the fence and, moreover, such exercise is fun.

The very day after the fence was first made, the students came jumping over it just as if it were not there at all. But they did not come near the living room of my master because they calculated that it would require too much time to run away if they came that far. They simply loitered where there was no danger of being caught. It was impossible for him to see what they were doing from the east room. In order to discover them loitering around the north lot, he would have to open the wooden gate in the garden and look from the corner of the house. From the toilet window, too, the whole situation could be seen at a glance. But though my master might see many of his natural enemies, there was no way of catching them—all he could do was to yell at them from behind the grille of the toilet window. If he made a detour through the garden to attack the enemy-held positions, his footsteps would be heard and his foe would simply retreat to the other side of the fence before my master arrived. It was like a boatload of fishermen trying to creep up to seals basking in the sun. My master could not keep a perpetual watch from the toilet window, nor could he open the gate and run out every time he heard the students. To remain on constant alert, he would have had to resign his post as a teacher and take up the pursuit of students as his sole career. What most frustrated my master was that he could hear the voices of the enemy from his study but could not see them; and from the toilet window he could see them but wouldn't be able to catch them or chase them away. But the enemy had fathomed my master's disadvantage and had devised their strategy accordingly.

When the students knew that my master was in his study, they would sing in loud voices. Then they'd commence making fun of my master, talking so that he would hear them but also so he could not know who was doing the talking. From the study it was impossible to tell whether the students were in the garden or on the other side of the fence. If they heard my master come out, they'd jump to their own side or, if already there, they'd act as if nothing had happened. When my master went into the toilet (by the way, I've been using this not-too-becoming word "toilet" very often and I find it extremely embarrassing, but in order to explain this battle, it is quite essential that I do so). Well, anyway, when the students knew that my master had entered the toilet, they would make it a point to roam about in the vicinity of the paulownia trees so my master could see them. My master would invariably yell out at them, so loud that the neighbors could hear him; and the enemy would leave for their base camp without any confusion. My master was greatly perplexed at this strategy. Knowing for sure that some of the boys were on his premises, my master would rush out with a cane in his hand—but would find no one. Then he'd take a look out of the toilet window and see several of these poachers back again. My master would then dash out once more only to find them gone— that is until he returned to look through the toilet window again; he would repeat this again and again and again. He would busy himself to exhaustion. His frenzy grew so much that it was difficult to tell exactly whether his job was that of a teacher or if his main occupation was to do battle with invaders. It was when this frenzy reached its peak that the following incident took place.

Some kind of incident almost always occurs when one loses one's head in a frenzy. A frenzy is a state in which the blood rushes to the head and reasoning powers are lost. In this point, Gelen, Paracelsus and even the out-moded Chinese doctor Pien-Ch'ueeh all agree. In the olden days of Europe, it was claimed that there were four kinds of fluid that circulated within the body. One was the fluid of anger. Another was the fluid of dullness. The third was the fluid of melancholy which, upon reaching the head, caused one to grieve. The last was the blood fluid which enlivened the four limbs of the body. With the progress of civilization, the fluids of anger, dullness and melancholy have disappeared, so it seems that now only blood remains to circulate in our bodies. Therefore, it is blood that goes rushing to the head when one gets in a frenzy today. But the amount of blood varies a little in each individual, according to his nature and temperament. It can be said, however, that most people have roughly two and a half gallons flowing through their veins. When excited, these two and a half gallons of blood rush to the head· so the rest of the body becomes cold.

I know of a good example that will give a clear picture of how this frenzy affects people. One day in September of 1905, several thousand people in Tokyo got mad at the authorities and many

My master would rush out with a cane in his hand—but . . .

police boxes were being set on fire. The policemen, instead of defending their posts, all rushed to headquarters, leaving not a single police box in the city occupied. Diagnosing this from the doctor's point of view, it can be called "police frenzy". In order to cure this malady, it is essential to restore normal circulation of the blood, that is, to bring the blood back down from the head. There are various methods.

The father of my master used to tie a damp cotton towel around his head and then heat his feet over a charcoal foot warmer. To cool the head and warm the feet is one of the best ways to insure longevity according to an old Chinese medical book. If you don't like this method, there's another one which priests used to try. While making a pilgrimage, like the nomadic Buddhist Priest Un-sui, they would sit on a rock under a tree all night. To sleep on a stone under a tree was not for the sake of penitence, but a method of bringing the blood back to its normal circulation. Hui-nêng, who was the sixth leader of Buddhism after the death of Dharma, thought of this one day when he was pounding rice. Just try sitting on a rock and you'll find your posterior getting cold. As your rear end cools off, the blood begins to circulate. This is in the order of nature so there is no room for doubt concerning its effectiveness.

And so, as you see, there are many ways to bring the blood down but, unfortunately, no method has yet been found to make the blood rush to the brain. It is generally believed that a person loses more than he gains by becoming excited but there are cases that prove such hasty conclusions questionable. In some occupations, it is of great importance to get excited and to have the blood rush to the brain. Those who must take this into grave consideration are poets. It is just as essential for the blood to rush to the brain of a poet as coal is indispensable to a steamer; if the supply stopped for even one day, poets would become just ordinary individuals, doing nothing but eating.

Actually, frenzy is only another term for madness, but it doesn't sound any too good to say that a person can't do his work unless he goes crazy. By agreement, literary people call this madness "inspiration"—ah! inspiration!—as if it were of great beauty.

This may deceive some people but it is still madness. Platon called this "divine" madness but, divine or not, the term still sounds to too many people like simply being crazy. So it is to their advantage to stick to calling it "inspiration"—a word that sounds to me like the name of some drug. Just as the base for ordinary boiled fish paste is the lowly yam, just as the image of the Goddess Kwannon is usually only a small decayed piece of wood two inches long, just as duck stew as served in most restaurants is really made from the flesh of crows, and just as the beef used in boarding-house sukiyaki is ordinarily horse meat—inspiration is nothing but temporary madness. The reason why most poets don't have to be locked up in the lunatic asylum in Sugamo is that their insanity is only temporary.

And it is quite difficult to attain this fleeting moment of insanity. It's comparatively simple for someone to be insane all his life; but God, who is good at creation, must have had a difficult time in making a man who would be insane only when he has a pen in his hand. For centuries, learned men have been racking their brains, trying to devise some method to induce blood to rush to the brain, besides bringing the circulation back to normal. There was once a man who ate twelve green persimmons every day in order to get inspiration. His theory was that by eating green persimmons, he would get constipated and this would cause the blood to rush to the brain. Another man would jump into an iron bathtub, heated from below, with a bottle of warm *sake*. He believed that the blood would rush to the brain by drinking in a hot bath. According to this same man, even better results can be expected by taking a hot bath in port wine instead of water. Unfortunately he died before he had saved enough money to put this into practice. It is a pity.

Then there was a man who hit upon the idea that if he imitated men of old he would get some inspiration. This was an application of an older theory, that is, by imitating the attitude and action of a given person, one's mental state becomes similar to that person's. If you imitate a drunkard and talk nonsense as he does, for example, your mind eventually becomes like the drunk's; and if you sit in religious contemplation like a priest and endure the uncomfortable position until a stick of incense burns down, you will feel as if you were a priest yourself.

It has been said from times of old that a person becomes excited if he imitates the conduct of famous inspired writers. I understand that Victor Hugo used to lie on his back in a sailboat to receive inspiration; so if you should get on a boat and look at the azure sky, you're bound to become excited, too. Robert Louis Stevenson is said to have written his novels while lying on his belly; if you do the same, the blood is bound to rush to your head. There have been many persons who have tried to devise ways of pumping blood to the brain, but no one has yet felt completely satisfied with the results. It's unfortunate. But perhaps there will come a time when we can all feel inspired at will. I, for the sake of civilization, sincerely hope that this day will come soon.

I believe that this is a sufficient explanation of frenzy, madness, insanity and excitement so now I would like to carry on with the great incident. But before I do, I should point out that there are generally quite a few smaller happenings which always seem to occur before any large outbreak. It has been the evil practice of most historians to leave out the small incidents which preceed their descriptions of more important events. The frenzy of my master, for example, became more and more extreme every time he met with the small incidents which finally accumulated to explode into the big turmoil. If I didn't explain how each developed in order, it would be quite difficult to understand the behavior of my master. And if it were not understood, my master's frenzy might only be considered as another case of his eccentricities, and its true significance underestimated. My master would be quite discouraged unless others recognized his frenzy as such because it caused him so much trouble.

Actually, the incidents which I am about to relate, whether large or small, will bring little honor to my master. But though I might bring him dishonor, I would like to say that his frenzies were genuine and certainly not of the inferior kind. My master has nothing in his character of which he can boast so if I didn't tell you about his eccentricities, there would be nothing whatsoever for me to make public.

The enemy troops at the Descending Cloud invented a game that proved to be similar to shooting dumdum bullets. They played it during their ten-minute recesses and after school, furiously firing into the lot on the north side. Their ammunition was what we usually call " balls " and they were discharged toward our house by using a stick that looked like a large overgrown wooden pestle. Since these bullets were being fired from the schoolground, there was no fear that my master would be hit by any one of them as long as he was in his study. Even his enemies knew that it would be quite impossible, but then that was a part of their military strategy. During the battle of Port Arthur in the Russo-Japanese War, the Japanese navy bombarded the port only indirectly but with great results. So there is no reason why the balls that roll and bounce into other people's lots cannot have great effect. Most important, though, the entire army of students would let out a big yell with every volley. As a result, my master's blood that had been circulating in his arms and legs could not but thin out; and instead of roaming about in his body as it should, it went up to his head. It must be admitted that the strategy of the enemy was extremely clever.

Long, long ago in Greece, there was a writer by the name of Aeschylus who had a head common to most scholarly writers. What I mean is, he was bald. A head becomes bald because it lacks nutrition, I'm pretty sure. Most scholarly writers live in poverty. They always use their heads and therefore use up all the necessary nutrition that hair generally needs. Aeschylus himself possessed a shining, round and slippery bald head.

One day this writer, rocking this head in question, went out for a walk and let it reflect the sunshine. His not covering his brilliant cranium proved to be a big mistake. When a bald head is in the sun, it can be seen from a great distance because it shines like anything. At the time of my story, there was an eagle flying high above Aeschylus and it had a live turtle in its claws. Turtles are delicious but even from Grecian times they have possessed extremely hard shells so eagles can't do much about them even if they are good to eat. We know of broiled lobsters but even today as there is no restaurant that serves broiled turtle on the half shell, so it's quite natural that the Greeks did not have them in those days either.

The eagle was quite at a loss as to what to do with the turtle when he espied, far below, something that shone. The eagle must have decided that if he were able to drop the turtle on the shining object, the shell would surely be cracked to pieces; it would be no trouble to fly down afterwards to dine on the flesh. So the eagle took careful aim and dropped the turtle without any word of warning whatsoever. Unfortunately, the head of the writer proved to be softer than the shell of the turtle, so his bald head was shattered. The renowned Aeschylus, therefore, met a merciless death.

What I don't understand for sure is the underlying object of the eagle. Did he drop the turtle knowing that the object was the bald head of a writer, or did he drop it thinking it to be a shiny rock? You might possibly compare this eagle with the army of the Descending Cloud School but my master's head is not like that of Aeschylus—nor does it shine like a famous scholar's. Still, my master must certainly be ranked as a scholarly writer because he sits all day in a room he calls a study, even though it might be only a six-mat room and even though he might really be sleeping with his head resting on a difficult book. That my master is not bald must mean that he does not yet have the qualifications to be a scholar, but he is most certainly doomed to meet that fate in the near future.

In any case, the students of the Descending Cloud seemed to be trying to hurry the future. After two weeks of their bombardment, the head of my master would have lacked nutrition and become as shiny as a loquat on a tree, like a shiny brass kettle, or maybe like a copper pot. But if the attacks continued for still another two weeks, his head would soon look more like a squashed loquat, a leaky brass kettle, or a cracked copper pot. My master, however, would continue to struggle against the enemy until the bitter end regardless of such consequences, I am sure. Mr. Kushami, the Invincible!

One afternoon while napping on the veranda, I dreamed that I was a tiger and that I had ordered my master to fetch me some chicken. With an obedient "yes", he timidly brought me some. Then Meitei appeared, so I told him that I wanted to eat some sukiyaki made of wild goose. As usual, Meitei commenced giving me a lot of wild theories. He said that pickled turnips mixed with salt crackers would taste like wild goose but to this I opened my jaws wide and gave a frightening roar. Terrified, he hastily explained that the restaurant Yamashita where they make wild goose sukiyaki was out of business. I compromised for some beef sukiyaki and commanded him to buy me a pound of the best meat at Nishikawa's, otherwise I'd begin eating him. Meitei, tucking the ends of his kimono in his *obi* to make it easier to run, dashed out to buy the beef for me. I then stretched myself out on the veranda and waited for Meitei to return; but before I could even sample the beef, I was awakened from my beautiful dream by a loud shout.

My master who had just a moment before prostrated himself timidly in front of me, came rushing out of the toilet, kicking me aside with all his might. He then hastily put on his garden clogs and ran around to the wooden gate that led to the Descending Cloud School. It was extremely embarrassing to have suddenly shrunk from a huge tiger to a tiny cat, but my master's threatening countenance and the pain he had caused by kicking me was so terrible that the thought of being a tiger soon disappeared. Believing that my master was finally going to do battle with the enemy, I endured the pain and followed him around to the garden.

I heard my master calling out "Thief!" At the same time, a sturdy-looking boy about eighteen or nineteen with a school cap on his head went climbing over the fence. Just as I thought my master might catch the culprit, the student crouched into a running position and fled toward his base camp like a shot. My master, finding that his shouting had caused the desired effect, again yelled "Thief!" But in order to catch up with the trespasser, he would have had to climb over the fence and, if he penetrated too far, he himself would become a trespasser, too. As I have often mentioned, my master is extremely excitable so he seemed to forget this. Just when one more step would have meant an invasion of alien territory, an officer of the enemy who wore a thin spiritless moustache came slowly forward. A conference began over the fence between these two generals.

" Yes, he's a student of this school."

" If he's a student, what business does he have entering private property? "

"A ball rolled into your place."

" Why doesn't he get permission before entering? "

" I'll tell them to be more considerate next time."

" That would be much better."

I had anticipated a heated argument, like a struggle between a dragon and a tiger, but it all ended quickly in mild talk and without either contestant losing his temper.

What's most admirable about my master is his enthusiasm. But when it comes to action, it amounts to nothing. It's like my suddenly becoming a cat after dreaming I was a tiger. This, by the way, is one of the little incidents I previously mentioned. Now I must describe the explosive outcome.

My master was lying on his belly in the living room, probably trying to think up some new ideas concerning defensive tactics against his enemy. Classes were being conducted at the Descending Cloud. The schoolground was comparatively quiet. Through my master's open paper door, however, the voice of an ethics instructor could be heard. It rang out clear and strong. I recognized the voice of the officer who had negotiated with my master the previous day.

" . . . and public morality is extremely important. France, Germany, England—all countries have great regard for public morality, even the most uncivilized. It is indeed sad, therefore, that we in Japan have such little regard for others. There might be some of you students who think morality is something new, something imported from abroad but that would be a great mistake. Our ancestors greatly admired the moral lessons of Confucius, and practiced faithfulness and forgiveness. Forgiveness is essential in all public morality. As I am also human, there are times when I want to sing out in a loud voice. But when I myself am studying and somebody in the next room is singing, I cannot concentrate no matter how hard I try. Therefore, even though I might feel refreshed by reciting some Chinese poems out loud, I remind myself that I might unknowingly be causing inconvenience to someone in the next room so I refrain from doing so. In that same way, you students must learn to respect public morality and refrain from doing anything that will cause a disturbance to others."

My master grinned when he heard this lecture. A cynic, seeing his grin, might believe that it was sarcastic, but my master is no such villain. His mind is not good enough to become villainous. The reason my master smiled was simply because he felt glad. He believed that since the instructor of ethics was giving such a lecture, he would be forever safe from the bombardment of dumdums. For the time being, at least, he needn't worry about getting bald. Though his frenzy might not disappear right away, it might dispel itself if given time. Now there would be no need to tie a wet towel around his head while warming his feet, or to sleep on a rock under a tree. He was dreaming of a happy future and that is why he grinned. His optimism was quite natural. Even though he lives in the twentieth century, he still believes that one should always repay one's debts. He considered this lecture as the end of the trouble.

Eventually recess time came and the lecture abruptly stopped. All the other classes were dismissed too, and the eight hundred boys who had been sealed within their classrooms gave a whoop and came tumbling out of the building. The noise they made was like a swarm of bees whose hive had just been knocked over. Buzzing and shouting, they streamed out of windows, doors and every other opening that would set them free. This was how the big incident began.

I'll first explain the battle array of the bees. You might think that there would be no such formalities in a skirmish as this, but you would be mistaken. When an ordinary person thinks of battles, he imagines such military engagements as those of Shaka, Mukden and Port Arthur—famous battles in the Russo-Japanese

War. Others, those savages who have a touch of the poetic, might think of Achilles dragging the corpse of Hector around the wall of Troy three times, or imagine Chang Fei, the great warrior of China, carrying a long snake-like halberd and glaring fiercely from a bridge at Ts'ao Ts'ao's great army of one million. It is perfectly all right for a person to dream whatever he wishes but it would be wrong to believe that there are no other kinds of wars. There may have been many foolish battles throughout history, but it would take a miracle to produce one greater than this in such a pacific period as today in the Great Japanese Empire. Though there are sometimes minor disturbances as caused by people burning police boxes, the clash between Mr. Kushami, the master of the *Den of Sleeping Dragons*, and the eight hundred students of the Descending Cloud School must certainly be considered as one of the great battles fought since the establishment of the city of Tokyo.

Tso Ch'iu-Ming, the Chinese scholar, described the Battle of Yenling by first explaining the strength of the enemy, and since then his style has been followed by all the best historians. Therefore I myself will commence by explaining the battle array of the bees: one long column lined up on the other side of the rough fence. It seemed as if their first object was to draw my master to their line of battle.

"Do you think he'll give up soon?" "Not him!" "It's no use, he won't come out." "I wonder if we'll really win." "No reason why not." "Come on, everybody, let's yell." Shouts, shouts, shouts, and still more shouts then shattered the air. This was the students' battle cry. A little to the right of the long column, still on the schoolground, the artillery took up its position. There, facing the *Den of Sleeping Dragons*, stood an officer with a great big wooden pestle in his hands. Ten or twelve yards opposite him stood another officer who acted as the gunner.

According to what I have only recently heard, this is called baseball practice. I was still ignorant about this sport but I now understand that baseball is a game imported from America and it is exceedingly popular in Japan. At the time, however, it was only natural that I mistook this skirmish for artillery training.

America must be a country full of eccentric notions to introduce a game to the Japanese that causes so much inconvenience to others. Americans might consider this fun but when a game can startle others as much as baseball disturbed my master, it can also be thought of as a bombardment.

Definitions change according to different expressions. By saying it is charity, one can practice fraud ; or calling it inspiration, some enjoy their frenzy. Some might consider baseball simply a game, but the way the students of the Descending Cloud played it, it was more like an artillery attack.

One of the boys would throw the dumdum with his right hand at the student with the wooden pestle in his grasp. As for the ammunition itself, I couldn't distinguish what it was made of. It was round and as hard as a stone, covered and sewn up with leather. It left the hand of the gunner and flew swiftly through the air. The student standing with the wooden pestle in his hands raised his weapon in the air and tried to hit the round object. Sometimes he missed but in most cases he hit it with a loud smack. The speed and the power of the dumdum is most extraordinary, easily enough to smash the head of my nervous, weak-stomached master. This is about all the action but around the players there was a mob, and every time the wooden pestle smacked the ammunition, these boys clapped their hands and yelled out, " Good for you ! We've made another hit ! " " It won't be long now. Do you want to give up now or later ? "

This noise alone might have been endurable but almost every three shots came rolling into the yard of the *Den of Sleeping Dragons*. You see, if it didn't enter the place, the attack would have been for nothing. Although these special dumdums are now being manufactured in great numbers, they are still quite costly. The gunner of each military squad had one or two of them but they could not afford to buy a new ball every time one of them was smacked over a fence. For that reason, the boys had a whole platoon of men whose job it was to go around retrieving these wild shots. There was little trouble except when the ammunition fell in a high clump of grass or in somebody else's estate. Ordinarily when playing baseball, the ball is supposed to be hit so that it falls in some convenient place—but not so in this case. On the contrary, the students' aim was not simply to play baseball but to do battle with my master. Therefore they would deliberately smack the dumdums so they would fall into his yard. That being the case, they'd *have* to enter my master's property. The easiest way was of course to climb over the rough fence but then my master would have become angry. If not, my master would have had to take off his helmet as a sign of surrender. Due to this unendurable state of affairs, his head would certainly become bald soon.

Once a shot from the enemy, true to its aim, came flying high, snapping off a leaf from a paulownia tree before its flight hit the second line of defense or, in other words, the bamboo fence. It hit with a loud crack. According to Newton's first law of motion, once an object attains such movement, it would keep on moving at a set speed in a straight line if no other power were added to it. If baseballs were controlled by this law only, it would mean that the head of my master would have met the same fate as the pate of Aeschylus . Fortunately, Newton's second law saved my master's head from that calamity because although the change in movement is in ratio to the added power, it causes some effect to the straight line due to that same power. I don't understand what all this means but, whatever the case, the fact that the dumdums did not pierce the bamboo fence and continue flying through the paper sliding door to crash into my master's head was, without mistake, due to Newton.

Presently, as expected, we heard the bamboo grass being threshed about with a stick, and one of the boys screeched, " Some place around here." " More to the left." Whenever the enemy entered my master's place looking for balls, they would at all times speak in especially loud voices. Their sport would have been incomplete should they have come quietly and left quietly. Of course the dumdums were precious but what was even more important was to irritate my master. In this case, they could easily have found their ball because they heard it hit the bamboo fence. Its location was clearly known. It would have been easy to come in quietly and pick it up. According to Leibniz, however, order is necessary in all possible relationships. The alphabet, then, must always be listed in the same order—A, B, C, D, etc; there should always be a group of loaches in the water under a weeping willow tree; and bats should always fly only by the light of the moon. Though a ball might seem to have little connection with a fence, the process that is followed by those who always throw balls into someone else's property shows there is a close link. The students of the Descending Cloud did not have to make such a row about looking for a ball but this was really the strategy they meant to employ in order to draw my master into battle.

Even though my master is a passive man, he could not but accept this challenge. Just as he had done many times before, he resolutely stood up and dashed outside. Running full tilt, he was able to catch one of the enemy; this was a great feat for my master. His catch was a little boy of about fourteen or fifteen, however, somewhat unworthy of my mustachioed master. Believing that this boy was good enough as a prisoner of war, my master forcibly dragged him to the veranda in spite of the boy's pleas. It is here that I must mention the enemy's strategy again.

They had anticipated that my master would again appear, especially because of his threatening attitude the previous day. If a big student were caught, some serious trouble could have developed so they sent out small first-year or second-year boys to recover the balls. The strategy was that if my master caught one of the small boys, it would not reflect as much on the honor of the Descending Cloud. Besides, a grown-up man like my master would deal less harshly with a small boy. Such was the enemy's plan, a scheme any ordinary person would have to consider logical.

But the enemy had forgotten that my master is not an ordinary person. If my master had had enough sense, he would not have attacked them the day before. Frenzy makes great changes in a person; to a man of wisdom, it brings a lack of common sense. As long as a person has presence of mind enough to tell the difference between girls, little boys, rickshawmen and pack-horse drivers, he can't truly be considered as being in a frenzy. A man out of his senses, however, can, like my master, catch a little first-year boy and consider him to be a prisoner of war.

It was the prisoner himself who was most to be pitied. On orders issued by his upperclassmen, he was carrying out the duties of a common soldier. Once caught by the opposing general, who not only lacked common sense but who was also at the height of a frenzy, the boy found himself in a tight corner. His officers could not just stand by quietly, looking at the shame he was experiencing, so one after another they came climbing over the fence or through the wooden gate. Soon there were about twelve of them standing in a row in front of my master.

Most of them had taken off their coats and vests, the sleeves of their white shirts were rolled up and most of them stood with folded arms. One or two boys had their worn-out cotton flannel shirts flung over the shoulder perfunctorily. Besides, there was one dandy who wore a shirt of white duck, bordered in black with his initials sewn on the front. Every one of them seemed to be in excellent condition with well-developed muscles and sunburned faces. They could have just arrived from Sasayama in the Province of Tamba. It seems a shame to force such sturdy specimens to study in a junior high school. They were of such splendid stature that the nation would surely benefit if they would become fishermen or boatmen. All of them were barefooted with their trousers rolled up high, as if they were about to go and help somebody whose house was on fire. For some time, both sides just glared at each other. There was something deadly about the way their eyes met.

Finally my master broke out with great vehemence, " You boys are trespassing!" It was as if he had set off a firecracker between his teeth; his nostrils were quivering with rage. I have heard, by the way, that the nose of the paper lion used in Japanese dances is copied from the nose of a man in anger, otherwise it would not seem so terrible.

" We're students of the Descending Cloud."

" Oh? Students of the Descending Cloud wouldn't trespass other people's property."

" But you can see that we're wearing the badge of our school on our caps."

" Maybe you stole the badges. If you're students of the Descending Cloud, why did you enter someone else's yard without
permission? "

" Our ball came into the place."

" Why did you let the ball come this far? "

" Well—ah—it just came."

" Fools ! "

' " We'll be careful next time."

" Do you think ·I'll let you off that easily? Especially when
I'm not even sure who and what you are."

" But we're all students of the Descending Cloud."

" Then what year are you in? "

" The third year."

" You're sure? "

" Sure."

My master then called out to the maid, " Go to the Descending
Cloud School and bring somebody."

" Who shall I call? "

"Anybody, but get him here."

The maid answered, " Yes, sir." But as the scene was so
funny and as she did not clearly understand the mission of her
errand, she couldn't help grinning. My master was carrying on
a big war, exerting himself to the utmost, but his own maid only
grinned. This made my master's frenzy all the more acute.

"I said to get somebody! It doesn't make any difference who.
Do you understand? The principal, a member of the staff, the
chief instructor—anybody."

" Then the principal— " The maid only knew the word
" principal."

" I said the principal or a member of the staff or the chief
instructor—now do you understand? "

" If nobody else is there, shall I bring the janitor? "

" Stupid! What can a janitor do? "

The maid finally left but it was easy to see that she did not yet
grasp the reason of her errand. I was afraid that she would really
bring the janitor but after a while I saw, to my surprise, the
instructor of ethics coming in through the front gate. My master

[275]

waited until the instructor was seated and then commenced with the negotiations.

"Just a moment ago these young boys entered my property." His statement was made in an old-fashioned way, as if he were reciting *The Loyal League of the Forty-seven Ronin.* "Are they really students of your distinguished school?" My master ended his speech somewhat sarcastically.

The instructor of ethics did not seem surprised in the least. He looked over at the brave students standing in the yard and then, turning his eyes to my master, replied. "Yes, they're all students of mine. Only this morning I was trying to impress them with the value of being considerate so nothing like this would occur. It's difficult, yes. Now, boys, why did you climb over the fence?"

As the students were like students you find anywhere, they found they had nothing to say when confronted by their instructor of ethics. They just stood there like a flock of snowed-in sheep, huddled together in a corner of the yard.

"I guess they can't help it if their balls fly into my yard sometimes but the boys don't have to be so inconsiderate when they come to get them. They could climb over the fence quietly, pick the ball up, and leave. That shouldn't be too much to ask."

"Truly. It's just as you say. I try to watch the students but, as you see, there are so many of them. Hereafter I want you boys to be more careful. If a ball flies over the fence, go around to the front gate and ask permission to fetch it. Do you understand? Sports are essential in education. We cannot very well prohibit them from playing baseball but I would like to apologize for so much inconvenience. From now on, the boys will go to the front gate and ask permission before they enter your property."

"Well, I'm glad you are so cooperative. I won't mind the balls if the boys will only ask permission to retrieve them. I'm sorry to have caused you trouble by coming here." My master, as usual, had commenced brilliantly but ended dully. The instructor of ethics then led the "arrivals from Sasayama of the Province of Tamba" through the front gate and returned to the Descending

Cloud. And thus the big incident came to an end.

You might laugh at this being considered a major incident but if you do, it only proves that you do not realize how much it effected my master. This was a big incident to my master—not necessarily big for those who laugh. If you speak ill of my master because of this, saying that he is like a spent arrow shot from a strong bow, I only ask you to remember that this is an essential characteristic of my master. I also want to remind you that my master is good material for comic stories. If you say that it's absurd to fight with little boys of fourteen or fifteen, then I also agree with you. My master is definitely absurd. That is why Keigetsu Omachi says that my master has not as yet emerged from his infancy.

I have now related the small incidents as well as the big one, so now I would like to describe the aftermath to bring my story to a close. Some of you might believe that I am writing all this at random with my tongue in my cheek, but I am not a cat of such hasty judgment. There is a philosophy behind every word and every phrase; when words and phrases are joined together, the beginnings and ends correspond and reflect that philosophy. But if those same words and phrases were read only as nonsense, the philosophy would change until it would be more like preaching sermons.

Nobody, then, should be so insulting as to read while lying down or to read five lines all at once with the feet stretched out. When Liu Tsung-Yuan read the works of Han T'ui-Chih, a Chinese politician and a man of letters, he always made it a rule to wash his hands and to purify them in rose water first. In reading my work, however, I would only like to ask you to be enthusiastic enough to buy your own copies; do not borrow my books from your friends.

But what I am going to relate now is what I myself claim to be the aftermath. As an aftermath, you might think that it won't be worth reading but that would be a great mistake you would learn to regret. Read everything to the very end.

On the day following this big incident, I felt like taking a walk, so I went outside. Just as I was going to turn the corner to go down the alley across the street, I happened to see Mr. Kaneda and Suzuki deeply engrossed in conversation. They had met by chance; Kaneda had just come home in a rickshaw and Suzuki was just leaving after having visited Kaneda's home. The Kaneda estate had not been a place of much interest for a long time so my feet had not trodden in that direction for several weeks. It was good to see Kaneda and Suzuki again, however. As I walked toward them, their conversation, of course, fell upon my ears. This was not any crime on my part. If they did not want to be overheard, they shouldn't have been talking there in the first place. Kaneda, above all, should not get mad at my eavesdropping because his conscience did not disturb him after dispatching detectives to find out about my master's activities. If Kaneda got angry with me, it would only prove that he does not know the meaning of impartial justice. In any case, I happened to hear their conversation although I had no intention of listening.

" I've just been visiting your family, sir. It's nice to see you, too," said Suzuki courteously after bringing his head down in a quick bow.

" Hmmm. I've been wanting to see you for some time, Suzuki."

" And what do you want to see me about? "

" Actually it's not much, but you're the only person I know who can manage it."

" If I can be of any service to you, I'll gladly do anything, sir. What is it? "

" Well—hmmm," hummed Kaneda, still thinking.

" If you prefer that I call some other day, I'll do that. When will it be most convenient for you? "

" Oh, no. It's not as important as that. As long as you're here, I think I'll ask you right now. Remember that queer individual, that friend of yours? What's his name?—Kushami or something."

" It's Kushami. Now what has he been up to? "

" Nothing, but he still fills me with disgust."

" That is only natural. Kushami should take his social position into more consideration. He seems to believe he's the sole master of the universe."

"That's it. He says such pert things, such as how he won't bow his head to money or to businessmen. I myself decided to show him the power of one businessman and I think he's weakening a little. It still surprises me how stubborn he has been."

"He doesn' know the difference between advantage and disadvantage so it's easy for him to be stubborn. He's a hard nut to crack."

"Ha, ha, ha! That's right. But I mean to crack that nut. Now I'm having the students of the school nearby torment him."

"That should do it. Is it working?"

"He seems to be weakening rapidly. He's bound to surrender to power pretty soon."

"There's no contending against the inevitable."

"Right. He must be just about ready to give up now so I was wondering if I could get you to go and see how he's managing."

"Oh, that would be no trouble at all. I can go right away and make my report to you later today. It will be wonderful to see him less sure of himself."

"Yes, drop in on your way back. I'll be waiting for you."

Here I discovered another secret design against my master, and I again realized the power that businessmen yield is great. Because of one businessman, my master had become frenzied although he is usually like a dead ash, doomed to have a head so bald that it would be a dangerous place for flies to land on. His crown was also likely to meet the same fate as that of Aeschylus, all because of the power of one businessman. I don't understand exactly how the earth twirls around its axis but I *do* know now that money is what moves the world. Those who understand this even better are none other than the businessmen themselves. That the sun rises in the east and sets in the west without mishap must also be entirely due to men of business.

Though I didn't really realize it until then, it is quite stupid of me to be brought up under the roof of a poor educator instead of receiving the divine favors of a man of wealth. Even my master would have to comprehend the powers that businessmen hold this time. If he remained stubborn, the very life he so ardently clings to would be in danger. Curious to know how my master would greet Suzuki, I decided not to loiter around any longer. Even cats can be greatly worried about their masters. I ran past Suzuki and made my way home as fast as I could.

Suzuki began, as could be expected, very smoothly. He did not mention Kaneda at all but turned the conversation to more ordinary topics.

" By the way, you don't look any too well. Is there anything wrong with you? "

" There's nothing especially wrong with me."

" But you look pale. You'll have to learn to take better care of yourself. Are you sleeping well? "

" Sure."

" Do you have anything that's worrying you? If so, I'll do whatever I can to help. Don't hesitate to say so."

" Worry? About what? "

" Worrying is bad for the health. It's wiser to live laughing and to be happy. You look terribly melancholy."

" Well, it's not good to laugh too much. If you laugh for no reason, you're liable to die."

" Nonsense! Laughter brings happiness. Fortune comes in by the merry gate."

" Do you know the Greek philosopher Chrysippus? "

" No. What about him? "

" He laughed himself to death."

" But that happened a long time ago! "

" What's the difference? He saw a donkey eating figs out of a silver bowl and, finding this funny, he began to laugh. Then he found that he couldn't stop and so he finally died laughing."

" Well, of course I don't mean for you to laugh that much. Just laugh—you know what I mean—just right—and you'll find yourself feeling wonderful in no time."

Suzuki was putting out feelers the best he could. At that moment, the front door slid open with a rumble as if a guest had dropped in. This was not the case, however.

" Can I come for the ball in your yard? "

The maid gave him permission from the kitchen and the student went around to the back garden. Suzuki made a funny face and asked the reason for this interruption.

" The students behind the house keep throwing their balls into my place."

" The students behind the house? Are there students there? "

" The name of the school is the Descending Cloud."

" So? It's a school then? It must be very noisy."

" Noisy isn't the word for it! I can't even study. If I were the Minister of Education, I'd close the school down right away."

" Ha, ha, ha! You're quite mad. Are you irritated about something? "

" Yes, I am! The boys bother me from morning till night."

" Then why don't you move? "

" Move? Of all the impertinence! "

" Don't get mad at me. Well, they're only children. Why don't you let them be? "

" That's easy for you to say, but you don't have to put up with the noise. I had a teacher come yesterday and we talked over the problem."

" That must have been interesting! Was he very apologetic? "

" Uhuh."

Just then the front door slid open again and another voice was heard. " May we come for the ball that's in your yard? "

" They keep coming, don't they? "

" The teacher and I decided that they should come by the front gate."

" Is that why they come so often? Well, well! Now I see."

" What do you see? "

" Why they come for the ball."

" That was the sixteenth time today."

" Terrible! Why don't you arrange it so they won't come? "

"Arrange it so that they won't enter? How can I help it if their balls keep flying over? "

" Well, if you say you can't help it, that's that. But you don't have to be so stubborn. If a man has corners it's difficult to roll smoothly through life. Sharp edges have their disadvantages.

A round object can roll along smoothly with ease whereas if there are corners, the edges get caught and it hurts. You're not the only person in this world and you can't always have people act according to your own wishes. The point is simply this; it's foolish to go against a man who has money. All you get for trying are worries; you break down in health and, moreover, people won't speak well of you. None of your suffering really hurts a rich man; all he has to do is to sit tight and order people around. You can't win against such heavy odds. It might be admirable to be stubborn at times but if you are stubborn all the time you will find it effects your studies and worries you during your daily routine. So much labor lost, so much fatigue gained."

"Pardon me but the ball has gone into the yard. Can I go around to the back to fetch it?"

"There's another one," laughed Suzuki.

"Inconsiderate people!" exclaimed my master, again getting red in the face.

Suzuki, finding that he had completed his mission, said that he would have to be leaving but asked my master to drop in to see him some day. Then he left.

Right after Suzuki's departure, Dr. Amaki came on a professional call. There are not many instances when a victim confesses that he himself is suffering from frenzy. When most people notice that something is wrong, they are generally past the peak and my master had reached the peak of his excitement during the big incident of the previous day. The negotiations had proved a rather tame ending but a solution was found to his troubles. After deep consideration, my master had at last realized that something was wrong with him. Of course there was much doubt about the source of his infirmity: was it the Descending Cloud or something internal? But in any case, a doctor was needed.

My master lived next to a school, but he was irritated the whole year round, even during school vacations. He wondered if his malady might possibly be an irritation that medicine might effectively pacify. That was why he called in Dr. Amaki, the family doctor. Let's not consider whether this move was necessarily wise or not but we ought to give him credit for his praiseworthy and clearheaded action when he noticed the affects of his frenzy.

Dr. Amaki was calm as usual and all smiles: "And what seems to be the trouble?" In almost all cases, doctors begin with " and what seems to be the trouble?" I for one would not have confidence in a doctor who didn't begin with " and what seems to be the trouble?"

"Doctor, I'm afraid I haven't much longer to live."

"Now, it can't be that serious."

"I'm wondering if medicines do me any good."

Dr. Amaki showed surprise at this statement but, being my master's senior and possessing a gentle disposition, he did not express his emotions in words.

"Take my stomach for instance. Though I've been taking medicines for a long time, it's always the same."

"That's not absolutely true."

"Is that so?" My master was again asking somebody else about the condition of his own stomach.

"You can't expect to get well all of a sudden; it takes time. It's much better now than it used to be."

"Is that so?"

"And do you still get irritated?"

"Oh, yes. I even get irritated in my dreams."

"I've told you to take more exercise."

"If I did, I'd get even more irritated."

Dr. Amaki seemed somewhat disgusted but managed to continue. "Now let me look you over." He then commenced his medical examination.

My master, in the middle of the examination, suddenly announced, "Doctor, the other day I read a book on hypnotism. It says that pilfering can be cured by hypnotism as well as many diseases. Is that true?"

"Yes, hypnotism is effective in some cases."

"Do they still practice it now?"

"Yes."

[283]

" Is it difficult to hypnotize a person? "

" Not at all. Sometime I do it myself."

" You do, really? "

" Do you want me to try it on you? Everybody can be controlled through the power of hypnotism."

" That's interesting. Yes, try it out on me. I've always wanted to have myself hypnotized—but can you bring me out of the trance? "

" There's no need to worry. Shall we try? "

And so my master was going to be hypnotized! I had never seen it practiced so I was naturally curious. I watched from a corner of the sitting room.

First of all, the doctor commenced massaging the eyes of my master, stroking the upper eyelids up and down. Presently the doctor said, " You feel your eyes getting heavy, don't you? "

" Yes, actually they are getting heavy," answered my master.

The doctor kept stroking the eyelids while repeating, " They will become gradually heavier—yes, they will." I supposed my master had begun to feel the effects for he kept silent. The massage was continued for three or four minutes until finally Dr. Amaki announced, " Now your eyes will not open." My poor master! He was blind!

" Can't I open them? "

" No, you will not be able to open your eyes." My master just sat there, mute, with his eyes closed. Then Dr. Amaki said, " If you think you can open them, just try. You won't be able to."

" Is that so? " As soon as my master said this, his eyes popped open. He then grinned. " It didn't work, did it? " Dr. Amaki also laughed, " No, it didn't." So the experiment on hypnotism ended in failure and Dr. Amaki left.

But soon there was another guest. It seems strange that so many people come to the house of my master since he has so few friends. It is difficult to understand but, whatever the case, they came. This visitor was a stranger to me. I am telling you about him only because he has a connection with the aftermath of the big incident. He cannot be neglected.

I don't know his name but besides having a long face, he had a beard like that of a billy goat. He must have been forty or thereabouts. I generally think of Meitei as an aesthete, but I plan to call this man a philosopher. If you ask me why, it is only because he did not try to show off like Meitei. He seemed to have been a former classmate of my master because they talked without reserve.

"Did you say Meitei? He's as unsteady as goldfish food floating on the surface of a pond. The other day, he was walking in front of the house of a peer with a friend. Meitei does not know the peer yet he invited his friend inside for a cup of tea. He's extremely eccentric."

"What happened after that?"

"I didn't even ask. He only floats around like goldfish food. And Suzuki? Does he come here, too? He doesn't have much reasoning power but he's pretty clever in getting around. He may wear a gold watch but he hasn't got any depth and he really isn't much good. Suzuki often talks about smoothness but he doesn't really understand it much himself. If Meitei can be compared with goldfish food, then Suzuki is like a dab of jelly—smooth but also trembling underneath."

My master seemed impressed with this witty parable because he laughed loudly, an almost immemorial occurrence.

"Then what about yourself?" my master asked.

"Me? Well, let's see—guess I might compare myself to a yam, stretched out and buried in mud. How's that?"

"You always seem free from worry. I envy you."

"I just do what most ordinary people do, that's all. It's nothing to be envious about. I'm lucky because I find it impossible to carry a grudge. That's my only strong point."

"How about your financial situation? Are you doing well nowadays?"

"It's just the same as always. I have only enough to get along. I'm able to eat so I don't worry much."

"I myself find life unpleasant; I sometimes get so irritated that I can't stand it. It's discontent everywhere I turn."

"Discontent isn't always bad. Learn to endure your discontent and dissatisfaction; you'll feel better for it after you have lost it. There are all kinds of people so you can't expect them all to be just as you yourself would prefer. Chopsticks should only be used like other people use them, otherwise it would be difficult to eat. When rich people order a suit, the tailor makes it so it will fit perfectly from the very first. But if you cannot afford a good tailor, don't worry. That's a good thing about this world because after you wear an ill-fitting suit for a while, it gradually takes shape and eventually fits. In the same way, it would be nice to be born with perfect adaptability, but if this is not the case, then learn to wait until the world adapts itself to you. It's the best way to be."

"I'm afraid that there would never be a meeting point in my case, no matter how long I waited. It's hopeless."

"Some people insist on wearing a suit too small for them. It rips and tears. In other words, they start fights, commit suicide, and make all kinds of trouble. But in your case, you're only disinterested and disappointed, that's all. I hardly believe that you would commit suicide or start fights. There's nothing to worry about."

"But I pick fights every day, even when I don't have anyone to fight with."

"You mean you fight all by yourself—this is interesting. Of course you can go ahead and fight this way all you want."

"But I'm tired of it."

"Then quit."

"I hate to admit it but I simply cannot."

"Well, what is it that disturbs you so much?"

It was then that my master related the incident he had had with the Descending Cloud School. He also told this philosopher about the insults handed out to him by the spies that the Kanedas had sent, about Pinsuke, Kishago and about many of his other troubles. The philospher silently listened and then started talking himself. "You don't have to worry about what Pinsuke or Kishago might say. It's probably quite senseless anyway. As for those junior-high-school boys, it's not worth the trouble to get so worked up. They might be a nuisance, sure, but you've talked with them and fought with them and now look at the situation. It really isn't much better, is it?

"Concerning such matters, I believe the Japanese of old were much more clever than most Westerners. Westerners want to be positive and this is quite the fashion in Japan today, but being so positive has a great defect. In the first place, there's no limit to the craving for satisfaction. A state of thorough completeness is never attained. Do you see those cypress trees over there? Well, you say to yourself that they're unsightly so you clear them away; then it would be the boarding house beyond them that irritates you. There would be no limit to your search for the perfect view. Westerners are like this. Neither Napoleon nor Alexander felt much satisfaction after their victories. If you're dissatisfied with a person you might commence quarrelling with him. If he doesn't give in you could sue him. You might think that you would be satisfied if you won the case, but you wouldn't be. It is impossible to reach a state of perfect happiness. Some say that limited government is not good so they change to representative government. This doesn't work either, so they change to something else. Thinking that a river is a nuisance, we build a bridge over it; believing that mountains are troublesome, we build tunnels through them. It's tiring to walk so we build railways. But we never attain the state of complete satisfaction.

"As humans, we cannot have our own way always. Western civilization might be considered as positive or progressive but it is a civilization made by people destined to be dissatisfied all their life. The traditional civilization of Japan did not attempt to find satisfaction through such changes but through the individual. The great difference between us Japanese and Westerners is that we realize that we cannot change our environment. When there is trouble between father and son, Westerners try to alter their relationship; but we Japanese believe that the relation between father and son cannot be altered no matter how hard we may try. Instead, we attempt to find a compromise within the relationship. It is the same with husband and wife, master and servant, between warriors and merchants, and it is also the same with nature itself. If there is a mountain blocking our way to a neighboring country, we don't have to move the mountain. Instead, we should find a way that would make it unnecessary to go to that foreign country. We should learn to build up a feeling in ourselves that would give us satisfaction by not having to go over the mountain. Members of the Zen Sect and Confucianists best understand this.

"No matter how powerful a person may become, he could never manage to control the will of the whole world. One cannot stop the sun from setting nor can one reverse the flow of the Kamo River. But what we can all manage to control is our own mind. If you yourself were able to train your mind better, you wouldn't worry so much about the students of the Descending Cloud, and I believe you could even forget about the spies Kaneda sends here. And if Pinsuke happens to make fun of you again, all you have to do is to call him a fool and be done with it.

"Once upon a time there was a priest who, when somebody slashed at him with a sword, quickly composed an ode: ' Flashing a sword like lightning, you've cut the spring breeze.' The assailant was awed with the priest's wit and ran away without taking his life. I think that we could all learn a lesson from this priest. I myself am not that clever but I believe it's a mistake to consider the positiveness of Westerners as the only good principle to follow.

"Take our own case for instance. No matter how positive you may act, can you ever really manage the students who come to tease you? It would be a different matter if you had the authority to close down the school or if you could go to the police with the problem. You would have to have money to make any such positive action bear fruit, however. Right now you are contending against heavy odds; you have to bow down to wealthy persons and you have to give way to the students who rely on number for strength. A poor person like you cannot fight all alone. The fact that you try is the main reason for your dissatisfaction. Do you understand now?"

My master listened but did not answer the last question.

After this unusual guest, the philosopher, had left, my master went into his study and, without opening any book, he just sat alone deep in thought.

Suzuki preached that it is better to go along with the majority and with those who are wealthy. Dr. Amaki had suggested that nerves could be soothed by hypnotism. Finally, the philosopher had implied that my master could attain satisfaction by training himself to be passive. Which course my master would select is his own business but, in any case, it seemed sure that the situation could not continue much longer as it had in the past.

IX

MY MASTER'S FACE is pockmarked. Before the Meiji era, it seems that pockmarked faces were quite the mode; but ever since the Japan-British Alliance, such blemishes have become unfashionable. The decline of the pockmark began at the same time that there was a great increase in population so these scars will probably be completely exterminated soon. This has already been proven by medical statistics. It has been shown so scientifically that even I, a cat, embrace no doubts about its being true. I don't know exactly how many living persons are pockmarked but I can say that there are none among cats. Actually, I only know one human so disfigured and that happens to be my master. What a pity!

Every time I glance up at my master, I wonder how he ever acquired such an odd face. At one time, his pockmarks might have brought him some influence. But not today. Today, when these deformities generally collect themselves on people's upper arms, my master still has them on top of his nose and they spread to his cheeks. The fact that they can't be removed might be something to boast about, especially for the pockmarks themselves. It would be a good thing if they could be done away with entirely but that would be discouraging for the scars. It is possible that during the first decline in their fashion, pockmarks pledged themselves not to leave until they could stop the sinking sun from going down any further. This determination might be the reason they occupy my master's face so impudently. If so, these pockmarks should not be looked upon with scorn. They have secured themselves forever, resisting the swift changes of time. That is certainly worthy of respect. The only big defect is that they are unsightly.

When my master was a little boy, there was a famous doctor of

Chinese medicine whose name was Sohaku Asada and he lived in Yamabushi-cho, in Ushigome. When this old doctor went to visit his patients, he traveled slowly, ever so slowly, in a palanquin. After the elderly Sohaku passed away, his son-in-law took over the profession and the palanquin was replaced by a rickshaw. Perhaps when this son-in-law dies and his son takes over the practice, he may even substitute *kakkonto*, the only medicine Sohaku and his son-in-law ever prescribed to their patients, with aspirin. To tell the truth, it was really quite a sight, even in the days of the elderly Sohaku, to see him winding through the streets of Tokyo in a palanquin. The only ones who could remain indifferent to this spectacle were old-fashioned ghosts, pigs on freight trains, and the elderly Sohaku himself.

The pockmarks of my master are quite as out-of-date as old Sohaku's palanquin and they cause a feeling of pity whenever seen. My master's stubbornness is not inferior to that of old Sohaku, however. He continues to attend school every day, exposing his disfigured face to his pupils while teaching the English reader.

When he stands on the platform of the classroom, the craters that were so popular a century ago offer the pupils a unique form of education. While my master repeats " Monkeys have hands," he is also silently giving a lecture on " The Influence of Pockmarks on the Face." When such speckled individuals as my master are teachers no more, the pupils will have to go to libraries and to museums in order to study this problem, just as they now have to do when trying to imagine what the Egyptians were like from examining mummies. Considering the pockmarks of my master in this light, they are not entirely without merit.

But my master does not endure those blemishes all over his face for the sake of merit. He was once vaccinated against measles on the arm but, unfortunately, the measles transferred themselves to his face in no time. Since he was only a little boy at the time, he had no interest in girls so he kept scratching his face because it itched so much. In that way he ruined the face he had been given by his mother at birth. Now he often tells the Mrs. that before getting the measles he used to be a boy perfect in form.

He boasts that he was so pretty that Westerners would turn back to look at him when he visited the temple of the goddess Kwannon in Asakusa. That might have been so but, unfortunately, he has no witness to back up his statement.

Even if his pockmarks render some merit, a thing that looks unclean is a thing unclean, any way you look at it. When my master became of age, he commenced to worry a great deal about his appearance and did everything possible to erase the unsightly scars. But they are different from the palanquin of the elderly Sohaku, and my master could not get rid of them. They will always remain distinctly on his face.

This seems to worry my master somewhat because every time he walks along a street, he counts the pockmarked people he sees. He jots down in his diary such details as how many he finds, whether they are men or women, and whether he sees them at the market in Ogawamachi or in Ueno Park. The other day, a friend who had gone abroad dropped in, and my master asked him if he had seen many Westerners with pockmarks. After thinking for some time, slanting his head to one side, the friend confessed, "Very few." My master asked again to make sure "Very few?. But there are some, aren't there?" Then the friend absent-mindedly replied, "Yes, but they're all beggars or hobos. I can't remember seeing any pockmarks on educated people." My master exclaimed, "Is that so? It seems to be a little different here in Japan, doesn't it?"

My master gave up any idea of continuing his feud against the Descending Cloud Junior High School after talking with the philosoper. Instead, he shut himself up in his study and brooded over something else. He might have been following the philosopher's advice and meant to try to culture his miraculous mind passively. But since he has always been passive, he could hardly expect results by continuing to fold his hands over his bosom. It seems to me that it would have been much better if he took his English books to the pawn shop and then, with the cash thus obtained, go to some geisha girl. She might even teach him the very popular song *Rappa Bushi*. But since he is such a warped individual, I know that he would not heed any advice given by a cat. Thinking it best for him to have his own way, I let him alone for several days.

Actually, I let him alone for seven days. It is a custom in the Zen sect to hold a divine enlightenment ceremony on the seventh day after a trial is begun. I myself hoped that after this period my master would have reached some important conclusions—to continue to live or to die. So on the seventh day I walked slowly from the veranda to the entrance of his study and surveyed the room.

It is a sunny six-mat room facing south with an enormous desk in it. The desk is not just big but huge—six feet long, three feet ten inches wide, and proportionately high. Of course, it is not a ready-made desk. This strange article was made to order at a neighborhood furniture shop. My master had ordered a desk that could also serve as a bed. Why my master had such an immense desk made and why he wanted to sleep on it is still a mystery to me. Did he design this monstrous object on the spur of the moment, or did he confuse two wholly unrelated pieces of furniture when he was drawing up his plans? In any case, the result is fantastic. The greatest fault is that as a bed it is not merely fantastic, but worthless. Once I happened to see my master fall off onto the veranda while sleeping on it. Since then, he does not often use the desk as a bed.

In front of the desk is a mousseline-de-laine cushion. Three holes have been burnt through by cigarettes so the grayish cotton padding inside can be seen. Looking into the room, I saw my master sitting ceremoniously on the cushion on his folded legs. His back was facing me. His dirty gray *obi* was tied in a knot behind, both ends dangling down until they touched the upturned soles of his feet. It was only the other day that I tried to play with the ends of this *obi* but was suddenly slapped on the head for my folly. It is an *obi* I do not often go near.

He was still thinking— Or was he? Well, there's a proverb that says one wastes a lot of time before making an important move. Anyway, I went around and took a peek. It was then that I saw something with a peculiar glitter on the desk. I thought this queer so I blinked my eyes a couple of times and then tried to endure its glare so I could see what it was. I found that the glitter was light reflecting from a mirror that was being moved about on the desk. Instantaneously a question popped into my mind: What in the world was my master doing with the mirror in his study? The reason I say " the " mirror is that there is only one in my master's household.

I had understood that mirrors were only supposed to be in washrooms. That very morning I had seen the mirror there; I had watched my master comb his hair after washing his face. By the way, some of my readers might not believe that my master ever combs his hair. It is true that he is lazy in doing most things but the lazier he becomes, the more careful he is about combing his hair. Since I came to this house, I have never seen my master with a half-inch haircut, even in the hottest weather. He always has his hair cut to the length of two and a half inches. And not only does he part it on the left with great care, but he also flips up the ends of his hair on the right side to give a nonchalant effect. This, too, might be considered as the act of an insane person.

This elegant way of arranging his hair does not harmonize with my master's old desk at all, but as his vanity does not cause harm to others, nobody ever criticizes him for it. My master himself is extremely proud of his hair style but actually the reason he wears his hair long is this:

His pockmarks have not only invaded his face but have encroached upon his scalp. If he had a half-inch or a third-of-an-inch crop like most people, a lot of the marks would show. No matter how hard he would try to smooth down a short haircut, the uneven surface of his head would still be in sight. It might sound quite poetic, but I could liken it to a withered field with fireflies glowing here and there. But this might be disagreeable to the Mrs.

By wearing his hair long, there is no fear of the pockmarks being exposed—there is really no need to emphasize their presence. Perhaps my master would like his hair to grow down over his face so he could cover the scars there, too. My master believes that there is no need whatsoever to pay for a short haircut only to advertise that he has pockmarks all over his crown. This is the reason my master wears his hair long; and because he wears it long, he often combs it; and this is also the reason he often looks into the mirror. Therefore it seems strange that there is only one mirror in the whole house.

That the looking glass which was supposed to be in the washroom was in the study meant that either the mirror itself had been sleepwalking, or that it had been purposely brought into the study by my master. Maybe he brought it to help culture his passiveness. Long ago, a scholar called on a famous Buddhist priest and found him stripped to the waist and polishing a piece of slate tile. When asked what he was doing, the priest replied that he was trying to make a mirror. The scholar was greatly surprised and said that it was not possible to polish a slate tile into a mirror. At this, the priest laughed heartily and said that he'd quit if that was the case, but added that this labor was no more foolish than reading books and getting no knowledge from them. My master must have had a smattering of such ideas. He was now moving the glass around and around. Thinking that the matter was becoming rather serious, I quietly continued to look.

My master was earnestly looking into his only mirror so he didn't see me. The looking glass, in the first place, is a weird object. I understand that it takes quite a bit of courage to look into a mirror when alone in the middle of the night in a big room lit only with a single candle. The first time one of my master's daughters shoved the mirror in front of my face, I was so frightened that I ran around the house three times. Even in the daytime, looking into a mirror as long as my master did, one would undoubtedly become terrified of his own face.

Presently he sighed to himself, "I'm really not at all handsome." His confession is worthy of praise. His actions were certainly those of an insane person, but what he said stood to reason. I felt sure that a little bit more of this and he'd become frightened of himself too. Unless a person realizes that he is a scoundrel, he cannot be considered worldly wise. And if he is not a world-wise person, it is absolutely impossible for him to attain enlightment.

My master, having gone this far, should have said, " I'm scared." But he didn't. I don't know what he was thinking after he had confessed his own ugliness but soon he puffed out both cheeks and slapped them a couple of times with his hand. I am at a loss to know what kind of a charm this might have been. It was when his cheeks were inflated that I realized he looked like somebody else I know. After some hard thinking, it dawned on me that it was Osan, the maid. By the way, while I'm on this subject perhaps I should describe Osan's features.

She has a puffed-out, swollen face. The other day someone gave my master a gift—a lantern made from a dried globefish—purchased at the Anamori Inari Shrine. Osan's face was puffed out just like this globefish. The swelling is so exaggerated that it is hard to distinguish her eyes. The puffed-out globefish is evenly round, like a ball, but the bone structure of Osan's face forms a few angles so she looks more like a dropsical hexagonal clock. If Osan heard this, she would be furious with me, so I'll return to my master.

As I have already explained, he had his cheeks puffed out and he kept slapping them. At the same time he murmured to himself, " If the skin were always as taut as this, no one would notice the pockmarks."

He then turned his face sideways so as to let the light fall from the left. " This way, they're extremely noticeable. It's best when the light falls fully on the face. Very queer, indeed! " He seemed to be greatly impressed. Then he held the mirror out as far as possible and intently looked into it.

"At a distance, it's not so bad; the marks show more from close up. But I guess that is true with almost everything." He was mumbling excitedly to himself, as if he had discovered a great truth.

His next move was to bring the mirror suddenly to a horizontal position under his chin. He then squinted his eyes and wrinkled his forehead and nose all at once. He must have realized how horrible he looked because he quickly stopped.

" I wonder why I'm so ugly," he mused, holding the mirror

about three inches from his eyes. He stroked his nose with the tip of his forefinger and then pressed the finger on a blotter lying on the desk. Grease formed a round blob on the paper. He seemed to know a lot of tricks. After wiping the grease off his finger tip on the blotter, he peeled open his right eyelid, succeeding admirably in making a ghostly face. At this stage, it became rather difficult to understand whether he was experimenting with his pockmarks or trying only to out-stare the mirror.

Trying to interpret this absurd spectacle favorably, perhaps he was trying to understand himself better in order to attain enlightment. In all studies, man must study himself first. The heaven and earth, mountains and rivers, the sun and the moon, the stars and other heavenly bodies—all are but reflections of man himself. It would be impossible to study other matters without taking one's own self into consideration. If a man were able to forget himself completely, he would no longer be himself. Nobody can ever know another person completely. Moreover, nobody besides you yourself can do any of your studying for you. Even if they wanted to do it or even if you asked them to do so, it would be something quite impossible. That's why heroes become heroes with no urging from others. If you could know yourself through others, it would be like having somebody else chew for you so you would know whether a piece of meat were tender or tough. To hear sermons in the morning, to listen to principles in the evening, and to handle books in a study are simply ways to make a person realize that he must learn to think for himself without the help of others.

There is no reason to smother oneself in the preachings of others, in the principles of others, or to bury oneself amid stacks of moth-eaten books written by others. If there is, it would be because your own ghost had been the inspiration. But even a ghost is better than no ghost. And if you go chasing a shadow, you cannot possibly deny that you might not meet your own real self. But in most cases, the shadow does not leave the body. So, if you interpret my master's actions in this sense, they should be considered as admirable. He could be considered a better man than the scholars who blindly accept the theories of Epictetus and boast about having someone else to think for them.

A mirror is a brewery of vanity and, at the same time, a sterilizer of pride. There's no other tool that can make someone a fool as quickly as when he peers into a looking-glass with the feeling of vanity. It can be said that two thirds of self-conceit, which not only harms the conceited person but also causes injury to others, is due to mirrors. Joseph Ignace Guillotin, a curious doctor, brought untold terror to himself as well as to others when he invented his head-cutting machine during the French Revolution. The inventor of the mirror must also have been conscience-strickened. But still, when one feels disgusted with himself, or all shrivelled up, there's nothing as reassuring as a look into a mirror.

Beauty and ugliness both become obvious so you'll wonder how you've been able to live so proudly in the past with such a face. And this realization should bring a feeling of gratitude because there's nothing so priceless in the education of a fool than to acknowledge the fact that one is a fool. Before this self-acknowledged fool, each and every self-important fellow should bow in respect. The fool himself, flushed with triumph, might despise this and laugh at those who admire him but it is his modesty that makes the others bow in the first place.

My master is not clever enough to acknowledge himself a fool, yet he looked at the pockmarks carved on his face frankly. To acknowledge one's own ugliness can be considered the first step towards acquiring humbleness of the heart. Perhaps my master is a man you can expect to hear about after all. But again, his moment of honesty might also have been due to the fact that he had been snubbed by a philosopher.

Still ignorant of my presence, my master made another face, one as bad as he could. "Hmmm, they're quite bloodshot—must be chronic conjunctivitis," he complained and then began to rub his blood-shot eyes vigorously. No matter how itchy they might have been, it was not wise to rub them the way he did. In the not too distant future, his eyes will look like those of a salted red snapper. Presently he looked into the mirror again. His eyes were as dull as the winter sky of northern countries, but then my master's eyes are never very bright. I could exaggerate and say that they are so vague with confusion that there was no dividing line between the whites of his eyes and the pupils.

Like his mind, his eyes are hazy and pointless, floating in their sockets unsteadily. This disorder can sometimes be attributed to congenital syphillis or to the measles. My master has tried to cure his dull look by gulping down reddish frogs and worms of willow trees ever since he was a child. The care his mother gave him has resulted in failure; he has been in this blank state ever since he was born. I myself know that my master's empty stare is not due to congenital syphillis or even to the measles. His eyeballs roam around in a state of indistinctness and muddiness simply because his brain is equally unclear. This look of dismay and gloom must have caused a great deal of worry to his mother who probably knew nothing about his weak brain. Smoke indicates fire and clouded eyes are sure signs of stupidity. My master's eyes are symbols of his mind: his brain must have a hole in it, like those coins used in the Tempo era; and his eyes, therefore, are like those Tempo coins, rather large but of practically no value.

The next thing my master did was to commence twisting his moustache. When my master first started growing a moustache, it had extremely bad manners; the hairs grew out in whatever way they pleased. Even today when individualism is admired, hairs growing out every which way would cause embarrassment to the owner of a moustache. My master had recently made great efforts to train it and his endeavors brought some fruit. The moustache seemed a little neater every day. At one time it was difficult to distinguish the moustache but now it grows more luxuriously. My master must believe that his moustache is something to cultivate with care, for every morning and evening he encourages it to grow more. His ambition in life is much the same as that of Wilhelm II, the Kaiser of Germany: to proudly display a moustache, a symbol of success.

Indifferent as to whether the pores slanted sideways or downward, he'd grasp a bunch of unruly hairs and pull them up high.

I should think the hairs would wither after such an ordeal, for this even seemed to hurt their possessor at times. But this is how the moustache was trained—simply by pulling the hairs the wrong way. Some people might think this an odd hobby, but it is quite the proper thing to do. This same painful procedure can also be seen when teachers, boasting about their ability, forcibly develop the characters of their students; so there is no reason to criticize it.

While my master was absorbed in pulling his moustache the many-cornered-faced Osan, the maid, came in from the kitchen, and held out some letters in her red hands. The mail had arrived. My master, still grasping his moustache with his right hand and holding the mirror in his left, turned his head around to face the intruder. The many-cornered Miss, seeing the moustache which usually droops down now straight up in the air, all of a sudden ran back into the kitchen and laughed herself out, supporting herself against the rice cooker.

My master did not seem bothered by this. He calmly put down the mirror and picked up one of the envelopes. The first was a printed letter, rather formal in style:

Dear Sir:

Allow us to offer our sincere best wishes for your happiness.

In reflecting on the past, we have enjoyed victory in every battle in the Russo-Japanese War. Our ever loyal officers and men are now returning amid shouts of " *Banzai* ". The joy of our nation is overwhelming. When called to take up arms in this just battle, our brave troops offered their lives for their country with admirable spirit. They had to endure the discomforts of hot and cold climates for a long time in strange lands thousands of miles away. Their efforts can never be forgotten.

The victorious return of almost all of our troops will soon be completed. With this in view, it is our humble aim, as representatives of this district, to hold a celebration on the twenty-fifth of this month to pay homage to the officers and men from our district who fought in this war, and also to console the families of those who died in action.

In regard to this, we would like to have the kind support and cooperation of all concerned in order to make this occasion a success. Any donation on your part will be used to further this worthy cause.

Yours sincerely,

The letter was signed by a peer. My master, after having read it, folded it again, inserted it back into its envelope and then forgot all about it.

It is not often that my master does much donating. Once when there was a crop failure in the northeastern districts, he donated two or three yen, but later he would repeatedly complain that he had been deprived of a great deal of money because of the donation. Everyone knows that a donation is made willingly—it's not as if a person were being robbed by a thief. Therefore my master's saying that he had been deprived of money is not appropriate. In any case, my master is hardly the kind of person to donate anything so troops could be honored, not even when asked by a peer in a printed letter. Of course it might have turned out differently if the peer had come and vigorously negotiated, however, it is even more probable that my master would be thinking that he himself should be honored first at any function. Afterwards, he might welcome the troops—or anyone else. Now that he was constantly in want, however, he probably thought it would be wiser to have the peer arrange such matters all by himself.

My master picked up the second letter. It was also printed:

Now that we are having cool autumn weather, we sincerely hope that you are taking the best possible care of your health.

The construction of our new school building, as you most probably know, has at last entered the final stage. With great determination and perseverance while sustaining bitter hardships, we have been fortunate to acquire means of obtaining almost all the funds essential for this purpose. We are also fortunate to be able to announce that we have published a book, " Essentials of Sewing Techniques ". This book is based on the principles and fundamentals of industrial art, acquired only after many years of research while experiencing untold-of difficulties.

It is my ardent wish that this book will be purchased by every household. It will certainly serve as a wonderful help to anyone interested in dressmaking. Besides, the small profit we can expect would help greatly to complete the school. We request your kind consideration and humbly ask you to obtain this book for your maid or some other interested person. Bowing nine times in humbly begging for your cooperation, I am,

Yours sincerely,
Shinsaku Nuida
Principal
Dai-Nippon Girls' Sewing High School
Postgraduate, Research Department

My master crumpled up this courteous letter and threw it carelessly into the wastepaper basket. It is a pity that Shinsaku's nine bows, along with his determination and perseverance, had gone to waste. Now for the third letter.

It was quite an extraordinary one. The envelope was covered with red and white parallel stripes, like a stick of peppermint. From the top to bottom, the address was written in a peculiar style in thick brush strokes: " To Mr. Kushami " Peppermint. sticks sold by street vendors generally have little tidbits in them to surprise the children who buy them. Though I couldn't promise that this letter would contain a special treat, the envelope was extremely pretty :

If I should judge heaven and earth, they might show their anger by drinking the river Hsi dry in one gulp; but if I were judged by heaven and earth, I would merely become like dust on the street. Tell me, then, what relation exists between heaven and earth and myself?

The first person who ate sea slugs should be respected for his pluck, and the first who tasted globefish should be given credit for his courage. He who introduced sea slugs to our everyday meals should be considered as great as Priest Shinran, and those who introduced globefish should be thought of in the same light as Nichiren, another famous priest.

As for you, Mr. Kushami, you only eat dried gourd shavings with vinegared bean paste. I have never as yet seen a truly distinguished person eating dried gourd shavings with vinegared bean paste.

Your best friends might betray you, your parents might keep secrets from you, your lover might cast you aside; riches and honors might be out of your reach forever and you might lose your respect and position overnight. The knowledge you have stored in your mind might commence to grow moldy. And to whom would you ask for help? Who in this wide world would help you? God?

God is only a dummy invented by those who are in desperate trouble. Such people are like the smelly remains of coagulated human excrement evacuated in moments of oppression. Did you say that you've found peace of mind by relying on God's compassion? Bad—very bad! A drunkard totters to his grave, then the oil is spent and the light goes out. Are the aged exempt from all worry? When your acts of good and evil are finished, what will you leave behind? Yes, Mr. Kushami, don't you think it's better to have your tea?

There's nothing to fear if you do not consider man as man. But if you do not consider a man as a man, why do you resent this world when you are not even yourself? This would be like admiring a hero who does not consider a man as a man. But the difference lies in the fact that he showed his colors when you did not even consider him to be a man. Therefore show your colors, you stupid idiot!

If men are men but you are not you, the discontented will descend from the heavens. We call this spasmodic action "revolution". Revolutions are not made by the discontented but are creations of distinguished heroes who produce them by preference.

My dear Mr. Kushami, there are many ginseng herbs in Korea. Why is it that you don't eat some?

Humbly bowing twice, I am,
Yours truly,
Kohei Tendo at Sugamo

Shinsaku had bowed nine times at the close of his letter, but this ended with only two. Well, of course, not being a letter requesting any donations, Kohei Tendo must have made it easier for himself by cancelling seven of them. This was not a letter asking for any money but it was practically impossible to understand. This letter would have been rejected even by the lowest type of magazine so therefore I thought my master would tear it to shreds. But no! He re-read it, again and again. He must have decided there was some hidden significance and he wanted to comprehend its full meaning.

There are many things in the universe which cannot be understood but there is nothing that we cannot attach some meaning to if we try hard enough. No matter how difficult a sentence happens to be, if we have the will to interpret some idea from it, we can. Whether humans are stupid or clever, they are still humans. But even if we considered humans as dogs or pigs, it would not be too much of a proposition to rack our brains over. It would make no difference if we said that mountains are low or that the universe is tiny. We could just as easily get away with saying that crows are white, or that Ono-no-Komachi* is an ugly woman, or that Mr. Kushami is a true gentleman. Therefore, such a nonsensical letter as this could be interpreted in any way, simply by finding some reason for the interpretation decided upon. A man like my master, who is used to giving lengthy definitions of English words without even knowing the actual meaning, would especially want to attach some significance to this foolish letter.

Once my master pondered for a whole week on a question asked by a student: " Why, on a nasty day, do you say ' Good

---

* Ono-no-Komachi was a famous and noted poetess during the reign of Emperor Montoku (850–858) of the Heian Era (794–1191), and who was known as one of the most beautiful women of Japan.

morning'?" It took him three days and nights to find out the meaning of "Columbus" in Japanese. Does the greatest hero in the world ever eat dried gourd shavings with vinegared bean paste? Can eating Korean ginseng bring about a revolution?—for such a man as my master, such puzzles are full of hidden significance.

My master, after having considered this difficult letter in the same way as he did the problem of "Good morning", seemed quite pleased with himself. He praised the letter exceedingly: "The meaning is deep. It must have been written by a person who has studied a lot of philosophy. A great view, indeed!" By this one statement, the stupidity of my master can be clearly proven. But there is at least one point which stands to reason; my master has the habit of praising anything he does not understand.

But this does not apply only to my master. In matters one doesn't understand, there are concealed bits of wisdom that one cannot mock; that which a person cannot fathom, gives him a feeling of nobleness. That is why most people generally praise what they do not comprehend, and why scholars lecture on subjects they have mastered as if they didn't understand what they themselves were talking about. This can be seen every day in universities; when explained in such a way that the students can't understand it, the lecture is well spoken of. But when a lecture is given in clear terms, it is not considered intellectual.

That my master thought highly of this letter was not because he clearly understood the significance. And no wonder, since it had no significance at all. Consider the sea slugs appearing all of a sudden as did the excrement. The only reason my master praised this letter was because he could not understand it at all —like the Lavismists highly praising the *Lao-tsze*, like the Confucians highly praising the *Book of Morality*, and like Zen priests highly praising the *Reminiscences of Lin-chi*. Of course they cannot admit that they do not understand these works, so they give the philosophies the interpretations that satisfy themselves and make believe they understand. To think highly of what is incomprehensible was fun even in the days of old.

My master reverently folded this letter and replaced it in its envelope. He then placed it on his desk and he put his hands into his bosom and sank into deep meditation.

Soon, however, a loud voice was heard from the entrance of the house. " Pardon, beg pardon." A visitor had come. The voice seemed as if it belonged to Meitei but unbecoming him because it sounded so excited. My master heard the voice but his hands remained inside his kimono and he did not stir. Most probably he had once decided that it was not for the master of the house to greet guests from his study because he never does so. The maid had gone to buy some laundry soap and the Mrs. was in the toilet. The only one left to greet the guest was myself but even I do not like this duty.

Then I heard the visitor jump onto the veranda and step into the house after opening the paper sliding door. My master was a queer man but then his guest was also queer. I knew by the footsteps that the caller was now coming from the parlor towards the study.

" Where is everybody? You're having visitors," boomed out Meitei.

" Oh, it's you!"

" What do you mean ' Oh, it's you!' If you're here, why don't you answer the door? The place is like an empty house."

" Well, I had some thinking to do."

" Even so, you could at least have said ' Please come in.' "

" No I couldn't."

" Pampering yourself as always!"

" I've been practicing some mental culture the last few days."

" It's hard on your guests when you can't even answer the door because of your mental culture. You shouldn't be that lost in your studies. By the way, I didn't come alone today. I brought a remarkable person with me. Come and meet him."

"And who did you bring?"

" Never mind who. Just come and meet him; he has been looking forward to seeing you."

" Who is it?"

" Never mind, just come."

My master stood up with his hands still in his bosom and said, " I hope you're not playing any tricks on me again." Going by way of the veranda, he nonchalantly strolled into the parlor. There, opposite the alcove, reverently sat an old man.

My master, upon seeing him, unconsciously took his hands out of his kimono and sat down right beside the paper sliding door. He was facing west and the old man also faced west, so there was no way of bowing to each other. And old-fashioned people are extremely strict about greetings.

" Please sit over here," urged the old man, pointing to the alcove while hinting to my master to take his proper place. Only two or three years ago, my master believed that it made no difference where he sat in a room; but ever since he attended a lecture and learned that the space in front of the alcove was for honored guests, he never sat in front of one. Moreover, here was an old man, a complete stranger, who solidly sat in the middle of the room. So my master only bowed and suggested that his guest take the honored position. As it turned out, he was only repeating what the old man had first said to him.

" Please sit over here."

" That would be going against etiquette, so please."

" No—please, you take that seat." My master was again imitating the old man without doing any thinking for himself at all.

" Really, your modesty puts me in a very embarrassing position. Please don't be so reserved. Please, over there."

" I'm sorry to cause you embarrassment, but please. Please." My master was all red in the face and mumbling his words terribly. It seems that his mental culture wasn't doing him much good. Meitei had kept standing behind the sliding door, smiling at the performance. But now, thinking it was about time to stop this foolishness, he shoved my master's rear over and commanded, " Move over. If you stay so close to the door, I'll have no place to sit. Now, don't be so modest and take your proper place." He then forced himself to where my master had been. Reluctantly my master slid forward.

" Kushami, this is the uncle from Shizuoka I've often told you about. Uncle, this is Kushami."

"Well, well, it's a great pleasure to meet you. I understand that Meitei comes here often and it has been my wish to visit you too for a long time. Fortunately, we were in the neighborhood today so we dropped in so I could thank you for your kindness to my nephew. I sincerely hope we can keep up a long friendship." The old gentleman's greeting flowed out without any hitch. My master, however, does not have many chances to meet other people and, besides, he is a man of few words. He looked overwhelmed by this old visitor and was at a loss as to how to deal with the situation. Having been addressed so eloquently, he forgot all about the Korean ginseng and the colorful envelope with red and white parallel stripes; in desperation, he stammered, "I—ah—I should have—ah—visited you—ah—yes, I wish to be honored—with your—friendship." He raised his bowed head a little from the floor but found that the old gentleman still had his head close to the mat. Obligingly, he brought his head down again.

After sucking in a deep breath, the elderly guest raised his head and said, "I myself used to have an estate here in Yedo (Tokyo) but when the government fell, I moved to Shizuoka. I haven't had a chance to visit my old home town until today. I seem to have lost my sense of direction. If it wasn't for Meitei I wouldn't have been able to find my way around. There have been many changes. It's three hundred years since the shogunate first established itself here in the shogun's estate."

Meitei, finding this discourse tiring, cut in, "The shogun's estate might have been wonderful but we are also fortunate to live during the present time. There was no Red Cross Association in the old days, for example, was there?"

"No, there was no Red Cross. The present is also glorious because it's now possible to see members of the Imperial Household; that is surely something that could not have been done in my younger days. I have lived for a long time, but I feel especially thankful that I was able to be present at the grand meeting today and to have listened to the voice of His Imperial Highness the Prince. I can die happily now."

"My uncle feels lucky to be able to do the sights of Tokyo after such a long time. He came from Shizuoka just to be present at the grand meeting of the Red Cross Association. We went to the meeting at Ueno Park today and dropped in here on our way home. That's the reason my uncle is wearing the frockcoat I ordered at the Shirokiya Department Store."

Meitei brought the frockcoat to my attention, and I took a look at it. It didn't fit the old man at all. The sleeves were too long, the collar was too small, and there was a depression along the back as deep as a pond. Besides, the coat was too tight at the armpits. It would have been difficult to make another fit as bad as this, even intentionally. The collar of the shirt had become unbuttoned so every time the old gentleman turned his head, I could see his Adam's apple. I couldn't tell whether his black tie was around his collar or his neck. Perhaps the frockcoat could be tolerated, but the uncle's topknot was a sight to be seen! Looking to see if he had his famous iron fan with him, I found it on the mat lying neatly beside his bent knees.

My master finally recovered himself and began applying the newly acquired powers of observation he had learned. His face showed special surprise at the old gentleman's suit. Meitei had told my master how strange his uncle looked, but my master found him even worse. If my master's pockmarks can be considered as material for future historical research work, then the topknot and the iron fan of this elderly gentleman must be even more valuable for preservation. My master wanted to know more about the iron fan but he could not very well ask directly. On the other hand, it would be impolite to stop the conversation so he commented, " I believe there must have been a big crowd at the Red Cross meeting." This was probably the safest way to continue the flow of talk.

" Yes, a tremendous crowd. And everybody seemed to be staring at me. It seems that people have become terribly curious. In my time they weren't like that."

" Exactly. They were not like that at all," imitated my master, as if he were an old man himself. This does not mean that he was pretending to know about such matters ; he was just saying whatever came to his hazy mind.

" They seemed especially curious about this helmet splitter."

"That iron fan of yours must be quite heavy."

"Just take hold of it," suggested Meitei. "It's really very heavy. Uncle, let him feel it."

The old man picked the iron object up and urged, "Please." My master received the offering in the same way worshippers accept models of the swords of Naozane Kumagai at the Kurodani Shrine in Kyoto. He held it for a while but returned it with only "I see."

"Everybody calls this a fan but actually it's a helmet splitter, altogether different from a fan."

"Oh? What do you do with it?"

"You split helmets with it. And when your enemy is dazed by the blow, you kill him. It's been used from the time of Masashige Kusunoki."

"Is that the helmet splitter of Masashige?"

"No. The possessor is not known. But it's old—it probably dates back to the Kenmu era [1334–1336]."

"By the way, Kushami, after the meeting today, my uncle and I dropped in to see Kangetsu at the College of Science. He was in the physics laboratory. My uncle's helmet splitter is pure iron, so a magnetic condenser there was effected and almost broke down."

"That couldn't be," the uncle interrupted. "The iron used for this helmet splitter was made in the Kenmu era. It's of the best possible quality so it couldn't happen."

"The quality of the iron wouldn't make any difference. You couldn't help it; even Kangetsu said so."

"By the way, is Kangetsu the fellow who was grinding glass balls? It's a pity, isn't it, being so young. He should have something better to do."

"I suppose he is to be pitied but once he completes his research, he's sure to become a doctor of science."

"Well, if you can become a scholar just by grinding glass balls, anybody can become one. I could become a scholar myself; the owner of a marble store would be the most excellent. In ancient China, ball polishers were considered of rather low social standing." The old man then looked at my master as if he were silently demanding approval.

"Is that so?" uttered my master respectfully.

"Today nobody seems to study anything except physics. Though that may seem admirable to you, physics won't help you at a critical moment. In my days, the training of a warrior was a matter of life and death. When a soldier's time came, he was so cultured that he did not panic. Such a life is not as easy as grinding glass balls or weaving wires."

My master again respectfully said, "Is that so?"

"Uncle, in order to cultivate the mind, you can sit with your hands at your bosom inside your kimono instead of grinding glass balls, can't you?"

"That's where you're wrong. It's not as simple as that. Mêng-tsŭ, the Chinese scholar, urged his disciples to develop a true conscience; Shao K'an-Chieh, another Chinese scholar, cautioned his followers against having their minds occupied with only one thought and he told them to acquire a wide view of the world. A Chinese Buddhist priest of the Zen sect, Chung-Fêng, considered constant participation in religious services as most important. These principles are more difficult to understand."

"Indeed, quite impossible."

"Have you ever read the works of the Zen priest Takuan?"

"No, I haven't even heard of him."

"Takuan asks, 'Where must you place your mind?' If you place it on the movements of your enemy, your mind would be possessed by the movements of your enemy. If you concentrate on the sword of your enemy, you would become possessed by the sword of your enemy. If your resolution is to slash at your enemy, your consciousness would be possessed by the thought of trying to slash your enemy. If you place all your confidence on your own sword, you would become possessed by the thoughts about your own sword. If you limit your mind to the thought that you cannot be defeated by your enemy, your whole being would be possessed by that one thought. So there would be no place to your keep mind. That's what Takuan says."

"Uncle, your memory is still very good, indeed. Kushami,

did you understand it all?"

"Hmmm. Is that so?" said my master, again repeating his same polite phrase.

"You see, don't you? Where must you place your mind? If you placed it on the movements of your enemy, your mind would be possessed by the movements of your enemy. If you concentrate on the sword of your enemy—"

"Don't worry, Uncle. Kushami knows all about these matters. He keeps himself in his study all day long cultivating his mind. He remains so deep in thought that he can't even come out to greet his guests. You needn't worry any about Kushami."

"That's extremely praiseworthy! Meitei, why don't you join him?"

"Ha, ha, ha! I haven't got the time. Just because you don't do anything yourself, you think that everybody else is free."

"But you don't do anything, do you?"

"But I'm engaged in leisure itself!"

"There! You see how unoccupied you are. That's why you should cultivate yourself more. I've heard of 'Leisure in intervals during one's business', but never of being 'Engaged in leisure itself'. Am I right, Mr. Kushami?"

"Well, I don't believe I have ever heard about it either."

"Ha, ha, ha! I surrender. By the way, Uncle, how about a dish of famous Tokyo eels? We could go to the restaurant Chiku-yo. It would take no time from here by streetcar."

"That sounds good but I promised to go to Suihara's today, so you'll have to excuse me."

"Sugihara's? Is that old man still alive?"

"It's not Sugihara but Suihara. It's insulting to mispronounce the names of others. Learn to be more careful."

"But the written characters are *sugi* and *hara*, aren't they?"

"Yes, but it is read Suihara, not Sugihara."

"That's queer."

"Nothing queer about it at all. Many of the characters written in Japanese have two or more meanings as well as pronunciations. The Chinese use the same character for 'earthworm' as we do, but pronounce it differently. In both languages it signifies a worm with no eyes. It's the same with the characters for the Chinese word 'toad' although we read it to signify 'frog'."

"I guess that's true."

"When you kill a toad [*gama*] by hitting it, it dies on its back. In Japanese we say that it has 'turned over' [*kaeru*] on its back. Therefore, we are actually calling a frog [*kaeru*] a 'thing turned over'. It's the same in reading my friend's name. Only a countryfied boy would read 'Suihara' as 'Sugihara', so if you don't watch out, everyone will laugh at you for your ignorance."

"Well, are you really going to see this Suihara now? I don't feel much like paying another visit."

"If you don't want to, you needn't come. I'll go alone."

"Can you?"

"I'll take a rickshaw if you'll call one for me."

My master obligingly had the maid go for a carriage and the old gentleman; after making a long and formal farewell, put his derby hat over his topknot and left. Meitei remained.

"So that's your old uncle!"

"That's him."

"Is that so?" said my master for the last time, putting his hands into his bosom while in deep thought.

"Ha, ha, ha! Don't you think he's wonderful? I'm lucky to have such an uncle. He's the same anywhere he goes. He must have surprised you." Meitei was delighted with the thought that he could surprise my master.

"Not much."

"If you weren't surprised, you are a calmer man than I had believed you to be."

"But I like the way he stressed the culture of the mind."

"Do you think that's worthwhile? When you become sixty, you'll probably seem just as old-fashioned as my old uncle does to us. Don't pay too much attention to such out-moded ideas."

"You keep telling me your uncle is old-fashioned but perhaps those older people have the right ideas while we're wrong. In the first place, the education given nowadays attempts too much —there's no limit to it. You're never satisfied. Our ancestors studied in the Oriental method, trained themselves to be more

[313]

passive and with finer tastes. That's because the mind and only the mind was being cultivated." My master was repeating the ideas of his philosopher friend as if they were his own.

"That's all foolish nonsense. You're beginning to sound like Dokusen Yagi."

Hearing the name of Dokusen Yagi, my master swallowed a quick breath in surprise because the philosopher who had visited the *Den of Sleeping Dragons* was none other than Dokusen Yagi himself. My master had no idea that Meitei knew him. Now Meitei had stumped my master into silence only by mentioning his name no sooner than my master had begun to warm up to saying his piece.

Realizing that he was on thin ice, my master asked, "Have you ever heard Dokusen's theory?"

"Have I ever heard it? It hasn't changed a bit since we were classmates ten years ago."

"Well, a good theory does not have to change."

"Because of people like you who will listen to him, Dokusen can still get along. The stupid goat! Just take a look at his whiskers. He looks exactly like a billy goat. Even in school he wore a beard. Once he came over to my place to spend the night and to preach his theory of passive culture. He'd keep repeating the same thing over and over again; he never knew when to stop. I suggested going to bed but you know what an idiot he is—he simply said that he wasn't sleepy and continued repeating his theory. A terrible nuisance! I told him that even if he didn't feel sleepy that *I did*. I finally got him to bed but just as he was going to sleep, a rat came and bit his nose. He made an awful fuss in the middle of the night. He talks about how little life means but he seemed terribly worried about dying from the rat bite. He kept telling me that the poison from the bite was spreading through his body. I was so annoyed that I went to the kitchen and fixed him a piece of paper smeared with mashed rice kernels."

"But why?"

"I explained that it was a plaster imported from Germany and that a famous doctor had invented it there. I told him that the people in India used it after being bitten by poisonous snakes. I praised it as much as I could. I told him he'd have nothing to worry about if he stuck it on his nose."

" You had a knack for fooling people even at that time, didn't you? "

"And as Dokusen is such an innocent boy, he believed every word I said. He went back to bed and was soon snoring. I almost died laughing the next morning when I saw a piece of thread hanging from his billy goat whiskers from under the paper plaster."

" It seems he's become more serious since that time."

" Did you meet him recently? "

" He came about a week ago."

" No wonder you're spreading the passive theory of the Dokusen school."

" I was greatly impressed at the time so I have begun cultivating my mind with great effort."

" It's good to be enthusiastic but if you take what everyone says so seriously, you'll only make a fool of yourself. You always seem to believe what others tell you right away. Dokusen, for instance, will tell you great theories but when an emergency arises, he's the same as any of us. Do you remember the earthquake we had nine years ago? The only student in the dormitory to jump from the second story was Dokusen and him alone. He really hurt himself."

" Did he have an explanation for his action? "

" Of course. According to him, he was very fortunâte. The spirit of the Zen doctrine is in learning to remain calm so when an emergency arises, the head is clear for acting fast. Dokusen said that when everyone else panicked during the earthquake, he alone had the presence of mind to leap out of the second-story window. He seemed proud of himself and actually boasted about his feat as he went limping around. He's really stubborn. I myself don't trust anybody that talks so much about the Zen sect and Buddhism."

" I wonder," mumbled Mr. Kushami, giving way a little.

" When Dokusen came to see you the other day, didn't he

quote a line that sounds like a Zen priest talking in his sleep?"

"He said something about flashing a sword like lightning and cutting the spring breeze."

"Sure, sure. That lightning stuff! That's always been his favorite. There wasn't anybody in the dormitory who didn't know that lightning business of the "Reverend Undiscerner", the nickname we gave Dokusen. It was especially fun to hear him recite that line when he got all excited. He'd get all tangled up and say, 'Flashing a sword like the spring breeze, you've cut lightning'. Try him out the next time he comes. He begins his preaching calmly but if you start opposing him, you'll get him all confused and he'll start contradicting himself and saying queer things."

"You're always trying to fool other people!"

"You can't always tell who is fooling who. As for me, I hate people who say that they're like Zen priests or that they can foretell the future. Near my house, there's a temple called the Nanzo-*in*. The retired head priest there is about eighty years old. The other day, during a shower, lightning struck a pine tree in the garden of the temple right outside the old priest's window. Everyone told me how self-composed he was but when I asked the priest himself about the lightning, I found that he was stone deaf. So, you see, most phenomena can be explained in some logical way. As for Dokusen, he wouldn't be a bad sort if he only kept his continual preachings to himself. There are times when he can convince others with his wild dreams and that's bad. Did you know that there are two people who went crazy because of him?"

"Who?"

"One of them is Tozen Rino. Because of Dokusen, he became interested in the study of Zen doctrines and went to Kamakura. It was there that he began to go crazy. Right in front of the Engaku-*ji* Temple there is a railroad crossing. Well, one day he jumped onto the rails and sat there like a Zen priest, boasting that he'd stop the oncoming train. Of course the train stopped and he was saved but he insisted that he was immortal and could not be burnt nor drowned. He tried to prove this by diving into a lotus pond in the temple gardens."

"And did he drown?"

" No, a priest of the seminary passed by and saved him. After that he returned to Tokyo but finally died of peritonitis. The reason he got peritonitis was because he ate boiled wheat in the temple instead of rice and overly seasoned pickled vegetables. Therefore you can say that in a way Dokusen actually killed him."

" That proves that it's sometimes dangerous to become too engrossed in any one subject," said my master, screwing his face up in anxiety.

" That's right. And I had another classmate who went crazy because of Dokusen."

"And who was he?"

" Robai Tachimachi. Poor fellow, he was also influenced by Dokusen and always kept saying that eels go to heaven. And he finally became like an eel himself."

" What do you mean by that?"

" That Tachimachi loved to eat. He was as greedy as a pig and, besides, he had the stubbornness of a Zen priest. He was a terrible nuisance. Nobody noticed just when it all began but he kept saying the queerest things. Once when he was visiting me, he asked whether beef cutlets ever came flying to the pine trees I had in my yard. He told me that in his home town, boiled fish paste often came floating down rivers on little boards. I don't mind a joke but when he suggested that we go digging for some sugared chestnuts in a ditch outside, I gave up. He was finally taken to the insane asylum in Sugamo and confined there. Pigs are not generally permitted to enter insane asylums but due to Dokusen, Robai was able to get that far. Dokusen's influence is very great."

"And is he still confined in Sugamo?"

" Oh, yes. And he's extremely proud of his insanity. I understand he's changed his name from Robai Tachimachi, which he claims is of no interest now, to Kohei Tendo. He believes himself to be Heaven incarnate. You ought to go and see him; it would be worth the trip."

[317]

" Did you say Kohei Tendo? "

" Yes. He's given himself a good name even though he is crazy. He insists that he can help save the people of the world who are in doubt and he sends letters to his friends telling them to go and visit him. I've received four or five of His letters myself. They're generally so long that I have had to pay for insufficient postage twice."

" Then the letter that just came to me was from Robai."

" Did you receive one, too? That's queer. And was the envelope red? "

" The middle was red from top to bottom but white on both sides. Quite an extraordinary envelope."

" He has to order them from China. The white parts represent the ways of heaven and earth, and the way of mankind is shown in between in red; this is the way Robai explains it anyway."

" The envelope has great meaning behind it, doesn't it? "

"Although he is kept busy boasting about his insanity, his greed for food still remains the same. Every time he writes he mentions something to eat. He must have written something about food in your letter, too. Am I right?'

" He wrote about sea slugs."

" Robai always liked sea slugs. Anything else? "

" He mentioned something about globefish and Korean ginseng."

" That was clever combining globefish and Korean ginseng. Maybe it was his intention to point out that if you're poisoned by eating globefish, boiled-down Korean ginseng will act as an antidote."

" It didn't sound like that, though."

" It doesn't make any difference. He's crazy. Was that all? "

" Oh, yes. There was also a place where it said, ' Mr. Kushami, drink some tea.' "

" Ha, ha, ha! Drink some tea! He must have thought that you would need some tea after the globefish. *Banzai* for Kohei Tendo! " Meitei seemed especially happy about this and commenced to laugh heartily.

My master, who had read and re-read this letter respectfully, now found that the sender was a notorious lunatic. He was furious with himself because all his enthusiasm and labor had been for nothing; he felt ashamed, too, to have relished a letter from a lunatic so much. He became doubtful about his own mental state since he had been so full of admiration for the work of a madman. His face expressed anguish due to the combination of his anger, shame and worry.

Just then, the entrance door screeched open and a couple of heavy footsteps were heard. Then a voice called out, "Beg pardon. I beg your pardon." Unlike my master, heavy in motion and slow to rise from a sitting position, Meitei is quick and light. Without waiting for the maid to receive the caller, Meitei replied, "Coming," and made his way to the entrance vestibule in two leaps. It was rather troublesome to have Meitei visit us unasked and unannounced, but once inside the house he was quite handy because he went about greeting visitors as if he were a house boy. But Meitei was, after all, a guest so it was wrong for my master to remain seated in the parlor and let him do the job of greeting callers. Most people would follow the guest if the visitor happened to answer the door but Mr. Kushami is different. He remained calmly seated on his cushion in the parlor. To be calmly seated does not necessarily mean that my master's nerves were calm, however.

I could hear Meitei talking away with two strangers, but presently he shouted, "Hey, Master of the house! Come here a moment. You're the only one that can handle this." My master resigned himself to duty and sluggishly stepped to the entrance, his hands still in his bosom. Meitei had a calling card in his hand, still talking with the two strangers in a crouching posture. His rear end was not in a very dignified position.

On the calling card was printed: "Torazo Yoshida, Police Detective, Metropolitan Police Board." There were two men in the vestibule. One was twenty-five or -six, high in stature and rather handsome, wearing a taffeta kimono. He stood there silently with his hands in his bosom, just like my master. I thought that I had seen that face before so I took a closer look. It really was a face I knew! He was the thief who had entered the house of my master and stole the yams! Aha! And now he was here again in broad daylight, and at the main entrance!

"This is a police detective. He has arrested this thief and now he wants you to go to headquarters."

Now that my master understood why the detective had come to his house, he lowered his head and bowed humbly. The thief was much better looking than the policeman so my master must have thought that he was the detective. It was to the thief, then, that my master bowed. The criminal must have been surprised but he couldn't very well say that he was a thief, so he just kept standing there without a word. He still had his hands inside his kimono. Since he was handcuffed, there was little else he could do with them.

For some strange reason, my master has a habit unbecoming a man of the present age; he feels it necessary to show gratitude to public officials and to the police. He believes that authority is to be greatly feared. Police officers are simply men paid by the public to work as watchmen, but my master cringes before them. The father of my master used to be the headman of a village on the outskirts of Tokyo, and he formed the habit of kowtowing to people in higher places. As a result of this, my master must also believe it necessary to humble himself before authority. It is extremely pitiful.

The detective must have thought it very funny for my master to bow to a thief and he couldn't help smile. "You're to come to the Nihon Zutsumi Branch Office Station at 9 a.m. tomorrow. What articles were stolen?"

"The stolen articles were—" began my master. But he had forgotten. All he remembered was the box of yams that Sampei Tatara had given him. The yams were of no importance at all, but it would be very embarrassing if he could not finish his sentence "The stolen articles were—" The articles had been taken from his own home and yet he could not answer. My master did not want to show how childish he really is so, making up his mind, he announced, "The stolen articles were—mmm—a box of yams."

The thief must have thought this extremely funny because he

suddenly bent his head down and buried his chin inside the collar of his kimono. Meitei commenced laughing loudly. "You must regret the loss of those yams very much."

Only the police officer remained serious. "I don't think you can get your yams back, but most of the other things have been found. When you see them, you'll most probably remember. We will have to have a receipt for the stolen goods so don't forget to bring your personal seal.* You must come before 9 a.m. It's the Nihon Zutsumi Police Branch which is within the jurisdiction of the Asakusa Police Station." After the policeman had finished this speech, he left. The thief followed him through the front door. As the prisoner couldn't take his hands out from his bosom, he had no way of closing the door so it was left open. Though humble before, my master seemed angry at this lack of courtesy because he slammed the door shut with a bang.

"Ha, ha ha! You certainly respect detectives, don't you? If you'd always be as humble as this, you'd be much better liked. It's strange that you're only nice to police officers."

"But he took the trouble to come and tell me about the thief."

"But that's his business. All you have to do is to treat police-men like anyone else."

"But his is not an ordinary business."

"I agree. His job is a nasty one. Being a detective is the lowest form of work."

"You'll get into trouble if you say such things."

"Ha, ha, ha! All right, I'll quit talking about detectives, but I still cannot but wonder at your respecting a thief!"

"Who respects thieves?"

"You! You humbly bowed to the thief, didn't you?"

"When?"

"Just now. You almost touched your head to the ground—and to the thief!"

"What are you trying to say? That was the detective."

"Do you think a detective would be dressed in a kimono?"

"He's wearing one because he's disguised."

---

* Seals are used on all official documents in Japan rather than the signature.

" Stubborn ! "

" You're the one that's stubborn."

" Look, do you think a detective would stand around with his hands in his bosom? "

" You can't say that detectives never do, can you? "

"All the while you were bowing humbly, he just kept standing and didn't return you even a nod."

" Well, being a detective perhaps he's not used to such courtesy."

" Oh, you don't even want to try to understand."

" No, I don't. You keep calling the policeman a thief, and that's nonsense. You didn't see the thief when he entered the house, did you? You're the one that's being stubborn."

Meitei must have at last realized that my master was a person incapable of understanding so, unlike his usual self, he didn't argue any more. My master was greatly elated at this because he thought he had won against Meitei, something extremely rare. Actually Meitei had decided against degrading himself more by arguing with such a stubborn person, but my master felt sure that his stubbornness had impressed Meitei. Well, there are many such topsy-turvy misunderstandings in this world. The funny thing about being so stubborn is that the most pigheaded people firmly believe they are protecting their honor; few of them realize that they are really objects of scorn.

" Well, in any case, are you going tomorrow? "

" Of course I am. The detective told me to be there by nine, so I'll leave around eight."

" How about school? "

" I'll take the day off. School, bah! " he seemed to spit out his contempt.

" Will it be all right to take the whole day off? "

" Sure. I'm paid a monthly salary and they don't deduct anything for being absent," confessed my master. You might consider this underhanded of my master but try to consider his simple mind. My master is just simple—not malicious.

" Do you know the way to the police station? "

" No. I mean to go by rickshaw." He was still fuming with anger.

"You don't seem to know any more about Tokyo than my uncle from Shizuoka."

"Go ahead and be as sarcastic as you want."

"Ha, ha, ha! The Nihon Zutsumi Branch Station isn't in just an ordinary place, did you know that? It's in Yoshiwara."

"What's that?"

"In Yoshiwara."

"You mean the Yoshiwara where all those licensed brothels are?"

"There's only one Yoshiwara here in Tokyo. How about it? Are you still planning to go?" Meitei was teasing him again.

Now that he knew the police station was in the red-light district, my master seemed somewhat hesitant. But after considering it more carefully, he exploded, "I don't care if it is in a licensed brothel area or not. I said I'd go so I'll go." Stupid people are generally especially stubborn when being teased.

Meitei suggested that the trip was going to be interesting. "Go and take a look around." And with this, the subject that had caused so much anger ended. Meitei then talked on more ordinary subjects for a while but finally left, saying that if he got home too late his uncle would be worried.

My master ate a hasty supper and then barricaded himself in his study again. There, with folded arms, he commenced thinking the following. I'll tell you how I read his thoughts later on.

"I had intended learning much from Dokusen Yagi but according to Meitei, he does not seem to be the proper person. Somehow his theory now seems senseless. Meitei tells me he is somewhat mentally deranged. Besides, he has driven at least two other people crazy. Really, I was in an extremely dangerous situation. If I became more friendly with him, I might eventually have to be confined to an asylum myself. I admired Robai Tachimachi, alias Kohei Tendo, and believed that he was a great man with great views, but he is now locked up in Sugamo. Meitei might have exaggerated, but Kohei Tendo probably firmly believes that he is the superintendent of heaven. Perhaps I became a little off-balanced myself. It is said that birds of a feather flock

[323]

together. Since I admired the theory of a lunatic—at least I was sympathetic to what was written in the letter—I must be a near relative of that lunatic. Am I cast in the same mold? If I were crazy and living in a room next to Kohei Tendo, I might feel tempted to tear down the dividing partition so I could sit with him and talk. That is a terrible thought!

" My brain has recently been acting so strange that I wonder about my own sanity. Such shocks probably affect a part of the brain and I have lost an amazing amount of equilibrium. Though there is no queer feeling on my tongue or under my armpits, I find a tingling at the base of my teeth and in my muscles. It has become terrible! Maybe, I am a perfect lunatic already. I wonder if I will be locked up in an asylum, too. Fortunately I haven't yet caused injury to another person or become too much of a nuisance to the community. Perhaps insanity can be detected by counting the pulse—no, there's nothing wrong with my pulse. A fever? No, I have no temperature. But, in any case, I'm worried.

" If I continue to compare myself with lunatics, maybe I'll go mad even sooner. My method is wrong. I worry about my sanity because I have been holding a lunatic as a model.

" Therefore, maybe I should try to reach the opposite conclusion by comparing myself to a normal person. How about beginning with Meitei's uncle in the frockcoat who came today? But that would involve the question ' Where must you place your mind? ' No, Meitei's uncle is a little balmy himself. Then how about Kangetsu? He's grinding away at his glass balls from morning till night, hardly taking time out for lunch. He's a little crazy, too. Meitei? He considers it his God-sent duty to do nothing more than go gamboling about. He must be happy, but he's still a lunatic. How about the wife of Kaneda? That evil character of hers is completely opposed to common sense. She is certainly mad, without mistake! Then there's Kaneda himself. Though I haven't met him as yet, I know that he has found it possible to live with his wife in harmony. He must be an extraordinary person! But ' extraordinary ' is just another word for insanity, so I must consider him along with the others. And then—oh, yes, there are those refined ruffians of the Descending Cloud Junior High School. They are still young but they will surely learn to surpass all the others in time.

"No, most people are more or less the same and this gives me unexpected hope. Society is a gathering of lunatics. Lunatics group together and fight among themselves—grabbing, pulling, plundering, and speaking ill of each other. Like microscopic cells they continue to survive—collapsing to rise, and rising to collapse. Is this, then, what we call society?

"Perhaps this is why we build insane asylums. We lock up those who cause trouble because they possess more understanding and have better reasoning powers than the rest of us. Are people in asylums sane and those outside the insane? As long as lunatics are considered different they will be locked up. But if those same people ever became organized and formed the majority of the population, they would no longer be thought of as being crazy. We often see examples of lunatics outside of the asylum who use their money and power to employ other lunatics to cause riots. Those are generally the men we consider as being great. It has become impossible to tell who is crazy and who is sane."

All this was in my master's mind as he sat deep in thought that night under the solitary lamp. This again shows how extremely shallow my master's brain is. Though he possesses a Kaiser moustache, he is so stupid that he cannot discriminate between a sane and insane person. Not only that; after all that thought, he could not arrive at any logical conclusion to his problem.

But my master does not have the capability of thinking with thoroughness. The vagueness of his reasoning is like the smoke of a cigarette blown from his nostrils—extremely hard to grasp.

I am a cat. There might be some question as to how I could read so precisely the mind of my master, but it is quite easy, simply because I *am* a cat. I can read people's minds through their countenance. How did I acquire this technique? Now, don't get so inquisitive. In any case, I possess this power. While napping on the laps of humans, I sometimes rub my soft fur against their bellies quietly. This creates a special kind of electricity which causes their thoughts to reflect in my mind's eye as clear as day. The other afternoon when my master was gently stroking my head, for example, it suddenly occurred to him that he wanted to skin me. He was thinking of making a fur-lined vest out of me! How nice and warm and comfortable, he thought. I instantly detected this diabolical plan and was frightened. But with this ability, it has become possible for me to relate all that took place in my master's mind that night.

Unfortunately, my master can only concentrate for a short time. Before he could solve his problem, he went soundly to sleep. Of course the following morning he had completely forgotten all about Kohei Tendo. If he ever begins to think about lunatics again, he will have to start all over from the beginning. Of course I cannot actually guarantee that he would arrive at exactly the same incomplete conclusion, yet I am sure that no matter how many times he attacked the problem, he would always arrive at the same answer: " It is impossible to tell who is crazy and who is sane."

X

"GET UP. It's seven o'clock," called the Mrs. from the other side of the paper door. I could not tell whether my master was asleep or awake because he had his face turned the other way and he did not answer his wife. He has the habit of not replying to others. When he must give an answer, it is generally simply an "uhuh", and even this is not easily said. Such people are not very well liked, especially by women. Even the Mrs. who has to live with him does not esteem my master too highly. When considering other members of the fair sex, my master's popularity is—well, better imagined than said.

My master is not even really liked by his parents or brothers, so there is no reason to believe that anybody else would love him. As he is not even warmly received by his wife, it is impossible to believe that he could ever become popular with other girls. There is really no need here to tell you all this, but my master believes that his wife does not love him any more because of his age. I am explaining all this only so you will better understand their relationship.

The Mrs., having been asked to wake up her husband at a designated time, had done so. Since my master had disregarded her call without even an "uhuh", the Mrs. reasoned that she could not be blamed if her husband were late to the police station. After having done her duty, she went into the study with a broom and a duster.

Like on every morning, I heard the duster being swished around. The Mrs. had again begun her housecleaning. I wonder whether this chore is done for the sake of exercise or for play because the motions the Mrs. goes through, I must confess, are absolutely meaningless. The Mrs. seems to clean merely as a formality. She dusts the paper doors and briefly slides the broom over the straw mats, and that is the extent of her housecleaning. She does not seem to consider at all the cause and effect of her efforts. The places that are generally cleaned are always nice and neat, whereas the corners, where dust and dirt accumulate, are that way forever.

In ancient China, a sheep used to be sacrificed at a temple on the first day of every month but now the worshippers only go through the motions without killing an animal. Well, the house-cleaning of the Mrs. is done in much the same way. It is only an empty formality. Yet she continues these rites every day. It is done so mechanically that the results are much the same as they must have been before the invention of the broom and the duster.

Unlike my master, I am an early riser so that by this time, I had become quite hungry. As the table had not even been set for the members of the family, it was unlikely that my breakfast would be ready as yet. It is sometimes wretched to be a cat. I kept thinking that there might possibly be some sweet-smelling steam rising from my abalone shell, so I could not stay still. Knowing it was unlikely but still looking forward to breakfast, I pictured the exquisite scene. Even though I realized it would be wiser to stay put, I could not resist going and investigating for myself.

Unable to resist the temptation, I went to my abalone shell beside the kitchen stove and looked in. Just as I had expected, I found the shell only blankly reflecting the early autumn light which came in from the sliding window near the ceiling. It was just as I had left it after eating the previous night. Osan had already transferred the boiled rice into the serving container and was stirring some soup in a pot over a small clay brazier. Hanging down from the edge of the rice cooker were paper-like bits of dried rice vapor. As both the rice and the soup were ready, it was about time the maid gave me something to eat.

There is no sense in being formal so I decided to demand my breakfast. I loudly meowed to Osan, coaxing, complaining and pleading; but it seemed as if Osan did not even notice me. Osan never really learned to like me but I was trying hard to gain her sympathy at the moment. I again tried, "Me-ow, me-ow".

My pleas sounded as pathetic as if I were grieving for my home in a far away land. Osan still took absolutely no notice of me.

Is Osan deaf? She couldn't be a maid very well if she were. Perhaps she is deaf only to the voice of cats. Some people are color blind. They might think that they have perfect eyesight but from the medical point of view, they are freaks.

If Osan can hear cats, then she is terribly unsympathetic. Some nights when I have to go out on business, I ask her to open the door but she seldom helps me. When she ever does let me out, she usually forgets to let me in again. Even in the summertime, night dew is bad for the health and frost is even worse. It is terrible to have to wait for the sun to rise while standing under the eaves. The other night I was shut out and some stray dogs attacked me. I was able to make the roof of a storage shack in time, but I had to spend the whole night shivering in the cold there. All these inconveniences are caused by Osan's lack of sympathy.

I knew from the beginning that I would get little response in dealing with her but I wished to get her attention, endeavoring whatever I could. Listen to the saying that goes: " When in hunger we pray to God ", or " To steal under pressure of poverty " and " Letters to a sweetheart never cease." Now for the third time I cried out, " Me-ow-ow, me-ow-ow." This screech should surely have caught her attention. As for myself, I considered my plea even better than a Beethoven symphony. But it did not have any effect on Osan.

Suddenly, she kneeled down and lifted one of the removable floor boards. She took out a piece of hard charcoal about five inches long and then struck it hard on the brazier. The long stick broke into three smaller pieces, showering black charcoal powder all over the place. Some of this dust even got into the soup but Osan is not the type to worry about such a trifle. She added these three pieces of charcoal to the brazier by inserting them under the bottom of the soup pot. Her actions clearly showed that she had not even heard my symphony. Helpless and dejected I returned to the sitting room. On my way, I passed the entrance of the washroom and saw the three little girls were washing their faces. The bath was doing a good business.

The two elder girls go to kindergarten but the smallest one is still too young. She is such a baby that she still can't even wash her face by herself in any sense of the word. The baby had taken a mop out of a bucket and was wiping her face all over with it. It must be sickening to wash one's face with a mop, but it wasn't anything to be surprised about with this small tot. Boya is the kind who would shout for joy right in the middle of an earthquake. Perhaps she can be classed along with Dokusen Yagi.

But the eldest sister understands her responsibilities as the eldest fairly well. She threw the gargling cup down with a clatter and tried to take the mop away from her baby sister.

But Boya has a mind of her own and does not often mind her sister. "Don't. Babu!" she screamed, tugging at the mop.

Nobody knows the meaning of this "babu" nor where it originated. It is only when Boya is angry that she uses it. The mop, in the meantime, was being pulled by the elder sister to the left and by Boya to the right, so the middle part began to drip. The water splashed not only on Boya's feet but also on her *genroku*. I have only recently discovered that by a *genroku*, Boya means any kind of a kimono covered with medium-sized patterns. I don't know from whom she might have learned this.

"Now, Boba, stop it. You'll get your kimono all wet," commanded the elder sister smartly. She may be the eldest girl but she still has much to learn. Until only recently she thought that *genroku* was *sugoroku*, a kind of backgammon.

But small children often make many mistakes with the language that make grownups laugh. For instance, instead of saying "*hinoko*" (flying sparks of a fire), my master's daughters say "*kinoko*" (mushrooms), or instead of correctly saying Ochanomizu, the name of a school, they say "*ocha-no-miso*" (paste made from tea). In the same way, they mispronounce "Ebisu Daikoku" (the god of wealth) as "Ebisu *daidoko* (a kitchen)." They also say that they are not children of a "*waradana*" (a house thatched with straw) instead of denying that their home is an "*uradana*" (a house in a back alley). My master only laughs at these errors but it is most probable that when he is teaching English, he makes even worse mistakes himself.

Boya doesn't call herself Boya, but refers to herself as Boba. And when "Boba" saw her *genroku* was wet, she commenced crying, complaining that her "*gendoko*" was cold. Osan came rushing in from the kitchen to wrestle the mop away from Boba and to wipe her kimono dry. But even during this confusion, the second daughter, Sunko, was comparatively quiet. A jar of white face paint had rolled down from the shelf, and Sunko was earnestly applying it. She first drew a white line down the ridge of her nose, highlighting it to look twice as big as usual. Next she dabbed the make-up around her cheeks in big white lumps. But by the time she had made her toilet this far, Osan had dashed in to wipe Boba's kimono and she wiped Sunko's face, too, much to Sunko's displeasure.

After the turmoil ended in the washroom, I went to my master's bedroom to see if he had got up. Upon arriving, I found that my master's head had completely disappeared, but one of his medium-sized feet was protruding from under the bedding. He had pulled his head under the bedclothes so he could sleep longer. Actually, he looked much like a turtle. The Mrs. had completed her cleaning in the study by now. With the broom and duster still in her hands, she called out through the paper door as before, "Are you up yet?"

She then opened the door and saw the headless quilts. The Mrs. had received no answer this time either, so she took a couple of steps into the room and poked the bedding with her broomstick. My master had pulled himself under the bedclothes, head and all, in order to be ready for the Mrs.'s attack. He must have had the foolish thought that he could continue his slumber if he didn't have his head out but that trick didn't work. At first the Mrs.'s voice sounded as if it had come from the threshold, so my master thought he was still safe. Therefore he was all the more surprised when he was poked by the broomstick. He finally gave up all hope and grunted in a small voice, " Uhuh."

" You're supposed to be there by nine. If you don't hurry, you'll be late."

" I know, I know. I'm getting up," grumbled my master from between the quilts. This was a sight to see.

The Mrs. is continually being fooled by this false promise. She gives up her vigil thinking that my master will really get up but then he goes to sleep again. The Mrs. cannot be off her guard. " I'm watching you. Now get up."

It is always disagreeable to be told to get out of bed even after you have promised to get up. This is especially true with my self-willed master. It might have been because of his wife's challenge but my master at last flung the bedding aside.

" Do you have to be so noisy about calling me? If I say I'll get up, I'll get up."

" But you generally stay in bed after you say so."

" Who? That's a lie!"

" It's every day."

" Don't talk nonsense."

" Nonsense? Is that all the thanks I get? " The Mrs. still stood with the broom in her hands. She looked dangerous. Just then Yatchan, the child of the rickshawman, started to brawl. The rickshawman's house almost touches the rear walls of my master's home and every time my master becomes angry, Yatchan's mother forces her baby to cry. The woman might be paid for this service by Mr. Kaneda but it must be very troublesome for her little boy.

If my master were more considerate, he would feel sorry for Yatchan and stop making so much noise when angry. To be so cruel with her own child only because of being paid for it by Mr. Kaneda, the rickshawman's wife is proving that she is even more insane than Kohei Tendo. Not only is the child made to bawl out every time my master gets angry but also every time Mr. Kaneda's henchmen came around to tease him. Even when all is quiet, there are times when the rickshawman's wife feels sure that my master will soon loose his temper, so she has Yatchan crying a little ahead of time. I often wonder if my master is really the master of his own house or whether Yatchan has more authority. In this way, it is not difficult to torment my master. All anyone has to do is to rebuff Yatchan a little and his tears will put my master in agony.

In Western countries long go, when a criminal escaped and could not be apprehended, the people used to make an image of him and burn the dummy at the stake instead. Many of my master's tormentors must also have knowledge of such matters because they so often use the same strategy. Take for instance the Descending Cloud Junior High School students and Yatchan's mother; both serve Mr. Kaneda's purposes perfectly.

My master, hearing the screams of Yatchan, seemed to have a fit that morning because he immediately got up and sat down on top of his bedding. He had evidently forgotten all about cultivating his mind and about Dokusen Yagi. My master began to scratch his head so hard with both hands that I was afraid he would hurt his scalp. Bits of dandruff which had accumulated for a month came floating down on the back of his neck and on the collar of his cotton sleeping kimono. It was a grand sight! Wondering about his moustache, I saw to my surprise that it was sticking out on end. The hairs must have thought that if their possessor was in such a rage, it would not be right for them to remain limp. Each and every one of them seemed filled with passion and the moustache stuck out in all directions. This was worth seeing. The day before, when confronted by a mirror, each hair lined up neatly side by side and formed a Kaiser's moustache. But after a night's sleep, their training meant nothing to them.

This is the same with my master. After cultivating his mind one day, he goes to sleep only to wake up to find all his culture disappeared. It is really a wonder that a wild man like my master with his wild moustache has never been fired from his teaching position. Perhaps that goes to show what a big country Japan is. And because it is easy to lose oneself in such a big country, maybe that's why Kaneda and his henchmen are able to pass as human. My master probably believes that as long as those kind of people can pass as human, there is no reason for his being fired. I myself would like to send a card to Sugamo and ask Kohei Tendo about this problem. He would know right away.

My master opened the hazy eyes I have already described as

wide as he could and stared intently at the closet in front of him. The closet is divided into halves horizontally, and the opening is covered by two sliding doors. My master's bedding was almost touching the paper partitions so they were directly in his line of vision. Both the closet doors were covered with colored paper. Bits of paper are torn here and there so it's possible to see the framework inside as well as other layers of protective paper. Various kinds of scraps were used as padding—printed matter and paper written on with a brush. Some of this literature had been pasted upside down or backwards. My master noticed these gory insides and suddenly felt like reading what was written on them.

Up until now, he had been in such a rage that he was tempted to grab the rickshawman's wife and rub her nose against a pine tree, so it might seem queer that he suddenly decided to commence reading old scraps of paper. Actually this is not a strange phenomenon for those who have such fits of passion.

My master is like a crying child who immediately begins to laugh once he receives a piece of cake. When a student, my master was boarding at a temple and he occupied a room right next to the living quarters of several priestesses. The rooms were only divided by paper sliding doors. Priestesses have always been famous for being the meanest of all mean women, and these priestesses tried hard to torment my poor master. They would bang their cooking pots every time my master was studying and sing out, " The crying crow has now laughed. The crying crow has now laughed." My master commenced hating priestesses from that time on.

But even so, the song aptly describes my master. He cries and laughs and is happy and sorry twice as passionately as most people. His moods never last very long, however. You might say that he does not have any persistence and that his mind frequently wanders but in reality he is shallow-minded and superficial—a defiant spoilt child. Because of his character, he got out of bed that day with the intention of fighting the rickshawman's wife, but he suddenly changed his mind and decided to read what was written on the padding of the ragged paper closet doors. For my master, this is not really at all strange.

The first scrap of paper that caught his eye included a picture of Hakubun Ito. The paper was pasted upside down but toward the top there was a date—the 28th of September in the 11th year of the Meiji era [1878]. What was Ito, the Resident-General of Korea, doing at that time? My master was probably curious but another scrap of paper covered the lower end. There my master read, "the Minister of Finance." Amazing! Ito had once been the Minister of Finance but he was now standing on his head! Looking a little to the left, "Minister of Finance" was again written but the letters were lying down horizontally, as if taking a nap. This was, of course, much better than being upside down. At the bottom of a large gap in the colored paper, there was written "You are" in wood-block print. The rest of the sentence was not exposed. On the next line, my master read, "with haste". Again, nothing followed.

If my master had been a detective of the Metropolitan Police Board, he might have torn the paper door apart. Detectives do not generally have a very high education so they do anything in order to find out all they want to know. The police are really difficult people to deal with. I wish they would be a little more reserved in their actions. If they were more refined, however, it's possible that they would never be able to find any clues. I have heard that at times the police go as far as to manufacture their own evidence so they can arrest an innocent person. Although they are hired by the taxpayers, they are often terrifying enemies of the public.

In turning my eyes to the center of the closet door, I found that a map of the Oita Prefecture was doing a loop-the-loop. Since Hakubun Ito was standing on his head, it did not surprise me to see the Oita Prefecture in this undignified position. My master, having read this far, now clenched his fists and lifted them high towards the ceiling. He was preparing a wide yawn.

This yawn resulted in something similar to the yowling of a whale, but afterwards my master slowly commenced to dress himself, and then he started for the washroom. The Mrs., impatiently waiting for him to get up, could now put away the

[335]

bedding in the closet and fold my master's sleeping kimono. Then, as every morning, she commenced to clean the room.

Just as the sweeping and dusting has become more of a formality than actual housecleaning, so is the procedure my master follows each morning when washing his face. It was the same that morning as it was ten long years ago. Of course he gargled as noisily as usual. Having carefully parted his hair, he stately made his way into the dining room with his towel still thrown across his shoulder. He then sat down at the table beside a rectangular handwarming brazier.

Now there's no telling what some of you might think the brazier was like. Perhaps you picture a brazier made of wood from the zelkova tree, with a delicate scale-like grain pattern. Or perhaps you imagine a receptacle lined with copper. The more romantic reader will see a pretty girl with freshly washed hair kneeling beside a brazier made of black persimmon, coquettishly tapping her long silver pipe against the edge.

Unfortunately, Mr. Kushami's brazier is not so stylish. It is so old that it is difficult to tell exactly what material it is made of. Most wooden braziers are quite beautiful when brightly polished but it is impossible to tell if my master's is made of the zelkova tree, of cherry or of paulownia because it is so neglected. It is dull and undistinguished. Neither my master nor his wife even remember purchasing it; the question once arose, and it seems the brazier was not a gift either. If my master were asked if he had stolen it, the answer would probably not be any too clear.

Quite some time ago, a relative died and my master and his family took care of the house for a while afterwards. Later, when my master was able to find a home of his own, he possibly packed the brazier with his own household goods before moving.

There are many similar cases in the world today. It is said that bankers begin to think that the money they handle is really their own. Government officials are servants of the people so they are given some authority to carry out their jobs; but as they continue to work, they get to thinking that their authority is only to torment the people who gave them that authority in the first place. Therefore, with so many such people in this topsy-turvy world today, it would be quite improper to condemn my master as a criminal only because of the brazier. If you insist on calling my master a thief, then you may as well say that everyone else is a criminal, too.

At the table with my master was Boba, the little girl who had wiped her face with a mop that morning; Tonko the eldest daughter who went to the " paste made from tea " school; and Sunko, who had stuck her finger into the white face paint. They were already eating their breakfast. My master looked around impartially at his three daughters. Tonko's face has the shape of a steel sword guard. Sunko resembles her elder sister but looks more like a red lacquered tray made in the Loochoo Islands. Boba does not look at all like her sisters; her face is long. There are few faces that are not long but this child's was long horizontally. Although we know that fashions often change, a face that's long sidewise will not ever have much of a chance to become very fashionable.

Even though they are his children, my master is sometimes frightened of them. Like all children, they have to grow up. And grow they do—as fast as the bamboo shoots in the Zen temple nearby. Every time my master realizes how tall they have grown, it worries him deeply. It is as if he were being pursued from behind. Though my master is terribly absent-minded, he at least knows that his daughters are not boys. He knows, too, that there will come a time when he must see that they get married. He is at a loss what to do about them. Since he can never hope to take care of them properly, he should not have had children in the first place. But this is a common failing in humans. Humans are continually accumulating what they do not need and then pitying themselves for the burden.

As may have been expected, the children were quite ignorant of the fact that their father was troubled because of them, so they happily enjoyed their meal. The most troublesome child at the moment is Boba. She is just three years old, so the Mrs. supplies her with a short pair of chopsticks and a small rice bowl, as befitting a three-year-old. But Boba is not pleased with having the smallest of everything so she often snatches her elder sister's rice bowl and takes possession of her longer chopsticks even though she cannot manage either. In looking around, we generally find that the person who most lacks ability is the one who tries hardest to act important. Such people are those who dream most of attaining high official positions. Such illogic almost always begins to bud when such people are about the same age as Boba. The roots go so deep that it is practically impossible to convince them of their folly, either by education or discipline.

Boba had again taken possession of her sister's large rice bowl and long chopsticks. As she was trying to do something she was incapable of, she only caused havoc. Boba had grasped the chopsticks too near the base and had stuck them into the rice bowl. The bowl was four fifths full of rice and the remaining fifth consisted of bean-paste soup. As soon as the rice bowl received the force of Boba's chopsticks, it heaved to a thirty-degree angle and the soup spilled out. Boba remained undaunted even though she was covered with rice and soup. Still determined, Boba brought her little mouth to the rim of the rice bowl and tried to catch as much rice as she could by shoveling in the contents with her chopsticks. Most of the rice, now sticky and yellowish because of the soup, splattered all over her nose, cheeks and chin. The few grains that missed her face scattered on the floor. This is a terribly reckless way to eat a meal.

It is here that I would like to mention a few words to Mr. Kaneda and all those other individuals who have great influence: If you try to deal with the world like Boba does with her rice bowl and chopsticks, you cannot expect to convey much rice to your mouth. Rice does not simply jump into one's mouth by natural force, but does so because it loses its sense of direction. Therefore I wish that you would reconsider your use of wielding power and exerting unnecessary force. Force does not befit men of ability, wise in the ways of the world.

Sister Tonko who had had her rice bowl and chopsticks taken away by Boba was being tolerant; but as Boba's bowl was too small for her, she'd consume a bowlful in three mouthfuls. This naturally led to her stretching her hands toward the rice container frequently. She had consumed four bowls already and was just going on to help herself to the fifth. She lifted the lid off the rice container and took hold of the ladle, but hesitated for a moment. It seemed as if she were asking herself whether she should eat another bowl or not. Presently she made up her mind and scooped up one more bowlful of uncharred rice. But she heaped the rice too high with the last scoop and the last ladleful rolled onto the straw mat in a lump. Tonko did not seem upset at all and commenced picking it up carefully. I wondered what she would do with it but soon saw her put it back into the rice container. It could not have been very clean.

As might have been expected of an elder sister, Tonko exclaimed at Boba's dirty face after she had finished eating: "Boba! Your face is covered with rice!" First, Tonko picked off the rice which had clustered around Boba's nose. I thought she would throw these remains away but, to my surprise, she put them into her own mouth instead. Next she picked off the kernels on the cheeks. The other sister, Sunko, who until this time had been quietly gnawing on a pickled radish, scooped up a piece of sweet potato from her soup and suddenly threw it into her mouth. Now, as you all know, there are few things hotter than a sweet potato when cooked in soup. Even grown-ups, if they are not careful, sometimes blister their mouths with them. Sunko was now in a panic. With a cry, she spat the sweet potato out onto the table. Somehow two or three morsels came rolling right in front of Boba—and Boba is very fond of sweet potatoes. When she saw her favorite food right in front of her, she threw away her chop-sticks, made a grab for the chunks of sweet potato and gobbled them up.

My master who had witnessed everything without saying a word, was now picking his teeth. As for his children, his is a strictly "let-alone" policy. His three children, while still school-girls in their sailorsuits, could run away from home with com-mon-law husbands and my master would probably still look upon the situation without any comment.

My master does absolutely nothing. Yet, on the other hand, look at the people who are considered industrious. They lie, trick, bluff and intimidate others in order to get ahead. It seems they all believe it is the only way to act. Little junior high school boys see all this and follow the same course. It all makes me blush for shame. But I do not want to imply that these people are really good workers—no; they should be classified as sloppy. As I am a Japanese cat and patriotic, when seeing such people, I feel like scratching out their eyes. Each time the number of these incompetent egoists increases, my nation becomes that much weaker. A school with such students is an insult to all schools, and a nation harboring such citizens insults itself as a nation. We all recognize this to be an insult so it is hard to understand why there are so many of these people roaming about the country today. Perhaps the Japanese people don't have as much pride as cats do. It is very unfortunate, indeed. I must confess that when I compare my master with such people, my master is the better human being. He is better because he is not ambitious, or efficient, or smart.

After he finished his own breakfast without any mishap, my master put on his Western clothes and ordered a rickshaw. When he asked the rickshawman whether he knew where Nihon Zutsumi was, the rickshawman made a sly smile for a reply. My master did not have to tell him that it was near Yoshiwara where the licensed brothels were.

After my master had left, the Mrs. finished her breakfast and then told the children to hurry so they wouldn't be late for school.

" But the teacher said that today was a holiday," said the elder sister.

The Mrs. became a little suspicious but looked at the calendar in the closet and found the date marked in red. It really was a holiday. My master had sent his notice of absence unnecessarily. Meitei should have told him but Meitei is a man difficult to understand. Perhaps he himself had forgotten about the holiday or maybe he only pretended not to know. So the Mrs. told the children to go ahead and play, and then she took out her sewing box.

During the thirty minutes that followed, the house was so peaceful that there is nothing for me to write about. But soon a young visitor came to the house, a schoolgirl about seventeen or eighteen years old. She wore shoes with crooked heels; her purple *hakama* skirt dragged on the ground, and her side locks were arranged to look like the round beads of an abacus. She entered by the back way without announcing herself. This was my master's niece who comes to visit at times on Sundays, and who generally returns home after quarrelling with her uncle. She had the lovely name of Yukie. Yet her face does not do justice to her name. You see girls with such faces every time you walk down the street.

" Hello, Auntie ! " She entered the room casually and sat down beside the sewing box.

" Why so early this morning ? "

" It's a national holiday today. I left home around eight-thirty. As I haven't seen you for such a long time, I just thought I'd drop in and say hello."

" I hope you can stay awhile. Your uncle will be back pretty soon."

" Has he gone some place already ? That's unusual, isn't it ? "

" Yes. He's gone to—the police station. Isn't that funny ? "

" Oh ? Why ? "

" They caught the thief that entered our house last spring."

"And so he had to go as a witness. What a nuisance ! "

" Oh, it's all for the best. A policeman came yesterday to tell us that the stolen articles have been recovered."

" If it wasn't for that, Uncle would still be in bed, wouldn't he ? "

" Your uncle certainly does like to sleep late. When I wake him up, he gets as mad as anything. He asked me to get him up by seven this morning but when I did he covered his head with his quilts and wouldn't answer me. The second time I called him, he insulted me. Really, it's disgusting."

" I wonder why he's always so sleepy. Maybe his nerves are worn out."

" No, it can't be that."

" But he keeps getting angry for no reason at all. It's a wonder he can keep his job at school."

" Well, they say that he's nicer at school."

" Then that's worse. It's like Konnyaku Emma—the King of Hell quivering like jelly."

" And he loves to contradict me. When I say right, he says left; and when I say left, he says right. Absolutely stubborn."

" Cross-grained, that's what he is. But that's Uncle's main pleasure. If you want him to do something, tell him not to. In that way you can make him do whatever you want. The other day I wanted a new umbrella. I kept telling Uncle that I didn't need one so he bought me one saying that there is no reason why I shouldn't have a new umbrella."

" Ho, ho, ho! That's wonderful! I'll do the same from now on."

" You won't get anything if you don't."

" Some time ago, an insurance salesman came and I certainly wish I could have tricked him into buying some. The salesman explained all the benefits that life insurance offers but he refused to buy. We don't have any money in the bank at all, so I naturally worry about the children. If he were insured, I would feel much more at ease "

" That's true. Something might happen." To talk so intimately about personal family matters does not become a girl of seventeen or eighteen.

" I listened to him talking to the salesman from the next room and it was really funny. He said that he recognized the value of insurance and insurance companies, but he stubbornly claimed that if a person were not destined to die, there was no need to buy insurance."

" Did Uncle say that? "

" Yes! The insurance man explained that life, though apparently long, is often cut surprisingly short. Then your uncle announced that he had decided not to die. Don't you think that unreasonable? "

" Even though he is determined, he'll have to die some day. I intended by all means to make high grades at school but I failed."

" That's what the insurance man said: life is something one

[342]

cannot manage as one would prefer. He said that if a person could live as long as he wanted to, nobody would die."

"The insurance man was right."

"Of course, but my husband refused to be reasonable. He again proudly said that he would never die—that he was under pledge not to die."

"Queer, isn't it?"

"He certainly is. Your uncle insists that if he ever has enough money to pay for an insurance policy, he'll put the money in the bank instead."

"Has he ever saved any money?"

"Not in the least! He gives no thought of what might happen after he's dead."

"Then of course you're worried. I wonder why Uncle's that way. His friends who come here aren't that strange too, are they?"

"Absolutely not. Why, your uncle is without comparison."

"You should have Uncle consult Mr. Suzuki about money matters. Maybe he could make him understand."

"Well, Mr. Suzuki is not very well liked by us."

"Then, how about that other man—the one who's so self-composed?"

"Do you mean Mr. Yagi?"

"That's him."

"We are somewhat annoyed with Mr. Yagi at the moment. Meitei came yesterday and said that Mr. Yagi might not be as clever as we had believed."

"Really?"

"Is Mr. Yagi one of your teachers, Yukie?"

"No, but last week he lectured at the Shukutoku Ladies Meeting."

"Was he interesting?"

"Well, not very. But he has such a long face and long beard —like that of Tenjin-sama, the deified spirit of Michizane Suga-wara—so everybody listened to him."

The Mrs. was just going to ask more about the lecture but the three children had heard Yukie talking by now, so they came tumbling into the tearoom from the veranda. They had probably been playing in the vacant lot on the other side of the bamboo fence.

"Oh! It's Yukie!" screamed the two elder sisters happily.

"Now, now. You don't have to be so noisy. Come, sit down quietly. Yukie was just about to begin an interesting story." Then the Mrs. began putting her sewing away.

"Oh, Yukie, I love to hear stories," said Tonko.

"Is it going to be *Kachi-kachi-yama* again?" asked Sunko.

"Boba like 'tories, too," lisped the third daughter as she squeezed in between her two sisters. She did not mean that she likes to listen to stories, however, but to tell them herself.

"Now Boba is going to tell a story," laughed the elder sisters.

"Boba, you're next. Let's hear Yukie first," scolded the Mrs. But Boba didn't seem to like that idea.

"No-o. I wanna be first—Babu!" she screamed.

"There, there. All right, Boba, what story are you going to tell us?" said Yukie.

"Bon-tan, Bon-tan, where you going?"

"That's good. And then?"

"To de paddy field to cut wice."

"That's right. How well you remember it!"

"If you tum, you'll be in de way."

"It's not 'tum', it's 'come'," cautioned Tonko. Boba again just cried "Babu!" and silenced her sister. But as her sister had cut in, Boba forgot the rest of her nursery rhyme and couldn't continue.

"Is that all?" asked Yukie.

"Can't remember. Damn!"

"Ho, ho, ho! Bad girl! Where did you learn to say such a thing?"

"From Otan."

"Bad Osan—to teach such a thing!" interjected the Mrs. with a forced smile. Then she continued, "Now, it's Yukie's turn. Boba, you're to listen quietly this time." Even tyrant Boba seemed to understand this for she immediately became silent.

"Well, according to Mr. Yagi's lecture," began Yukie, at last getting on with her story, "long ago, right in the middle of a crossroad, there was a big stone image of Jizo, the guardian deity of children. There was a continual passing of horses and wagons at this crossing and the Jizo was often in the way, so the people of the town got together and decided to move the stone image."

"Is this story about something that really happened?"

"Mr. Yagi didn't say. But anyway, after much consultation, the strongest man of the town was chosen to move the Jizo. He stripped himself to the waist and pulled and tugged at the Jizo but it would not budge an inch."

"It must have been quite a heavy Jizo."

"The strong man soon became so tired that he had to go home and to bed. Then the cleverest man of the town appeared and told the people to leave the matter to him. He filled a lunch box full of rice dumplings covered with bean paste, and showed it to the Jizo. 'Come, come. Come and eat these dumplings.' But the Jizo did not move at all. The clever man was still sure he could entice the stone image, so he brought a gourd full of *sake* and went up to the Jizo again. He told the Jizo that if he wanted a drink, all he had to do was to step forward. The man worked at this for about three hours but the Jizo would still not move."

"Yukie, doesn't the Jizo ever get hungry?" asked Tonko. Sunko then joined in with, "I want some rice dumplings, too!"

"The clever man had failed with both food and drink so next he made a lot of counterfeit paper money and told the Jizo to come and get it. Again the Jizo refused to move. It just remained as stubborn as ever."

"Something like your uncle."

"That's right. Exactly like Uncle. At last the clever man gave up, so a braggart appeared and said that he would be able to move the stone without fail. He began the task as if he were confident of success."

"And what did this braggart do?"

"This is the most interesting part. First he came wearing a policeman's uniform and a moustache. He stood in front of the Jizo and demanded that the Jizo move in the name of the law.

He acted as bossy as any real policeman. Of course today not many people pay much attention to the police, no matter how bossy they act."

"And did the Jizo move?"

"Move? No, not at all. It was still just as stubborn as Uncle."

"Yet your uncle respects the police very much."

"Oh, is that so? There's no need to be afraid of them, is there? But the lecturer said that the Jizo did not move. It stood as if nothing had happened. Then the braggart became extremely angry. He went home and took off the policeman's uniform and threw his fake moustache into a wastepaper basket. Then he approached the Jizo while wearing the clothes of a very rich man. He probably tried to look as much like Baron Iwasaki as possible. All he did was to make a face and to walk silently around the Jizo while smoking a big cigar."

"What did he expect to do?"

"He meant to daze the Jizo with the smoke."

"This sounds more and more like a joke of a professional story-teller. And did he daze the Jizo with the smoke?"

"No, the statue was made of stone, you know. The braggart should have stopped trying right then, but next he disguised himself as a prince. Isn't that terrible?"

"Truly. Did they have princes at that time, too?"

"I guess so. Mr. Yagi said that the man imitated one. It was a frightful thing to do, being so disrespectful to the Imperial Household!"

"But what prince did he disguise himself as?"

"It doesn't make any difference; it's disrespectful."

"Well, yes—"

"In any case, this trick didn't work either so the braggart finally gave up."

"It serves him right."

"Yes. He should have been jailed. Well, anyway, the people of the town gathered again to consult each other but no one else appeared to deal with the Jizo. No one knew what to do."

"Is that the end of the story?"

"No, there's more. The townspeople then hired a great many

[346]

rickshawmen and roughnecks to walk around the Jizo while making as much noise as possible. They believed that if they annoyed it, the Jizo would want to move to a quieter place. Well, the noise went on for many days and many nights."

" They were really determined, weren't they? "

" But the Jizo took no notice."

"And then what happened? " asked Tonko impatiently.

" Well, the people themselves got tired of all the noise but the rickshawmen and the roughnecks didn't want to stop because they were receiving wages for their trouble."

" Yukie, what's ' wages '? " asked Sunko.

" ' Wages' means money."

" What were they going to do with the money? "

" Oh, Sunko, I don't know. Now there was an idiot by the name of Baka-Take who nobody talked to. When he found out what all the racket was about, he called the people fools and said that a Jizo could not be moved like that."

" Clever for an idiot."

" Yes, he was clever. So the crowd laughed at him and asked Baka-Take to move the Jizo for them and Baka-Take at once consented. He told the rickshawmen and the roughnecks not to make so much of a disturbance and then he walked up to the Jizo with straightforwardness."

" Yukie, who is Straightforwardness? Was it a friend of Baka-Take? " Tonko interrupted with this queer question just at a critical moment but the Mrs. and Yukie burst out laughing.

" No, it wasn't his friend."

" Then who was it? "

" Straightforwardness means—I can't explain it."

" Oh, I see, ' straightforwardness ' means ' I can't explain it ', hmmm."

" No, no. It means— "

" Yes? "

"Well, you know Sampei Tatara, don't you? "

" Yes. He brought us some yams."

" Well, Tatara is quite straightforward."

" Then Tatara is ' straightforwardness ', is that it? "

" Well, something like that. Anyway, Baka-Take stood in front of the Jizo with his hands in his bosom and told it that the people of the town would like it to move to one side of the road. The Jizo at once agreed. It only complained that the people should have said so in the first place. It then took its place right where everyone had wanted it to be."

" What a funny Jizo ! "

"And now begins the lecture."

" Is there still more ? "

" Yes. Then Mr. Yagi explained that he had a good reason to tell that story at a meeting of ladies. He apologized before continuing but said that most women have the bad habit of beating around the bush instead of coming straight to the point. He admitted, though, that this is not limited only to women. He said that even many men living today had become somewhat womanish because of foreign influence; many men misunderstand Western culture and blindly accept all imported ideas, believing that by accepting them, they are becoming true gentlemen. Instead, Mr. Yagi pointed out, such men are only hampering the progress of civilization.

" But coming back to women, he asked us to remember this story so we will become as honest as Baka-Take in settling our problems. Mr. Yagi believes that if all women followed Baka-Take's example, many of the quarrels between husband and wife, and between a bride and her mother-in-law would disappear. He said that most people like to appear mysterious but that this is especially true of women. The average woman, therefore, is generally more discontented than the average man. In other words, Mr. Yagi suggested that we women become idiots. That was his conclusion."

" Well! And how about you, Yukie? Are you thinking of becoming an idiot yourself? "

" Nonsense! I don't want to become a Baka-Take. Tomiko Kaneda was at the meeting and became furious with Mr. Yagi's suggestion."

" Do you mean the Tomiko Kaneda who lives on the other side of the alley? "

" Yes, that stylish girl."

" Does she go to your school, Yukie? "

" No. But she belongs to the Ladies Club. She certainly wears beautiful clothes, doesn't she? It takes my breath away."

"And they say she's pretty, too."

" Oh, I don't think so. She's just ordinary. Any girl who uses so much make-up as she does would be pretty."

" Then if you used as much make-up, you'd be twice as beautiful."

" Now, don't tease me, Auntie. Actually those rich girls use too much make-up."

" It must be nice to be so rich."

" Yes, but Tomiko should become a little like Baka-Take. She's terribly bossy. She kept telling everybody at the meeting that a poet has dedicated a new book of poems to her."

" That must be Tofu."

" Tofu? Oh, that's funny! "

" But Tofu is a very serious-minded person. He thinks that he justly did her a great honor."

" It's people like Tofu that encourage Tomiko to be so foolish. She even told me that somebody sent her a love letter the other day."

" Really? Who sent it? "

" She said she didn't know."

" Wasn't the letter signed? "

" Yes, but nobody knows the name. She said that it was on a scroll six feet long and that the letter was very romantic. The man wrote that he worshipped her and that it would be a great honor if he could be sacrificed for her sake, like a lamb at the altar. The letter also said that Cupid had used a blowgun to shoot the arrow into his heart. It was full of such nonsense."

" I wonder if the man is really serious."

" Tomiko seems to think so. Three of my friends have read the letter."

" She shouldn't be showing such a letter to other people. Tomiko is supposed to marry Kangetsu."

" It might not be a nice thing to do but she's proud of having received it. The next time Kangetsu comes around you'd better tell him. He doesn't know about the letter, does he?"

"I don't know. He doesn't do anything except go to school to polish those glass balls so he probably doesn't know."

"I wonder if Kangetsu is really going to marry Tomiko. For his own sake, I hope he doesn't."

"But why? She has money and that would help his future a great deal."

"Oh, Auntie, you always talk about money, money, money. It's vulgar. Don't you think that love is more important? Without love, a couple can never find happiness together. Isn't that true?"

"Well, I suppose so. How about you, Yukie? What kind of a man do you intend to marry?"

"How would I know? I have nobody in mind."

Tonko who had been listening quietly up to this point without understanding anything, suddenly opened her mouth and announced, "I want to get married, too." Yukie, who is still at that awkward age, seemed a little shocked at this statement but the Mrs. remained calm and laughed. "And who do you want to marry?"

"I might marry the Shokonsha Shrine, where all of those soldiers killed in action are buried. But I'm not sure because I have to cross the Suido Bridge to go there."

At this smart answer of the little girl, both the Mrs. and Yukie forgot all about their own conversation and burst out laughing. Then Sunko faced her sister and suggested a plan.

"Tonko, I like the Shokonsha Shrine too, so let me get married to it with you. If you don't want to cross the Suido Bridge, I'll go by rickshaw all by myself."

"Boba going, too," shouted the baby. She also wanted to marry the Shokonsha Shrine. If all three of them could be enshrined there together, it would save my master a lot of future worry.

It was then that sounds of a rickshaw stopping in front of the house were heard. This was followed with a lively announcement by the rickshawman reporting my master's return. After having the maid take a big cloth-wrapped bundle from the rickshawman, my master entered the tearoom with perfect composure.

" So you've decided to visit us again?" my master said to Yukie as a greeting. He then dropped an earthenware object similar to a *sake* bottle beside the handwarming brazier.

" That's a queer *sake* bottle. Did the police give it to you?" asked Yukie as she uprighted the fallen receptacle. Her uncle answered with pride, " Do you like it? Doesn't it have a nice shape?"

" Does it? This thing here? Why, it's not so pretty. Why do you need this—ah—oil container?"

" It's not an oil container at all. It's a shame you don't have better taste."

" Then what is it?"

"A flower vase."

" But the mouth is too small and the base is too round."

" That's what makes it so unusual. You're really without taste—just like your aunt here. It's a shame, really a shame." My master picked up the pottery jar while mumbling to himself and held it toward the light to examine it more carefully."

" I still think it's strange that the police gave you an oil container, though. Don't you, Auntie?"

But Auntie was not much interested in the conversation. She had opened the cloth-wrapped bundle and was inspecting the returned articles with round saucer-like eyes. " Thieves are becoming more considerate nowadays. Look, everything has been washed and ironed."

" Don't be foolish. I didn't get this vase from the police. I was kept waiting, so I took a walk and happened to see this in a curio shop. You might not understand but this is an *objet d'art*."

"Just as you say, Uncle. But where did you go walking in that kind of a neighborhood?"

" Where? Just around Nihon Zutsumi. I entered the Yoshi-wara area, too. It's a very busy place. Have you ever seen the big iron gate? I guess not."

" There's no reason for me to go to Yoshiwara. It's a wonder how you, a teacher, could go into such a district where there are so many prostitutes. Isn't that so, Auntie? Auntie!"

"Yes, you're right. But I think some of the things are still missing. Is this all that's been returned?"

"The only thing missing is the box of yams. You know, I was told to be at the police station at nine o'clock sharp but I had to wait until eleven. The Japanese police are no good."

"But that's no excuse to go walking into the Yoshiwara area. If this were known, you'd probably be fired. Isn't that true, Auntie?"

"Yes, maybe. Oh, the lining of my *obi* is gone. I thought there was something missing."

"Don't complain about your *obi* lining. I had to wait for three hours—a terrible waste of my precious time."

My master then went to his bedroom, took off his Western clothes and changed into his more comfortable kimono. When he returned, he serenely leaned against the brazier and admired his new " oil container ". The Mrs., in the meantime, had put the stolen articles away in the closet and sat down near Yukie.

"Auntie, this oil container is supposed to be an *objet d'art.* Don't you think that's funny?"

"Did you buy it at Yoshiwara? Why?"

"Why? This vase is a thing of beauty!"

"But you could have bought one just like it here in the neighborhood. You didn't have to go to Yoshiwara for it."

"Don't believe that this is just an ordinary vase. You don't see one like this everywhere."

"Uncle, you're just as stubborn as a stone Jizo."

"You're being too impertinent for a schoolgirl. I advise you to read the *Onna-Daigaku;* it is a book of etiquette for girls written in the Yedo period but the lessons will never become old-fashioned."

"Uncle, which do you dislike most, insurance or schoolgirls?"

"Who says I don't like insurance? Anyone who worries about the future should be insured. But schoolgirls are worse than useless."

"I don't mind being useless. By the way, do you have an

insurance policy?

"I'm thinking of being insured next month."

"Sure?"

"No mistake about it!"

"But why? Instead of buying insurance, it would be better to do something else with the money. Don't you think so, Auntie?" The Mrs. just smirked.

But my master suddenly became serious. "You probably think that you'll live one-hundred or -two hundred years. When you grow up you'll realize the necessity of insurance. I'm getting insured next month sure."

"Well, that's that. If you can throw money away like on that umbrella you bought for me the other day, it might just as well be thrown away on insurance. I really didn't need a new umbrella at all."

"Don't you really need it?"

"No. I didn't even want a new one."

"If that's the case, you might as well give it back to me. Tonko wants one so I can give it to her. You didn't bring it with you today by any chance?"

"Why! Are you serious? You bought it for me and now you ask me to return it."

"You just said that you didn't want it, so what's so strange?"

"I don't need it, but it's outrageous to ask someone to give back a gift."

"You're talking in riddles. What's outrageous about asking you to return an umbrella you don't want?"

"Anyway—"

"Anyway what?"

"Anyway, it's outrageous."

"Foolish girl. You're saying the same thing over and over again."

"You're saying the same thing over and over again, too, aren't you?"

"But you said you didn't want it."

"That's true. I actually don't want the umbrella but I don't want to give it back to you either."

" You're being both unreasonable and stubborn. Don't they teach logic at your school?"

" Now you're calling me uneducated! But just imagine, asking a person to return a gift! You're being heartless. Maybe you should imitate Baka-Take a little."

" What's that? You want me to imitate what?"

" I'm telling you to be more honest and frank, that's all."

" You're not only stubborn but foolish besides. That's why you couldn't keep up your grades at school."

" Maybe I did fail, but you're not paying for my schooling."

Yukie now seemed unable to control herself any longer for a few drops of tears began to fall on her purple *hakama* skirt, splotching it with red stains. My master was dumbfounded at this show of emotion. He was saved from further embarrassment, however, because Osan came from the kitchen and announced a visitor.

Osan, after curiously glancing at the crying girl, said, " It's a student."

My master immediately left the room and I, with the intention of gathering more news and also to learn more about humans, stealthily followed by way of the veranda.

To make a study of humans, it is best to select a time of trouble. Ordinarily, humans are just usual so there's not much to learn by looking and listening to them. But when trouble occurs, all this usualness—due to some miraculously mysterious function—suddenly becomes lost; humans become eccentric, strange, and extraordinarily queer. Yukie's red tear drops are good examples of this phenomenon. Yukie is just as unpredictable as most humans. She did not seem unusual when she was talking with the Mrs.; but as soon as a man appeared, Yukie all at once became like another person. She suddenly revealed a deep and unknown beauty—ingenious, elegant, strange, and mysterious. This charm is common in all women but it does not always express itself so easily. My master is so perverse that he generally rubs my fur the wrong way, however, I am fortunate in being able to observe many such performances without the actors them-

[354]

selves knowing I am watching. For that reason, I go with my master wherever he goes. I want to learn as much as possible during my short lifetime.

But now, who would be the new guest?

I found a young student about seventeen or eighteen, the same age as Yukie, seated in one corner of the parlor. His hair had been so closely cropped that I could see his scalp. His round nose indicated the exact center of his face. There was nothing much characteristic about him except that his head was extraordinarily large. It looked huge even though he had his hair so short; if he had worn his hair as long as my master's, he would surely attract a great deal of attention. It is my master's belief that people with such large heads do not generally have much intelligence inside. This might be true but actually, at first sight, this student looked as great as a Napoleon.

He wore a splashed pattern *kasuri* kimono though I am not sure whether it was of a Satsuma, a Kurume or an Iyo-*gasuri* design. In any case, it was a lined garment with somewhat short sleeves. I doubt whether the student had any underwear on. They say that it's stylish not to wear an undershirt when dressed in kimono but this student impressed me as being shabby. Moreover, he had left three clear imprints of his bare feet on the straw mats. He was now sitting on the fourth imprint and he looked very uncomfortable.

There is generally nothing unusual about a person sitting quietly, but when this roughneck with his cropped hair and short kimono was seen in such a dignified position, it didn't seem at all natural. It must be a great ordeal for a student who does not even bow a greeting to a teacher on the street to sit for thirty minutes like an ordinary person. It was comical to me to see this student pretending to be honorable and of illustrious virtue, but it must have caused the boy a great deal of strain. It is a wonder how students can ever restrain themselves like that since they are so noisy in the schoolroom and on the schoolground.

Seeing my master's visitor, I was filled with pity in spite of the ridiculousness of the situation. Even though my master is a stupid man, he exerts great authority over individual students and, most probably, he is extremely proud of this ability. But I wonder what would happen if these individual students ever got together and began to defy their teachers collectively. A coward becomes bold under the influence of liquor and a mob becomes intoxicated by the realization that it is powerful as a group. But this Satsuma-*gasuri*-cladded student had come alone and was therefore forced to show respect to my master who has the honorable title, at least, of teacher.

My master offered a cushion to the student by shoving it toward him and saying, " Go ahead and use it." But the cropped-haired fellow just sat tight. He mumbled a " Thank you " but didn't move. It always surprises me, a cat, that visitors so often refuse the use of the fading calico cushion for fear of not being considered modest enough. The Mrs. did not purchase the cushion for people to stare at; it was expressly made to be sat upon. It must surely bring disgrace to the cushion itself and a rejection also means that my master somewhat loses face. The crop-headed student did not refuse because he disliked the cushion itself. The truth is that he hardly ever sits on his legs in the formal style except during the annual Buddhist services of his deceased grandfather, so by this time his legs had gone to sleep and therefore difficult to manage. The cushion simply laid there in a useless heap. A troublesome crop-head! It would have made everyone happy if he were that reserved at school and in his boarding house. He had become reserved now when he needn't, but is wilful when he should be reserved.

It was then that the paper door slid softly open and Yukie entered with a cup of tea and ceremoniously offered it to the student. The boy might have been tempted to jeer " Savage tea! " But that was impossible because he was facing my master himself, and he felt greatly honored to be offered the tea by this pretty girl. Yukie had just learned how to serve guests properly according to the Ogasawara school of tea ceremony. The student was in a very awkward position but Yukie, in closing the door behind her, slyly smiled at him. Girls almost always show more courage in times like this than boys of the same age. Besides, as Yukie smiled so soon after shedding her red tears in mortification, her face was all the more bright.

After Yukie had left, the room remained silent for some time but finally my master, who thought that this interview would be like taking an ascetic exercise, opened his mouth and asked, "By the way, what is your name?"

"Furui."

"Furui? Furui what? What's your first name?'

"Furui. Buemon Furui."

"Buemon Furui—hmmm. That's quite an elegant name—very classical. You're in the fourth year, aren't you?"

"No."

"In the third?"

"No, I'm in the second year."

"Are you in A class?"

"No, in B."

"If it's B class, then you're under my supervision. Isn't that so?" My master seemed impressed. Actually, my master had noticed this boy's large head before and had even dreamed about it, so impressed was he. He had previously associated this head with the classic name, but my master had not connected it with the B class of the second year. When he heard that this impressive head was under his supervision, he unconsciously applauded his good fortune.

But why this large head had come to him, he could not surmise at all. In the first place, my master is not popular with his students; boys do not come to visit him even on New Year's Day or at the end of the year. As a matter of fact, this Buemon Furui was the first student ever to call and my master was at a great loss as to know how to treat him. There was no reason to believe that he had come just for a friendly visit; but if he had come to advise my master to quit teaching, he would at least have shown more animation. It did not seem reasonable that Buemon had come to consult my master on any personal or private matter, so, all in all, my master was quite confused by the visit. Even Buemon himself did not seem to know exactly why he was there. Not knowing what else to do, my master came straight to the point.

"Did you come to pay me a friendly visit?"

" No. I didn't come for that."

" Then what did you come for? "

" Well— "

" Something about school? "

" Yes. I want to tell you something."

" Hmmm. Well, what is it? You're free to talk," said my master. But Buemon kept his eyes cast down and didn't say anything. Usually Buemon is very eloquent for a second-year student. Though his large head is not a good measure of his rather low intelligence, he is generally considered as the most skilful speaker in Class B. It was he, by the way, who had put my master in a difficult position by asking him the meaning of Columbus. That a boy with so much skill should sit there fidgeting like a stammering princess only meant that there was something serious behind his unexpected call. My master became a little suspicious.

" If you have something to tell me, get on with it."

" It's hard to know how to begin."

" Something hard to begin? " repeated my master looking into Buemon's face. The student's eyes were still downcast so my master couldn't read any thoughts from them. Therefore the teacher changed his attitude a little: " It's all right. You can say whatever you want. There's nobody listening and I won't repeat what you say to anybody."

"Are you sure it's all right? " Buemon was still in doubt.

" I think so," guessed my master.

" Then I'll begin," said the student. He lifted his close-cropped head and looked at my master as if his triangular-shaped eyes hurt. My master half filled his cheeks with smoke from his cigarette, and then blew it out and faced sidewise.

" To tell the truth, I'm in trouble."

" What kind of trouble? "

" I'm in great trouble so that's why I came here."

" Tell me about it."

" I didn't think much about it at the time but as Hamada asked me to lend it to him, I did."

" Is Hamada that Heisuke Hamada? "

" Yes."

" Did you lend him your boarding fee or something? "

" No, nothing like that."

" Then what did you lend him? "

" My name."

"And why did Hamada want to borrow your name? "

" He sent a love letter."

" What? "

" I told Hamada that I would mail the letter for him but that I didn't want him to use my name."

" Now you're talking in riddles. Start from the beginning and tell me who did what."

"A love letter was written."

"A love letter. To whom? "

"Well, that's why I said it was hard to begin."

" Did you write this letter to some girl? "

" I didn't write it."

" Then did Hamada send it? "

" No. It wasn't Hamada either."

" Then who sent it? "

" I don't know."

" You're still talking in riddles. Didn't anybody send the letter? "

" Only the name was mine."

" Only the name was yours. That doesn't make sense. Now, look. Tell me about it more slowly and more logically. Who was the love letter written to? "

" That Kaneda girl who lives across the alley from here."

" The businessman's daughter? "

" Yes."

" You said that you lent your name. What does that mean? "

" That Kaneda girl is so silly that we sent a love letter to her. Hamada said we needed a good name for the signature so I told him to write his own. He said his name wasn't very romantic but that Buemon Furui was an ideal name. So I finally let him use mine."

"And do you know this girl? Have you ever met her? "

"I don't even know what she looks like."

"That's outrageous—sending a love letter to a girl you haven't ever even seen. What induced you to do such a thing?"

"Everybody said that she was fresh and bossy so we did it just to tease her."

"That's even more outrageous. And was the letter sent?"

"Yes. Hamada wrote the letter, I lent my name for the signature, and Endo dropped it into her mailbox one night."

"Then, there were three of you in the plot."

"Yes, but I began thinking that I might be expelled if anybody found out. I haven't slept for two or three nights."

"What a foolish thing you've done! Did you write 'Buemon Furui, Second-year Student, Bunmei Junior High School'?"

"No. I didn't write the name of the school."

"That, at least, is fortunate. This could reflect on the honor of the school."

"Ah—what do you think? Do you think I'll have to leave school?"

"I'm afraid so."

"Oh, Mr. Kushami. My father is terribly strict and I have a foster mother. If I have to leave school, I wouldn't know what to do. Do you really think I'll have to leave?"

"You should have thought about the consequences before you signed your name."

"But honest, it just happened, that's all. Can't you arrange it so that I wouldn't have to leave school?" Buemon was almost crying but behind the paper door the Mrs. and Yukie were trying hard to stifle their laughter. My master himself assumed an air of importance and repeated, "Well, well, well." This visit had proved to be very interesting.

Some of you might ask what's so interesting about it, and that is a reasonable question. Be it man or beast, to know one's self is to have a better understanding of the world. Humans would be more respected by cats if they understood themselves better. Few people know even the height of their own nose, much less anything about their own souls. Though humans are conceited, there is no good reason for this conceit. They go around claiming that they are the lords of all creation, but at the same time they don't even know the height of their own nose. You'd think that they would learn to be more humble, but few of them ever lose their conceit. Humans serenely insist on this contradiction but it only proves them to be terrible fools.

That my master, the Mrs. and Yukie were enjoying the discomfort of Buemon is not, I believe, unusual in humans. But each one felt a different reason for the enjoyment. First of all, my master: he was completely indifferent to Buemon's future. He did not care at all if the father of Buemon was strict or whether his foster mother treated him like an orphan. Of course there wasn't any reason for my master to worry—even if Buemon had to leave school, my master's job would not be affected in the least. If all of the students had to leave school, then my master's livelihood might suffer. But the fate of one Buemon Furui meant nothing and did not influence the daily life of my master at all. Where there is little self-interest, there is scant sympathy. My master does not know how to wrinkle his brow and sigh for others while blowing his nose. Humans are not generally very sympathetic or obliging animals. When they shed tears for others, they are only assuming sympathetic countenances for the sake of self-interest. In other words, they are cheating. The people who are best at this kind of cheating are generally those who possess an artistic temperament. They are highly valued by the public but they are also the humans I consider most suspicious. My master is awkward and therefore he is not much valued. With nothing to lose, he can express his cold feelings quite easily. And you can tell how cold he is by his constantly repeating nothing more than " Well, well, well " to Buemon.

But an honest man like my master is not to be altogether despised. Lack of interest and indifference are inborn traits of all men, and those who do not strive to hide this failing are the most honest. And in the world today, honesty is scant. It is difficult to imagine that there will ever be many honest men either, not until Shino, Kobungo, and the other six virtuous characters come walking out of the *Life of the Eight Dogs** and start living across the street.

But enough of my master for the time being. Now I will tell you about the women laughing in the tearoom. They did not share my master's indifference but they were greatly enjoying the case of Buemon's love letter. There was no special reason for their mirth—they just found it funny. But ask a girl some day if she would ever laugh at somebody in trouble. The girl would most probably feel insulted. The insult itself would be a fact, but then laughing at someone in trouble is also a fact. I myself sometimes steal, but I don't like others to tell me that I am being immoral—the accusation would be a stain on my good name. It would be an insult. The situation is the same as that of the women laughing at Buemon's troubles.

But all human males must learn to remain calm when they are stamped on, kicked at and shouted at if they want to remain friends with the gentle sex. They must also learn to consider it pleasant to have girls spit on them and laugh at their discomfort. Buemon was feeling extremely repentant for having done something which came about by a very slight error on his part; and he would have probably believed it insulting that others were laughing at his predicament. But this is childish—a conclusion arrived at by one who is not as yet a grown-up. When a person makes an unintentional breach of etiquette, he gets mad at anyone criticizing him and accuses his tormentors of not being broadminded. It is generally best to stay quiet.

Buemon himself was the incarnation of worry. Unlike Napoleon's brain, which was filled with dreams of glorious deeds, Buemon's great head contained nothing but practical worries. At times, his round nose wriggled because the worries in his head reflected themselves through the nerves of his face. He had been troubled for three days; his fear remained like a cannon-ball lodged in his stomach, as if he had swallowed a big round piece of candy. Since he could not find a solution with his own reason-

---

* *Life of the Eight Dogs* (*Nanso Satomi Hakken-den*) is a novel written by Bakin Takizawa about some warriors called the Eight Dogs. Each one represented a virtue—benevolence, justice, courtesy, wisdom, loyalty, fidelity, filial piety, and fraternity.

ing power, he had come to the home of a teacher he disliked so much that he even hated to bow his great head to him. Buemon had altogether forgotten how he had pestered my master at school and how he had encouraged his classmates to tease him. He only knew that it was the duty of this supervisor to come to his help in time of need. How simple-minded!

My master was certainly not a supervisor because he wanted the responsibility. He was a supervisor only because the principal had made him one. As the hat of Meitei's uncle was a derby in name only, my master was a supervisor only in name. If things could always be managed according to what they are called, then Yukie would be able, just by her beautiful name, to have a marriage arranged for her. Not only was Buemon self-centered but he firmly believed that others should always be kind to him.

This opinion was born from having too much faith in others. Of course, he could not have imagined that he would be laughed at because of his trouble. Buemon, after having visited the home of his supervisor, must have learned a new truth about his fellow-men and, because of this discovery, he might learn to be all the more human in the future. He will become indifferent to the worries of others; he will laugh loudly when his friends are in trouble. And thus, future generations will be made up of such people as this Buemon, just as the world is already composed of such people as Mr. and Mrs. Kaneda. For his own sake, I prefer that Buemon learns to know himself as soon as possible so he can become a more ordinary person. If he does not learn, he will not be able to succeed in life like Mr. Kaneda has done. And if Buemon never learns to be indifferent to the suffering of others, he will be purged from the society of his fellow creatures and that would be worse than simply having to leave school.

As I was enjoying this interesting lesson on human behavior, the front door slid open with a loud grating and a face appeared from behind it.

"Mr. Kushami."

My master was still repeating his "Well, well, well" to Buemon when this unexpected visitor called from the entrance. Looking, he found Kangetsu's head sticking out from behind the door.

"Come on in," my master shouted, still in a seated position.

"Do you have company?"

"It's all right. Just come in."

"To tell the truth, I've come to take you out."

"Where to? To Akasaka again? If that's the case, no thanks. The other day you walked me around so much that my legs are still stiff."

"That was a long time ago. Come on, let's go out."

"Where to? Well, anyway, come on in for a few minutes."

"I want to take you to Ueno Zoo to listen to the roaring of the tiger there."

"That's senseless. But anyway, come in for a second."

Kangetsu was too far away for any argument, so he reluctantly took his shoes off and came into the room. As usual, he had on his gray trousers but there was a patch at the seat of his pants. It was not there because the pants were so old or that his rear end was so heavy; Kangetsu claims that the patch was necessary because he had recently taken up bicycle riding which caused considerable friction to his posterior. After Kangetsu had entered, he nodded a greeting to Buemon, not dreaming in the least that this boy had sent a love letter to the girl he considered his future wife.

"It would be foolish to go all the way to Ueno just to hear a tiger roar."

"We wouldn't go there right away. I was hoping to just walk around for a while and then visit Ueno about 11 o'clock at night."

"What?"

"Then the old trees in the park will be quiet and spooky."

"I should believe so! It would be a lot more lonesome than in the daytime."

"And then we'll go walking where the trees are most dense and sit down where people don't go even in the daytime. Presently we'll get the feeling that we're not living in a city with its clouds of dust, but lost somewhere in the mountains."

"What are we going to do once we get that feeling?"

"We'll wait for a while and soon, from within the zoo, the

tiger will let out its roar."

"Do you think it'll roar on order?"

"It'll roar all right. I can hear it even in the daytime from the College of Science. But in the deep solitude of the night, when not a soul is around and when the devilish air comes creeping up around us, and when a beast with the face of a man stinks in my nose—"

"What do you mean by a beast with the face of a man stinking in your nose?"

"Don't you know that people smell differently when they're frightened?"

"Oh? Well, what then?"

"Well, then the tiger will let out a roar that will shake and tremble all the leaves of the old cryptomerias. It's going to be horrible."

"Horrible is right!"

"Don't you want to go? You can't say that you've heard a tiger roar unless you've heard one at night."

"Well, well, well," replied my master. He remained as indifferent to the adventure proposed by Kangetsu as he has been to the pleadings of Buemon.

Buemon, in the meantime, had been listening enviously to Kangetsu in silence but he must have remembered his own plight when he heard my master's "Well, well, well" because he suddenly interrupted, "I'm worried. What am I to do?"

Kangetsu then looked at the large head in wonder. As for me, I had something else in mind so I excused myself and stepped into the tearoom.

The Mrs. was still giggling while pouring some tea into a cheap Kyoto teacup. After putting it onto a saucer made of antimony, she asked Yukie to take it to Kangetsu.

"Me? I don't mind but—"

"But what?" asked the Mrs. a little surprised, and she abruptly stopped her giggling.

"There's no reason," said Yukie. But she did not move. Instead she bent her head and let her eyes fall on the *Yomiuri* newspaper beside her.

The Mrs. tried again to ask her the favor. "You're acting queer today. It's only Kangetsu. You don't mind, do you?"

"But—I don't want to," mumbled Yukie without taking her eyes off the newspaper. She couldn't have been able to read a word. But if this was disclosed, then there was no mistake that she'd begin to cry again.

"There's no reason to be so shy, is there?" asked the Mrs., this time with a smile. She placed the teacup and saucer on the newspaper.

"Oh, you're being mean," blurted out Yukie as she tried to pull the newspaper out from under the teacup. But the newspaper caught the saucer, and the tea spilled onto the paper and ran in between the seams of the straw mats.

"Now look what you've done."

"Oh, this is terrible," said Yukie, and she ran out to the kitchen for a mop rag. To me, this scene was extremely interesting.

Kangetsu, not knowing what was happening on the other side of the paper partitions, was still talking in the parlor.

"I see you've repapered the sliding doors. Who did it?"

"A girl. Don't you think it's done well?"

"Exceedingly well. Was it the girl who comes here so often?"

"She also helped. She was bragging that since she can paste paper on doors this well, she is qualified to get married."

"I find that the paper here is stretched tight while that on the right-hand side is a little wrinkled."

"The women started on the right side so they had more experience by the time they were repapering the left."

"I see. The surface on the right shows transcendental curves which any ordinary function does not express," theorized Kangetsu as if he were explaining a scientific problem.

"Well, well, well." Buemon at last realized that he had been forgotten and had no reason for staying any longer to plead his case, so he suddenly bowed his great cranium to the floor to announce his departure. My master said, "Are you leaving?"

Dejectedly, Buemon put on his wooden sandals and dragged them along the ground as he passed through the gate. A pitiful sight!

If worse comes to worse, Buemon might write "A Poem by the Rock" and then throw himself into the Kegon Waterfall. All of his troubles were actually caused by Kaneda's daughter's being so coquettish. Therefore if Buemon kills himself, he could become a ghost and then take the girl's life, too. If more such girls disappeared from the world, there would be less trouble for other boys. Even Kangetsu might find a more suitable girl to marry.

"Is that a student, Mr. Kushami?"

"Uhuh."

"What a large head! Is he smart?"

"Not as smart as what you might believe by looking at his head, but he asks some interesting questions at times. The other day he asked me to translate 'Columbus' and I was at a loss."

"And what did you tell him?"

"Oh, I just said the first thing that came to mind. You know, little boys wouldn't have faith in me as a teacher unless I gave them some kind of an answer."

"Teachers have to be like politicians, don't they?

"Well, now he got himself into some trouble, the fool."

"What happened? I noticed that he was worried. What's it all about?"

"It's all foolishness. He sent a love letter to the Kaneda girl."

"What? That big head? Students are certainly getting presumptuous nowadays."

"I guess you must be worried about the incident, too."

"On the contrary, I find it fascinating. I don't care how many love letters Tomiko receives."

"It's good to know that you're so assured of yourself."

"It doesn't make any difference to me. But when I think about that big head writing a love letter—well!"

"And he only did it as a joke. You see, the boys think that the girl is too bossy, so three of them got together and decided to tease her."

"Do you mean that three boys wrote one letter? This is getting even more intriguing. It's like three people eating one serving of food."

"One boy wrote the letter, another went to put it into her mailbox and the other lent his name. The student here today was the one whose name was used. He was probably the most foolish. And, besides, he claims that he has never even seen Kaneda's daughter. How can anyone be so absurd?"

"Now, this is a big event of recent times—it's great! But don't you think it's comical that such a big head could write a love letter to a girl?"

"But it might develop into something serious."

"It doesn't make any difference. You don't have to worry about the Kanedas."

"But you might marry the girl."

"That doesn't make any difference either because I only *might*, that's all."

"Even if you don't care there might be—"

"It wouldn't make any difference to the Kanedas, either. There's nothing to worry about, I tell you."

"Well, then, we'll let it rest at that. The boy's conscience is now bothering him so he came here."

"So that's why he looked so dejected. But why did he come to you?"

"He's afraid he might be expelled. That's what worries him the most."

"Why would he have to leave school?"

"Because he did something bad, something immoral—that's why."

"That's nothing you can call immoral. It doesn't make any difference to me, and the Kanedas probably consider the letter an honor and are telling their friends about it."

"I don't believe it."

"In any case, it's a pity. Maybe he shouldn't have written the letter but it's not right of you to let him worry so much either. It's as if you were strangling him to death. His big head is ridiculous but his face shows that inside he's not so bad. The poor boy was so upset he could only wiggle his nose."

"You've become as light-hearted as Meitei, haven't you?"

"Whatever you want to say, but people are quicker to excuse

.others today. You, Mr. Kushami, are too old-fashioned."

" But to send a love letter just for the fun of it ! And to somebody he doesn't even know ! It goes against all common sense."

" Jokes aren't generally very reasonable. Why don't you try
to help him. You would feel better for it. By his looks, he's
heading for the Kegon Falls."

" Well— "

" Sure, go ahead. Grown-ups who are supposed to have
more judgment often do worse things than write love letters.
They play bad jokes and then pretend to be innocent. If you
expel that boy, you would have to punish all the grown-ups
who are just as foolish—otherwise it wouldn't be fair."

" That's true."

" Well ! Now that that's settled, how about going to Ueno to
hear the tiger roar ? "

" The tiger ? "

" Yes. Let's go. To tell the truth, I have to return to my
home town in a couple of days so I won't have another chance to
go out with you for some time. That's why I came today."

" Do you have something important to do at home ? "

" There's something I've got to do right away. In any case,
let's get going."

"All right, then. Let's go."

" It's going to be my treat today. So after having something
to eat, we'll walk to Ueno and arrive just in time for the roar of
the tiger." Kangetsu was so enthusiastic that my master became
excited too.

After they had left, the Mrs. and Yukie continued giggling while
talking about the events of the day.

XI

IN FRONT of the alcove, Meitei and Dokusen were facing each other with a checkerboard between them.

"The one that loses has to invite the other to a dinner. Do you consent?" Meitei wanted to make sure that he had made the point clear. Dokusen pulled at his goatee and answered, "It's not fun to play when your feelings are carried away by thoughts of winning money. Let's forget who wins and who loses, but have a game with spirit. It will be as if we had just come out from a dark cave and were standing under fleecy white clouds. The game will be a lot more interesting."

"Aha! At it again, are you? You old hermit!"

"It will be like playing a no-stringed harp."

"Like sending a note on a wireless apparatus."

"Well, in any case, let's play."

"Do you want the white stones?"

"It doesn't make any difference."

"Being a hermit, you're as big-hearted as usual. If you take the white stones, that means, according to the nature of things, that I'll have to take the black—let's begin. You can start."

"The rules call for the black stones to make the first move."

"Is that so? All right. I'll be modest about it and begin from here according to the rules."

"Wait! There's no rule saying that you can put your stone there."

"It's a newly discovered rule."

That day I saw this checkerboard for the first time. It is designed for a strange game. The board itself was square, not too large, and divided by lines into many smaller squares on which the white and black stones were laid in such an array that they blurred my eyes. And then the two players got all excited, saying that they had won or lost, and that one stone was dead or alive. The surface of the board only covers a space of about one square foot. I could have easily scattered the stones with my paw and spoiled the game.

When the stones are lined up in rows, a player builds a "hermitage"; but when they are scattered, it's considered as returning to the former "battlefield"—really a useless amusement! It would be much easier for the players simply to place their hands at their bosom inside their kimonos and just keep staring at the board.

There's not much problem when the first thirty or forty stones are laid out but at the climax of the game, all the stones are on the board and it becomes bewildering. There are so many white and black stones that they almost fall off the edges. They must be squeezed so closely that they seem to creak against one another. It's not possible to ask the next stone to move, no matter how crowded it becomes; nor can the stone in front be ordered out of the way. Each stone can only stay put, resigning itself to fate in this tight position. Humans invented this game of gobang so the stones can be said to represent men. Assuming this to be true, we must admit that humans like to limit themselves within self-imposed boundaries so they cannot move freely. In short, humans purposely seek hardship.

I don't know how it all began, but the easy-going Meitei and the Zen-witty Dokusen had found an old checkerboard in the closet and had commenced with the game. At first each played following his own rules and according to his own whim, freely placing the respective white or black stones wherever he wanted. But there's a limit to the board and with each move the space became smaller. It therefore became difficult even for easy-going and Zen-witted players.

" No, Meitei! You can't move to that place."

" Oh? Well, none of your Zen-priest books might carry a rule like this but it's permitted by the Hon-inbo school of gobang."

" But it's only going to be a dead stone there."

" 'A warrior fears not death, much less the partaking of pork.' How about this move then?"

" So that's your move, eh? Now let me see—' Perfumed breezes come from the south, bringing coolness to the palace '— If I put a stone in this spot, all's well."

" Hmmm—you bridged the gap, eh? I didn't think you'd notice it. ' Oh, don't bridge the moat nor strike the hour bell at the Hachiman Shrine, or else you will awake my darling.' Now, how about this move? How will you take it? "

" No trouble at all. ' You shiver at seeing a sword in the air inclining towards you.' I'll cut through like this, and—there."

" Wait! I'm all through if you cut me there. Wait a minute now."

" I told you not to make that move."

" You were right. A thousand pardons. Kindly, if you please, remove that white stone."

" What? "

"And while you're at it, take away that next stone, too."

" But that's cheating."

" Hmmm. ' Do you see the boy? '—Hmmm. Come on, don't be so unfriendly. It's just between you and me, isn't it? It's a matter of life and death for me. Hmmm. ' One moment, one moment, please.' Just a scene that I'm coming down the ramp onto the stage."

" Do you give up? "

" But take that one away, too."

" You've asked me to take away six of my stones! "

" You have a good memory. Hereafter I'll be asking you more requests. Why don't you take that stone back? Don't be so stubborn. Since you have practiced sitting on your legs in the Zen style so long, you should have learned to be more apprehensive by now."

" But if I don't kill that stone of yours, you can kill two of mine."

" Yours was the ' it-doesn't-make-any-difference-if-I-lose ' attitude when we began."

" I don't mind if I lose, but I don't want you to win."

" That's a terrible philosophy. Well, anyway it's ' Flashing a sword as the spring breeze, you've cut lightning ', isn't it? "

"You've got that wrong. It's 'Flashing a sword as lightning, you've cut the spring breeze'—not the other way round."

"Ha, ha, ha! I thought that you might begin to misquote yourself by now, but I see you're still in your normal mind. Well, if that's the case, there's nothing more for me to do but to give up."

"'Today red, tomorrow dead.' Better give up."

"Amen," said Meitei as he slapped one last stone down on the board with a sharp clap.

While Meitei and Dokusen were earnestly engrossed in their game in front of the alcove, Kangetsu and Tofu sat at the entrance of the parlor talking with my master. In front of Kangetsu were three dried bonitos, lined neatly in a row.

Kangetsu had carried them to the house inside his kimono and they still felt warm to the touch. The eyes of both Tofu and my master were centered on these dried bonitos. Presently Kangetsu opened his mouth and uttered, "Actually I returned from my home town about four days ago. But as I have had several matters to attend to, including many visits, I could not drop in to see you sooner."

"There was no need to come in such a hurry," replied my master in his usual curt way.

"But I was worried about getting these fish to you as soon as possible."

"They're dried, aren't they?"

"Yes. Dried bonito is the most famous product of my home town."

"Famous? Well, I believe we have some bonitos here in Tokyo too," emphasized my master as he picked up the biggest fish and smelled it.

"You can't tell if a dried bonito is good or bad just by smelling it."

"Are they famous because they're somewhat larger than those here in Tokyo?"

"Well, just taste one and see."

"But look, this fish is chipped on the end."

"That's the reason I wanted to bring them here quickly."

" Oh ? "

" You see, some rats got to it."

" I might get pest ! "

" Don't worry.   There's no danger when rats nibble away only that much."

" But how did the rats get at it ? "

" On board the ship.   As I didn't have any other place to keep them, I carried the fish in my violin case.   I wouldn't have minded their eating the dried bonito but they also gnawed at my precious violin a little, too.'.'

" What a stupid rat ! I wonder if all rats on ships are so foolish," commented my master for some strange reason.

" They'd be just as stupid anywhere else.   But anyway, I was afraid rats might get at the bonitos again even in my boarding house so I took them to bed and slept with them."

" That wasn't very sanitary."

" So just before eating them, be sure and wash them a little."

" Just a little bit won't be enough."

" Well, you can always soak them in lye and scrub them to a polish."

" Did you also take your violin to bed with you ? "

"A violin is too bulky to take to bed so— "

" What?   You say you took a violin to bed?   How elegant ! There's a poem which goes : ' The departing spring, when one feels heavy, as if a lute were in his bosom.'   Of course this refers to the more poetic days of the past.   Talented violinists of the Meiji era today should take their violins to bed with them or else they will never be able to surpass the musicians of old. How about this one: ' The long wintry night, when one hugs a violin under a sleeved coverlet and watches through the night'? Tofu, can you compose a new-styled poem about taking violins to bed?" Meitei was talking in a loud voice, getting himself involved in the conversation on the other side of the room.

Tofu replied seriously, "As new-styled poetry is so different from *haiku* poems, it is difficult to compose in a hurry.   But when modern verse is complete, it has a sweeter voice and it touches the secrets of the soul."

"Is that so? I thought that spirits could only be attracted by burning hemp reed. Can you lure them back to earth with those new-styled poems, too?" Meitei was still neglecting his game of gobang.

"You'll lose your game if you keep chattering away like that," cautioned my master. Meitei didn't pay any attention, however.

"My rival is just like an octopus in a pot; he can't stretch out either his legs or his arms so I joined the conversation to forget my discomfort."

Dokusen, his equal, pretended to be enraged and he shouted, "Come on. It's your move."

"What? You've made your move already?"

"Long ago."

"Where to?"

"I just lengthened this line of white stones diagonally."

"Hmmm. 'Lengthening this line of white stones diagonally and you've already lost the game.' Is that what you mean? Well, let me see—my move will be—will be—and 'While I'm thinking it over, it will be—will be—it has already gotten dark!' Let me see now—can't do that. Listen, I'll let you reconsider that last move. You can put the stone any other place you want."

"What kind of a game is this?"

"Uhuh. All right, then, I'll make a move—here—right around this corner. I'll place my stone here—how's that? By the way Kangetsu, your violin can't be very expensive if even rats don't like it. Buy yourself a better one. Do you want me to get you one from Italy that's three hundred years old?"

"If you kindly would. And while you're at it, pay for it, too."

"A violin that old wouldn't be worth much." My master knew nothing about violins but he strongly spoke his mind to Meitei.

"You're thinking that an old violin is like an old man. Even some old men, like a certain Mr. Kaneda, are still worth a lot of money. But as for violins, the older they are the better. Now, Dokusen, may I ask you to be a little quicker? I'm not quoting the part of Keimasa played by *kabuki* actors but, as you know, because ' Autumn days end rather quickly '."

" Playing a game of gobang with a restless person like you isn't any fun. Give me a chance to think. All right, I'll place a stone here to complete my square."

" Well, well. So you've finally made your stones tell. Isn't that a shame! I was afraid you'd notice that spot. I was racking my brains in order to talk trash so I could distract you. But you've finally made it."

" Naturally. You don't play the game; you only cheat."

" This is what you call the Hon-inbo school, the Kaneda school, the Gentlemen of Today school of gobang. You know, Kushami, maybe those highly seasoned pickles in Kamakura were good for Dokusen after all. As far as gobang is concerned, he has my great admiration and respect He doesn't play very well but he at least tries."

" Maybe a person as lighthearted as you should imitate him," returned my master with his back to Meitei. Just as my master had finished saying this, Meitei stuck out his big red tongue. But Dokusen, as if this argument were of no concern to him, just said, " Your turn next."

" When did you start playing the violin? " asked Tofu of Kangetsu. " I would like to study it but they say it's quite difficult."

"Anybody can manage to play it a little."

" They say that anybody who has an interest in poetry can make rapid progress in music. What do you think? "

" I guess so. You would probably pick it up fast."

" When did you start studying? "

" While I was in high school. By the way, Mr. Kushami, did I ever tell you why I started playing the violin? "

" No, not yet."

" Did you study it from a teacher in high school? "

" There wasn't any music teacher in my school. I studied it by myself."

" You're a born artist."

" Studying by oneself doesn't make a person a born artist," was Kangetsu's grim reply. Kangetsu is the only person I

[376]

know who would look grim when called a born artist.

"But tell us how you studied. I'd like to hear it."

"Sure, if you want me to. Is it all right, Mr. Kushami?"

"Sure, sure. Go ahead."

"Nowadays we see many young people in the street carrying violin cases, but when I was a boy practically no high-school student studied Western music. Moreover, the school I attended was in the back country. The people there were so simple that they didn't wear anything more elegant than hemp-soled sandals. Of course, there wasn't anyone who played the violin at school."

"Look, Dokusen, it seems that Kangetsu is telling some interesting story over there. How about stopping this game halfway?"

"There's still a couple of spots that can't wait."

"You're being rather mundane for a scholar of the Zen doctrine. All right, but let's finish in a hurry. By the way, Kangetsu, did you go to that high school where all the students are barefooted?"

"That's not true."

"Still, they say that the students who took military training there developed awfully tough feet because of making so many 'turn rights' when drilling."

"Absurd. Where did you ever hear that?"

"I also heard that each student took a great big rice ball to school for lunch. They carried it around by hanging it down from their belts on a string, like a Chinese citron. And as they ate it—maybe I'd better say as they gobbled it down—they would find a pickled plum in the center. One of their greatest joys was to eat down to the red plum, full of anticipation. Those boys are indeed all full of vigor. Dokusen, you might find this story interesting."

"Yes. Boys with a promising disposition of simplicity and intrepidity."

"And there's something more that I heard. They don't sell any ashtrays made of bamboo tubes there. I have a friend who used to work there and once he tried to buy one near your home town. The storekeeper told this friend that all he had to do was to go to the back of his house and cut one for himself, so there—

fore bamboo tubes used for ashtrays were not in demand. Don't you think that is a praiseworthy example of simplicity and intrepidity, Dokusen?

" Hmmm. That's that—but I guess I'll put a stone here to play it safe."

"All right. Play it safe. Now, that takes care of the game. By the way, you're really quite amazing, Kangetsu, to have begun to study the violin at such a place. It's worthy of admiration. ' Remaining a bachelor and excelling all others ' is what the *Ch'utz'u* of the Han dynasty suggested in its anthology. Maybe Kangetsu is the Ch'ü-Yüan of the Meiji Era."

" I don't like the name of Ch'ü-Yüan."

" Then be the Werther of the twentieth century. What? Are you counting the stones? What an honest fellow! But you don't have to worry about the score because I know that I lost the game."

" But I want to know the score."

"All right, then. But you'll have to count my stones for me. If I miss hearing about how the Werther of the century began to study the violin, I would never be forgiven by my ancestors." Meitei then left his seat at the checkerboard and slid towards Kangetsu. But Dokusen picked up each of the scattered stones and lined them together in neat rows; his lips moved as he counted to himself. Kangetsu continued his story:

"As I lived in such a rural area, everybody in my home town was terribly Spartan. If anyone showed the least tendency towards the arts, they'd say that it was shameful; they would say that the students of other prefectures would laugh, so any artistic person was strictly disciplined. It was very troublesome."

" The people in your home town don't show much sense. Why, for instance, do the students only wear those dark blue *hakama* skirts? That seems especially odd because everybody there is so dark complexioned anyway—they're always exposed to the salty wind. It might be all right for boys to be so dark but the girls can't be very pretty." Whenever Meitei joined any conversation, the story almost always strayed away from the main subject.

"Are the girls as dark as the boys? "

[378]

" Yes, they are."

" It's a wonder they can find husbands."

" It doesn't make any difference when everybody else is so dark in complexion."

"A case of cause and effect, don't you think so, Kushami?"

" It's best to be dark. A person with a light complexion is conceited and keeps looking at himself in the mirror. Women would be especially difficult to manage," lamented my master.

" But when everybody is dark, maybe the darkest are the most conceited." Tofu's theory stood to reason.

" Well, whatever the case, it would be a better world if there were no women," grumbled my master. To this Meitei laughed a warning, " If you keep on saying such things, your wife will have a fit."

" You don't have to worry."

" She's not at home?"

" She went out with the children a little while ago."

" I thought it was especially quiet. Where did they go?"

" I don't know. She goes out whenever she likes."

"And she comes back whenever she likes, is that it?"

" Well, something like that. You two are lucky to be single." At this statement, Tofu made a grimace of discontent but Kangetsu just kept grinning.

Then Meitei stated, " Most married men feel that way. How about you, Dokusen? You're always having trouble with your wife, aren't you?"

" Me? Wait a minute. Four times six is twenty-four—twenty-five, twenty-six, twenty-seven—. Hmmm, there are forty-six squares. I thought I had won more than this but there's only a difference of eighteen spaces. Now, what were you saying?"

" I just said that you're always having trouble with your wife, that's all."

" Ha, ha, ha! No trouble at all. You know something? My wife loves me."

" Well, pardon me!"

" There are a lot of happy marriages," emphasized Kangetsu, taking the trouble to speak up for all the wives in the world.

" I agree with Kangetsu," argued Tofu. " In my way of thinking, there are only two ways in which a man can attain perfect
happiness, and they are through art and love. Love between a
husband and wife is one of the most important forms of love.
A man should absolutely marry so that he can enjoy this happiness.
The man who remains single is going against the will of Heaven.
What do you think, Meitei? "

"An honorable opinion. Maybe I'll never be able to enjoy
that absolute happiness."

" You'll be even less happy once you get yourself a wife,"
remarked my master glumly.

" In that case, we young single men should try to attain that
spiritual happiness through art. That's why I am planning to
study the violin, and the reason I asked Kangetsu about his own
experience."

" That's right. We were supposed to listen to the violin story
of our friend Werther here, weren't we? Begin again. I won't
interrupt any more," promised Meitei, finally realizing his bad
habit.

But Dokusen interrupted: " You can't find perfect happiness
only through the violin: that would be too easy a way to find the
hidden truths of the universe. If you wish to attain the sublime,
you would have to have enough spirit to let yourself plunge over
a cliff, fall dead, and then return to life." Dokusen was again
putting on airs and lecturing, but Tofu did not understand even
the first principle of the Zen doctrine so he did not understand
anything Dokusen had said.

" You may be right, but I believe that art is what best expresses
the extremity of man's devoutness, and it cannot be disregarded."

" Since you seem to understand the importance of art, I might
as well continue my story. And so, as I already said, I had great
trouble. I even had difficulty in buying a violin, Mr. Kushami."

" I should think so. They wouldn't be able to sell many
violins at a place where nobody even had hemp-soled sandals."

" It's not exactly that. They had violins for sale all right, and
I had enough money, but I still couldn't buy one easily."

" Oh? "

"As my home town is so small, everybody would have known that I bought a violin. I would have been accused of being presumptuous and then disciplined."

"Great talent has always been oppressed," nodded Tofu sympathetically.

"There you go with your 'talented' again. I wish you would kindly refrain from using that word. But every time I'd walk in front of the store window and see the violin, I would imagine how wonderful it would be if I could buy one and how it would feel in my hands. Not a day passed without my thinking about that violin."

"That's only natural." This was Meitei talking.

"I don't understand how you could have become so attached to a musical instrument," grumbled my master again. He could not fathom such enthusiasm.

"All in all, it only proves I'm right to say that you're talented," said Tofu with respect.

Only Dokusen, twisting his goatee, kept himself aloof.

"You might be wondering why violins were sold at such a place as this; there was a girls' school nearby and the girls had to practice the violin so it's not particularly strange. Of course none of the instruments were of any real quality. The storekeeper himself did not put too much value on the violins but hung them in bunches of two or three in front of the store. When walking in front of the shop, I'd see them move with the wind and, at times, an errand boy would finger them so I'd hear the quivering sounds of the strings. I'd feel as if my heart would burst and I wouldn't know what to do with myself."

"That's a dangerous sign. I've heard that some people have epileptic fits when they see water, and others get fits when they see crowds; but as for you, my young Werther, you seem to be attacked by fits from violins," joked Meitei.

"Well, one's senses have to be that acute in order to become an artist. There's no doubt about your being a talented person," repeated Tofu, in even more admiration.

"Yes, you might say I had fits, but the sounds I heard at that time were unique. I've played my violin a lot since then but I never hear as beautiful a tone as I heard at that time."

"Emitting sounds as beautiful as precious gems."—It was a pity nobody took notice of Dokusen's poetic verse.

"The third time I heard that miraculous sound, I firmly resolved to have a violin. Even if I were going to be rebuked by the townsfolk, or scorned by people in other prefectures, or even if I were disciplined and fell down to my last breath, or, worse, even if I were expelled from school—I knew that I had to have a violin."

"That's what you call a really talented person. If you didn't have talent, you would never get a feeling like that. I envy you. I've also been trying to work myself into such an emotion all these years, but the feeling never comes. When I go to concerts I try my best to listen with enthusiasm but I can't get truly interested," said Tofu with envy.

"Maybe you're lucky that you aren't so intense because the suffering I went through at the time was something words cannot express. But I finally bought the violin. It was the evening before the Emperor's birthday in November. My landlord had planned on spending the holiday at a hot spring resort but I told him that I was ill. I even stayed away from school. I laid in bed all day thinking how that evening I'd go and buy my violin."

"Did you stay away from school saying you were ill?"

"I certainly did."

"You were talented in many ways," chuckled Meitei a little obligingly.

"I found that I became too impatient with my head out of the bedding so I snuggled inside, closed my eyes, and waited. But I was too restless to stay like that long, so I stuck my head out and saw the strong autumn sun shining flat on the other side of the paper door. On the upper part of the door, I noticed a cluster of narrow shadows waving in the wind."

"And what were the narrow shadows?"

"Bitter persimmons were hanging from the eaves."

"Hmmm. And then?"

"I got out of bed and went out to the veranda and ate one."

"Was it good?" asked my master, just like a little child.

" The persimmons around my home town are all good. You can't find any like them in Tokyo."

" Never mind about the persimmons," snapped Tofu. " What happened after that?"

" I went back to bed, closed my eyes and prayed that the gods would make the sun go down quickly. After what I thought to be three or four hours, I poked my head out but the strong autumn sun was still shining brightly on the paper door and the narrow cluster of shadows was still waving in the wind."

" You already told us that part."

" It happened a lot of times. I got up again and ate another persimmon, and then went to bed and prayed to the gods once more."

" You're repeating yourself, Kangetsu."

" Don't be so impatient, Mr. Kushami. Listen carefully. Then I endured another three or four hours and stuck my head out of the cover. As before, the strong autumn sun still shone on the paper door and above it, the narrow silhouettes still swayed in the breeze."

" But you're saying the same thing over and over again."

" So I got out of bed, opened the door, picked a persimmon, and ate it."

" You must certainly like persimmons."

" I'm getting impatient for autumn when the persimmons are ripe again," admitted Kangetsu.

" In the meantime, your audience is getting even more impatient."

" Mr. Kushami, you're so restless that it's hard for me to stick to my story."

" It's hard on us, too," complained Tofu.

" Well, if all of you agree, I'll cut the story short. In any case, after eating a persimmon I'd go back to bed but after staying in bed awhile I'd go and get another persimmon. Eventually I ate all the persimmons that were hanging from the eaves."

" It must have been pretty dark by then."

"After eating the last persimmon, I thought it would be dark, too. I stuck my head out, but—what do you think? The strong autumn sun was still shining all over the paper door and—"

"I give up. Go ahead and repeat yourself all you want. There's no ending."

"It's hard on me, the storyteller, too."

"But since you have so much stamina, even when telling a simple story, you're bound to succeed in almost any enterprise. If we let you go on talking, you'll continue your descriptions of the bright autumn sun until tomorrow morning. Let me ask you this : just when do you expect to buy that violin?" Meitei was just as impatient as everyone else. Only Dokusen remained composed. He looked as if he were perfectly willing to wait until the following morning or, for that matter, even until the morning after that. He seemed content to let the autumn sun continue shining brightly. He showed no sign of annoyance.

Kangetsu himself remained calm : "I kept waiting for night to come so I could buy my violin but every time I stuck my head out of bed, the autumn sun was shining ever so brightly. The impatience you are enduring now is nothing in comparison with the suffering I myself felt at that time. Even after I had eaten the last persimmon, I found that the sun was still shining brightly. I was so discouraged, Tofu, that I broke down and cried in spite of myself."

"I should think so. I know that all artists are sentimental and emotional and I sympathize with you, but I wish you would get on with the story." Tofu was such a nice fellow that he remained serious even when saying something funny.

"Sure, sure. I want to carry on with the story much faster, too, but the sun wouldn't go down. I cannot hurry even if I tried."

"If we have to wait until the sun goes down, you'd better stop right now." My master didn't seem to be able to stand it any longer.

"But I can't stop here. Anyway, I'm going to begin the most interesting part now."

"All right, then. But how about having the day end so you can get on with your story?"

"That will be difficult but as you are a teacher, I'll give in.

Let's say that the day has now ended."

" That's very convenient," murmured Dokusen nonchalantly, and the rest of the men burst out laughing without knowing it.

" Finally night came. Thinking that all was safe, I left my boarding house. It was in the village of Kurakake. You see, I don't like noisy places so I had secluded myself in a hermitage fit for a snail. I lived in a trackless part of the country with some farmers— "

" Don't you think it's a little exaggerated to say that you lived on a trackless farm? " complained my master. Meitei also protested. " You're overdoing it as well by saying a hermitage fit for a snail. It would be a much more truthful description to say a four-and-a-half-mat room without any alcove."

Only Tofu praised the choice of words: " Whether it's exact or not, the description is poetic and understandable." Dokusen remained more serious: " It must have been pretty hard to go to school from such a place. How far was it? "

" Only a distance of about four or five blocks. The school was in the country, too."

" Then most of the students lived nearby."

" That's right. There was a student or two in almost every farmer's home."

"And you want us to believe that you were living in a trackless part of the country."

" Sure. If there hadn't been a school, it would have been a trackless place. Well, anyway, that night I wore a padded kimono besides the overcoat of my school uniform with the gilded buttons. I covered my head and face with the hood of the overcoat so nobody would recognize me. I was being very careful. As I said, it was November so the leaves of the persimmon trees had all fallen. The road from my boarding house to the Nango highway was covered all over with dead leaves and they rustled at every step. I felt as if somebody were following me. In the gathering darkness, I saw the woods of the Torei-*ji* Temple looming even blacker in the night. This secluded Buddhist temple is also the family cemetery of the Matsudairas and is at the foot of Mount Koshin, about one block from my boarding house.

Above the trees I saw an endless number of stars. The Milky Way seemed to hover over the river Nagase diagonally and ended up at—at, well, somewhere—around Hawaii, I guess."

"Hawaii sounds somewhat beyond the point of the story," commented Meitei.

"After walking about two blocks along the Nango highway, I entered the city by way of Takano-dai. I then passed along Kojo and turned up Sengoku street. With Kuishiro street on the one hand, I sneaked through Tori Ward and from there I zigzagged by way of Owari, Nagoya, Shachihoko, and Kamaboko streets."

"You don't have to go into so many streets. Did you ever buy the violin or didn't you?" asked my master impatiently.

"The shop was called Kanezen, a sort of general hardware store, and it's still further down the street."

"I don't care where it is, just get there and buy your violin."

"Thank you. So when I arrived at the store of Kanezen, I found a lamp shining brightly over—"

"Now, it's a lamp that's shining brightly! Now you won't be satisfied unless you've explained how brightly the lamp shone." Meitei was reminding the speaker not to repeat himself.

"I'll explain the lamp only once so you needn't worry. I looked inside and saw the beautifully shaped violins faintly reflecting the light of autumn evening. The taut strings could have been of silver."

"Very descriptive," mumbled Tofu in praise.

"'That's it! That's the violin I want!' My heart began thumping and my knees became weak."

"Hmmm?" Dokusen, at this description, sneered through his nose.

"Without thinking, I ran inside. I pulled my wallet out of my pocket and took two five-yen notes from it."

"So you finally did buy it then?" My master seemed much happier now.

"I was just going to ask for it but then I realized what an important moment it was so I hesitated."

"You didn't buy it after all? It's amazing how the purchase of a violin can drag along so."

" I'm sorry that I can't tell my story any faster but I couldn't buy it just then."

" But why? "

" It was still early evening and a lot of people were walking in the street."

" What's wrong about that? What difference could it make, even if there were one-hundred or two-hundred people around? " exploded my master.

" It wouldn't have made any difference if they were just ordinary people, but most of them were students of my school. They had their sleeves rolled up and they carried big canes, especially those who were always at the very bottom of the class. If they found out that I had bought myself a violin, there's no telling what they would have done to me. Almost all of the boys were proud of being good at judo. I wanted the violin, but life was even more dear to me. I decided it was better to live and not play the violin than to lose my life."

" Then you finally decided not to buy it. Is that so? " My master was trying hard to receive a clear answer.

" Oh, I bought it."

" You're being extremely irritating. If you're going to buy it, why don't you buy it right away? Why couldn't you make up your mind? "

" Ha, ha, ha. The world doesn't always go the way we want it to go," laughed Kangetsu while coolly lighting a cigarette.

But my master became tired of the long and drawnout story. He suddenly stood up and went into his study, only to return with an old book. He then lay down on his stomach and commenced reading. Dokusen also disappeared from the group. He had returned to his former position in front of the alcove and was playing a game of gobang all by himself. Kangetsu's audience was deserting him. Tofu, however, ever faithful to art, stayed and so did Meitei who is never defeated by boredom.

Kangetsu meanwhile nonchalantly puffed on his cigarette. When he continued with his story, it was at the same speed as before.

" I was afraid I wouldn't be able to manage my purchase so early in the evening. But if I returned around midnight, Kanezen would have gone to bed and it would have been even more difficult. I therefore decided to wait until just before Kanezen went to bed because few students would be around at that time."

" That seems like a good plan."

" I decided that ten o'clock would be just about the right time, but that meant I would have to kill several more hours. It would have been troublesome for me to go home and I didn't feel like visiting any friends. Usually it was no trouble at all to pass two or three hours walking around but on that night, time seemed to stand still. I know what is meant when people say they've waited ' on tiptoes ' for somebody." Kangetsu then looked at Meitei purposely.

Meitei returned, " Old people still say ' Waiting alone impatiently at a foot warmer,' or 'A watched pot never boils.' Maybe the violin that hung from the ceiling was impatient, too. The time must have passed especially slowly for you, walking around like a detective but with no object. Maybe that's how a homeless dog feels. Really, there's nothing more pitiful than a homeless dog whimpering in misery."

"A dog? That's not a very nice way of putting it. I've never been compared with a dog before."

" You know," said Tofu, " while listening to your story I can't help compare your sufferings with the hardships most great artists have to face. Of course Meitei was only joking when he mentioned the dog. But get on with your story." Tofu meant to console Kangetsu, but Kangetsu would have continued whether consoled or not.

" So, after wandering through Okachi street and Hyakki street, I arrived at Takajo Ward through Ryogae street. While there, I counted the old willow trees in front of the prefectural government building and then I counted the lighted windows of the hospital. Afterwards I smoked two cigarettes while sitting on the Konya Bridge. Then I looked at the time."

" Was it ten? "

" Not yet. So I walked across the Konya Bridge and went

east along the river where I saw three massagists returning home. And I heard dogs howling."

"Howling dogs on a long autumn night beside a river sounds dramatic, something a fugitive would be impressed with."

"Do I sound like a fugitive from justice?"

"No, but you're about to commit a crime."

"If it is a crime to buy a violin, all of the students in music schools are criminals."

"If you commit an act so secretly, you're like a criminal even if the purpose is honorable. Christ, in his lifetime, was a criminal, too. Good-looking Kangetsu can also be considered a criminal because he bought a violin, violating the rules of that small-town society."

"If that's the case, I'll let you consider me a criminal. But it still wasn't ten o'clock."

"Well, you could count the names of the streets again. You might even get the autumn sun to shine brightly once more. If you need something else to do, you might even eat another three dozen dried persimmons. I'll wait as long as you want for the rest of the story, so go ahead."

Kangetsu smiled slyly.

"I'll have to surrender if you're going to tell the story ahead of me. All right, then, I'll say it's ten o'clock all of a sudden. Now that the promised hour had arrived, I walked to the store again. As the nights are cold in November, there were few people in Ryogae street, the busiest quarter of the town. The muffled sound of their wooden sandals seemed lonely and quite sad. The storm windows had already been closed on Kanezen's store; only the low side door remained open. I felt as if that howling dog had followed me as I entered the store."

Just then, my master raised his eyes from the dogeared book he was reading: "Did you buy the violin yet?" Tofu replied, "No, but he will in just a minute." "Not yet? It certainly takes a long time!" My master then commenced reading again. Dokusen remained silent. He had covered most of the checkerboard with the white and black stones.

"With my hood still covering my face, I asked for the violin.

There were several clerks clustered around a hand-warming brazier, talking among themselves. They looked up in surprise so I pulled the hood down further over my face with my right hand. I had to ask for the violin a second time but finally the boy sitting nearest me stood up and took down a bunch of three or four violins. He told me that the price was five yen twenty sen."

"That cheap? Are you sure they weren't just toys?"

"The clerk said that all of the violins cost the same but that they were all made with patience and were strong. I took out one five-yen note and twenty sen in coins from my wallet and then I wrapped the instrument in a large cloth I had brought for this purpose. During my purchase, the other clerks stopped talking and kept looking at me. I knew that there was no fear of their recognizing me because I had my hood over my face, but even at that I was impatient to get out into the street as soon as possible. At last I finished wrapping the violin. I tucked it under my overcoat and left the store. But when the employees chanted out "Thank you" all together, it almost chilled my bones. Going out into the street I found, much to my relief, almost no one around. Soon, however, I heard two or three people about a block away coming in my direction. They were reciting poems as if they wanted their voices to echo thoughout the town. Being frightened, I turned west from Kanezen's store. I followed the canal to Yaku-oji Road and from there I arrived at the foot of Mount Koshin by way of Hannoki Village. When I reached my boarding house I found that it was 1 : 50."

"That means you had been walking almost all night," sympathized Tofu.

"But you finally bought your violin. What a long, long journey! It's something like playing travelling backgammon!" exclaimed Meitei, greatly relieved.

"And now comes the part that's really worth hearing. You've only heard the beginning."

"Is there more? This is going to be awful. I'll bet you could out-talk almost anybody."

"If I stop here, it would be like shaping an image of Buddha but not putting its eyes in. Listen just a little more."

" How about you, Mr. Kushami? Are you listening? The violin has at last been purchased."

" What now? He's probably going to sell the violin. And if that's the case, I don't want to listen."

" I didn't sell it."

" Then I'll try all the harder not to listen."

" Tofu, you're the only one that's listening to me with any interest. It's a little discouraging but I guess it can't be helped. I'll just tell you the gist of the rest."

" Go ahead and tell it in full detail. It's all very interesting."

" Well, I was finally able to buy the violin but now I didn't know where to keep it. There were always a lot of friends coming to my place, and they would be sure to have seen it. I could have dug a hole and buried it, but then it would be too troublesome to dig up again."

" Did you hide it in the ceiling? " guessed Tofu.

" I didn't have any ceiling. I was living in a farmer's house."

" Well, where did you put it? "

" Where do you think? "

" I don't know. Inside the storm-window boxes? "

" No."

" Did you wrap it up with your bedding in the closet? "

" Not that either."

While Tofu and Kangetsu were talking about where the violin might be kept, my master and Meitei were also discussing something in earnest.

" How do you read this? " asked my master.

" What? "

" These two lines here."

" Oh, this? It's ' *Quid aliud est mulier nisi amiticiæ inimica* '. That's Latin."

" I know it's Latin, but how do you read it? "

" You have repeatedly told me that you can read Latin yourself." Meitei had sensed danger and was trying to keep himself clear of it.

" Of course I can read it. I can read it, but what does this mean? "

"You say you can read Latin but you don't understand it? That's outrageous!"

"Translate it into English."

"You sound as if you were ordering a servant around."

"Don't be foolish. What does it mean?"

"Let's take up this Latin business later on. I want to listen to Kangetsu for a while. He's at an extremely interesting part now. It's like being at the barrier of Ataka where success or failure is at a balance. I want to know whether his violin will be discovered or not. Now, Kangetsu, what happened after that?" Metei was suddenly very interested in the story about the violin so my master was sadly left abandoned. Kangetsu, encouraged by Meitei's show of enthusiasm, continued:

"So I finally hid it inside an old clothes box. This clothes box had been given to me by my grandma when I left home. She told me that she had brought it with her when she first got married."

"An old box like that couldn't have harmonized very well with the new violin. What do you think, Tofu?"

"True. They could hardly harmonize."

"The ceiling wouldn't have harmonized either," argued Kangetsu.

"Maybe we can make a poem out of this. How about this: 'Hidden in a clothes box was a violin, lonesome autumn!'"

"You're in the mood to compose *haiku* poems today, aren't you, Meitei?"

"Not only today. I always have some *haiku* poems in me. I have such a profound knowledge of *haiku* that the late Shiki Masaoka was speechless with admiration."

"Oh? Did you know Shiki?" asked honest Tofu.

"Well, even if I wasn't terribly close to him, he and I always agreed in our inmost thoughts, as if we were connected to each other by a wireless telegraph." Tofu seemed disgusted with this incoherent answer and did not ask Meitei more. Kangetsu continued with his story.

"At last I had found a place to put my violin but I was still greatly troubled. Of course I could take it out often without

[392]

attracting attention, but the violin isn't made only to be looked at. A violin is nothing unless it is played, but that involves noise and, therefore, discovery. To the south, just over a rose-covered fence, was the boarding house of the leader of a bunch of bullies. I couldn't play it so near."

"That wasn't very fortunate, was it?" Tofu again expressed his sympathy.

"It was a pity. Even history reveals how sounds can betray the whereabouts of a person. Once Lady Kogo was discovered because she was playing a *koto*. If I were stealing food or making counterfeit money, the situation would have been different; but the sound of music cannot be completely hidden."

"Wait a minute. You are only talking about sounds. There are other things that can give a person away just as thoroughly. When I was a student, I lived in a temple near Koishikawa with another friend, Tojuro Suzuki. Now Tojuro liked sweet *sake* very much. He used to keep some in a beer bottle but would never invite anybody to join him. One day Tojuro went out for a walk, and Kushami stole a drink out of the bottle. He should not have done it but—"

"Who did you say drank Tojuro's *sake*?" shouted my master. "It was you who kept stealing it."

"I should have been more careful. I didn't think you would hear what I was saying because you were reading a book. You're the type we call 'all ears, all eyes.' But you're right. I drank some of it from time to time, but it was you who was caught. Now listen, you two. Kushami here can't drink, but knowing that the sweet *sake* was somebody else's, he drank as much as he could. You can imagine how red he got."

"Shut up! You can't even read Latin."

"Ha, ha, ha! Tojuro returned and found that more than half of his beer bottle was empty. He knew that somebody had been at it, so he took a look around and found Kushami lying rigid in one corner of the room, like a doll made of red clay."

Everyone burst out laughing at this. Even my master, though still pretending to read, also chuckled. It was only Dokusen who kept quiet. He had evidently become overly engrossed in his solitary game of gobang because he was now crumpled over the checkerboard fast asleep.

"There are a lot of ways to detect secrets besides sound. Another time, a long time ago, I went to the Ubako Hot Springs and shared the same room with an old man, a retired tailor from Tokyo. It didn't make any difference to me whether he was a tailor or a second-hand clothes dealer, but after the first three days the old man began to annoy me. I had run out of cigarettes and, as you all know, Ubako is located in the mountains and the hotel is the only indication of civilization around there. There's nothing to do but to soak in the mineral water and to eat. And it was there that I ran out of cigarettes—a disaster! It's funny but when a person is denied something, he begins to crave it very badly. I myself had a sudden craving for cigarettes though I usually don't pay too much attention. And what was most annoying was that the old man had come with a whole bagful of cigarettes. He'd sit cross-legged in the room right in front of me and smoke one cigarette after another. It wouldn't have been so intolerable if he had just smoked in the ordinary way. But he'd make smoke rings, blow the smoke out vertically and then horizontally and then up in the air. He would also exhale the smoke out from his nostrils and—. In other words, he was just showing off his smoking."

"Showing off his smoking?"

"Well, when a person parades in front of someone else in new clothes, you would call it showing off of clothing. But as this was concerning cigarettes, the old man was showing off his smoking. Do you understand?"

"Instead of enduring this torture, why didn't you ask him for some?"

"I don't beg. I'm a proud man."

"But what would be the matter with that?"

"I don't know, but anyway I wouldn't beg."

"So what did you do?"

"I stole some."

"Well, well."

"Once when the old gentleman went to take his bath, I told

myself that if I was ever going to smoke, this was the time. So I helped myself and began puffing away on his cigarettes as fast as I could. Actually, I didn't have much time because the door slid open after only a few minutes and the owner of the cigarettes again entered the room."

" Didn't he take his bath? "

" He was going to, but he found that he had forgotten his wallet so he came back for it. Nobody would have taken his money—very insulting of him to even worry about it."

" Maybe he was worried about his cigarettes."

" Ha, ha, ha! Perhaps, but let's forget about the wallet. Anyway, when he opened the door, he saw the room filled with cigarette smoke. I had tried to make up for two days in five minutes. 'An evil deed will become known a thousand miles off.' And so, my crime was exposed."

"And what did the old man say? "

" In spite of this— Well, he was at the age of wisdom. He didn't say anything. He only wrapped up fifty or sixty cigarettes in a paper and offered them to me. He said that though they were only a poor brand of cigarettes, I could have them if I wanted to. Then he went down and took his bath."

" I wonder if that's what they call a typical Tokyo man."

" I wouldn't know if he were a typical man of Tokyo or a typical tailor, but anyway we soon became good friends. So after an interesting two weeks there I came home."

" Were you supplied with cigarettes for the whole two weeks? "

" Well, that's about what happened."

"Are you all through with the violin story? " asked my master. He closed his book and stood up, thereby declaring his surrender.

" Not yet. But I've just come to the most interesting part so be sure and listen carefully. While you're at it, wake up that man who's sleeping on the checkerboard. What's his name now —oh, yes, Mr. Dokusen. I would like for him to listen too. Besides, it's not good for the health to sleep that much."

" Hey, Dokusen, wake up. Wake up, Dokusen. Come and

listen to this story. Come on, get up. Your Mrs. is worried."

" Wha-at? " exclaimed Dokusen. When he lifted his head, a trail of slobber could be seen running down his goatee. It looked like the shiny trail of a snail.

" Oh, I was sleeping like ' white clouds on the mountain tops '. I sure had a wonderful nap."

" We've all witnessed your wonderful nap but how about trying to keep awake for a while."

" I guess it's about time I did wake up. Did anything interesting happen? "

" Here's where the violin— Where did Kangetsu leave off, Kushami? "

" How would I know? I wasn't listening."

" He was getting ready to play it."

" That's right. He's going to tell us how he began to play his new violin. All right, come over here and listen to his story."

" What? Are you still on the violin? How annoying."

" You play the no-stringed harp, so you don't bother other people. But Kangetsu's playing screeches and groans so loudly that the neighbors can hear it. That's what is most annoying."

" Is that so? Kangetsu, did you ever find out any way of playing the violin without having the neighbors hear it? "

" If there is a way, I'd like to know about it."

" You don't have to know about it; all you have to do is to look at the pure white ox that lives in a place where no worldly desires exist—you'll understand right away," chanted Dokusen. But nobody understood him. Kangetsu had purposely tried to change the subject anticipating that Dokusen, being half-asleep, might say such a strange thing. Then Kangetsu continued with his tale.

" The following day was the Emperor's birthday. I stayed at home but was restless from morning till night. I kept opening the lid of the clothes box and shutting it. I also kept a cricket in this box. When evening came, the cricket began to chirp and I took out the violin and bow."

" So finally it came out," cheered Tofu. Meitei followed this with a warning: "It will be dangerous if you play it in your room."

"First I picked up the bow and examined it from the tip to the base."

"You're beginning to sound like an inexperienced sword dealer," coldly criticized Meitei.

"When I held it in my hands, I had the sensation a samurai must have felt when he drew his finely whetted sword from its sheath under the candlelight in late autumn. Holding the bow in my hand, I trembled all over."

"Really a born artist!" exclaimed Tofu again. But Meitei followed with "More probably a case of epilepsy." My master urged Kangetsu on: "Why don't you begin playing it?" Dokusen only made a face as if to say that all this was a bore.

"I was happy to find that the bow was safe so now I took out the violin and examined it closely under the lamp. All this took about five minutes. And don't forget that the cricket was chirping all during this time."

"We'll remember whatever you want us to, but get going with your playing the violin."

"I'm not playing yet— Well, the violin had no scratches. When I had satisfied myself that the instrument was all right, I stood up."

"To go some place?"

"Oh, shut up! If you're going to interrupt me every few seconds, I'll never be able to finish."

"Listen everybody, Kangetsu wants us to keep quiet."

"Very well, we'll only listen from now on."

"Sorry, very sorry. Let's listen more carefully now."

"I put on my straw sandals and with the violin under my arm I took two or three steps from the door. But then I hesitated again."

"There he goes. I knew for sure that he was going to stop some place."

"There aren't any more dried persimmons so there's no reason to go back."

"Now if you gentlemen are going to cut in every few minutes

and stir things up, it's going to take a long time to finish—and Tofu wants to hear this story. So after taking two or three steps, I returned to get a red blanket; I had bought it for three yen twenty sen before I left home. I covered my head with the blanket and then blew out the lamp. It was so dark that I couldn't even see where my sandals were."

" Where were you going? "

" Just keep quiet and listen. It took me some time to find my sandals and when I stepped outside I saw that it was a bright moonlit night. Digging my toes into the ground through the dead persimmon leaves, I climbed up Mount Koshin. Suddenly the temple bell of the Torei-*ji* Temple gonged and the sound came floating through the red blanket and into my ears. Tofu, what time do you think it was? "

" I wouldn't know."

" It was nine. I was climbing to a place called O-daira. As you know, I am a cowardly fellow so it was all very frightening. I would not have been able to continue unless I had my heart so set on playing the violin. That desire was much stronger than my fear. O-daira is a clearing located on the south side of Mount Koshin. On nice days, a castle and its surroundings below can be seen through the red pine trees—a majestic view. And the clearing itself—let me see—was about sixty by sixty feet in area, and right in the middle of this clearing was a big stone slab about twelve by twelve feet square. Beyond the clearing to the north were many large camphor trees which surrounded a swamp by the name of Unonuma. It would take three people to touch hands by stretching their arms around the trunks. The only house around there was a hut which belonged to a man who went about collecting camphor. It was eerie even in the daytime. Once some army engineers on maneuvers cut a road through the mountain, though, so it wasn't difficult to climb. I finally reached the big stone slab and spread my red blanket on it so I could sit down. This was the first time that I had ever climbed the mountain on such a cold night. I began to feel a creeping sensation in my belly but after a while I became more calm. When alone in the mountains like that, what generally most disturbs the mind is the feeling of fear; once that is lost, a brilliant, piercingly cold, and mysterious inspiration enters the soul. I sat there with this feeling for about twenty minutes. I felt as if I were living alone in a crystal palace. My body—no, not only my body but my soul, my whole being—seemed to turn to gelatine, so transparent had my emotions become. Now it was I who had turned to crystal, not like living in a crystal palace at all."

Meitei said jokingly with a straight face, "This has become serious!" But Dokusen sighed in admiration, "Amazing!"

"If this sensation had continued, I might have sat there until morning without playing the violin."

Tofu suggested, "Maybe a fox had set a spell over you."

"I had lost all consciousness of myself and of others. I didn't have a thought as to whether I was alive or dead. Then, all of a sudden, a piercing cry rang out from the direction of the old swamp to my rear."

"So finally something has appeared."

"This cry, like a searing blast of wind in late autumn, vibrated far above the tree tops and all through the mountain. I came back to myself."

"Well, that's a relief," whistled Meitei, exaggerating his concern by patting his chest.

"'When you throw away your life, it renews heaven and earth,' isn't that so?" commented Dokusen with a wink. Kangetsu understood nothing of this statement.

"I took a look around and found that everything on Mount Koshin was quiet—so quiet that I could hear the fall of dripping rain water. I still don't know what it was that made the cry. It was too piercing to be a human scream and too loud for a bird. It might have been a monkey—but no, there are no monkeys in that vicinity. When I was trying to figure out what the screech had been, I found that the quiet that had previously occupied my mind was now replaced by confusion and disorder, all jumbled together. It was a feeling that Prince Arthur of Connaught must have experienced when the Japanese were jubilantly welcoming his visit in 1906. The pores of my body suddenly opened, and my courage and composure evaporated as quickly as alcohol vanishes when rubbed on hairy shins. My heart was dancing a jig underneath my ribs and my legs began to tremble like the humming string attached to a flying kite. It was unbearable. I picked up the violin, covered my head with the blanket, and staggered from the rock. I ran down the mountain as fast as I could and then I crawled into my bed and went to sleep. There has been no time that I was so frightened in my life."

"And then what?"

" That's the end of the story."

" Didn't you play the violin?"

" I couldn't have played it even if I had tried—not with that cry ringing in my ears."

" Your story sounds somewhat incomplete."

" Well, that's probably because I told it exactly as it happened. Did you like it?" asked Kangetsu as he looked around proudly.

" Ha, ha, ha! It must have been hard on you to bring that story to an end. I thought you were going to tell us that you had become the male Sandra Belloni of the East." Meitei was hoping that somebody would ask him more about Sandra Belloni. Nobody did, but he continued anyway. " You see, Sandra Belloni played the harp and sang in the moonlight in a forest. Kangetsu carried his violin up Mount Koshin, which is somewhat similar, but with a different result. Sandra Belloni surprised Phoebe but Kangetsu was surprised by a spooky old badger. Just a slight difference, but one story is beautiful and the other is comical."

" It's really not as funny as you think," replied Kangetsu, unexpectedly calm.

Then my master criticized Kangetsu. " It serves you right to have been frightened—trying to act so smart with your violin on the top of a mountain." Dokusen added, " You'll have to learn to use your head if you want to enter the dark cave of the devil and still survive." It is indeed unfortunate that nobody understands what Dokusen is generally trying to say.

" Oh, by the way, Kangetsu, are you still polishing those glass balls at school? Meitei was changing the subject of conversation.

" No. My trip back home has held the work up. Actually I'm getting tired of it and am thinking of quitting altogether."

" But you won't be able to earn your doctor's degree if you stop," warned my master with his brows drawn together. Kangetsu, however, gave an unexpectedly flippant answer. " Me? A doctor? He, he he! I don't have to become a doctor now."

" That's going to interfere with your marriage plans and maybe the Kanedas won't like that."

" Marriage? Whose? "

" Yours, of course."

"And who am I supposed to marry? "

" Kaneda's daughter."

" What? "

" Don't you remember that you promised to marry the girl? "

" I made no promises. I can't help what the Kanedas are telling everybody."

" I never expected anything like this! What do you think, Meitei? You know the secret, don't you? "

" What secret? The one about the Nose? If that's what you're talking about, it's not a secret any more. Everybody knows. The *Mancho* newspaper keeps asking me when they will receive the honor to print the pictures of the bride and bridegroom. Tofu knows about it, too. He has composed a long poem entitled *The Song of Mandarin Ducks*. He had been waiting for Kangetsu to get married for three months now. But if Kangetsu doesn't get his degree, Tofu's masterpiece will be a treasure written in vain. He's worried about it very much, too. Isn't that so, Tofu? "

" Please don't worry about me. Maybe I can make public that poem on some other occasion."

" There, you see, Kangetsu. A lot of people are counting on your earning the degree of a doctor. Get back to business and get those balls polished."

" He, he, he! Sorry to have caused you so much trouble, but actually there's no need for the degree any more."

"And why? "

" Because I already have a wife, that's why."

" Is it possible? When did you elope? You can't trust anybody any more. Kushami, did you hear? Kangetsu has a

[401]

wife and a baby already?"

"No child yet. After all, I've only been married one month."

"And just when and where did you get married?" asked my master, as if he were a judge of the preliminary court.

"Well, when I went back to my home town, there she was waiting for me. The dried bonitos I brought you today are wedding presents from my relatives."

"A wedding present of only three dried fish? Your relatives must be a little stingy."

"Don't worry. I received a lot more."

"Then your wife is from your home town, too. Is she quite dark?"

"Well, yes, she's dark complexioned. Just about right for me."

"But what do you intend to do about the Kanedas?"

"Nothing."

"That wouldn't be very nice. What do you think, Meitei?"

"Tomiko can easily marry somebody else. Couples often get married for no better reason than that they bump heads in the dark. And it doesn't seem to make much difference who bumps whose head. I still think that the person who's to be pitied most is Tofu."

"That's all right. I'll still give *The Song of Mandarin Ducks* to Kangetsu. I'll compose another poem for Kaneda's daughter."

"For a poet, you are certainly generous with your creations."

"But you should have told the Kanedas about this." My master was still worrying.

"But there's no need. I didn't do the proposing so all I mean to do is to keep silent. Besides, the Kanedas probably know already. I'm surrounded by the people they send to spy on me. There must be ten or twenty of their detectives watching me."

When my master heard the word *detective*, he made a sour face. "Huh? If that's the case, it's best to keep quiet." In spite of his own suggestion to drop the subject, however, my master started talking about detectives as if he were giving a lecture.

"To steal from a person when he is off his guard on the street or in the train is what you call picking pockets, but to get people to admit a fault when they are off their guard is the business of a detective. The man who lifts sliding doors out of their grooves without being noticed and takes what belong to others is called a robber, whereas those who can read people's minds by making them talk without their knowing what they are saying are detectives. Those who stick broad swords into floor mats and forcibly take cash hidden underneath are called burglars, but the detectives uses strong language in order to get people to say what they do not wish to speak about. Therefore, a detective belongs to the same family as pickpockets, robbers and burglars. So don't pay any attention to them because that would only promote their vice. Don't be influenced by them."

"Don't worry. One or two thousand detectives could attack me from the windward side and there would still be nothing to be afraid of. Don't forget that I'm the famous Glass Ball Polisher, Bachelor of Science, Kangetsu Mizushima!"

"Hear, hear! It's wonderful to know that our newly wedded scientist is so full of confidence. By the way, Kushami, since a detective is the same as a pickpocket, a robber or a burglar, what kind of a specimen is Kaneda—one who employs detectives?"

"He's something like Chohan Kumasaka, the famous bandit chieftain."

"Chohan Kumasaka! That's good! In noh plays, Chohan becomes two different people after being cut in half during a fight even though both of his bodies soon disappear. But the 'Chohan' that lives across the street has become wealthy through usury. He is such a stubborn and stingy person that he would never disappear, no matter how many times he were cut in two. If he wants to revenge himself, he could cause you trouble for the rest of your life. So be careful, Kangetsu."

"Oh, don't worry. I'll just call him a boasting robber and then threaten him with revenge." Kangetsu remained undisturbed and in high spirits, just like the hero in most noh dramas.

"It seems to me that almost everyone living in the twentieth century has become somewhat of a detective. I wonder why that's so." Dokusen in his unique way, was putting forth a question which had no connection at all with the topic at hand.

"It's probably because of today's high prices," replied Kangetsu.

"I think it's because people don't fully comprehend art any more," Tofu answered.

Meitei theorized, "It's because we have begun to sprout horns of civilization and those horns are as useless as confetti."

It was now my master's turn again. He began with a voice that sounded somewhat pompous. "I've been thinking about this problem for quite a long time now, and I have decided that the people of today have the tendency to become like detectives because they have developed too strong a consciousness. The consciousness I mean is not that which Dokusen calls the faith to perceive Buddha's retributions through the mentality which one had been born with, nor does it mean the spiritual enlightenment that tells a person that he is the same as heaven and earth, nor—"

"You're making the discussion a little too complicated, Kushami. But as long as you've troubled the tip of your tongue to make such a scholarly disclosure, I would like to say that I, your humble servant Meitei, also want to make a complaint about our present civilization."

"You're of course free to do so if you wish, though you generally just talk but don't say anything."

"But I have much to say. The other afternoon you bowed down to the police-detective as if he were a god, but today you are comparing a detective to a pickpocket and a robber. This is a great contradiction. But I have held the same opinion of detectives ever since before my father and mother were born."

"A police-detective is a police-detective, and another day is another day. But today is today. If you don't change an opinion, you're not progressing. A stupid person cannot occupy a seat with learned men, and that's what you are."

"That's rather strong language. If a detective expressed himself in this way, he would be considered amusing."

"Are you calling me a detective?"

" On the contrary. You're too honest to be a detective and I like you for it. But let's hear the rest of your great argument."

" The people of today have become too self-conscious—we all recognize too well the wide gap in interests between ourselves and others. And each day civilization progresses, this self-consciousness becomes more sensitive. We have become aware of every movement of our hands and feet. A man by the name of William Ernest Henley, in criticizing Robert Louis Stevenson, said that whenever Stevenson passed in front of a mirror, he would not be satisfied unless he looked at his own image. That's how little Stevenson could forget himself. But this is the trend all of us are following today. In sleep we think of ourselves; when awake we think of ourselves. Our self is stuck in our mind wherever we go, so our every speech and action has become artificial and forced. We are living our every moment with the same painful feeling a young man and woman experience when they are about to meet each other for the first time at a marriage meeting. Such words as self-composure and tranquility sound impressive but they have no meaning any more. In this respect, the people of today are like detectives and robbers. As the work of a detective demands that nobody will notice him, he couldn't possibly be a good detective unless he had a strong self-consciousness. As for robbers, they are constantly worried about being caught or found out so naturally they have developed a strong self-consciousness, too. We people of today, both asleep and awake, keep thinking about our own interests and about potential losses. Therefore, like detectives and robbers, we have also developed a strong self-consciousness. Twenty-four hours a day we are restless and sneaky and worried—this is present-day man. That is the curse of civilization. Foolish, extremely foolish ! "

When it comes to such subjects, Dokusen is not a person to maintain silence. " Kushami's theory has my approval. Our ancestors were taught to forget themselves; today we are told never to forget ourselves. This is a sharp contradiction. During the full twenty-four hours of the day our minds are filled with thoughts of ourselves; therefore there is no time for tranquility. It's a hellish world we are living in. There would be no better way to help the people of the world today than to help them to forget themselves. Only the poets seem to know the importance of sitting under the moon, far away from evil passions, to search truth. There are still many acts of kindness but true generosity is lacking. Today, an act that Englishmen call 'nice' also includes a feeling of self-praise or of self-interest; the British are so full of self-consciousness that it is always ready to burst out. Once an English prince went on a visit to India and was asked to dine at the palace of a maharajah. Forgetting for a moment that he was in the presence of the prince, the maharajah indulged in the custom of his country by picking up a potato with his fingers and passing it onto his plate. Right away he realized this breach of etiquette and became red with shame. So the prince nonchalantly picked up a potato with his fingers and— "

" Is that the custom of England? " asked Kangetsu.

My master followed this up with another tale. " This is also about England. One evening some regimental officers were giving a dinner for a private who had distinguished himself in action. When the last course had been served and the fingerbowls brought out, the private, unfamiliar with table manners, put the bowl to his lips and drank the water in one gulp. It was just as the commanding officer was going to make a toast to the noncom, so the commanding officer drank the water from his fingerbowl in one gulp and the rest of the officers followed suit."

" I know one too," explained Meitei who could never stay quiet for long. " When Thomas Carlyle was first received by the Queen, he was not accustomed to the ways of the court. He sat down in a chair first and then asked the Queen to take her seat. The lords and ladies-in-waiting who were standing behind the Queen commenced to giggle—no, but they were about to giggle —when the Queen turned her head and gave them a sign to sit down, too. In no time, all the Queen's attendants were seated, so Carlyle did not lose face. This was an act of kindness elaborately offered."

" Since it was Carlyle, the attendants should have kept standing," commented Kangetsu, trying to show his admiration for Meitei.

" Self-consciousness on the part of the person offering kindness is not bad," continued Dokusen, " but because the person does possess that self-consciousness, his kindness is the result of an exertion. It is a pity that kindness cannot be more natural. With the progress of civilization, it is believed that savageness diminishes and intercourse between different people becomes peaceful. But this is not necessarily true. With self-consciousness as strong as it is, how can true peace be possible? At a glance, everything might appear peaceful but there is always a constant struggle going on between men. When we see two *sumo* wrestlers in each other's grips in the middle of the ring without moving, all looks quiet. But actually the bellies of the wrestlers are tense with tumult." .

" Disputes in the olden days were settled by strength and they were fairly innocent, but nowadays victory depends more on wit. This also helps increase our self-consciousness." Meitei felt as if it were his turn to do some talking. "According to Francis Bacon, if we abide by the rules of nature, we can learn to win against nature. It is strange to find that victories nowadays are won just as Bacon said. It's something like judo, overcoming an opponent by taking advantage of his strength."

" It's also like hydro-electricity. The power of water is not opposed, but encouraged, and in this way electricity is generated with excellent results." Kangetsu had only begun but Dokusen interrupted. " So self-consciousness will trap a person in poverty, in wealth, in a mood of melancholy, and when he's feeling happy. A talented person will be overcome by talent, a man of knowledge will be defeated by his knowledge, and a man like Kushami who is short-tempered will be tricked by his enemy who can take advantage of his temper."

" Hear, hear!" exclaimed Meitei, clapping his hands. My master just made a sly smile and said, " But this doesn't always go as smoothly as you seem to believe." To this, everyone in the room laughed out all at once.

" By the way, how would the Kanedas be overcome?"

" The wife will be overcome by her nose, Kaneda himself will be defeated by his own hardness, and his henchmen will fall victims to their own detective work."

"And the daughter?"

" The daughter? I haven't seen her so I can't say. But most probably she'll be overcome by clothes, or by food or maybe by drink. It is quite unlikely that she will ever be overwhelmed by love. There is even the possibility that she will die in the streets like poor Ono-no-Komachi."

" Don't you think you're being too hard on her?" protested Tofu. After all, he had gone so far as to present her with a poem.

" The saying ' Less greed, less poverty ' once had a very important meaning. If we never learn to understand this, man will keep struggling forever." Dokusen looked as if he had been enlightened himself.

" You can't remain indifferent, either, Dokusen. You might be overcome by the ' Flashing-a-sword-as-lightning ' stuff."

" When considering civilization today, I myself don't feel like living any more," complained my master.

" Go ahead and die if that's the case," Meitei promptly replied.

" I don't want to die, either." My master is insensibly stubborn.

" Nobody worries much when they are being born, but when they are about to die they take it hard," said Kangetsu, stating another truism.

" When you borrow money, you don't think much about it. But when you have to return it, you worry a lot. There are many similar examples." Meitei was very quick in giving such answers.

" Those who don't worry about repaying their loans are lucky in the same sense as those who don't worry about dying," commented Dokusen, standing aloof and looking very unworldly.

" You seem to believe that the most audacious people are the most enlightened."

"According to the Zen doctrines, an iron bull with a stern face has an iron-willed heart; and an iron-willed heart, therefore, only dwells in iron bulls with stern faces."

" Do you mean to say that you're an example of an iron bull?"

"Not exactly. But the reason a person worries so much about death is only because such a sickness as nervous prostration was discovered."

"I see. But you were born before the discovery of nervous prostration."

Meitei and Dokusen became further involved in this queer dialogue but my master continued talking with Kangetsu and Tofu about his own dissatisfaction with civilization.

"How not to pay back borrowed money is a great problem."

"That's true. But you must return it."

"Look. I'm talking so shut up and just listen. Not to repay money is as great a problem as not dying. Alchemy might offer a solution but alchemy has always ended in failure. It is definitely clear that man must die."

"That was clear even before alchemy."

"Look. I haven't finished talking yet. When it became evident that man had to die, a second problem came to light."

"What?"

"The question of how to die naturally arose. A Suicide Club is one way of solving this second problem."

"I see."

"It's painful to die but it would be much worse if you could not die. People who are stricken with nervous prostration are in more agony alive than dead. Still they worry about death, not because they are afraid to die but about why it is best to die. Most such people do not have good brains so they leave the problem unsolved. Eventually, other people abuse them to death. But those who have a trait of character are not willing to be abused to death so they study the problem more thoroughly. The only reasonable solution is in suicide. Some day everyone will leave the world simply by doing away with himself."

"The world will become quite insecure, won't it?"

"Probably. Henry Arthur Jones once wrote about a philosopher who strongly advocated suicide."

"And did he kill himself?"

"Unfortunately not. But in another thousand years, everybody will be committing suicide. In ten thousand years, people will talk about death in no other way than as self-destruction."

" That's going to be a terrible mess."

" Ways of committing suicide will be extensively studied and it will be considered a fine science. At the Descending Cloud Junior High School, they'll be teaching methods of suicide instead of holding classes in ethics."

" It's kind of fun to listen to this lecture on suicide. Meitiei, did you hear Mr. Kushami's theory? "

" I heard it. I'd love to hear the teacher of ethics in the Descending Cloud tell his students that they should not adhere to the barbaric custom of public morality any more, but that, as future leaders, their first duty is to commit suicide. But the lesson could easily go one step further and make it lawful to kill others. That poor scholar Mr. Kushami who lives near the Descending Cloud Junior High School, says he is tired of living so the students might consider it their duty to put him to death as quickly as possible. As we are now in a period of enlightenment, they mustn't be as cowardly as in the past and employ lances, halberds or missiles. By only speaking ironically, they could kill Mr. Kushami. It would be a charitable deed and, moreover, it would mean honor."

" Your lecture is interesting, too."

" There's still something more. At present, the main object of the police is to protect life and property. But in the future the policemen will go around with sticks, like dog catchers, killing the citizens throughout the country."

" But why? "

" Why? The people of today value their lives, so the police protect them; but in the future the people will find life unbearable, so policemen will beat them to death in mercy. That's why. But the people who have some sense will commit suicide, so the only ones left for the policemen will be those exceedingly poor-spirited fellows, idiots, and the disabled who don't have the ability to destroy themselves. Those who don't want to live, but hesitate to do away with themselves, will put up notices on their front doors saying that a man or a woman, whichever the case may be, living in that house desires death. The policemen will come around when it's convenient and fulfill that wish. The body? Oh, the policemen will come around with a cart to pick it up later. Then there's something else—"

"Your joke has no end," murmured Tofu with admiration. Dokusen, nervous about his billy-goat whiskers as always, now expressed his opinion.

"If you consider this story a joke, it can be called a joke. But, again, if you consider it as a prophecy, it can be just that. That which lacks logic is often found to be an accepted fact when repeated, and right under your nose. There is also the tendency to accept a frothy dream as an everlasting truth. Some other people, hearing a new and different idea, right away take it as a joke."

"Just as 'a swallow or a sparrow cannot comprehend the mind of a great wild goose', it is impossible for a little man to understand a great man." Kangetsu felt quite pleased with himself when Dokusen nodded in agreement to this statement. Dokusen continued, "There was, once upon a time, a place in Spain named Cordova and—"

"Isn't it still there?"

"Maybe. But never mind about that. There was a strange custom in Cordova. When the Angelus rang at the end of the day, all the girls and women left their homes and went to bathe in the river."

"Even in winter?"

"I'm not sure about that. But anyway, all of them went splashing in the river. No man could take part in this daily routine but many of them looked at the scene from far off. On the waves, in the gray of the evening, the white-skinned girls could be vaguely seen moving in the water."

"That sounds quite poetic. You could make a new-styled poem out of this. What was the name of the place again?" Tofu eagerly leaned forward when hearing something said about naked women.

"The name's Cordova. The local lads could only watch the girls from a great distance. But the boys once rebelled and decided to play a joke."

" In what way? " asked Meitei, glad to know there would be another joke.

" They bribed the bellkeeper to ring the Angelus one hour early. As the women in Cordova are frivolous as all other women, one and all ran out in their undershirts and underpants as usual when they heard the bell. But when they jumped into the river, it was still light."

" Wasn't the fierce autumn sun still shining bright? "

"And up on a bridge, they saw all the men looking down at them. Embarrassed, all the women blushed with shame."

"And what then? "

" So you see, people are sometimes led astray by custom. We too often forget the fundamental principles and are deceived by habit."

" I see. That's a good piece of advice. Now let me tell a story about being led astray by custom. I read about this technique in a magazine the other day. Let's pretend that I am running an antique store and that I have many masterpieces out in front. Of course they are genuine works of art so the price I am asking is quite high. One day, a curious customer comes and asks the price of a picture by Motonobu, the successor to Masanobu, the originator of the Kanoo school of painting. I tell him it costs six hundred yen. The customer then expresses his regret that he doesn't have the cash on hand and that he is unable to buy it."

" Does he have to use those exact words? " asked my unsociable master.

Meitei retorted, " This is only a story. Let's pretend that he says so. Then I tell him that since he is so pleased with it, he can take it and pay me later. Of course the customer hesitates, so I suggest a monthly payment, though it will take quite a long time. As I am happy for his patronage, he does not have to worry about causing me any trouble. I suggest ten yen a month, or five if he thinks that too much. After some talk with him I finally sell him the picture by Motonobu Kanoo Hogen at six hundred yen, to be paid by monthly instalments at ten yen a month."

" It's something like buying the *Encyclopedia Britannica* by paying the London *Times* a little each month, isn't it?"

"But the London *Times* is reliable. I am being extremely unreliable, because now I begin with a cunning swindle. Listen carefully. Now, when you're paying six hundred yen at the rate of ten yen per month, how long do you think it'll take, Kangetsu?"

"It'll take five years of course."

"Of course, five years. Now, Dokusen, do you think the period of five years is short or long?"

"One minute can give us a feeling of lasting for ten thousand years, just as ten thousand years can make us feel as if it passed in only one minute. At times it's short, and then again it may seem not too short. In other words, it all depends on how you look at it."

"What's that? A didactic poem? If so, it's without reasoning. Now, the customer will have to give me ten yen every month for the next five years or, in other words, he will have to pay me sixty times. These payments will eventually become a habit. After he gives me ten yen sixty times, he will feel that he must still pay ten yen for the sixty-first time, also. Then for the sixty-second, and the sixty-third. In other words, after having repeatedly paid me on a certain day each month for such a long time, he feels unsatisfied unless he keeps paying me ten yen on that date. Man seems clever but we are sometimes led astray by custom, as Dokusen just said. By knowing this weak point, I can get ten yen every month for doing nothing."

"Ha, ha, ha! Nobody is as forgetful as that," laughed Kangetsu.

My master admitted, rather seriously, "But Meitei is right. I paid for my university tuition in small payments each month and I lost track. The university authorities had to tell me I didn't owe any more the last time I went." My master considered his own disgrace as if it were the disgrace of everybody in general.

"There, you see. The moral of my story is sound because here's a person who has proved such forgetfulness as possible. Therefore, those of you who only laughed at my story about the art of suicide should take it more seriously. Especially such young men as Kangetsu and Tofu who lack experience should listen carefully so they can learn more about life."

" Much obliged. Then hereafter, we'll make it a rule to pay our monthly instalments only sixty times."

" You might still consider it a joke but you could learn much from the story, Kangetsu," said Dokusen. He continued, " Now, let's suppose that Kushami or Meitei tells you that you must apologize to a certain Kaneda because you did not let him know about your wedding. What would you do? Would you apologize? "

" I'd argue that it wasn't at all necessary. If the Kaneda's wanted to apologize to me, that would be different but there would be no need for me to talk to them."

" What if the police told you to apologize? "

" I'd protest all the more."

" What if a cabinet minister or a peer ordered an apology? "

" I would refuse even more strongly."

" There! You see? That's the big difference between our fathers and you of the younger generation. Only a few years ago authority was respected, but there will soon come a time when the authorities will be completely powerless. Even now a nobleman cannot influence others any more than anybody else. If you want me to put it strongly, the more authority one person possesses the more that person's authority will be resisted. People in high places can no longer do everything they wish. This phenomenon is still bewildering to the older people. Great changes occur in social conditions and in human nature with each generation, so Meitei's story of the future cannot only be considered as a joke."

" Since I have such an appreciative friend, I will continue my story of the future. It is just as Dokusen said: the people who shelter themselves under authority, or insist on relying on a couple of hundred bamboo spears to defend themselves, are just as out-of-date as a man in a palanquin desperately trying to run a race with a train. My theory concerns a special phenomenon which can affect the fate of all mankind. After carefully observing the tendency followed at present and prophesizing its future trend, I believe even marriage will eventually become an impossibility.

"As I mentioned before, society is now centered on the individual. At one time, a family was represented by the father, a district by its magistrate, and a province by its lord; nobody's personality was recognized except that of the representatives. But now everybody is trying to emphasize his own personality. You became you alone, and I became I. When two people meet on a road they immediately begin to defend their individualities— ' He is a man but so am I '. But because his personality has become strong, the individual himself has become proportionately weak. Today a man cannot easily cause injury to others, so we might believe that by escaping injury we have become strong; but then since we can seldomly harm others also shows that we are actually weaker than our ancestors. But nobody likes to be considered weak; we want to prove our strength even when defending trifles.

" Because of our newly developed individuality, there is now no peace between man and man. We strain ourselves to the utmost to prove our individual strength, so we are living in agony. Because of this constant conflict, we have tried to find ways of separating ourselves from others. The first step was to have parents and children live separately. Just go to an old-fashioned mountain village in Japan some day and you'll find all the members of a family still crowded under one roof. They have no individuality to claim; and even if their personalities were developed, they wouldn't insist upon them. So their life runs smoothly. But when it comes to the more highly civilized people, we try to express our egoism as much as possible. We believed that if we didn't show off our self-importance, it would be to our disadvantage. Therefore, to maintain security, parents and their married children live separately.

" Europe has progressed much more in civilization so they adopted this system much earlier than in Japan. If you happen to find a father and his grown son living together in Europe, the son will be paying for his room and board just like an outsider; and if he borrows money from his father, he will return it with interest. This laudable custom can exist because the father recognizes and respects the individuality of the son. This custom will surely be imported into Japan sooner or later.

"So families today are separated; now we are able to endure our individuality in every way except the feeling of respect which is lost because of this development of individuality. We will not relax until we become even more separated. But since father and son and brothers and sisters have separated, there is nothing more to be desired except the separation of man and wife. In the days of old, they talked about 'two in body but one in mind.' 'To be united forever as man and wife for weal or woe' is what was said, and even after death they became like badgers in one hole. Barbarous! But now it's different. The husband is an individual forever and so is the wife. The wife marries after having cultured her personality at a girls' school; she no longer does everything her husband wants her to do. If she did, she would be considered only a doll, not a wife. The more civilized she is, the stronger her personality. And the more her individuality is developed, the more unsuitable she becomes for her husband. There is naturally a conflict, and the husband and wife fight from morning till night. There is now a boundary between the husband and the wife, as distinct and clear as between water and oil. And as our civilization progresses, this difference will become even more acute, and gradually it will become even more disadvantageous for a man and wife to live together."

"Is that why there are so many divorces? You have me worried now," said Kangetsu.

"Divorce, yes, divorce! Couples throughout the world will separate. Those living together hereafter will be considered eccentrics."

"Then that means people like myself will be thought of as crazy?" asked Kangetsu, speaking of his new marital status.

"Fortunately, you are living during the reign of Emperor Meiji. I am only speaking about the future. But as my mind is one or two steps ahead of the times, I will remain single. People make a row about my not getting married and accuse me of being frustrated in love, but such people are really very short-sighted. But never mind this. I want to continue with my story.

"A philosopher once descended from heaven and preached against conformity. According to his advocacy, man is an animal of personality. If this personality were exterminated, man himself would no longer exist. In order for man to become significant, no price is too high to pay to maintain his personality and to develop it. Bounded by corrupted customs, something barbarous goes against the natural inclination of a man and he gets married. This was understandable during the uncivilized period when the personality was not developed. But today, it is different. Since we have attained such a high degree of development, there is no reason why two personalities must marry. That there are still so many uncivilized young men and women who, indifferent to logic and caught by temporary passion, permit themselves to enter matrimony is worse than immorality and corruption. As educated men, for the sake of humanity, of civilization and of preserving the personalities of these young men and women, we should do our utmost to resist this barbarous custom."

" I cannot possibly agree with this theory of yours," exclaimed Tofu as he resolutely slapped his knee. " I believe that the most precious and priceless attainments in this world today are love and beauty. Because of love and beauty, we are comforted; we are made complete and happy. It is because of these two expressions that our characters can become noble and pure, and our feelings more refined. Love gives a meaning to life whereas beauty brings delight in the form of poems, songs and music. I believe that as long as mankind exists, love and art will exist."

" If so, very good. But the philosopher I just mentioned said that they will necessarily be exterminated. Art is bound to meet the same fate as that of marriage. When we talk about the development of personality, we mean freedom of personality. And by that, we are implying ' you are you ' and ' others are others '. For exactly the same reason, art cannot exist forever. The reason art flourishes today is that there is still a meeting point between the personality of the artist and those who enjoy that artist's creations. You yourself compose new-styled poems, but if no one reads them except yourself, you would be wasting your time. You are fortunate enough to be living in the Meiji era so you are read, but in the future—"

"I'm still not convinced."

"It's not that they won't read your works only because they are your compositions. It will be because each individual will have his own respective personality so highly individualized that it won't be fun reading what other people write. Even now, in England, we can find this tendency. Just take a look at Meredith and at James. They are contemporary writers and they express their own personalities to a great extent in their works. But they have few readers and there's a reason for this. Their works are only interesting to those who have the same personality as the writers. And when this tendency becomes even more pronounced, art, the same as marriage, will be completely forgotten. Now do you understand? When the time comes that I cannot understand what you write, and you cannot understand what I write, there will be nothing between us—art or anything else."

"Well, that might be. But I still can't visualize it intuitively."

"If you can't understand it intuitively, try to understand it circuitously."

Then Dokusen butted in: "But it's quite true. Once you give man freedom of individuality, their relations with each other become cramped. Nietzsche's superman was invented mainly because the philosopher could not dispose of this cramped feeling. At a glance, you might think that this superman was Nietzsche's ideal but that's not so. It was a complaint. Cramped because of the development of individuality even in the nineteenth century, Nietzsche could not roll in his bed freely. He felt that he was always causing an inconvenience to others so the old man scribbled his wild fantasy in desperation. When you read Nietzsche, you feel sorry for him instead of finding him exciting. His voice of dauntless progressiveness is really a display of great indignation.

"In olden days, when one man became great, the whole world came gathering under his flag—it must have been wonderful! If such power could still be exacted, there would have been no need for a Nietzsche. There's a great difference between the characters depicted by Homer, and the superman of Nietzsche.

Homer and Chevy Chase are cheerful. They simply transfer interesting episodes onto paper and there is no bitterness. It was different with Nietzche. Not one hero appears in his works. There used to be only one Confucius so he could make use of his influence. But now there are lots of Confuciuses. Everybody living today probably considers himself a Confucius. Therefore when a person claims to be a great philosopher, nobody takes him seriously. And as nobody pays any attention to him, he complains. He writes about supermen in order to voice his complaints. Man has asked for freedom but has not been able to feel satisfied with it. That is why Western civilization is not as admirable as it appears on the surface. In the East, disciplining of the mind used to be considered the righteous way. But now, due to the insistence on individuality, the people have become mentally worn out. They are now beginning to understand the saying ' Peaceful are the subjects of the sovereign.' But we have realized our mistakes too late, like an alcoholic complaining that he should not have drunk so much."

" You gentlemen seem terribly pessimistic about the future but I don't feel that way at all. Why is this?" asked Kangetsu.

" That's because you're still a newlywed," was Meitei's immediate explanation. Then my master suddenly interrupted.

" If you think that you're lucky to have found a wife, you're making a great mistake. I'm going to read something for your future reference." My master then produced the old book he had been reading. " This book was written a long time ago but even then it was clear that women are bad."

Kangetsu inquired, "And how old is the book?"

" It was written by Thomas Nashe in the sixteenth century."

" It's surprising that somebody could have criticized my wife four hundred years ago."

" There has been much written against women, and some of the complaints might fit your wife so you'd better listen."

" I'll listen. I couldn't have asked for more appropriate instruction."

" I will introduce some views on womanhood that have been handed down from antiquity. Are you listening?"

" Sure, we're all listening, Even a bachelor like me is inter-ested," agreed Meitei.

"Aristotle said that because all women are worthless, it is best to marry a little bride. She will do less harm than a big woman."

" Is Kangetsu's wife large or small? "

" She's of the bigger variety."

" Ha, ha, ha! That's a wonderful book. Go on, let's hear the rest of it."

"A man once asked what the greatest miracle in the world might be, and a wise man replied: A faithful wife."

" Who was the wise man? "

" It does not mention any names."

" Maybe he was a wise man, frustrated in love."

" The next to appear in this book is Diogenes. He was asked when the best time to get married would be. Diogenes replied that it's too soon when you're a young man, and it's too late when you're old. That's what the book says."

" Maybe Diogenes had been thinking about this in his barrel."

" Pythagoras said that there were three things in this world to be greatly feared: fire, quote; water, quote; and woman, unquote."

" The Greek philosophers had some stupid ideas, didn't they? If you ask me, there's nothing in this world to be afraid of. Few people are destroyed by fire, or drowned in water, or—" Dokusen got stuck by the time he had come this far.

" —or melted by meeting a woman. Is that what you want to say? " Meitei had come to Dokusen's help. But my master continued to read on without paying attention to what was going on around him.

" Socrates said that the most difficult feat for a man is to manage women. Demosthenes advised revenging yourself by giving your wife to the enemy; day in and day out his enemy would be pestered until he would beg for mercy. Seneca remarked that women and ignorance are the two greatest calamities in the world; Marcus Aurelius wrote that the difficulties involved in managing a woman are like trying to manage a ship in a hurricane; and Plautus suggested that women probably like to wear gorgeous dresses mainly in order to hide their inborn ugliness. Valerius once mentioned in a letter to a friend that there was nothing in this world women wouldn't endure to satisfy their ultimate desire. He asked Providence to take pity on him so he would not be caught by their craftiness. Valerius also asked: Are women not enemies of friendship? Are they not inevitable suffering? Are they not certain disaster? Are they not natural temptation? And are they not poison in the form of honey? To forsake a woman shows lack of virtue, but to endure a woman means nothing but torture."

"That's enough now, sir. After listening to that much evil about my humble wife, I don't want to hear more."

"But there are still several more pages."

"It's better to forget about the rest. Anyway, it's just about time your wife was coming home," teased Meitei. Then from the tearoom came a voice. The Mrs. was calling the maid.

"What should we do? Your wife is back already."

"He, he, he!" giggled my master. "Why worry?"

"Oh, ma'am, when did you return?"

There was only silence in the tearoom.

"Oh, ma'am. Did you hear what we were just talking about?" Still no answer.

"The ideas your husband was expressing now weren't his own opinions. He was reading a book by Nashe written in the sixteenth century."

"I wouldn't know." This curt answer of the Mrs. seemed to come from a great distance. Kangetsu commenced giggling nervously.

"I wouldn't know either, and I'm sorry. Ha, ha, ha!" Meitei could not restrain his laughter. Just then the front door was roughly opened and loud footsteps were heard entering the house. There was no usual greeting but presently the sliding door of the room was brusquely opened and Sampei Tatara stuck his head in.

Somehow Sampei did not look himself. He was wearing a clean white shirt and a brand-new frockcoat—inconceivable!— and in his right hand he was carrying four bottles of beer bound tightly together with straw rope. He placed the beer next to the dried bonitos and, at the same time, still with no greeting, sat down. The ease in which he sat down made Sampei seem very worldly.

" Sir, how is your stomach nowadays? It's not good for you to stay at home like this all the time."

" I didn't say that my stomach was worse."

" No, but your complexion tells me the whole story. You're looking terribly sallow. Maybe you should go fishing. I rented a boat at Shinagawa and went fishing myself last Sunday."

" Did you catch many fish? "

" I caught nothing."

" What's fun about fishing if you don't catch anything? "

" You see, sir, it lightened my spirit. How about you? Have you ever gone fishing? It's a lot of fun to be in a small boat with the big sea all around," he explained, not caring who was listening to him.

" What I want to do is to take a big ship and ride around on a little sea," answered Meitei, helping Sampei along with his conversation.

" I wouldn't like fishing much unless I could catch a whale or a mermaid or something," said Kangetsu.

" You couldn't catch anything like that. That's why they say a man of letters doesn't have any practical sense." Sampei was as critical as always.

" I'm not a man of letters."

" Oh? Then what do you do? You know, for a businessman like me, common sense is absolutely essential. Sir, I've become rich in common sense nowadays. I'm greatly influenced by the people I meet every day."

" How do they influence you? "

" Cigarettes are also helpful. You can't cut much of a picture by smoking only cheap brands like Asahis and Shikishimas." Sampei then took out a gold-tipped cigarette of Egyptian make and commenced puffing on it.

" Can you really afford to be so extravagant? "

" No, but I will be able to be extravagant pretty soon. But

for the moment I can impress a lot of important people by smoking imported cigarettes."

"It's an easier way to impress people than polishing glass balls like Kangetsu does." Meitei was saying this to Kangetsu but before Kangetsu could answer, Sampei exclaimed, "Oh, so you're Mr. Mizushima. I heard that you have given up studying for your doctor's degree, so I decided to accept."

"What? The doctor's degree?"

"No, the daughter of the Kanedas. I'm sorry, sir, but, you see, the Kanedas have approached me again and again so I finally decided to marry her. Again let me say how sorry I am, Mr. Mizushima."

"There's no need to feel sorry," replied Kangetsu. My master suggested, "Sampei, as long as you want to, why don't you?" This sounded quite ambiguous.

"That's a very happy ending to the Kaneda problem. Just as I said a little while ago, there was bound to be somebody willing to marry her, and now look. See what a fine gentleman came along. Now, Tofu, you can start writing another new-styled poem." Meitei was getting himself somewhat worked up.

Sampei then said, "So you're Tofu. Won't you please compose something for my wedding? I'll have it printed immediately and distributed. I'll also have it published in the *Taiyo* magazine."

"Sure, I'll write something. When will you need it?"

"Any time will do. It can even be one you've already composed. And for that, I'll invite you to my wedding. Have you ever tasted champagne? I'm planning on serving champagne and I'm going to call in an orchestra. What do you think of having them play an accompaniment for Tofu's composition, sir?"

"Just as you wish."

"Sir, won't you kindly arrange the poem to music?"

"Kangetsu here, the flunker of exams, is good with the violin. Ask him. He won't consent only because of the champagne, though."

"Speaking of champagne, it's not very good when it only costs four or five yen a bottle. I mean to serve the best. But

I hope you'll compose some music for me."

" I would be very happy to. It doesn't make any difference whether the champagne costs you twenty sen a bottle or twenty yen. For that matter, I will compose the music for nothing."

" I can't accept it for nothing. If you don't like champagne, how about something like this?" Sampei then took out seven or eight photographs from his coat pocket and spread them on the straw mat. Some of the pictures showed only the upper half of a woman and others were taken full length; some were standing while others were sitting down; some wore *hakama* skirts and some displayed their long *furisode* kimono sleeves. A few even wore their hair in the traditional lacquered style, but all of them were pictures of young girls.

" Sir, all of these girls were candidates for my marriage. I could arrange to introduce some of them to Kangetsu and Tofu. How about this one?" Sampei handed a picture to Kangetsu.

" She's very pretty. Maybe I'll accept that favor."

"And what do you think of this girl?" Sampei passed Kangetsu still another picture.

" She is lovely, too. Go ahead and arrange a meeting."

" For which one?"

"Any one would do."

" You certainly have a lot of passion! Sir, this girl is a niece of a doctor."

" Is that so?"

" This one has a very nice personality and she's young, too—only seventeen. And she's going to bring someone a dowry of one thousand yen. Oh, that one is the daughter of the governor." Sampei was talking all by himself.

" I wonder if there's any chance of getting married to all of them."

" Don't be so greedy. Are you a follower of polygamy by any chance?"

" I'm not what you call a polygamist but I'm carnivorous."

" He's only joking, Sampei. You had better put the pictures away," suggested my master.

" Then you don't really want any of them, do you?" To give

Kangetsu a chance to change his mind, Sampei put the photographs back into his pocket slowly, one at a time.

"What's the beer for?"

"Just a present. I bought it at the store around the corner to celebrate my coming marriage. Please enjoy yourselves."

My master clapped his hands for the maid and had her open the bottles. Then, assuming great respect, Meitei, Dokusen, Kangetsu, Tofu and my master raised their glasses to toast Sampei and his future bride. Sampei was carried away with emotion. "I want to invite all of you here to my wedding. You'll come, won't you?"

"I don't want to," responded my master immediately.

"Why? It will be the biggest day in my life."

"I don't want to seem unkind, but I'm not going to be present."

"If you don't have anything to wear for the occasion, I can manage to get a *haori* coat and a *hakama* skirt for you. It would be good for you to mingle with others more often, sir. I'll introduce you to a lot of famous people."

"You'll have to excuse me."

"Maybe you'll cure your stomach."

"I don't have to get well."

"If you're going to be so stubborn about it, there's nothing I can do. How about you, Mr. Meitei? Will you come?"

"Me? Sure. If it's still possible, I'd like to be honored by being your go-between and watch the three-times-three exchange of the nuptial cup of champagne! What? Tojuro Suzuki is already the go-between? Well, that's a shame, but I guess it can't be helped. You can't have two go-betweens, so I'll just be present as another guest."

"And how about you, Mr. Dokusen?"

"Me? 'The joys a rod brings give us a quiet and easy living; men angle between the white duckweeds and the red smartweeds.'"

"What's that? Is it one of the Chinese poems from the T'ang dynasty?"

"I don't know. It might be, or it might not."

" You don't know? Anyway, I hope you'll be present, Kangetsu. You have a special reason to be there."

" I'll try to go. I'd hate to miss hearing the orchestra play my composition."

" That's right. And how about you, Tofu? "

" Well, I'd like to read my poem in front of the newlyweds."

" Sir, I've never had a happier moment in my life, so I'll drink another glass of that beer." Sampei drank a tumbler full in one draught which suddenly made him become very red in the face.

That short autumn day was coming to an end. The ashes in the handwarming brazier were studded with the corpses of many cigarette butts; the charcoal embers in the brazier had gone out long ago. Even these friends of my master seemed to have talked themselves out. Dokusen stood up and said, " Well, it's getting pretty late. How about leaving? " The rest followed suit and soon the room felt like an empty theater after a vaudeville show had come to an end, so lonely it was.

Having finished his supper, my master entered his study. Because of the chilly night air, the Mrs. adjusted the collar of her undergarment and continued her sewing, mending her worn-out everyday kimono. The children had gone to bed and were all sleeping in a neat row. The maid had gone to the public bath.

If a person went tapping the bottom of the hearts of those people who looked so optimistic, he would hear some sad groans. Dokusen, who seems to understand everything, still walks on the ground like everybody else. The world of Meitei might seem free from all worries but his is not a world as drawn in pictures. Kangetsu had quit polishing glass balls and had brought a wife with him from his home town. Such happenings are natural. Yet, the repetition of the ordinary becomes a bore. In ten years from now, Tofu might find that to compose poems, only to give them away, is not profitable. As for Sampei, it is difficult to say whether he will be living in the clouds or lying in a ditch. If he can always feel proud to be able to serve his friends champagne, all will be well. Tojuro Suzuki will probably go rolling along forever, and by rolling, he'll gather mud. Still, he will be more impressive than those who can't roll at all.

It is now more than two years since I began living with humans.
I once thought that my insight was unique but the other day
I happened to meet one of my own kind. His name was Kater
Murr. I had never seen him before, but he talked so impressively
that I was somewhat amazed. Upon investigation, however,
I found that Kater Murr had actually died one hundred years ago
but, due to a sudden spirit of curiosity, had become a ghost
and left Hades in order to surprise me.

This cat is now in Hell because he was once carrying a fish in
his mouth for his mother, and he proved to be such an undutiful
son that he couldn't endure the temptation and ate the fish himself.
It is said that Kater Murr had a talent not unequal to that of a
man. At one time he even composed a poem to surprise his
master. Becanse a no-good cat like me can never hope to realize
such achievements, I ought to say goodbye to this world and go
to Hell myself.

My master will die, sooner or later, from his stomach ailment.
Old Kaneda is already as good as dead because of his greed. The
autumn leaves have fallen and most of the trees are bare. All
living creatures are destined to die so if you can't make much
use of yourself while living, it might be just as well to die right
away.

According to Meitei's theory, man is destined to become sui-
cidal. If we are not careful, even cats might become influenced
by this cramped world. That would be terrible.

That evening, such talk had made me feel so depressed that I
decided to drink some of the beer that Sampei had brought. Perhaps it would brighten me up.

I went around to the kitchen. The lamp had most probably
been blown out by the autumn wind which came in from the door
left ajar. It was dark but some moonbeams filtered through the
window.

I could see three glasses on a tray, and two of them were still
half filled with the brownish liquid. The glasses, shining bright
in the moonlight, stood beside the charcoal extinguisher and looked

cool; but even hot water looks cool in a glass. I didn't really feel like drinking the beer any more but there is nothing like trying. When Sampei drank, he became red in the face and commenced to breathe heavily. Would a cat become gay by drinking beer, too? Well, I am bound to die some time so it is best to do all things while still alive. After I'm dead, I don't want to feel regret so I made up my mind to drink some of it anyway.

I stuck my tongue out fast, and quickly lapped up some beer in one glass—and I was greatly surprised. I felt the tip of my tongue prickle as if needles were being stuck into it. I could not fathom for what freakish reason humans like to drink such bitter liquid. Any way you looked at it, beer and cats do not go hand in hand. It was terrible!

I retracted my tongue but then had a second thought. Humans often say that the best medicine is the most bitter to the taste. When they catch cold, I have often seen them take some obscure medicine while making a sour face. I was never sure whether they got well because of the medicine or in spite of it, but this was a good chance to find out. If my stomach became bitter after drinking the beer, that would be that. But if I became joyful, forgetting everything like Sampei, it would be an epoch-making discovery, and I'd tell all the cats in Japan about my experience. I felt I had to see what would happen so, leaving everything to fate, I stuck my tongue out again. It was difficult to drink with my eyes open so I shut them tight and began lapping up the beer again.

With great effort, I was finally able to drink a little more and then I felt a queer sensation. At first, my tongue burned and it seemed as if my cheeks were being pressed from outside. It was somewhat painful but, as I drank more, this feeling eased off. And when I had finished the glass, there was nothing painful about it any more. I knew it was safe now, so I drank the second glassful very easily. Then, just for good measure, I lapped up all the beer that had been spilled on the tray.

Then, in order to find out how I felt, I stayed in a crouched position for a while. Gradually, my body became warm. My eyelids began to swell. My ears became hot. I suddenly wanted

I stuck my tongue out fast, and quickly
lapped up some beer in one glass—

The water of the barrel was about five inches
below the rim.   No matter how far I stretched
my paws I could not reach the top.

to sing. I felt like dancing to the old folksong *E'en Though You Say 'Twas a Cat, 'Twas a Cat.* I felt like telling my master, Meitei and Dokusen to go to hell. I wanted to scratch old man Kaneda; I wanted to bite off Mrs. Kaneda's nose; I wanted to do a lot of things. Finally, I wanted to stand up. And when I stood up I wanted to walk with a sway. Finding this great fun, I went outside. There I wanted to greet the moon good evening —" *Hai! Konban-wa!* " This was wonderful!

Realizing that this was what is called being gloriously drunk, I went aimlessly around as if taking a walk. Then again, it was as if I wasn't taking a walk. I took a few unsteady steps and became somewhat sleepy. I don't know myself whether I was sleeping or walking. I meant to keep my eyes open but they were extremely heavy. But I wasn't afraid of anything! I limply made one more step and then heard a splash.

Suddenly I was floating on some water. It was terribly disagreeable so I began to struggle but I could only claw at the water. I kicked with my hind feet and clawed with my forepaws. There was a grating sound. I had touched a solid object. My head only barely floated above the water but it was enough to see where I was. I had fallen into a clay rainbarrel. Now, this barrel had been filled with some water-shield plants during the summertime, but in early autumn, Kanko the crow came along and ate them all up. Afterwards he took a bath in the barrel. Since Kanko's first bath, much water had evaporated so the crow stopped coming. But I never dreamed that I would be taking a bath in the barrel instead of crow.

The water in the barrel was about five inches below the rim. No matter how far I stretched my paws I could not reach the top. Nor did jumping do any good. If I did nothing, I would sink. When I struggled, my claws would scratch the sides of the barrel and I'd feel for a moment as if I were floating a little. But right away I'd sink again. Going under water was a terrible feeling so I'd begin clawing again. Presently my body began to tire. I became bewildered and my paws would not work the way I wanted them to. Finally I didn't know whether I was clawing to sink or if I was sinking to claw.

The reason I was undergoing such terrible torment was only because I had wanted to climb on top of the barrel. Of course I now know it was impossible. My paws are less than three inches long. If I could have floated on the water and stretched my front paws as far as possible, I would have still been about two inches away from the rim. Since my claws could not hook onto the rim of the barrel, it would have made no difference whether I clawed, or if I became bewildered, or whether I simply worked myself to death—I couldn't make it. Knowing that I couldn't get out but still trying, I was attempting the impossible. And when attempting the impossible, the anguish is horrible. What nonsense! I was only prolonging my agony.

"I'm going to quit. Don't care what happens now." I then let my front paws relax, and then my hind legs, my head and my tail. I didn't resist any more.

Gradually I felt uncommonly comfortable. Could this feeling of thankfulness be agony? Was I still in the water or in the middle of a room? But of course it didn't make much difference where I was, or what I was doing. The only thing that counted was that I felt comfortable. Then I could hardly even feel this comfort. I'll cut the sun and the moon down from the sky. I'll pulverize the heaven and the earth. I am entering the mysterious but wonderful realm of peace!

I die.

I die and receive peace.

Peace cannot be had without dying.

Save us, merciful Buddha!

Save us, merciful Buddha!

Gracious blessings,

Gracious blessings.

ABOUT THE AUTHOR

Natsume Soseki, one of Japan's most distinguished writers, was born in Tokyo in 1867. At an early age he studied the Chinese classics, and though later intending to become an architect, he changed his mind, and entered Tokyo Imperial University to take up literature. In 1900 he was sent to London by the Japanese Ministry of Education to study English literature for two years. On his return he was appointed lecturer in English at Tokyo University. After publishing his first novel, *I Am a Cat*, in 1905, he immediately rose to fame. Shortly after this he resigned his post at the university to become literary editor of the Asahi newspaper. Many more novels followed, and Soseki became the leading voice of the age, often ruthlessly criticizing his contemporary society for its acceptance of westernization. He died in 1916 at the age of forty-nine.